Candy CRAVINGS

Nina Nash ~ Arianna Hart
K. Z. Snow ~ Marissa Alwin
Cris Anson ~ Aubrey Ross
Alexa & Patrick Silver

ELLORA'S CAVE
ROMANTICA PUBLISHING

ANIMAL ATTRACTION
Alexa & Patrick Silver

Wes' Valentine's Day surprise has turned into a nightmare. Grounded with thousands of other travelers at an airport by a storm, he and his wife will never make their cruise. A romantic holiday atmosphere this is assuredly not!

Brand, a feline shifter, is desperate. Sexual arousal is heavy in the airport and his flight has been canceled. He needs to join with another shifter soon or risk going feral.

When Brand spots Wes and Tabitha, the raw sexuality of these fellow shifters calls to his primal needs. But they aren't average shifters. Secrets and reclaimed heritage may pull them all together or rip them apart.

ASSIGNMENT
Nina Nash

When Aphrodite, reigning goddess of love, sends Diana on a mission to give a mortal woman the push she needs to be open to romance—just a few days before Valentine's Day—the "assignment" seems to be an easy one. Nudge the woman toward the handsome, interesting man and hope for the best, right? That's exactly what Diana does and Kate and Trevor, the mortals, find happiness in time for the big day.

When Diana realizes that there is a second being from the realm of love among the mortals she assumes that he is along to help with her assignment. Art, however, has an assignment of his own to attend to—one that is, to him, much more important than any other.

CHEER GIVERS & MISCHIEF MAKERS
K.Z. Snow

This story within a story concerns opposites in the world of Fae Rhy—the Cheer Givers and the Mischief Makers. Both are bound by duty to interact with humans on every holiday—the former, by enhancing the holiday; the latter, by undermining it.

Isabelle is a Cheer Giver who enjoys her body. For Valentine's Day, she finds a hunky "Recipient" at a singles club—the romantically unlucky Bryce could benefit from some cheering. But Isabelle is more strongly drawn to another man—the mysterious, alluring Daniel, who, alas, isn't needful enough to require her services.

When Daniel unexpectedly appears at her hotel suite while she's entertaining Bryce, Isabelle knows she cannot abandon her mission. Cheering both men seems the more equitable option.

It's a carnival of carnal delights...until Daniel begins to captivate Isabelle, body and soul—proving opposites do indeed attract.

DISCOVERY
Cris Anson

Something's missing from Becca's life. Maybe she needs...a Master?

A friend arranges for her to spend a weekend with one, to see if she's cut out for the life of a sub. The man who answers the door when she knocks makes her uneasy. He's huge, bald, leather-clad and every inch a Dom.

But she gets more than she bargained for. Three Doms, to be exact. Three sexy, lusty males who each turn her on in different ways. Becca discovers it's not only the submission she craves but the right Master to submit to. Only how can she make the giant understand which Master she wants when she's forbidden to speak?

HEART ON HIS SLEEVE
Marissa Alwin

Waryn of Lysky is annoyed to find a St. Valentine's Day celebration taking place at his duchy when he returns home from battle. Worse, his meddlesome aunt insists on drawing names for "sweethearts". But when he sees Sibil, the maiden whose name he is to wear on his sleeve for a year, Waryn is filled with lust. Maintaining honorable intentions around her will not be easy.

Sibil recognizes Waryn immediately. She once came to his aid and has never forgotten his face. He, however, does not seem to remember her. It's just as well, for she will soon be off to enter the Lord's service. But before she becomes a nun, Sibil hopes Waryn can teach her a bit about love — courtly and otherwise.

SCREW CUPID
Arianna Hart

When Reannah Mason receives a mysterious invitation to a Valentine's Day party at the House of Eros, she thinks it's a joke. After all, no one knows about her secret fantasies. The party promises to satisfy her every wish and desire. Unfortunately, it can't possibly know her deepest yearning — to be loved by the charming Kiefer Brown.

Kiefer has been trying to get Reannah to go out with him for months but she won't mix business with pleasure. When he spies an invitation to a Valentine's Day orgy on her computer he knows he has to go. With any luck, if he can seduce her body, her heart won't be far behind.

SOUL KISSES
Aubrey Ross

On an ancient holiday called Valentine's Day, in a hostile corner of space, a "scrapper" named Rage encounters a mysterious entity. She offers him pleasure for energy and their erotic journey begins. Fueled by sensual curiosity and bittersweet memories, each encounter is more intense than the last. Will their sexual adventure leave him satisfied or hungry for more of her sweet soul kisses?

An Ellora's Cave Romantica Publication

www.ellorascave.com

Candy Cravings

ISBN 9781419957185
ALL RIGHTS RESERVED.
Animal Attraction Copyright © 2007 Alexa & Patrick Silver
Assignment Copyright © 2007 Nina Nash
Cheer Givers & Mischief Makers Copyright © 2007 K.Z. Snow
Discovery Copyright © 2007 Cris Anson
Heart on His Sleeve Copyright © 2007 Marissa Alwin
Screw Cupid Copyright © 2007 Arianna Hart
Soul Kisses Copyright © 2007 Aubrey Ross
Cover art by Syneca.

This book printed in the U.S.A. by Jasmine–Jade Enterprises, LLC.

Trade paperback Publication Decemeber 2007

CANDY CRAVINGS

ജ

ANIMAL ATTRACTION

Alexa & Patrick Silver

ଇଚ

Chapter One

හ

"All flights are delayed. Please do not leave the airport. Your airlines will inform you when we have further details. I repeat, a strong storm has developed off Lake Michigan and..."

Tabitha Downes tuned out the announcement. She and her husband Wes had heard it a half-hour ago and again fifteen minutes ago. She understood. Their flight was delayed. They were going to miss their cruise and spend Valentine's Day in this miserably overcrowded airport. Message received, check!

If they had been wise, they would have rushed to the doors and taken a room at the one airport hotel. When she had suggested this, Wes hadn't been interested. He was sure this would be a brief delay and still held out hope that they would catch their cruise. Tab, on the other hand, knew the Murphy's Law Fairy had been flying overhead, dive-bombing them. The flight was almost four hours long and the cruise was set to leave in six hours.

Now, they and the other few thousand folks in the airport wanted to get on the first flight to the warmth of Florida. The lines at the ticket counters had been ridiculous, so Wes had dialed the airline 800 number, only to be told that all departing planes from this airport were going to be held on the ground for now, even the craft in the taxi line. The deicing machines were running full tilt and the plows could be seen clearing the runways but no planes were going out and very few were coming in.

"Dammit. This ruined everything!"

Tab winced at the angry tone of Wes' voice. Wes had been pinning a great deal of hope on this cruise. He saw it as their last chance for a new beginning. She thought the gesture meant the world. At least Wes seemed to care again, and that was the first step in saving their marriage.

"Wes, it's okay." She rubbed his arm in a comforting gesture. "Let's get away from the crowds here and find a quieter place where we can sit down."

Her husband scanned the packed lounge area and the restaurants overflowing with harried travelers, and nodded. She picked up her overnight bag and started walking toward a corridor.

"I think this is where they have all those fancy lounges. Want to stop here?" Tab questioned. Her husband groaned but his overnight bag fell to the floor with a thump, Wes following it down. Tabitha sank to the carpet beside him, rubbing his arm. This was going to be a long day, and if Wes was in a rage, it could turn out to be very stressful for her as well.

When Wes settled his head in her lap, Tabitha began stroking his light brown hair. He'd always loved her backrubs and massages—sensual and therapeutic—and she hoped this would soothe him. He shifted, resting his head against her pussy, and she felt the first twinges of arousal.

She and Wes hadn't been intimate in some time. Their marriage was on the rocks, and neither had been ready to risk emotional intimacy with the other. There hadn't been any fireworks or huge fights, just a dull, boring rut of work, home improvement projects, time spent with friends and awkward silences in their home life. They had been drifting apart for months—maybe even years.

Tabitha hadn't expected *any* Valentine's Day gift. She and Wes had never been huge gift givers. So she was shocked when he tugged her back into bed this morning and informed her that he'd arranged for her to have a two-week vacation and that they were going away. He'd even packed her bags for her!

The romance of the day just kept getting better when Wes brought her breakfast in bed, a necklace and a ring. She was wearing both of them now, the small rose pendant nestling close to her heart and the ring sparkling on her finger.

And now, Wes was most definitely nestling his head deeper between her legs. He wasn't acting overtly sexual, but her body didn't care. She began to moisten anyway. As she combed back his hair she nestled his head lower, trying to increase the delicious pleasure on her pussy.

She dug her fingers deeper into his scalp and he moaned happily. His nostrils quivered. *Can he smell my arousal?* Sure, they were in an empty corridor, but who knew how long they would remain alone in this little oasis of peace.

A small gush of liquid moistened her crotch at the thought. She'd never been someone who had taken chances, and neither had Wes, but right now it seemed as if they were shucking their conservative everyday lives for this romantic getaway. And Tabitha was more than ready to play along.

* * * * *

"Great! Wonderful! Are we going to sit on the tarmac any longer?" Brand Hove was getting deeply concerned. They had been sitting on this plane for some two hours. The last cockpit announcement was that they were eighth in line for deicing. He glanced out the window, knowing full well that the plane wouldn't be departing today. Hell, the plows couldn't even keep up with the snowfall.

He glanced at the flight attendant sitting in the seat across the aisle. Thankfully, he was the only one in the first-class section, so he was able to stretch his legs and pace when the restlessness got to be too much for him. But if he went *furry*, there would be hell to pay! And the longer he sat in this overgrown tin can, the more likely he'd go quadruped. And then he'd be in a mess!

"Mr. Hove, can I get you anything?" The flight attendant—Janis, according to her nametag—had been watching him quite closely, flirting with him, wafting her pheromones his way.

"Yeah. I need to get off the plane." He motioned to his cell phone, which was charging in one of the power ports. "You may have heard that I'm having a family emergency."

She didn't have to know that the emergency was that he was worried about any stranded brethren who hadn't yet checked in. He jiggled his leg and then began to pace the small aisle. Three steps forward, pivot, three steps back. The walls seemed to be closing in on him.

"We're still readying for takeoff. Please sit down. Can I get you something to drink?"

Brand shook his head and threw himself back in his seat. "No. I just have to get off. I can't just continue to sit here. Can't we deplane? I'm not stupid, nobody has taken off in hours."

The flight attendant consulted her watch. "I'll get a status update from the cockpit. Please fasten your seat belt."

He did as told. Janis called another flight attendant to the front and asked the pilot to open the secured door. As he waited for her to come back, Brand drummed his hands on his thighs. The first sign of an impending change was this burst of energy. He couldn't repress it, didn't want to, in fact. That would just lead to bigger and more *furry* problems.

"Mr. Hove? The captain just informed me that airport management and the air traffic controllers will be making an announcement at the top of the hour. That is less than ten minutes away. We request your patience until that time."

Brand nodded and picked up his cell phone. At least they hadn't asked for electronic devices to be turned off. For the last couple of hours, he'd had the in-seat satellite television on, hoping that none of his brethren had shown themselves to the public. So far, so good, but their luck could run out any minute now. Starting with him if he didn't get off this plane soon.

He grabbed his phone and connected immediately to the Council headquarters. He needed a status report. None of the rest of the ruling body had been caught in this storm, and many of the shifters on getaways with their spouses were either driving or had been diverted to other airports. The eastern half of the United States was in for a nasty storm, so his office informed him, and he was stuck in it. *Must be my lucky day.*

This snowfall meant that his meeting with the owners of Blood Anonymous, a vampire-shifter coalition, would be postponed. Denver, his assistant, would take care of rescheduling. For now, all Brand Hove, President of the International Shifter Council, needed to do was stay human until he had secured a hotel room. Easier said than done. He, more than any other shifter, was affected by human pheromones. If it was almost overwhelming in a plane that held maybe a hundred humans, what would the airport and city's hotels be like? Stupid question. He'd be swimming in a sea of human arousal. This day of the year, of all of them, guaranteed that.

Unable to stop himself, Brand pressed the heel of his hand against his cock, enjoying the thrill that the pressure provided. It had been aching for the better part of the hour, but had not become fully erect yet. He thanked every deity he could that he had been able to retain some control, because Janis was looking at him as if he was the prey and she was the big-game hunter. She had no idea she was hunting a dangerous wild animal. When *furry,* he could snap her neck in an instant, controlled only by the animal raging within. Not that he'd ever killed anyone. His parents had made sure of that, raising and rearing him to be a responsible human and shifter.

But today would test his inner strength and willpower. If he lost the struggle, not only could innocent human lives be lost, but his lapse could take down the entire shifter society.

Breathe deeply, he ordered himself, his entire body strung tightly. He was on the razor's edge of control. He clenched his fists and jaw and stared out the window, lost in thought.

"Mr. Hove?" Janis was leaning over him, her voice sounding extra sharp to his sensitive hearing. He was torn between wanting to thrust her away and pull her close, grinding his hard cock against her. But he didn't want her, and he was above using women.

"Got news?" He bit the words out through his clenched teeth.

"Yes. We're going back to the terminal. All flights have been canceled."

"Fine." Thank God and Bast, he'd finally be able to end this trip.

"But there is a problem. Visibility is so bad that the city is mostly closed down. Please take advantage of our first-class lounge."

Great. Just brilliant! He might be stuck in an airport teeming with sexual arousal. He must have pissed off someone in a past life. Otherwise, his personal visit to hell would have never occurred. He would have flown to Pittsburgh, met with the bloodsuckers and stayed at a nice respectable five-star hotel, where his inner kitty could come out to play. Staying in an airport was *not* in the cards. At least the shifters had their own lounge at O'Hare.

While he was pondering his woulda, coulda, shoulda, the airplane had been towed back to the gate. Brand grabbed his microfiber carryon — no leather for him, he wasn't about to use *animal* skins to clothe himself — and strode off the plane, purposely ignoring Janis' hopeful look. She didn't want to play with the kitty, and he had no interest in encouraging her. If he was going to mate, he'd have to find another shifter, vamp or other paranormal. They were the only ones who could match his stamina.

As he approached the end of the jetway, the faint, outdoorsy scent of shifter pheromones assaulted him. Desire coursed through him, making him stumble and fall to his knees. He nodded at the helping hand of a man, thankful that a woman hadn't grabbed him. He had no latent desire for men in general, and thus his arousal did not flare out of control. For now, anyway. He needed relief and he needed it fast. Otherwise, Chicago might just see its first runaway lion in airport story. Yeah, great, being plastered on the news was *just* what he needed!

Recovering slightly and driven by instinct and rising lust, he jogged through the gate area. There wasn't time to get a cab and find a hotel. He needed satisfaction and he needed it now.

Following the distinctive shifter scent, he rounded a corner and almost stumbled into a couple who were on the ground, her hands in his hair, his hard-on almost saluting Brand as he skidded to a stop.

Shifters. One of them was a shifter. He didn't care which one was—hell, he'd have both right now.

"Come on." He hauled the man up and then pulled the woman to her feet as well. Brand dragged the confused pair along the corridor past the first-class lounge to a plain, unmarked door. He fumbled with a credit card. "This is a special lounge for our kind. Sorry to be so abrupt, but I can't wait. I need you."

Chapter Two

ຂບ

Tabitha could only gape at the man. She had felt arousal stirring within her, rising irresistibly before this man grabbed her. Exchanging a look with Wes, she was reassured by his slight nod. It made sense to take advantage of the private lounge and the man's generosity. Whatever he couldn't wait to do—presumably to rebook his flight or a hotel—could work out for them too.

Tab followed the tall blond man into the exclusive lounge. With a shrug to Wes, she followed. This guy seemed to know what he was doing. Maybe the best phone services were in there.

As she and her husband entered the room, the man breezed by them, securing the door. She looked around cautiously, taking in the warm décor, the comfortable chairs and the huge bed that dominated the room. There was even a bathroom attached. It looked like a luxury hotel room, hidden right here in the airport! The man's heavy breathing brought her attention back to him and she noticed a film of sweat on his forehead. Though he looked sick, Tab guessed there was some other reason for his discomfort. An emotion she couldn't quite place shimmered toward her in waves, bringing with it a scent both woodsy and warm. It tantalized her and she squirmed, her heartbeat racing and breathing quickening.

"Are you okay?" Tab automatically reached up to touch Brand's forehead. He was burning up! Was illness responsible for this behavior or were she and Wes in a heap of trouble?

"Don't!" The man reached up to push her away then seemed to think better of it. He extended his hand in a gesture she interpreted to mean that he meant no harm. "You should know not to touch me when I'm in this state, sweetheart. The kitty might take a nice big bite out of you."

"Sweetheart? Excuse me, do I know you?" She was getting offended by his familiarity and unsettled by the way her body was reacting to his nearness.

He shook his head. "No, but you know our kind. All the pheromones and all the damn romance. I have to release this."

What the heck was he talking about? "Back up. Start from the beginning, what do you—" She stopped abruptly. Why was the man pulling off his coat and ripping off his tie? Yanking his shirt off in a jerky motion? Looking to her husband for help and guidance, Tab started to edge toward the door. This was too strange. She began to think seriously about getting out of there.

"What do you think you're doing?" At least Wes sounded strong and in control. Tab exhaled slowly, trying to will her body to calm down.

"Do you want to do it for me? I didn't stop to consider…well, okay. Take my pants off." The man invaded Wes' personal space, thrusting his hips out in carnal invitation.

Gasping in shock, Tab spoke up. "Um, enough is enough. Who are you and what specifically do you want?"

A test. It had to be a test. The man had a hungry look in his eyes as he took in Brand's chest. The woman was playing coy. He had scented shifter blood in both of them, but he couldn't work out which one was dominant—the gorgeous blonde or the handsome quiet guy. Their pheromones and desire hung heavy in the air. As he breathed it in, his cock twitched and his stomach clenched. Dammit, he wanted both of them now.

"What division are you with? Northland? Pacifica? Sucks that you got stranded here, but we can make the most of it."

"Division?" The woman was still playing the confused role. It turned him on almost as much as the musky spice of her pussy did.

"Yes, division. Shifter Division to be precise. Or are you independent?"

The woman exchanged looks with the man and then reluctantly sat on the big bed, the man crossing the room to take her hand. "We're from north of Green Bay," he said.

At least the other guy wasn't wasting his time. "That's the Great Lakes Division. Makes sense that I wouldn't know you. But look, I don't have much time. I have to fuck her, or both of you if you're willing."

"Name," Tabitha asked. She had a husky voice full of sexual promise. The woman still appeared to be dazed, though she was responding to the way her man stroked her hand and arm. "I want to know your name."

Brand ran a hand through his hair. "Fine, but can we please stop dicking around? I'm Brand Hove, Council President. And you are?"

"Wes and Tabitha Downes. She doesn't...she hasn't found hers yet. That's why she's so confused. I'm only half, but...I have those desires as well. What is your animal?"

"Lion," Brand responded, "And yours?"

"Panther. I think hers is feline too. Must be why you're so attracted." Wes turned to look at his wife. "I can't explain much now, Tab, but we have to do this. Please trust me here."

The woman gave her man another look. "I want answers, Wes. What is going on?"

She was resistant and it sounded like she was a cub that had not yet made her first shift. At her age, she should have had at least ten years of changes behind her. She'd likely be feeling the desires, her shifter scent had been tantalizing his. But she'd have no idea how to deal with these thoughts and feelings in her body.

Brand had to take matters into his own hands. His need burned within him but the woman needed to be handled carefully. He crossed the room and stroked her face with one fingertip. Her body shuddered with clear-cut need. "Just relax and let it happen, Tabitha Downes. My touch feels good, doesn't it?"

She shifted on the bed, seemingly unsure of his touch. She clearly wanted to master her reactions, but as her shifter heritage rose within her, she'd feel the need to couple very soon. Multiple times. And with both of them. This was going to be a hell of a weather-related emergency.

What's happening to me? This man, this total stranger, was just running a finger over her cheek and eyelid. His touch shouldn't be making her entire body tremble and quake, her pussy gush and her body physically ache for his touch. All of a sudden, a rush of yearning heated her body. It didn't make sense but she needed this man.

Tab moaned deeply, arching her back. Her nipples were swollen little darts of desire, her pussy liquid heat. She wanted to rub herself wantonly for this man, and that shocked her almost as much as the sexy shirtless man in front of them.

Tab moved onto her husband's lap. Wes' erection pressed against her ass and she ground against it mercilessly. Her caution had disappeared sometime between her nipples stiffening and her cunt gushing. She needed sexual satisfaction so badly. Normally reserved, Tabitha was buried in a storm of lust. Her pussy was tingling, the lips swollen, and her breasts aching.

She stared at Brand's chest and abdomen. Lightly brushed with burnished gold hair, every muscle stood out sharply, a few scars weaving silvery lines over the tanned skin. His cock was outlined sharply by his pants—long, hard and rampant. She had not desired another man since meeting Wes, but this sexy blond god turned her on beyond rational thought or reason.

Wes had buried his face in her hair. Reaching around to cup her breasts, he settled her more firmly on his lap. Her husband hadn't been this aroused in ages and she took full advantage of it, rubbing and grinding against it despite the intensely disturbing presence of the strange man who attracted her so.

The touch of Wes' hands on her breasts was almost too much. He cupped them gently, his fingers branding her flesh. Suddenly she realized that she had too many clothes on and stood, yanking her shirt and bra off, exposing her nipples to the air. She thrust her chest out toward Brand, offering herself to him without words.

"Oh!" Her gasp broke the silence of the room. As the air brushed over her breasts, her sensitivity and sensations were magnified. The air itself was alive, caressing and stroking her, licking teasingly over her nipples and caressing the fullness of her breasts. While she missed the touch of Wes' hands on them, this sensation was new and altogether overwhelming.

The stranger — Brand — reached for the button on her jeans and opened it, pushing the fabric down her legs. She automatically stepped out her pants, socks and shoes. Clad only in a pair of silky panties, Tab was neither embarrassed nor scared. Everything made sense all of a sudden. She was going to have sex with both this man and her husband and it thrilled her.

She stretched and then looked up at the man. He was tall, topping six feet by a few inches. And he was all sun-burnished, from his hair to his golden skin. A rugged man who had an air of command, he was quite different from laid-back Wes, her one and only lover before tonight.

He stepped back a pace, never breaking his gaze. She was vaguely aware of Wes rustling behind her but couldn't spare the mental energy for him.

My God, he's beautiful. I just want to touch him. Tab's newly awakened sexual urges were spiraling out of control. Rational thought left her, even more intense desire taking its place.

Then Brand lowered her back to the bed and bent down to caress her nipple with his mouth. Fire. Aching fire rushed through her veins. His light stubble abraded her overstimulated skin. Her hand crept down to her panty-clad pussy and started rubbing urgently. She had never been one for masturbation, but as her body opened up to her own touch, she moaned. She skinned her saturated panties off, spreading her legs wide, almost embarrassed by the way her scent hung in the air.

Brand suckled more urgently now, and Tab's finger moved from her clit and began delving into her cunt. She was hardly aware of where Wes was until his lips fastened on her sensitized clit.

"Oh God, you two..." Rational thought was impossible at the moment. Brand began plucking her other nipple and two of Wes' fingers dove into her soaked pussy. Tab's head lolled on the cushion and she concentrated on trying to breathe. She was burning up, both from the outside and inside. She was so aware of her body's responses that her blood roared in her ears and every bit of pleasure these men were wringing out of her was increased to an almost maddening level.

She brought her hand up to Brand's head and the scent of her drew his attention away from her nipple for the moment. He captured her moist finger and suckled deeply, awakening all new feelings inside Tab's body.

When he flicked playfully at her nipple, her whole body tensed. She was climbing the hill and knew she'd crest it soon if these men allowed her a release. Just then, Wes began to tap her cunt, finding her G-spot with unerring accuracy.

One, two, three taps. She was going insane with need, arching up to her husband and Brand. "Let me come! Please!"

Brand fastened himself on her other nipple, pulling and tugging. Wes sucked hard on her clit in time with his insistent tapping. The sensations of two men working on her at the same time, as well as the erotic strangeness of the whole scene, overwhelmed her.

Her world exploded. With a scream she felt herself tumbling over the edge. The orgasm shattered her, reducing her to a pile of need. Fire and ice raced through her body and then something else replaced them, a wonderful tingling.

Tab pulled Brand's head up and kissed him, tasting the subtle vestiges of her cream.

Brand watched the woman carefully for any signs of transformation. He knew that she was primed and ready, could smell her feline form within, a deeper musk that called to the primal animal inside him. "Tabitha, you're safe here. Let the change happen."

As her extremities trembled, her husband pulled her into his arms. His panther should be able to handle her cat, and after all, they were the established couple here.

His lust almost out of control, Brand jerked the rest of his clothes off and began pacing the room. This was torture. Who had he screwed in a past life to be stuck like this, in a room teeming with shifter desire?

"Hey," Wes said softly. "If you want to you can come over here, behind me. I don't mind. Right now, I want it. I want you to fuck me."

Was he serious? Brand regarded the man for only a second before crossing the room. At some point, Wes had dropped his clothes and from what Brand could see of his naked body, he was well formed. Though men weren't his preferred sex partners, he wasn't against anything that gave him pleasure, and that tight ass would give him a climax to remember.

Tabitha hadn't yet changed, but it was obvious that the process had begun. A first shift could take anywhere from ten minutes to ten hours. Given the fact that she was beyond her teens, the usual age for a first shifting, Brand bet that it wouldn't take long at all. And in the meantime he could amuse himself with her mate's muscular back and ass. And that cock looked damn tasty too.

"Nice." Resting his chin comfortably on Wes' shoulder, Brand reached over and stroked Tabitha's hair, her mewing sounds calling to his inner lion.

He nipped the back of Wes' neck, gathering the skin at the base and working it between his teeth, suckling slightly. Brand knew he was going to leave a mark, his mark of ownership, however brief.

Wes groaned and thrust his ass back. Brand relished the feel of those tight glutes clenching and releasing. It had been a long time since he'd experienced a man and the animal inside wasn't choosy, right now it just demanded release. Wes was good-looking and not alpha enough to be a challenge. Brand wasn't interested in a testosterone-laden fight for dominance, he just wanted to fuck with animal pride, animal lust.

"Do you want this? Then prepare your woman for me while we play. When the shift comes upon her, I'll fuck her. I want you to hold her and keep your human form so she has something comfortable and familiar. If things get out of control feel free to shift and dominate her. Then, when she's rested, we'll all have some fun."

Tabitha's whole body was tingling and a feeling not unlike panic was overcoming her. She didn't feel fear, but her emotions were tightly strung, her body wound like a spring. Strange things were happening inside her, a stretching. Something was exerting a great deal of pressure on her insides. She threw her head back, moaning. The feeling was altogether new to her, yet somehow it centered her as well. And she loved the sensitivity of her skin, her hearing, all her senses seemed stronger.

Wes' cock pressed against her lower back. Was it her imagination or did he seem more erect than ever? Their celibacy had obviously added to his desire. She luxuriated in the feel of her husband's rampant cock.

As Brand spoke, Tab tuned out, focusing inward. She was curious but not frightened about these changes in her body. Everything was so surreal. Tab knew she should be feeling her emotions more deeply but all these changes were fascinating.

Her mouth was overfull all of a sudden. When she parted her lips, the small prick of a fang scraped her mouth. Fangs? She never had fangs before. Tab wriggled out from under Wes and ran to a small mirror across the room. "Oh my God! Wes?"

Her body was covered in a luxurious spotted pelt of short silky fur, her face elongating as she watched. She stroked her hands up her body in shock, unable to understand these changes in herself. As she stared at this strange human-animal hybrid in the mirror, she became aware of the man growling behind Wes.

"Wes! Is he hurting you?" She hurried over, skidding to a stop when she saw the man's hand wrap around her husband's cock. Her desire was almost painful. She wanted to share her husband's cock with Brand, but more importantly she had to focus on what was going on in her body.

"What is happening to me?"

Brand lifted his head from her husband's shoulder. There was sure to be a love-bite there. "Tell her, friend. Tell her what you can right now."

Wes swallowed hard. Did he appear more hairy too? "Tab, please don't worry. This is part of our heritage. We're shifters."

Shifters? What did he mean? Shifters weren't real! Sure, Wes had been fascinated by the phenomena, but she always figured it was his love for animals coming out.

"I...I..." She couldn't form words.

"It's true, honey. You're a leopard shifter. See the pattern on your fur? Very shortly, you'll understand. Don't resist. All of us are safe in here."

Tabitha sat on the bed and tucked her legs under her chin, desire pushed into the background by her shock at this fanciful tale.

"Are you all right?" Brand asked.

Tabitha bit off a brittle laugh. "Um, no. This is all a bit to deal with."

Brand nodded. "We'll leave you alone for now. Join in if you feel ready."

Brand moved to Wes and sank onto his knees in front of the panther shifter. It had been quite some time since he had taken another male, either orally or otherwise, and he found himself hungering for the taste of cock. Wes had a great cock, not too thick and about seven inches long. It was coated in pre-cum, the foreskin exposing the blunt head.

He ran his jaw over the other man's leg, up to his inner thigh. When Wes was gasping for air, Brand took the other man's cock in a hand now transformed with paw pads and small claws. He stroked up and down a few times then plunged his head down on the hard shaft. Brand's throat opened up and he began suctioning hard, delivering a sensation that was two parts pleasure, one part pain. His fangs added to the stimulation by scraping over sensitive skin.

When his initial hunger was satisfied, Brand lifted his head, making a sound of pure feline satisfaction. He swiped his tongue over Wes' cock head, knowing that the rough texture would add a higher level of sensation. He worked the cock head like a master, smearing and devouring the constant stream of creamy pre-cum. Wes' lubrication had a wild taste to it, almost sweet, and the lion in Brand was responding wholly.

Wes appeared to have given himself over to a blowjob from a master. His head was thrown back and fists were clenched. Brand brought one of Wes' hands to his head, encouraging the panther to fist his hair. The bed rustled a bit as Wes' wife moved in agitation. She was getting hotter too, her spice joining her husband's in the air. Watching a near-stranger suck off her husband was probably increasing her shock. The beginning of the shift was lowering her inhibitions and raising her libido. At least Brand hoped so!

"Suck me...suck me some more, man. I want to come in your mouth," Wes' entreaty was tortured and Brand wasn't about to make him wait any longer. He sealed his mouth around the other man's cock, scraping his lion claws ever so gently over the man's tightly drawn-up scrotum.

"I want..." Tabitha's voice was needy and barely penetrated his haze of lust. Then he felt her small paws on his ass, opening him wide. Was she going to rim him? She hadn't looked *that* kinky, but her inner feline was probably bringing all her desires, no matter how nasty or kinky, to the foreground.

When his legs were fully apart, the woman settled herself on the ground and began tonguing his balls and stroking his shaft with those paws. She wasn't adept at using them and pricked him a few times, but the pain was quickly forgotten as she stroked him. She couldn't maneuver enough to suck him, a fact that was causing her endless frustration. Finally she spoke.

"Please fuck my husband. I want to have him in my mouth as you're fucking him."

That was all the encouragement Brand needed. He crossed the room, yanked a condom out of his bag and sheathed himself carefully, considerate of his claws on the fragile rubber. He was tremblingly eager to be buried in the other man's ass.

Tabitha had helped her husband arrange himself on hands and knees. As Brand applied some lube to the condom, Tabitha settled under Wes, his cock dangling an inch away from her lips.

Brand wished he could capture this moment, these two beautiful people waiting for him to mate with them. Unlike most of his matings, this one was devoid of political overtones.

It was just about sex and shifting. These people weren't using him for any reasons other than physical satisfaction. These people only wanted his body and semen, not to solidify their position or marry him for material gain. The change was quite refreshing. It had been too long since he'd been desired for his body instead of his position.

"Are you ready, Wes?" Brand questioned. The other man nodded silently. Brand gently stroked the woman's soft abdominal pelt for a moment before settling himself against Wes' back. The soft sounds of Tabitha slurping Wes' cock were the most erotic soundtrack Brand had heard in ages.

He stroked his sheathed cock over Wes' perineum, exerting enough pressure to further arouse the other man. Wes' anus seemed to relax for Brand, who pressed his cock gently but firmly against the puckered hole. It gave and Wes pulled Brand's entire cock head inside.

Fuck. Wes' tightness and heat were incredible. Brand trembled, trying to keep his desire under tight rein. He was incredibly tempted to just pound home in one thrust, chancing that the superior shifter genetics would heal any damage he made. No, instead of risking that, he'd enter slowly, stretching out the pleasure, making it sweet instead of brutal and deny his lion satisfaction for the moment.

Another inch in. God, the tightness was getting to him. And then Tabitha ran her claws over his balls, the pricking of the sharp appendages soothed by the spongy soft paw pad and the silky fur. He tried to wait, to let Wes adjust but then the other man rocked back, seeking more of his cock, and he was lost. He pushed in with one long, deep thrust.

"YES!" Wes' voice was full of triumph and satisfaction. Brand began thrusting in and out slowly, wanting Tabitha to keep her mouth on her husband's cock. When he could tell that she was keeping up, he let loose and fucked Wes' tight ass in deep stabbing strokes, trying to wring every bit of pleasure and passion out of the other man.

His wife took Brand's hint, rolling and stroking her husband's balls and sucking him urgently. "Come on, Wes. Come in your sweet wife's mouth while I come up your ass."

The veins popped out on Wes' arms, his trembles increasing. He was so close to the edge! Brand could feel his struggle to extend the enjoyment, but he had to realize that he wasn't the one in control here. Brand was, and he had to come.

Brand rammed home and steadied himself, pulsing in the other man's ass. He reached down, fondling Wes' balls and brushed his wife's hair against those full orbs. Brand was ready to let go, but he wanted this to be a shared orgasm. He wanted Wes' climax to push him over the edge.

The soft silk of Tab's hair on the tender skin of his sac seemed to do the job. Wes began growling and thrusting forward and back faster and faster, plunging into his wife's mouth then impaling himself on Brand's shaft. Brand fastened himself on the other man's neck, growling his triumph. Wes' muscles clenched firmly around his tortured cock and Brand's world shattered in bright bursts of light. The woman scooted out of the way and Brand collapsed on the panther shifter, spent for the moment.

"That was…" The woman's voice shook.

"Incredible?" Brand supplied. "Fantastic? Erotic? Or just the beginning?"

Chapter Three

෨

Tabitha giggled nervously when Brand spoke. He lay atop her husband, sprawled on the huge bed. Tab's pussy was liquid, her scent perfuming the room, her body so ready for either of their cocks. Or both of their cocks. She didn't care right now. She just wanted to be fucked.

The changes in her body had added to her arousal and while she still had questions, *many* questions, she knew she'd better absorb the information after she'd had her release as well.

What she'd just seen, someone penetrating her husband, had been a total turn-on. She'd had a great vantage point of Brand's sheathed cock pounding into Wes' ass, admiring the slight differences in their cocks and balls from only inches away. Their enthusiasm had taken her to another place entirely, and instead of being put off by the close view of anal sex, she was even more aroused. Her strong-and-silent type husband had allowed another man to give him pleasure. It was both touching and arousing at the same time. And she wanted to see much more of it!

She watched Brand lever himself off her husband and disappear into the bathroom.

"Wes, are you okay?"

He looked up into her eyes, his own burning with desire. "Yeah, I'm good. Did you mind what happened?"

Tabitha's cheeks heated and she knew that her face was bright red. "No, it was actually…sexy." Her voice sounded seductive, even to her own ears.

"Good, my little leopard, because as soon as Brand gets back, we're going to take you together. Don't worry about pregnancy or diseases. You can't become pregnant until after you've fully shifted for the first time and our kind are immune to all social diseases."

A thrill coursed through her at the thought of having both of them together. "I have so many questions, Wes. All of this..." She gestured with a paw. "I need to know who—*what*—exactly I am becoming. And how this happened. And how come you knew and I didn't."

Wes nodded, a sober expression chasing away the naughty glint in his eyes. "We'll explain that all to you, just as soon as you've been satisfied. Can you wait that long?"

Tabitha absolutely categorically needed these two men, so she would grant her husband a reprieve. In any event, her desire was so intense that she knew she wouldn't be able to concentrate on what they had to tell her. The fact that Wes knew and understood this was enough of a comfort for her. She still trusted her husband implicitly and the fact that he'd allowed her to watch him taking and getting satisfaction from a man had deepened their level of intimacy in new and exciting ways.

"All right. But you better make it worth my while."

Wes rose and gave her a gentle kiss, infusing tenderness that had been sorely missing in their marriage for years. She opened her mouth, inviting his tongue inside. He kissed her with a passion she had though was long dead and buried. It felt so good to be this emotionally close with her husband. She melted against him, her arousal building again, her love for him overshadowing the strangeness of the day.

"Happy Valentine's Day, my tabby cat. You've given yourself the best gift ever. You've found the other half of yourself. Cast your inhibitions away for just this day and let us take you to heights you never could have imagined. We've only just begun."

Tabitha stroked his strong jaw, deep in thought. Though she should be frightened, withdrawing from her husband, on some deep intuitive level Wes had calmed her fears and pushed her questions to the back of her mind. She felt safe with him, as always, and she knew he'd lead her through any confusion this new part of her life caused.

"I love you, Wes. Never doubt that." She had so much more to say but just couldn't find the words. If there were even words for the glow deep in her soul.

"Good." He smiled, brushing her hair away gently. "I think this new part of you is even more gorgeous than you usually are. This soft fur, the gleam in your eyes, the graceful way you move. You're stunning, Tab, and I've never loved you more than right at this moment. Stick with me, honey. Take this journey as my wife."

As she nodded, soul-deep wounds and cuts began to heal. Her spirit was mending, becoming whole again.

When Brand cleared his throat, Tab found herself wondering how much he had heard. She tore her gaze away from Wes, meeting the challenge in the other man's eyes.

"Are you ready for us, little kitty?"

He looked dangerous, almost a little wild. His blond hair was mussed and there were emotions swirling in his eyes. She glanced down his body, gaze hovering at his crotch. He was either still hard or had a hellofa recovery time.

"I'm ready. Take me, both of you."

Brand sat on the bed and tugged her paw, pulling her toward him. She crouched over the man, her breasts dangling in his face. He seemed unable to resist her reddened nipples, playfully snapping his mouth over one, then the other.

"Mmm," Tab moaned, rubbing her moisture over his cock, marking him.

"Not yet. Wes gets you this time. Then I'll take you while he sucks your clit."

The frank language added another level to her desire. She didn't want these men to be civilized right now, she wanted their animal attraction to take over.

She relaxed and laid down on Brand's body, pressing her cheek against his comforting chest and thrusting her ass in the air, exposing her cunt to her husband. Then she spread her pussy lips to expose the pink flesh inside. "Take me, Wes. Please." Her desire for her husband's cock and cum was overwhelming.

She sensed Wes moving but didn't expect a long slow lick. He swiped his tongue from her clit to her ass slowly, so slowly she wanted to scream. It felt so damn good! She arched her back, lifting her ass, gasping when Brand began raking his claws gently over the tops of the breasts flattened against his chest. His hard cock pressed into her belly insistently, igniting a fire that only a cock inside her would put out. She didn't care whose.

Darts of pleasure made their way from her pussy and breasts to the center of her being and radiated outward in increasing pre-orgasmic ripples. "Inside me now, please." Desire turned to demand. She simply *had* to have both of these men. Gone was the safe, staid Tab and in its place was this new person with desires that overwhelmed and controlled her. Instead of being upset or worried about this change, Tab felt liberated. She knew on some deep level that she was in touch with the deepest part of her soul.

Her husband's strong hands gripped her hips, his hands coming around to hold her breasts in a tender gesture, a counterpoint to the urgent need simmering around all of them. They encountered Brand, still softly caressing Tabitha's breasts with his shrinking claws. The other man made small satisfied sounds as Wes began stroking his flank and shoulder. Wes flicked Tab's nipple on each pass over Brand's body as he seated himself against her cunt.

This was the moment she loved the most, when her husband's length rested at her opening. He knew it and usually extended the torture until his patience was maddening. But she knew the game. He would penetrate her, he would control the depth and the timing, and if she rocked back, impaling herself on him, he'd fully withdraw and keep her at the edge for minutes.

I can't wait! Her thighs quivered, her willpower nearly depleted. One of Brand's hands went between her legs, stroking her husband's cock, flicking a fingertip over her clit in the upstroke. His hands had finished changing back from paws, but hers hadn't yet. She dug those claws into the fabric of a cushion, rubbing her husband's cock head against her clit and extending the stimulation from Brand's questing fingers.

"Little cat, let your husband fill you."

Tabitha was beyond listening, though she stopped short of impaling herself on Wes' cock.

"Little cat, enough." Brand's tone was full of authority.

Wes began moaning and rocking, almost but not quite penetrating her. She needed more sensation, *more* dammit! "Give it to me!"

In response, Brand spanked her cunt lightly, just enough pain mixed with the pleasure to cause her to jump in shock and moan.

"More. Please." Her swollen pussy needed any stimulation she could get, and the spanking was such a turn-on.

Was that needy growl really hers? She cried out as Wes penetrated her quickly and started a slow back-and-forth thrust. He filled her, every ridge and vein in his cock caressing her inner walls as if he was created for only her pleasure.

Brand pulled her head down onto his chest and she eagerly lapped at one of his nipples. He tasted of the outdoors, of wood smoke, snow, and the trace of mint, spice and herbs, a blend that was entirely masculine. She began laving his chest, paying special attention to his nipples, encouraged as his breathing got harsher. Her tongue glided over the silky golden fur of his pectorals. The sensation was sexy and almost decadent. He was wild, he was civilized and the blend of both was almost too much for her to comprehend.

"Brand, you have no idea how sexy you are."

His hands were buried in her hair, stroking from her scalp outward. Both soothing and arousing, his touch and the sensations of his muscled body against her softer one pushed her toward the edge.

Wes' magnificent cock was pounding into her, his hard thighs pressing against hers with every thrust, his hand fisted in her hair. He kept emitting small growls and moans that signaled his climax was looming. Tab was elated. Her husband had *never* been anything but tender and caring in bed. Here he was, fucking her hard and without concern for her needs, causing her just a little pain that urged the pleasure onto a higher plane. She loved the wildness that had come over him.

She'd never been fucked like this before! He drove into her with renewed desire and lust, making her cunt spark and fire into an inferno. He didn't just push her over the edge, he propelled her over with the force of his thrusts and the sounds he was making.

"Wes!" Tabitha dug her claws into Brand's shoulders, screaming. Her orgasm came over her with a force that reduced her to a quaking bundle of nerves. Lights exploded behind her closed eyelids and all she could hear was her labored breathing and her blood rushing throughout her body.

Just as Wes pulled out, Brand lifted her, settling her on his cock and thrusting home. Wes moved to the edge of the bed, his cock still hard and coated with both their cum. She was stunned when Brand began lapping at her husband's wet dick, tasting them both. The aftershocks of her orgasm were still rippling through her body and it all seemed so decadent.

Tabitha panted. "I want some too." Brand guided Wes' cock head into her mouth. She dipped her tongue into his slit, drawing out the last vestiges of her husband's semen. The combined flavor of cunt and dick was ambrosia to her.

Tabitha's cunt was rippling around the full length of Brand's cock. He was allowing her to control the up-and-down movements, skimming his hands down her sides. The sensations this almost-touch aroused were incredible!

"Let me have more." Brand's face was only a millimeter away. When her husband's cock popped out of her mouth, Brand captured it and they began to kiss each other, tongues winding around Wes' cock as she thrust her pelvis against him in short, hard strokes. Tasting. Licking. Kissing. Fucking. All the while Brand was wringing mini-orgasms out of her. This would be a quick fuck, ultimately to end in joint orgasms.

She loved the carnality of the act, it had been too long since she'd been used sexually. In the early days, she and Wes had coupled with intensity, but in the last years it had been safe, boring. Which this was decidedly not!

Brand picked up the speed, meeting her thrusts with new intensity. Tab released her husband's cock and rested her head on Brand's chest, whimpering as her body flooded with sensation. All rational thought left her mind as both Brand and Wes came, the former drenching her cunt, the latter drenching both of their faces.

Wes moved down to kiss both of them, tongues tangling, lips moving against each other's mouths. This felt so right to Tab. She didn't want this to end.

Chapter Four

ဆ

Wes watched his wife and Brand as they broke apart. Each took a hand and tugged Wes toward the bathroom. His mind whirled with the newness and the excitement of the day. *Happy Valentine's Day to me! I got my ultimate fantasy fulfilled.* Wes had known he was bisexual for most of his life, but had never experimented heavily with men. Yeah, he'd had his fun, especially in his college years, but the often soulless predatory way men approached other men had turned him off.

He'd married Tab when he was a fresh college grad and had put his bisexuality in the past. Whatever he fantasized about wouldn't hurt his marriage. Wes had been disappointed in their marriage because unlike most shifter couples, whose sex lives were enhanced by their shared genes adding a wild edge to their matings, theirs had settled into mediocrity. Though Tab never knew it, their shared shifter heritage *had* deepened their bond, just not as intensely as Wes had hoped. He'd always wondered if, because Tab had never shifted, her passions were hidden under her humanity.

His normal and boring marriage had sure ended today! Having Brand initiate his wife into life as a shifter should have aroused the most predatory protective alpha instincts in him. He should never have let the other man touch his wife. Yet Wes felt as if this was right, as if they were meant to share her.

He stood still as she and Brand washed him off gently, wanting to fondle Tab, but the exhaustion in her eyes told a compelling tale. She was drained, emotionally as well as physically. She just stood still as Brand washed their juices off her body.

"Hey, Brand. Can you find all of us a place to bunk?" They could not stay in this room much longer...surely there were other shifters in as much need of the privacy it offered as they were! "Tab has a lot of questions in her..." Since the other guy was a big muckety-muck in the Council, evident by the fact that he'd been able to get into this ultra-exclusive shifter lounge, he should be able to score them a room somewhere. Behind closed doors and in total privacy, they could monitor Tab's first full shift.

Thankfully, her fur was fading, her paws turning back into graceful human hands. In only a few minutes, she'd look fully like herself again.

"I'll see what I can do. The storm is fierce out there."

Wes nodded, this wasn't anything he didn't already know. "We need a place for us to stay for now. And Tab will need some sleep."

"I know." Brand walked out of the bathroom and reached for his cell phone. Wes closed the door that separated the rooms before he turned to Tab.

"Are you okay? A lot has happened today."

Tab cracked a wan smile. "It is a Valentine's Day to remember. I have so many questions, but yeah, I'm okay. You? You were so worried about the cruise."

Wes jerked his head toward the door. "I got a little distracted by the hunk out there. Was what he did with me okay?"

"Yeah, it was..." Her voice faded and a blush colored her skin.

"It was what?"

"Sexy. Seeing you two together was sexy." Tab chewed on her bottom lip.

"I'm glad." Wes pulled her into his arms, rubbing her back in small circles. "We should get dressed. Brand is going to try to find us some place to stay. Your exciting day isn't over yet."

"Oh?" Tab's expression turned serious. "I'm a bit overwhelmed. It'll be okay?"

"It'll be wonderful, Tab. I've been wanting to share this with you for so long... Just be patient and you'll see."

Finding a place for them to stay was a tall order. Even calling in every favor he could didn't seem to work, until Denver, his assistant, located a shifter manager at a local hotel. The manager offered to give them one suite, which was usually held for any VIPs. Now the problem would be getting there. Thankfully, the hotel was in the shadow of the airport. Hopefully Denver could locate a shifter cab driver who might be willing to ferry them to the hotel despite the weather and zero visibility. If that didn't work, they'd just have to walk, warming Tabitha between them. At least the sex had taken the edge off his lust. The human pheromones beyond the lounge were only an annoying buzz for now and by the time they'd become so intense that they'd steal his will, he'd be in a comfortable hotel suite with this intriguing couple and their special shifter pheromones would be all for him.

Brand noted that the couple had stayed inside the bathroom for some minutes. He wished he didn't feel so left out. That emotion was just silly. The man and wife let him share the most intimate act with both of them just now. Of course they wanted a little time to deal with everything.

He threw himself on the bed, trying to ignore their mingled scents marking the fabric. He could try to be patient. *Try* anyway. As he closed his eyes, Brand played back the events that had transpired earlier.

His cock swelled almost immediately and he wrapped a fist around it, stroking his dick up and down. His eyes snapped open when he felt not one but two mouths working on him. Tab was licking his balls while Wes was sucking his cock. It was obvious that the other man was not an expert cock sucker, but his enthusiasm more than made up for any lack of experience. Wes was making love to his cock, sucking it then licking up and down the shaft.

"So nice..." He could fall in love with these two. They seemed so open to giving pleasure to him—to Brand the man, the average everyday shifter, instead of Brand Hove, President of the Council. They didn't seem interested in any favors he could get them, just in him giving them pleasure. He had not experienced sex without strings attached for many long years and damn, it felt nice.

The couple worked his cock with enthusiasm and soon he was ready to come again, his third time in a couple of hours. He pulled Tab upright and kissed her deeply, Wes coaxing his cum out in a mild orgasm.

When Brand was able to catch his breath, he kissed first Tab then Wes gently, stroking their faces with his shaking hands. He didn't know how to put into words how they made him feel. Even if he had the words, he wouldn't say them. Always the president, he couldn't afford to let his weakness— or his vulnerability—show.

"Thanks." He settled for the simple instead, hoping they noted just how tender his voice was.

"So, what happens now?" Wes spoke, regarding Brand with a gaze full of mystery and promise.

"Right now, we make our way toward the Royal Hotel. I've secured us a suite there. We can wait out the storm and your wife's first shift there."

Wes' eyes widened in shock. "How did you manage to get a room there? That hotel is so exclusive."

Brand shrugged. Did Wes really not know how much influence he held? Within the shifter world, he was one of the most powerful men. "We just got lucky. Get dressed you two, then cancel your plans and collect your baggage. You're spending the night as my guests at the best hotel in the city."

* * * * *

Even though they had agreed on a meeting place near the airport's outer doors and were all booked with the same airline, it took almost two hours to cancel their tickets and collect their luggage. The airport was packed and people's tempers were fraying. The sooner they got out of there, the better, Wes thought. Tab looked exhausted, and every once in a while she'd shiver. The human pheromones in the air had to be driving her crazy. They sure were spiking his lust and he was used to the benefits of shifting.

Finally, they saw Brand in the distance, his height and presence making him stand out in the crowd. A dart of pure lust spiked through Wes as he observed the other man's magnetic presence.

"Do you like him?"

He regarded Tab as he considered her question. "I lust for him, and there is something very compelling about him. What about you?"

She giggled. His wife actually giggled! "He's very interesting…and so sexy. I'm not sure I want this to end."

"Maybe we don't have to." Though Wes wasn't active in the shifter society, he knew that permanent ménages were tolerated, even encouraged. Most of these involved two females, but two males and one woman wasn't an unheard-of concept.

"Really?" Tab's voice held confusion but there was a definite thread of interest.

"Maybe. It's not unknown among our kind. See how you feel in the morning and if you want to try it, we'll see what his thoughts on the matter are."

"He's a big deal, isn't he? Famous and all?"

Wes tried to recall what little he knew about Brand Hove. Since he was with a latent shifter, he had been reluctant to join the local and state-wide societies, though their newsletters still came to his office. Joining one would have meant awkward absences that would had to have been explained to Tabby.

He couldn't give her the details in this teeming mass of humanity. "I'll tell you about it later, Tab, or maybe Brand will. Let's get over to him and out of this place."

"Please." Relief was evident in her voice. It was clear that the crowd was getting to her. His hands were filled with their rolling bags, but what he really wanted to do was guide her through the morass and into the fresh cold air. When Brand suddenly appeared at their side, his bags slung over one arm, Wes handed their two suitcases to him without a word, then wrapped his arms around Tab, tucking her under his arm.

Brand's status in the community was evident. As soon as they stepped outside the terminal, a black sedan pulled up. Brand and the driver consulted for a moment, then he tossed their bags into the trunk. "Hop in. Sherman here is going to get us to the hotel. It'll be slow going. How many inches have dropped so far today, Sherman?"

"Four so far, sir. Upward of two feet expected from this freak storm. I'm heading home as soon as you're settled, sir. It ain't fit for man or beast out here."

"Indeed. We won't call on you again while the weather is so severe."

The check-in at the hotel was expedient and soon they were in an elevator riding to the top of the high-rise. Brand had taken care of everything, ordering room service—five porterhouse steaks, rare—and their bags had been whisked upstairs. Clothes would be laid out, the bed turned back and after the food was delivered they'd be totally alone to help Tab through her first shift.

* * * * *

"So, what do you think?" Brand asked softly.

Tab had her hands pressed against the large window in the living room area of their suite. Snow drifted down onto an idyllic scene. It was strange how all the ugliness of a city was masked by the frozen white crystals falling from the sky.

"It is beautiful. I want to be out there frolicking in it. That's so silly, though. I've never been someone who plays in the snow. And I'm near thirty, a little old for a delayed childhood." She winced, as if her words were somehow embarrassing.

Brand couldn't wait to take both Tab and Wes to the shifter retreat in South Dakota. She'd love romping in the snow with the other animals, shifter and otherwise.

"Tabitha, life as you know it has changed now. You will never be the same. You'll have to make every life decision while considering your shifter needs and desires. You've changed both inside and outside. I'll be here to help you and Wes with it. After you eat, we're going to bring that pretty kitty out to play."

She rubbed her arms in what appeared to be a gesture of comfort. "I have so many questions…"

Brand led her to the couch and settled her beside her husband. He chose to sit in the desk chair, a short distance away. If he touched either of them, he'd lose control and fuck them and Tab needed her rest right now.

Ignoring his desires for the moment, Brand began explaining the shifter society to Tab, starting with birth. He could tell that she was trying to wrap her mind around the fact that her parents had been shifters as well and wasn't surprised when she mentioned that they'd passed away when she was very young.

Without parents to lead the way, Tab must have been at sea. The Council tried to keep track of latent shifters, but clearly Tab had slipped through the cracks. Brand was impressed with the way she asked clear and well-thought questions. She was shocked and stunned, but seemed to be handling the revelation as best as could be expected.

After they ate, Tabitha told the men she needed a nap. Brand stayed behind as her husband tenderly tucked her in. He was really falling for this couple, an unexpected but welcomed magical serendipity. This all felt so *right*.

All of a sudden, he felt the need to speak to his spirit father, Nekhema. The wise man would be able to help him sort through his feelings. Decision made, he left Wes and Tab a note, took one of the room keys and his cell phone and walked down the corridor toward the stairs leading to the roof. Since the storm had brought them together, it only seemed right for him to be within it now.

The wind was cold but refreshing, the snow falling heavily. Brand was comfortable in the cold weather, his shifter metabolism adjusting to his body's needs.

"Spirit Father," he spoke into the phone. Brand regarded Nekhema as his second father. The man's wisdom and compassion made him Brand's most trusted advisor in Council matters.

"My son. Destiny has found you, I see."

"You see?" Brand had no idea Nekhema was a seer as well, but very little surprised him.

"You don't deny it, lion cub. This is very telling. I dreamed of them, a man and a woman, both cats. You have shared yourself with them. They have touched your heart and soul, Brand. To not pursue this connection would mean that you are lying to yourself, denying yourself happiness for the greater good of your position. A leader especially must have happiness and mates to keep him calm and centered while making decisions. Let your responsibilities wait a while until you pursue this. All work and no play makes for a very grouchy shifter."

Brand began pacing, agitated. "Why them, Father? I have walked alone for so many years and now…"

"And now your soul wants to love. Stop thinking with your head, cub. Think with your spirit and soul. Are these two your intended? If so, why fight it?"

"The politics—" Brand began, but the older man cut him off.

"The politics will not keep you or them warm at night! I have told you many times that when you find your intended, you will know it. Do you know it, my son?"

Brand sighed. Of course he knew it. He just didn't know how to rationalize it. "Yes, Father. I know."

Nekhema chuckled. "What is it you know, Brand?"

The old coot was going to make him say it. "I know that these two people are somehow my destiny. I feel complete with them. I must follow my heart and stop being a workaholic. The Council will manage without me for a short while. Shifter society won't collapse in ruin if I'm not as attentive. Is that what you want to hear?"

"Exactly. Good. Now let an old man roam the woods. Go chase your destiny and I will chase mine. Perhaps a small stewed rabbit will do. They give such good chase."

"Father! Please leave Leslie and Bronwyn alone. Eating my cousins is not the way to stay in my good books!"

The older man sighed quite dramatically. "Fine then. I will go to the market like a human. Now go, son. I'll smooth over things here and prepare your family for the announcement. And Brand? I'm very happy for you. Your voice projects your sense of peace and this is a peace I have long worried would pass you by. Open your heart, love and live. Allow them to see inside you. The leopard and the panther will never harm you."

Chapter Five

&

Wes paced the hotel suite, waiting for Brand. The man had left a brief note saying he'd be back soon. The weather outside was awful. He hoped that Brand hadn't ventured outside. Even with the added strength of the shifter blood, Wes knew it was dangerous for both man and beast out there right now.

His worry for the virtual stranger had rocked him. How could he have such a depth of worry and care for a man they'd just met? It was as if the entire day was just meant to be. He'd let another man take the reins and had been perfectly comfortable with that. Socially as well as sexually, they all seemed to fit together.

Unable to settle down, Wes paced the room, his worry allowing his panther to rule his motions. In a few seconds, he had his clothes off, the change coming over him, familiar and comforting. Now a sleek feline, he padded around the room, sniffing Brand's belongings. A small sound rumbled up from his throat. He liked this man even more in panther form—his scent was intoxicating.

Brand made his way back to the suite. Tab would probably sleep for a couple of hours, and he wanted to use that time to get to know Wes better. The other man intrigued him, Wes' quiet nature held a lot of mysteries.

As Brand opened the door, he heard a strange noise, a throaty snuffle. "Hi there, kitty." He spoke softy and low, entering the room in measured steps. The cat made a small noise—satisfaction mixed with healthy interest—and came closer, pawing at Brand's pants.

"Whoa. Wait just a minute, Wes. I'm not into blood sports." He could have sworn that the big cat smiled. Brand crossed to the bathroom, closing the panther out, and removed his clothes. This would be better than trying to remove them with a randy panther clawing at them. With luck, he'd still have some clothes intact. Shifting for him was instantaneous and painless, even in the small confines of the bathroom. Thankful that he had reopened the bathroom door before turning *furry*, he nosed the door the rest of the way open and padded over to the panther, emitting a small warning growl. They needed to establish the pecking order in this new feline pack and it was best they did it before Tabitha changed.

He *would* win. He knew it, Wes probably knew it as well, but they had to come to physical blows in animal form before they could have peace as a human ménage. It was just the way it had to be. Brand wouldn't draw the panther's blood if he could help it and would never strike a debilitating blow.

He began to circle the other man, lunging suddenly and striking a strong blow that pushed the panther back. Wes huffed out a breath, then jumped on him and the game began.

They sparred for what seemed like an eternity, dodging and lunging, catching fur in fangs and swiping claws shallowly across pelts. Finally, Brand had the upper hand in this well-matched fight. Wes was almost as dominant as him.

Brand stood behind Wes in the classically dominant pose, the other man's neck clamped firmly in his teeth. Both men had grown very aroused, but Brand wouldn't penetrate anyone when he was fully *furry*, though he wanted to plunge inside the other man so badly. It skirted too close to the bestiality line for him.

Tabitha awakened slowly. She wondered if the Valentine's Day events had been just a dream. But the sheets here were much crisper than hers and she couldn't smell Wes beside her. Something didn't seem quite right.

She lifted her hand to scratch her nose and then squeaked, a lethal-looking claw extended from a spotted paw. She'd nearly taken her eye out! Tabitha moved without legendary feline grace, her claws catching on the bedding. She slid out of bed in a heap, shook herself off. She caught her reflection in a mirror and stopped, shocked. Gleaming tan and brown fur covered her body in a thick luxurious pelt. Her face was fully feline, only her eyes stayed the same color. And she had a muscular tail. She twitched it, accidentally knocking a vase off a table. Tab let out a low growl as she was splashed with water, the shock offending her more than the sensation.

Now that she had seen her transformation, she padded to the door, nosing it open a bit more. There was a lion in the room! The lion looked almost as though he was having sex with a gorgeous black panther. Both made low guttural sounds, the lion pressing the panther down.

Tabitha maneuvered the door until it was open enough for her to walk through. As she approached, the lion looked up, his nose quivering, his eyes curious. It was instinct that made her move closer, rubbing her cheek against his, huffing into his gorgeous mane. This magnificent creature had to be Brand.

Tabitha lowered herself to the ground, nose to nose with the panther now, and stropped her forehead against his nose. His long pink tongue came out to lick her face. Her emotions flowed pure and simple through her and she reveled in the ease and rightness of being a shifter. She had found some small part of her soul that had always been lost.

So this was what shifting was all about!

She wanted to feel these big luxurious cats against her, she wanted to know the similarities and differences between them. Hoping they would follow, Tab curled up under the window, tucking her face under her paws. Within seconds, one cat then the other snuggled against her, their rumbling sounds soothing.

She was home now. Her new life was with both of these exciting and sensual shifters. She burrowed close to both of them, thankful for the gift they had brought out in her. She'd never be the same again.

Wes awoke to find both Tabitha and Brand sleeping in human form beside him. While his neck ached a bit, all of the small cuts and bruises the lion had inflicted were gone now. He glanced at Brand, no bruises or cuts marred the perfection of the other man's skin.

Being submissive to the alpha was something he'd have to get used to, but he trusted Brand enough to know that this was the best thing for them all. Although he had been the dominant partner in his marriage, there was a certain freedom in submitting to this man's leadership. And it really couldn't have worked any other way. Brand held the highest office in the shifter world—what message would it send if he was second to Wes?

Wes moved closer to the blond, brushing his hair back and kissing him tenderly. For this man and this man alone, he'd take his place at Brand's side. He had ignored his heritage and yearnings for far too long.

"Hi, Wes." Tabitha's sleepy voice and sensual smile energized him.

"Hello, little spotted one. How do you feel?"

She sat up and stretched, lifting her beautiful breasts high. "Energized. Fully alive. I don't quite know how to describe it. I feel like I can conquer the world."

"Well, what about conquering us instead?" Brand's voice was similarly sleepy and mellow.

Tabitha wormed her way between the two men, stroking both cocks at the same time. Each man found and fondled a nipple. They were relaxed and enjoying this intimate time together. The ultimate goal wasn't orgasm, it was in their shared togetherness, in the rightness of their triad.

"This is forever." Wes had to voice the words.

"Forever," his two lovers echoed.

Chapter Six

ᏚᎧ

It took a few days to get Wes and Tabitha's affairs in order. Both quit their jobs — they'd find new ones in California. They sold the furniture they didn't love and movers packed the belongings they wanted. Now they were ready to leave Wisconsin and their former lives behind.

Tabitha took Brand's and Wes' hands as they surveyed the empty house. Both husband and wife were a little sad at the transformation of their lives, but eagerly looked forward to their life in California with their new husband. Brand smiled fondly at them. They were a unit within the overall triad, but instead of being angry or jealous of this, Brand learned to take their bond as one facet of the whole. He and Tabitha had begun to relate on a deeper level and he was looking forward to creating a deeper connection with Wes.

Without speaking, husband and wife said silent goodbyes to their former life and the three shifters walked out the door into a brilliant sunny day. They were ready for this new chapter.

Four hours later, after being cramped in overgrown tin cans with wings and wheels, they arrived at a sprawling property. Acres and acres of trees were dusted with snow and the only structure was a sprawling ranch house set in a small grove.

"Time to meet your family," Brand announced.

Brand kissed Tabitha's nose and pulled his new family toward the door. As they approached, Nekhema threw the door open and ran outside.

"Brand! My son! Welcome home!" The wizened older man pulled Brand into a tight embrace. "Welcome home, my son. You have been missed. And who are these beautiful people?" Nekhema's dark eyes twinkled with merriment.

"Spirit Father, I bring many gifts. The biggest and most important is my new triad. I wish to present my new family to you. Please bless them and make them welcome at your hearth. Please share your wisdom, your knowledge and your love with them. Father, please meet Tabitha and Wesley Downes-Hove. My beloved, my soul."

Nekhema kissed both Tab and Wes on each cheek. When he stepped back, the tracks of his tears were visible. "Welcome, my new son and daughter. May you live long and happy lives with your husband Brand. Now, come inside and meet the rest of your family. We have been waiting an eternity for Brand to find the other parts of his soul. You are most welcomed in my heart and hearth. I just have one rule. Don't eat the rabbits."

Tabitha, Wes and Brand linked arms, walking confidently into their new lives.

About the Authors

❧

Alexa and Patrick Silver are a happily married couple who share their love of reading and happily ever afters.

Patrick is the technical geek and he makes sure everything makes sense. This superhero (in Alexa's mind, anyway) can leap tall plot holes in a single bound and defeat logic issues with a slash of his mighty sword.

Alexa is the creative type and she makes sure the romance is high on spice. This love chef mixes Alpha heroes with self-assured heroines, adds a liberal dash of sexual tension and bakes.

Their combined love of books, animal rescue and their family are only a few of the interests they share. While Alexa can often be found at her computer plotting their next project, or reading electronic books, Patrick prefers the challenge of computer games. Their reading tastes are quite different. Patrick loves to read stories from some of the latest and greatest authors in science fiction, while Alexa prefers to curl up with some of her favorite romance authors. They are each other's best friend and maintain that romance, like fine wine, only gets stronger and richer with age.

Alexa and Patrick live in the Northeast with their family.

Alexa and Patrick welcome comments from readers. You can find their website and email addresses on their author bio page at www.ellorascave.com.

Tell Us What You Think

We appreciate hearing reader opinions about our books. You can email us at Comments@EllorasCave.com.

ASSIGNMENT
Nina Nash

သ

Dedication

ૹ

To every love god, goddess and mortal whose heart beats
faster as the big day approaches.
Happy Valentine's Day!

Prologue

ɛɔ

The tinkling musical notes faded into the background, disappearing behind the sound of their racing hearts, feverish kisses and the soft, slippery scraping of skin against skin. Sighs, moans and whispered endearments were the only sounds that mattered.

His body, hard and muscular, covered hers completely and her hands clutched his broad back as his swollen cock brushed her sensitive skin, sending shivers up her spine in delicate waves.

Reaching down, she gripped his erection and pulled it closer to her warm, wet pussy. She touched his pink tip to her clit and pressed against him, knowing it wouldn't be long before she climaxed. With a steady hand she guided his cock to her opening and gasped as he slid into her.

The first thrust was only a tease—they both knew it. With a small smile he pulled his cock from her depths, turned his body so his mouth was near her pussy and straddled her shoulders, dangling his erection just above her face.

"Suck me. Suck me until I can't stand it—and then suck me some more," he said, his voice deep and throaty. Pressing his tongue to her slit, he parted her pussy lips and began to lap her nectar as she pulled his cock into her mouth and stroked him with her lips.

When he began to moan, thrusting against her mouth, she licked a finger and pushed it up his ass, expertly massaging his tight brown hole. The vibrations of his mouth against her clit as he struggled for control made her drip, her excitement pooling on the sleeping platform beneath them.

Lifting his mouth from her cleft, he pulled his penis free of her lips, rotated above her and impaled her with his hardness.

A few short thrusts and she tumbled toward her satisfaction, bursts of color exploding behind her eyelids as time stopped. The final flutters of her orgasm touched her as the first bursts of his release flooded her. He came as easily as she had, his cock twitching a final time before it lay still within her.

"So sweet, making love with you," he murmured against her ear. One thick finger pushed a lock of curly chestnut hair off her damp forehead and he kissed a spot above her brow as he smiled. "So easy, isn't it?"

She nodded.

Of course it's easy. Isn't that the way pleasures of the body are supposed to be? Free for the taking and deliciously easy to find?

"It always is, isn't it?" She shifted, clenching her pussy muscles around his still-erect cock. It would take but a tiny bit of encouragement to coax him into readiness… She wondered if she desired his carnal attention a second time. Perhaps…

The knock on the door was a mere formality and it was immediately followed by the entrance of a small woman dressed in flowing white robes. Crossing to the sleeping platform where the lovers were still joined, she looked down into the eyes of the love-filled woman.

"Diana, I trust that you are satisfied," said the newcomer with a smile. "This is a good time for us to talk, is it not?"

"It is always a good time to talk with you, Aphrodite," Diana answered. The man whose cock was still within her body paid no attention to the discussion, his head bent to her breasts. Her nipples stiffened beneath the touch of his warm, wet tongue. "And yes, I am satisfied. For now."

"Good. I waited until your pleasure was complete before disturbing you," the goddess said. "This won't take long. I have a new assignment for you. A Valentine's Day assignment—and it's an important one. All of the details are in the folder." As Aphrodite watched, the handsome man pulled Diana's nipple between his firm lips, suckling her with such force that his tan cheeks moved in undulating waves and she felt a wetness begin beneath her own robes.

Diana's eyes fell to the photo attached to the file. The woman's face, with large blue eyes and long blonde hair, was smiling but the smile stopped short of reaching her eyes.

Shifting to wrap her legs around the man's back, Diana pressed her clit against the base of his throbbing cock before she spoke.

"But, Aphrodite, this woman doesn't look like the kind that needs any help in the love department," Diana said, her voice husky. She arched her back, pressing her breasts into the hot mouth that serviced her body. Twinges of arousal gripped her and her pussy grew slipperier with each tug of his mouth on her nipples. Her body quivered at his touch, her breathing quickened and her concentration faltered. "She looks like she could make a successful love connection on her own. Are you sure my help is required?"

The man tugged his cock from Diana's wetness and stroked it as his fingers played with her swollen clit. He shone slickly with the juices of their passion and his large hand moved with ease over his skin. A tiny drop glittered at the tip of his member and he passed his thumb over it, massaging the wetness onto the rosy pink skin.

Releasing his erection, he knelt between Diana's legs and pressed his face to her folds. Parting her plump lips with his tongue, he licked her glossy opening, greedily lapping the sweetness that dripped from her hot center. When he rose to his knees, his hand dropping unselfconsciously to his penis, his face was shiny, the evidence of her arousal on his chin, lips and nose.

With a groan, he waved his cock between them, its meaty thickness commanding attention. There was no need to move quickly, now that their first desires had been satisfied and he slid his cock across Diana's hairless cleft with slow, sensual movements. It pressed against her clit, teasing it with the silky feel of its round cap before he buried it inside her again.

Aphrodite watched the process with unabashed interest. Lovemaking wasn't a matter to be concealed in the world of gods and goddesses and she considered joining the pair, considered dropping her robes and taking her place beside the couple. An additional body was always welcome when pleasures of the skin were being shared and she knew that her presence on the platform would be acceptable.

As tempting as the idea of making love was, she knew that it wasn't the proper moment for such a diversion. She had duties to assign and scant time to dispense them. The Earthly celebration was just days away and there with so many mortals in need of their assistance her own pleasure would have to wait.

"I am sure, Diana. This woman, Kate Patterson, is at a crossroads. The last boyfriend broke it off with her in a disagreeable manner, she's afraid to give anyone else a chance to hurt her again. Although she's met a man she's being resistant—she needs a push," Aphrodite said.

The couple began to thrust, the man's cock sliding in and out of the woman's wet center as Diana's puckered nipples grew pinker and harder. Snaking her hand between their pumping hips, Diana grasped the base of his penis and squeezed it before her fingertips began to stroke him, pushing his skin in the opposite direction of every thrust. The effect was instant, his breathing began to come in short, hitching gasps and his eyes widened as he fought for control. The women grinned as he became a captive—prisoner to the tight pussy that clenched him, hostage to the traitorous sensations of his own skin. The first telltale signs of his release, the tightening of his full, round testicles as they slapped against Diana's ass with each thrust, excited Diana and she felt a faint flush cover her breasts, spreading to her neck and face.

Aphrodite saw that their orgasms were nearly upon them and turned to cross the room, calling back over one shoulder. "Your job, Diana, is to give this Kate Patterson a push. And push her hard, too. I want her to learn to love, once and for all."

Before the door closed completely Aphrodite heard the couple's orgasmic cries fill the air. For a heartbeat she wished she'd taken the time to join them.

Chapter One

ဆ

Kate struggled to balance two plastic grocery bags, briefcase, purse and the bouquet of flowers stuck beneath her arm while she groped blindly in the brown leather tote bag that dangled from her wrist. Just as she felt the whole mess begin to slide toward the floor she felt a pair of hands grab the grocery bags.

"Here, let me help you."

In no position to argue, Kate smiled gratefully at the woman who'd materialized on her doorstep. With clear brown eyes, curly brown hair and a dazzling smile the woman could have been anyone—a typical girl-next-door type. Whoever she was, Kate was thankful to see her.

"Thanks," said Kate, her fingers closing around the door key. She poked it at the lock blindly, stabbing the door several times before the other woman reached out and took it from her.

"Let me do it. You've got your hands full." Pushing the door open with her hip, the stranger turned and grabbed the tote bag. "There, that should make it easier for you."

Kate walked into her apartment, dumped her bags on the kitchen table and motioned for the other woman to do the same. When their hands were empty Kate held one of hers out to her rescuer.

"I don't know where you came from, but I'm glad for the help," she said. "Hi. I'm Kate Patterson. Thanks for saving me."

"No problem. I'm Diana Billings. I'm living upstairs in 2A. I moved in last week."

Pulling a pint of chocolate ice cream from one of the grocery bags, Kate headed toward the fridge and stuck it in the freezer compartment. Then she leaned down and retrieved a bottle of white wine. Smiling, she held it toward her guest.

"Can I interest you in a glass of wine?"

Diana nodded as she gathered up the flowers and gave them an appreciative sniff. "I'd like that. I confess I haven't met anyone else yet and I'm a bit lonely. I'd love a glass of wine. Do you have a vase for these?"

As she reached for two glasses Kate tilted her head toward an upper cabinet. "In there. Any one will do, as long as it holds water. They were one of those impulse purchases. Figured no one's going to be buying me flowers anytime soon so I might as well buy them for myself. Silly, isn't it?"

"I don't think so. Why should we wait for someone to give us what we want? I think that sometimes we have to take care of our own needs," Diana said, arranging the carnations and lilies in a glass vase.

Kate waited until the flowers were arranged before she tilted her head toward the living room. She watched her new friend put the flowers on a side table as she opened the wine and poured two glasses, passed one to Diana, then raised hers in a salute toward the bouquet.

"To flowers, no matter where they come from," Kate said, taking a long swallow.

"To flowers. And friends."

"My idiot boyfriend dumped me. I could use a friend," Kate said as she finished the contents of her glass and poured a second. "It's so shitty, to get dumped right before Valentine's Day. He could have at least waited until the fifteenth. Would that have been too damn much to ask for? Shit, I hate being alone on the holidays—especially this one."

Diana's eyes scanned Kate, noting everything about her new assignment. Good-looking, with long blonde hair, teal blue eyes, a curvy figure with big breasts and long legs, Kate was a woman who could easily attract any man. If she put her mind to it.

But the mind, that's the issue with this one. No confidence — she's been trampled too often to know she has what it takes to find — and keep — love. Well, that's my job. I'll just give her a push, like Aphrodite instructed. Then things will change.

"I know how you feel. But really, whenever I've been dumped it's turned out to be a good thing. Maybe there's someone new who's waiting to step into your life. Isn't there anyone who interests you? Even a little bit?" Half the wine bottle was already empty.

Leaning forward conspiratorially, Kate grinned. "Actually there is. A guy from my office has been asking me out but I don't know if I can get involved with anyone again. Sex without a relationship? Sure, I can do that — I mean we all have *needs.* But love? Uh-uh. Jeff was so damn mean that I don't know if I can stand the idea of giving someone new the chance to walk all over me. I don't think I can stand it — being dumped again."

"But not every guy is like Jeff. And you don't know that the new one — what's his name?"

"Trevor."

"You don't know that Trevor would break up with you, anyway. He might be a really nice guy — he might be your love match," Diana said. She watched Kate pour the last of the wine, saw the reddened cheeks and glazed look on her face.

Mortals. Amazing how they react to wine.

Kate put her glass on the coffee table, kicked off her pumps and tugged her blazer down her arms. She threw it over the arm of the sofa. "That's better. Thank God it's Friday — finally. Some weeks seem to be twice as long as others, don't you think?"

And some go by really quickly. This one is going to speed by unless I'm careful. I've got to give you a nudge — one that'll get you moving in the right direction.

"The way I see it, some weeks are way too short," said Diana.

Here goes. A nudge — a double-decker push.

A ringing sound filled the apartment and Diana raised her eyebrows, feigning surprise. "Are you expecting anyone?"

"No. It's probably a salesman. I'll be right back," Kate said as she headed for the door.

Masculine laughter mingled with the sound of Kate's voice and two blond men appeared at the door, each carrying a bottle of wine.

"Diana, this is Bill, a guy I used to...um—"

"Sleep with. And this is my buddy Sean. He's someone I still sleep with—from time to time," Bill said, laughing.

"What else are friends for?" Shrugging, Sean took a swallow from a glass he was holding and raised the bottle in the air. "So, ladies, should we begin this little party?"

* * * * *

Bill's long thin cock, neatly sheathed in a ridged blue condom, slipped between Kate's legs and pressed against her cunt as she lay on her back on the rug in front of the big bay window. Outside, breaking the darkness into spasms of bright light, a huge neon sign flashed, sending rhythmic bursts of color over their naked bodies. Sean reached out and touched the other man's penis, stroking it as he slapped it against Kate's pussy. Angling it, Sean held it against Kate's wet opening as Bill thrust himself inside her body.

Diana felt heat build in her body as she watched Bill slip into her new friend's cunt. Fingering her own slick folds, she watched as Kate reached for Sean's erection and tugged it closer to her lips. When Kate wrapped her lips on his hardness she moaned, a sound that sent tremors down every spine and Diana quickened the strokes of her fingers on her clit.

Kate's body writhed as she was fucked by two cocks, the men matching their tempo so that they pumped against her in unison.

Grinning from his kneeling position over Kate's mouth, his cock buried between her lips, Sean reached for Diana and pulled her closer to him. He leaned down and put his mouth on her cunt, licking her honey slowly as she continued to finger her clit. When his tongue swept over her finger, pushing it aside, she began to quiver and his tongue increased the pressure on her, pushing her closer to her climax.

The scent of sex was in the air. Warm, wild and musky, their odors combined to make a unique aroma that fueled their passions. As juices covered hot flesh and skin stretched, strained and pulled they began to move together toward mutual gratification.

Diana's pussy spasmed, her back arched and she moaned, her orgasm gripping her at the same instant that cocks twitched and filled Kate with waves of wet come. Swallowing greedily, Kate's cries of release were muffled by the pulsing cock buried in her mouth.

In a heated heartbeat everyone was satisfied.

* * * * *

The knock on the door was answered almost instantly, as if her arrival had been anticipated.

"Hi," said Kate as she stood behind the door and pulled it open. "Come on in."

All traces of the previous night's activities were gone. No wine bottle or glasses, no tote bags or kicked-off shoes. The living room was clean of any hint of what had gone on just a few hours earlier.

Diana held out a string-tied bakery box. "I picked up some Danish. Hungry?"

"I just made a pot of coffee," said Kate. She pulled two mugs out of a cupboard and set them on the counter before she grabbed a knife and cut the string on the box. When she turned to look at Diana, it was with a look that was filled with a multitude of emotions.

I expected this, Kate. It's all right, I knew you'd feel this way this morning. Let's get this out of the way so we can concentrate on the real issues of this assignment.

"Listen, Diana, I think I should be up front with you about a few things," Kate began. She put the knife in the sink and braced her hands on the table before she continued. "Last night was great but I don't think I can do that again—at least not right away. Don't get me wrong, I loved it...I mean, I really needed it too." She colored slightly and arched her brows. "It was probably easy for you to tell that I was...well, a little bit...."

"Orgasmically challenged?"

Their laughter was fast and filled the kitchen. Any residual tension dissipated between them and Kate, still smiling, nodded. "That's a good way to put it. Yeah, I guess I was a little bit frustrated and I needed to feel desirable and...well, I just needed to be touched. Can you understand that? I've felt so shitty since Jeff dumped me. It felt so great to have someone touch me—and believe me, the orgasm was incredible."

"It rocked my world, too. Listen, Kate, I think I know what you're trying to say. I feel the same way. It's just something that happened. Something incredible, but not an every-night thing, right?"

"Right."

Great, you're interested in human contact. You're past feeling crappy and are feeling sexy again.

"I think it was just a question of being in the right place at the right time. Two horny women and a couple of bottles of wine with a pair of sexy guys—what else could have happened? But what I want to know is whether or not you know any men you could introduce to me. I'm new in town, remember?"

Kate finished her coffee before she responded. When she did it was with words that were slow and deliberate.

"I did get invited out tonight. Trevor asked me to go to a club with him. Trevor. He said something about a friend of his, too—some guy who's new at the health club. He asked if I knew anyone who'd like to go with us—sort of a double date, you know? I haven't told him I'd go yet. Are you interested? In going out with Trevor's friend?"

Diana smiled, sat back in the chair and crossed her legs.

"I am. Very interested."

Things are going so much better than I'd hoped.

* * * * *

Club Tango was packed. The two couples occupied a small table in a dark corner, a nearly empty pitcher of margaritas beside the remains of several platters of finger food. On one side of the table Trevor and Kate were pressed together, their heads touching as they talked in low voices. They seemed to have forgotten that there was anyone else at the table.

Kate turned to Art and felt her stomach drop. Handsome, with deep brown eyes and thick black hair, he smiled at her with a smile that was so bright she felt as if the lights dimmed every time he grinned. Powerless to stop the delicious trembling in her body, a definite reaction to the broad-shouldered man, she decided instead to relax and enjoy the unexpected stimulation.

Kate and Trevor look like they're getting hotter over there without any help from me. Why shouldn't I partake of pleasures of the body, too? Especially when there's such a yummy hunk pressing his hot body closer to mine. And hell, we know I'm hot—all the time.

"Kate said that you're new in town. Where do you come from?" she asked. Leaning toward him, she caught a whiff of his masculine, spicy scent and her pussy tingled as she felt the slipperiness grow inside her panties.

"Oh, here and there. I've been a bunch of places in the past few years."

"Army? Hobo? Why have you moved so much?"

"No, nothing as exciting as that, I'm afraid. My job—my calling—you could say, takes me all over," he said, staring into her eyes and telegraphing a silent message to her.

In a flash she knew. It was so glaringly obvious that she wondered how she hadn't seen it immediately. His good looks, oozing sensuality, charm and stellar personality—now it made sense.

Lowering her voice, she arched a brow. "You're...?"

"Uh-huh." When he nodded a lock of curly black hair fell over his brow and she reached up instinctively to smooth it off his skin. A jolt of electricity rocketed through her body and there was a wash of warmth that began low in her center and spread rapidly outward. It filled her as surely as ice cream fills a cone, making each and every one of her secret nooks quiver with desire. "Sent by Aphrodite. Just like you were, Diana."

"How come I didn't know? Why two of us—and why wasn't I told?"

It's not usual protocol, having both of us here at the same time! Everyone knows that there's only one god or goddess assigned to a case at any moment—what in the name of Hades is happening?

Looking up at Kate and Trevor, who were completely unaware of the drama that was unfolding on the opposite side of the table, Diana took in a deep breath. Usually placid, her temper didn't often flare up but in this instance she found herself battling the urge to speed back to Aphrodite and give her a piece of her mind.

As if I'd ever do that. The last love goddess that dared to spout off to the love leader got reduced to encouraging dogs to mate at a kennel somewhere in Argentina. Fat chance I'd have doing that— dogs make me sneeze and besides, what the heck does one do to make dogs feel more amorous toward each other? Ick. No. I think I'll keep my temper to myself.

Besides, Aphrodite must have had a reason for sending Art. She has a reason for everything.

"Dance?"

The full, rich voice broke into her thoughts like a light in a dark room. Nodding, she brought her eyes to his.

What the hell? Kate's doing fine on her own. I may as well have some fun.

The dance floor was crowded but not so crowded that it was uncomfortable. Art led her to a secluded corner and pulled her into his arms and she nestled against him, her body beginning to move effortlessly with his. An exceptional dancer, he was light-footed and easy to follow. As they danced she felt the tension leave her body, felt her apprehension fade and felt herself beginning to enjoy the touch of his hard maleness against her softer skin.

"Are you more relaxed now? I'm sorry it came as such a shock to you. I know it's against most protocol but I just figured that Aphrodite had her reasons," Art said as he looked down at her, locking his gaze on hers. "She always does." His breath was spicy, scented by the exotic flavors of the foods they'd eaten, when it washed over her. Leaning into it and into him, Diana savored every deliciously sensual aroma, licking her lips in response to the imagined taste of him.

"You're right about that," agreed Diana, passing her eyes over his ripe mouth. "She never does anything without a reason. And it's always a good reason."

"I guess we'd better just enjoy the assignment."

"That seems to be the best thing to do." It surprised her that her voice sounded husky to her own ears.

They both felt the familiar surges of sexual arousal and would have acted upon them without hesitation had they not been in the realm of mortals. The constraints of their present location made them grin as the signs of their lust grew more evident.

Diana's nipples were hard, pressing against his shirt with every step she took and her crotch was moist. She felt slippery and hot, eager to be touched and her breath began to hitch as Art's erection pressed against her hip, its rock-hard thickness beating a steady pulse as he made his desire known to her. The situation would have been comical had it not been so demanding.

"I'd like to tear your clothes off," Diana said as she pressed her cheek to his. "I'd like to pull your throbbing cock into my cunt and ride you until we both feel the waves of release fill our bodies. That's what I'd like, Art."

"Artemis," he said hoarsely. "God of lust in the forest, at your service. And, dear Goddess Diana, I would like nothing more than to let you fulfill your desires, thus fulfilling my own. We both know that that if we were back in our own land, we would be naked and my cock would be buried in your slipperiness at this very moment."

"Oh! It's too—I can't wait—I—oh!" A shudder gripped her body and he held her closely while she enjoyed a mild climax.

"But alas, we are not in our own world," he continued, pressing his hardness against her swaying body. "And my poor staff is doomed to eternal tumescence."

A giggle escaped her and she concealed the shaking of her body in the tight circle of his arms.

He feigned gruffness as he spoke into her ear.

"Oh? So it's funny to you, is it? Funny to think that me and my swollen cock will have no relief save my own hand? Does that amuse you, Diana?" Art nipped at her ear as they danced, sending a new wave of heat through her body.

"A little bit," she admitted. "But I have an apartment, you know. We could do as mortals do, if we desired. We could go to my apartment and..."

"I desire. I desire very much," Art answered, taking her hand in his and winding their way through the crush of dancers that were between them and their table.

He knew he'd have to convince Trevor and Kate it was time for more private pleasures.

Chapter Two

ഇ

Beside the parking lot at Club Tango there was a small dark alleyway. It wasn't an optimal setting for romance but it would have to do.

Her fingers slid his zipper down immediately but he didn't even feel her touch. With his hands beneath her shirt he was so completely absorbed in what his own fingers were fondling he had no idea she'd undressed him until she dropped to her knees and pulled his penis between her lips. Placing his palms against the concrete wall before him, he savored every sensation of her tongue swirling over his taut flesh, pressing himself farther down her throat as she cupped his testicles and squeezed them gently.

"I can't take this, Diana! I'm not a mortal man—I need more than this torture," he groaned, pulling her to her feet. "I can't be toyed with. I need to feel your body around my cock. And I need to feel it now, dammit."

When her jeans were around her thighs he turned her body and moved behind her. Pressing his cock against the crack of her exposed ass, he reached down, separated her cheeks and positioned his penis at her tight brown hole. There was a temptation to ram into her but he resisted—just barely. Yielding to his slow, steady pressure, her ass expanded to grip him until he was inside. As he reached around her body and found her engorged clit with his fingertips he began to thrust, pushing them both toward the edge of their already-stretched sensibilities.

"Yes, Art—do it like that! Harder—pinch me harder," Diana moaned, clenching her thighs around his hand as he tweaked her nub sharply. Bending toward the wall, she climaxed, his hand, his cock and the cold concrete the only things keeping her upright.

"That's right...like that, just like that. Now feel me, feel me baby. Here it comes—here comes my—oh gods!"

Arching his back, Art buried his cock to the hilt in her ass and gripped her hips as come flew from him in long, wet streams that seemed—to both of them—to go on for a very long time.

* * * * *

The apartment was sparsely furnished but neither of them cared. They'd barely closed the door behind them before they began pulling their clothes off.

"Damn mortal trousers!" Art muttered as he struggled with her zipper. "Zippers—who ever invented these blasted things? I've been having a deuce of a time getting my rod out of my trousers every time I need to use it. And now I can't get into yours when I need to get—ah, there. That's it."

Pushing her jeans down to her ankles and lifting her out of them, he struggled with his own jeans. With a few well-aimed swats, she pressed his hands away and slid his zipper down smoothly. Opening the fabric wide, she reached inside and tugged his hard-on out of his pants, gave it a quick wipe with a cleansing pad she took from her pocket, as he dropped his jeans and stepped out of them.

Fat, thick and hard enough to make any love god proud, his cock bounced in the air between them, giving no hint that its excitement had been recently relieved. Once they were naked he pulled her toward him, pressed her against his body as he devoured her lips with his own and ground his erection against her hip.

Waiting—any sort of slow, sensual exploration—was impossible for either of them. They wanted gratification instantly.

Art stroked her bare slit, moaned at the wetness he found and reached for his cock. Squeezing the base of his shaft between his thick fingers, he shook it as he struggled for control over his throbbing body.

"Don't make me wait, Art," she begged. "Please. I want you inside me. Now. We can be slower next time."

Turning away from him, she moved quickly toward the only piece of furniture in the apartment's small dining room. A heavy oak table stood in the center of the room, a mirrored wall the only other distinctive feature.

Leaning over the table, she propped herself on her elbows and watched her reflection in the mirror. Seeing her breasts dangle above the polished oak surface, her nipples, as hard as tiny pebbles, brushing over it, sent exquisite surges of pleasure through her already-tingling body. Diana spread her legs and watched as he stepped behind her and rested his heavy cock briefly on her ass. They stared in the mirror at each other for several heartbeats, smiling in recognition of the pleasure they were about to share.

With a low, thick moan Art pressed his penis to her wet pussy, pausing before he slid into her. His muscular arms circled her and he palmed her breasts as he thrust into her, rocking her body on the table with each pumping movement of his hips.

There wasn't enough satisfaction to be found for either of them with the rear entry position and they both knew it. Sliding himself from her body, Art lifted her to the table and she let her body relax on its hard surface. A shuffling sound came from beside the table when he bent down, gone from her sight for moments that felt endless.

Where are you, Art? I want you inside me again...I feel the emptiness you've left and I need your cock again. Bring it back, please.

The items he held in his hands were ones they were familiar with and he used them to tie her wrists to the strong legs of the massive table. Her bra, wrapped twice around her skin and his black leather belt, looped in a thick bundle, held her tightly.

Art climbed onto the table, straddling her body on his knees as he ignored Diana and began to stroke himself, watching every movement in the wall of mirrors. His cock stood straight out from his body, the skin so tight that it was pink and silky as he slid his fist from base to tip, stopping to massage the fat red cap before pressing his hand toward his abdomen again. A drop of glistening moisture seeped from his tiny hole and he looked down at it, holding his tip just inches from Diana's face.

"Do you see that?" he whispered, grinning. "That is only the first taste of my eruption, the first drop of the flood that's going to burst from this sweet little hole. Lick it, Diana. Lick it and taste my wetness."

Pressing his erection closer, he rubbed his cock across her tongue and watched as his wetness became one with hers. A hoarse chuckle came from deep within him as he ran his turgid organ across her lips, denying her the pleasure of sucking on his throbbing flesh. With his fingertips he pulled his tip from her tongue over and over again—each time she attempted to grab him he tugged it just out of her reach.

You tease, you rotten tease—I want that. I want it so badly.

"Art, for the love of Aphrodite, stop teasing me! You've spent too much time with mortal men...you've learned the ways of pleasuring women but goddesses—we can't be toyed with. Remember that, Art," Diana said, twisting her wrists against the ties that bound her. "Now. Put it inside my pussy now!"

Kneeling between her knees, he positioned himself and slid into her dripping cunt in one swift motion. As he began to pump into her his balls tightened, slapping her ass with each stroke, every slap bringing him nearer to the moment of his eruption.

I can't wait. I feel it starting, feel the first bits of—oh! That's it! So good, so incredibly good! Yes, oh yes...YES! Oh, yes...Now you—it's your turn. Do it now, Art—I want to feel you lose control.

Squeezing his cock with the still-quivering muscles inside her pussy, she let her muscles stroke him as she felt his breath begin to hitch. Watching him, wide-eyed and openmouthed as he emptied his cock into her body was a turn-on. Every pulsing spasm of his penis brought her closer to her second orgasm and it washed over her as the last drops of his pleasure filled her.

When they'd both stopped shaking, he grinned at her in the mirror. His cock, still turgid despite his climax, was securely nestled in her warm, wet pussy. Neither of them had made any move to dislodge it and it didn't seem likely that their pleasure would be ending anytime soon.

Diana gripped him with her muscles and grinned in response.

Thank Zeus he's not a mortal man! Imagine that being the end of it—it's almost too cruel to believe. Just when I'm ready to give it a second go, to think that his penis would be all soft and shriveled— ugh! Mortals, who can figure them out?

"Wonder how Trevor's doing downstairs?" asked Art as he began to move his hips against her ass. Sliding his cock out of her wetness with delicate deliberation, he tantalized her sensitive skin with inch after inch of male hardness. "Do you think he's doing a good job with her?"

Inhaling softly as his fingers found her clit, she pushed herself against his cock and pressed his throbbing shaft into her.

"Not as well as you're doing, I'd wager."

Chapter Three

😘

Diana reached for the garlic salt and shook it liberally onto her pizza. Topped with some extra crushed red pepper flakes and a fine dusting of grated cheese, it met with her approval and she took a first bite, moaning as the fine layering of flavors exploded in her mouth.

Sex always gives me an appetite. For food…and for more sex. I can't believe I had so much fun with Art. By Zeus, I can't wait to see him again. Mmm…it's hard to believe that I can still desire him after last night. By all rights I should be exhausted, not looking for sex for another day or two, at least. But there it is, a definite twinge of longing in my pussy…yeah, I want him again. Soon.

"So tell me, how did it go last night with Trevor? What did the two of you find to do after we left you?"

Kate blushed, taking her time chewing and swallowing before she answered. When she wiped her face with a paper napkin, it was impossible to wipe the look of satisfaction off her face.

"We talked," she said, smiling. "For a long time. Actually, Trevor didn't leave until this morning. Early this morning."

"Really? That sounds promising."

An answer didn't come immediately and Diana's hopes fell slightly. She wondered if Art would have to give Trevor another nudge toward Kate. Maybe Kate wasn't as ready for a new love as she'd thought she was. Not on her own, anyway.

Yeah, we might need another nudge here. It's taking too long for her to say anything. Way too long.

Looking up from her half-eaten pizza, Kate seemed to consider her words carefully.

"I don't want to get my hopes up but he's nice—really nice. I like him a lot."

"And that's a problem?" asked Diana. "You don't sound like it's an especially good thing and I've got to admit that I'm surprised. I thought being *really nice* was something desirable."

A loud slurping noise came from Kate's empty cup and she blushed as she put it on the table.

"Oops, I guess I wasn't paying attention. It is good, I guess. I mean, we were up all night, talking about everything and anything. I feel like I've known him forever and it feels really, really great... Except that's how it felt with Jeff, too. In the beginning it was great but then at the end it was horrible." Kate made circles on the tabletop with the moist bottom of her empty cup. "I don't want to do that again, fall in love and have my heart broken. I don't think I can stand it if it happens one more time."

The pizzeria was packed with the usual Sunday afternoon crowd. Young families with small children, elderly couples who still held hands and teenagers all filled the space. No one paid any attention to the two women in the corner booth who were dressed in jeans, sweatshirts and sneakers. No one cared that they were discussing matters of the heart, matters that would affect one woman's entire future.

Ah, that's the thing, Kate. You've got to be willing to step out of your comfort zone, be willing to give love another try. Haven't you heard the try, try again thing? I thought all mortals knew that one.

"What, haven't you heard the try, try again thing?" asked Diana. She chewed on the last bit of her pizza crust and stared at her new friend, a fleeting smile her only reward for the witty suggestion. Apparently the try, try again jingle wasn't as popular on Earth as it used to be.

"Yeah, of course I've heard that. But that's only for small children and...I don't know—for pets. I don't think it works for adults and their love lives, Diana. No, I don't think I can try again. Being dumped by Jeff was too terrible for me to take the risk again."

Kate gathered up her garbage and carried it to the trash can. When she returned to the booth she had a look of infinite sadness on her face, a look that shook Diana to her core.

How quickly mortals can go from joyful to tearful. It must be terribly tiring to feel so many emotions in such a short span of time. Honestly, how do they do it? It's making me tired just watching it.

"I don't want to butt into your life, Kate, but you are my new friend. And we have been rather close, don't you think?" said Diana, lowering her voice conspiratorially. When Kate met her eyes and nodded, they shared a secret smile. "So I think, being that we have been almost intimately joined, that I can speak freely."

Kate waved her hand in the air between them with a small grin. "In light of the fact that you've...um, been closer to me than any of my other friends have been, I think you've earned the right to say whatever you want to say. Really, I don't think that I can have any secrets from you after...well, you know."

Diana felt a ripple of pleasure move through her swiftly. By the telltale beads poking against Kate's sweatshirt, it was obvious that hers wasn't the only pussy that was suddenly moist and slippery. It was a good feeling to know that the time she and Kate had spent together with the guys on the first night had been as pleasurable to Kate as it had been for her.

"Yeah, I know and when I see your nipples like that," she whispered, staring pointedly at Kate's firm buds. "It's hard for me to not think about it. I've got to admit, Kate, that there's a sudden slippery feeling in certain parts of my body."

Leaning forward, Kate opened her eyes and whispered, "Really?"

"Really."

"Me too."

"Those two guys were great. Really great."

They grinned and sat back against the booth. In that moment it was like they were the only two members of an elite sorority and the knowledge they shared gave them the courage to push forward.

"So, as I was saying before your boobs interrupted me," Diana said, giggling. "I think that in affairs of the heart the try, try again thing works overtime. You should definitely give Trevor a fair shake. He deserves it and so do you. Why should you both pay forever for Jeff's bad behavior and definite lack of taste? Why?"

"You've got a point. Maybe I should give Trevor a fair shake—as you put it."

"Good. So, have you shaken him yet?"

"Diana!"

"Well? Have you?"

Kate scanned the room. It had emptied out considerably and when she was sure that there wasn't anyone who could overhear their conversation, she smiled. Widely.

"Well, I wouldn't say I've shaken him yet—not exactly. But I will say that I've given his...um—his equipment—an initial feel."

"And? How did it feel?"

Kate shivered. "It felt great. I can't wait to get my hands on it—without his jeans in the way, that is!"

* * * * *

The two couples were lingering over coffee when it happened. They'd had a delicious meal, talked and laughed and shared stories that made each of them feel the familiar bonds of friendship. But as they took their time drinking second cups of coffee, hesitant to end the evening—it happened.

Art and Diana recognized it immediately.

"Well, I don't know about that, but I can tell you that it was something I don't want to try again," said Trevor, shaking his head and smiling at the memory. "When I got down the slope I was so scared that I don't know how I didn't pass out right in front of everyone. I'll tell you, my legs were shaking so hard I thought for sure that everyone could hear my knees bashing together. Can you believe that I confused the bunny slope with the bullet slope? That's the last time I go skiing."

They all laughed at the easy way he told the story, not at all embarrassed at his horrific athletic adventure on Stowe Mountain. To the contrary, he acted like it was simply part of his overall learning experience—a part to be shared and giggled over.

"Sometimes it's hard to know what kind of things are worth trying a second time," said Kate. "It's easy to decide not to do something just because it didn't work out the first time. Not that I'm saying you should try skiing again, not unless you want to, that is. But I'm a pretty good skier and I'd be happy to give you some lessons if you'd like them."

"Promise we'll stay on the bunny slope?"

Trevor and Kate passed a long, meaningful moment staring into each other's eyes. Diana and Art knew that they and everyone else in the crowded Italian restaurant were momentarily forgotten. They didn't mind being forgotten.

"I promise," said Kate. "At least until you're ready to move on to something harder."

"It's a deal, then," answered Trevor, reaching across the table and covering Kate's hand with his own.

In that instant Diana knew that her assignment was complete. She'd managed to push Kate toward love, away from hurt and onward toward happiness and it filled her with joy to know she'd helped someone as deserving of love as Kate. There was a feeling of satisfaction knowing that Kate wouldn't be spending a long, lonely Valentine's Day. She'd be with Trevor, hopefully getting her hands on everything the guy had hidden beneath his clothes.

Art winked at Diana and she nodded. He reached into his wallet and tucked a wad of cash beside his plate before he held out his hand to her. She put her hand in his, feeling a shiver of excitement at his touch.

This guy drives me over the edge with just a touch. I can't believe he has the power to do that to me. No one—not god or mortal—has ever made me shudder like this—with a mere touch. No one.

"Listen, you two, we're going to shove off," said Art. They all stood and hugged and the other couple tried halfheartedly to get them to stay but Art insisted that they'd decided on going for a walk at a nearby lake. "Thanks anyway, but I promised Diana that I'd show her the lake at sunset. It's gorgeous and I want her to see it. So you two have a good night. We'll see you guys tomorrow."

As the women hugged Kate whispered two words that filled Diana's heart. They let her know her assignment had been a worthwhile one.

"Thank you."

* * * * *

Great Swan Lake was deserted when Art parked beside the path that led down to the water's edge. Loosening his tie, he removed it and threw it on the backseat along with his dinner jacket. Staring pointedly at her dress shoes, he raised an eyebrow and she kicked them off.

"Step carefully on the path," he said as he opened the car door for her. "After that it's all sand at the lake, so you'll be fine. Just step where I step."

Following him through the forest, putting her feet precisely where his bare feet had been, she felt like a child on a great adventure. She couldn't remember the last time she'd had so much fun on a love assignment. Maybe it was the idea that she'd helped to make two lovers find each other in time for the most important holiday in the love goddess's year or perhaps it was simply that she really cared about what happened to Trevor and Kate. Whatever the case, she knew that this assignment might just be her all-time favorite.

When they reached the lake she was awestruck by its beauty. Wide, shimmering and the most incredible shade of iridescent teal blue she'd ever seen, Great Swan Lake literally robbed Diana of her breath. Standing in the soft sand for long, silent moments, she felt contentment wash over her.

This place is gorgeous. And I'm so happy about Kate and Trevor. What else could I want?

"It's something else, isn't it?" The voice was so close that she could feel the movement of warm air near her ear as he spoke.

Ah, Art. Yes, how could I have forgotten you, handsome love god? Maybe this assignment is going to get a little better before it's over. I didn't think it was possible, but just maybe...

"It sure is," Diana agreed. They began to walk along the shoreline, pausing only to roll up their pant legs and wet their feet. "How did you find this place?"

Art watched a loon take flight before he answered. "I found it on my last assignment. I had some spare time and you know I just like to look around whenever I get a chance to visit a new place. I found this lake, saw the place I'm taking you to see and I don't know, I guess I just fell in love."

They had reached a remote part of the beach. When Art left the sand and headed toward the tree line, she followed him. They walked beneath towering pine trees, over a carpet of soft pine needles and into the forest.

"Taking me to see? You mean there's more here than just the lake?"

Nodding, he paused beside the trunk of a wide, ancient oak tree. With a wide grin, he pointed at a spot just up the sloping ground from where they stood.

"There is," Art said. "Up there."

Following his fingertip with her eyes, she scanned the trees until she saw it. When she found it, nestled in the trees, her heart jumped.

"Whose is it?"

"Mine," he answered proudly. Folding her hand in his, he pulled her forward. When they reached a set of wide wooden steps he lifted her as effortlessly as if she was a bottle of champagne and carried her upward until he reached the top step and set her down on her feet. They were standing on the wide deck of a hand-hewn log cabin. Perched high above the ground, looking down onto the lake, it felt as if they were in the clouds. The scent of pine mixed with the fresh, clean aroma of what could only be pristine mountain air.

"Yours? Oh, Art, how beautiful!" Diana perched on the edge of the wide deck, on a built-in platform that hung over the trees and gave an unobstructed view of the lake. The sun was beginning its descent as Art settled onto the platform beside her, putting his arm around her shoulders and pulling her close.

"Do you like what you see, Diana? Do you really like it?"

I do. But why, in the name of Zeus, is my heart bashing around in my chest like that? I feel...I feel decidedly flustered. Kind of like — no, it can't be. I'm a goddess, not a mortal. No, it's foolishness, that's what it is. No. It can't be.

But it was. When she turned to answer him she felt as if she was being sucked into a vacuum, felt the swirling, toppling, head-over-foot tumbling that could only mean one thing.

And he saw it. In that instant he saw it and the whoop of exhilaration that escaped from his lungs filled the air, bouncing off trees and sending birds out of their nests in a flurry of squawks and squeaks.

Art bent his head to hers, crushing her lips with his and his tongue slid into her mouth, claiming it for his own. There was no hesitation on the part of her mouth either. Her body and her heart responded instantly to his touch.

It took only seconds for them to pull off their clothes. A tangled heap of garments fell to the wide deck as they struggled to get closer to each other. When they were finally free to explore without encumbrance, Art paused. His fingers brushed across one erect nipple, teasing it to further tightness, before he covered her breast with his large hand and looked deeply into her eyes.

The pounding of her heart against his palm was undeniable, but he had to hear it from her lips. He had to hear it, even though he knew it was so.

"Tell me, Diana. Tell me the one thing you've never told another," he said softly. As he watched her eyes search his, he willed his heart to open, to be without barriers before her. It was something he had never done before, something he had never wanted to do. "Tell me," he urged. "I need to hear it. And you need to say it."

As he waited his cock stiffened. He could no sooner control the throbbing meatiness than he could control the weather and he had less desire to control either than he had to hear the words of her heart.

He kissed her, a soft, gentle kiss. When he pulled back he saw the faintest glimmer of wetness in her eyes.

"Tell me, Diana. We both need to hear it."

"I love you, Artemis. I love you as I have never loved another," she said quietly. They were words that would change their destinies forever and they both knew it.

"I know. I love you, too, dearest. I will love you until the end of time and further."

His mouth fell to hers and their passion, fueled by the depth of their emotions, carried them along on a delicious ride. He rose to his knees between her legs, a glorious sight that made Diana's heart thud double-time, before he reached for her with his mouth and licked her wetness, making her squirm with desire. His tongue stroked her folds until she thought she'd lose her mind at the unreleased sensations before he pulled her clit into his mouth and sucked. Hard. The delicious tingling that began deep within her body erupted in pulsing, shuddering waves of delight. Diana's back arched and she pressed herself to his mouth as she climaxed.

When the first waves of her pleasure subsided she pulled Art's body up so that he lay beside her, pushed him back against the platform and reached for his turgid cock. Hot and solid beneath her fingertips, he moaned as she tugged him gently. The tip of his penis held one glistening drop of moisture and she rubbed it into his rosy skin before she dropped her mouth to taste him.

Winding his fingers into her curly hair, he held her head as she sucked his cock deeply into her mouth. He tasted warm and woodsy, as if he, too, were a being native to the forest. Lips on skin, tongue on throbbing flesh, she stroked him, pulling him closer with each flick of her tongue toward his climax.

"Diana…. I don't think I can—oh! I don't think I can wait much longer," Art gasped.

With a final squeeze of her lips against his swollen skin she released him from her mouth. His cock bounced as she shifted and slid down onto him until she felt his balls touch her ass before she raised herself, squeezing his penis as she rose. The shock at the squeezing sensation was evident in his eyes and it gave Diana a feeling of power that made her even more excited.

Ah, Art…maybe I love you, my darling, but I'm not going to give you power over me. No, we'll share everything equally, not only in the mortal realm but in our world as well. And especially, darling Art, in the bedroom. We'll share everything there—especially.

Diana felt the sudden stiffening of his back, the quick, shallow breathing that told her that his release was upon them. As the first spasms of his climax pushed his wetness into her she pressed down against his shuddering cock and his twitching flesh touched her sensitive clit so forcefully that she climaxed with him, shaking with delight as he filled her.

If I had only known before what love feels like. No wonder mortals all yearn for it. No wonder Aphrodite is so set on making sure we bring it to every realm. It's divine — if I had only known sooner.

Art shifted Diana in his strong arms until she was lying beside him. He hadn't removed his still-firm cock from her depths and if he had his way they'd remain joined for quite some time yet.

When he kissed her she felt his penis jump and it made her giggle.

"Funny, is it? When I kiss you are you always going to giggle?" he asked with a wide grin.

"Only when your cock jumps inside me. That's going to make me giggle every time, I can guarantee it."

He nodded and stroked her nipple thoughtfully. "That sounds fair enough. I think I can accept that, giggling when the cock jumps."

Diana shifted so that he had better access to her breasts. The stroking was beginning to send a new round of shaking through her body.

"Mmm. Make me giggle, Art. Make me giggle *really* loudly," she whispered as her body began to heat again.

Moving her hips with slow, circular movements, she stroked his cock languidly and his hardness grew stiffer. He repositioned his legs, scissoring one of hers and pressed against her clit with the base of his cock so that every undulation of their bodies brought a fresh wave of pleasure to her.

"Does that make you giggle? Or maybe this will do it," he said, gripping her ass with his large hand. Running his hand down her thigh, he pulled her leg up until it draped over his shoulder. Using the added leverage, Art pumped his cock into her pussy until he felt her twitch beneath him. Only then did he allow his own pleasure to surface and he flooded her again.

When their breathing slowed, he lowered her leg, running his hand up her thigh and back up to cup her breast. He knew he'd never tire of touching the silky soft skin that he'd dreamed of for so long.

"I'm glad our assignment was completed easily," she said. "Aren't you?"

"Our assignment?"

"Mmm-hmm…Trevor and Kate, remember? Our assignment."

Art rolled an erect nipple gently between his fingertips. Her body was beginning to tremble again and he could feel the first flutters growing inside her as he fondled her. The thought was making his cock grow harder and he pressed his hips forward, moving within her.

"Oh…Trevor and Kate. They were *your* assignment, Diana—not mine," Art said. He began to thrust slowly, sliding his erection in and out of the warmth with studied deliberateness.

Oh, that feels so good. His cock is so big and hard and it's sending delicious shivers up my spine and—what? My assignment?

"Um, Art? What do you mean? Weren't they your assignment, too?"

Pushing his cock deep into her warm, wet pussy, he shook his head.

"No."

"No?"

"No."

She pressed herself against him, shuddering as the base of his cock stroked her engorged clit.

"What was your assignment, then?"

"This was my chance to let you know how much I love you. I have loved you ever since I first saw you. After all, darling Diana, even gods and goddesses should find happiness in time for Valentine's Day."

Also by Nina Nash

ဢ

Cairo by Moonlight
North Pole Naughty
Recipe for Love
Violet Moons

About the Author

ဢ

Nina Nash loves romance. She loves steamy kisses, hand holding, walking on the beach at moonlight and mostly, she loves love. The feeling that your feet have left the ground and your heart has begun to sing—that's what Nina is all about. Writing romance? It comes easily to a woman who believes in it as passionately as she does.

Nina divides her time between Key West and Manhattan. An accomplished pianist, she'll often be found tickling the ivories while contemplating her next novel. When she's not writing romance or making music, she likes to snorkel, scuba dive and rock climb.

Life in the Nash household is never dull. And Nina doesn't think it should be, either. As far as she's concerned, life is too short for dull. What do you think? Nina loves to hear from fans!

Nina Nash welcomes comments from readers. You can find her website and email address on her author bio page at www.ellorascave.com.

Tell Us What You Think
We appreciate hearing reader opinions about our books. You can email us at Comments@EllorasCave.com.

CHEER GIVERS & MISCHIEF MAKERS

K.Z. Snow

೮౩

Prologue

ഔ

Come on, don't sleep on the couch." Ron balanced on the edge of a cushion and stroked Mattie's bare leg.

She jerked it away from him, drawing it up toward her midriff. The position gave him a nice view of her ass and pussy, because neither was covered very effectively by her skimpy panties. Ron was tempted to run a finger along the soft, low ridge between her thighs. But she'd probably break his wrist. Despite that possibility, his cock had already begun thickening. It felt as if he had a third arm growing from his groin.

"Can't you say something?" he crooned, hoping to melt at least the top layer of ice.

"You have the most hideously awesome ability to say and do the wrong thing at the wrong time." The back of the couch muffled Mattie's voice but didn't filter the disgust from her tone.

Ron continued to debate with himself whether or not to touch her. "I must have been born with it."

"Gee, ya think?" she tossed over her shoulder.

"Old habits die hard. But you know I'm getting a lot better at doing and saying the *right* things." Ron craned his upper body toward Mattie's concealed face. "Wouldn't you agree?"

She neither agreed nor disagreed but clung petulantly to her silence.

"Don't I even get credit for trying?"

"I'm never cooking for you again," the couch seemed to mutter.

Great! *Is that a promise*? At least he wasn't brash or idiotic enough to say it. Ron sighed. Apparently no credit for his efforts was forthcoming.

Slapping his thighs in lieu of slapping Mattie's luscious little fanny, Ron said, "All right. Have it your way."

He rose from the couch, still uncomfortably aware of his hard-on, and walked across their cavernous loft to the bedroom at its northern end. He opened the closet and pulled a book from beneath his stack of jeans. Putting it on the bed for a moment, he stripped naked. After snatching up the book, he again traversed the living area and stopped before the coffee table.

"Happy Valentine's Day. I'm going to bed." Ron laid the book on the coffee table. Mattie's back was still turned to it. "Here's your present."

As he walked back to the bedroom, taking his usual long and leisurely strides, Ron could feel Mattie's gaze spilling over his shoulders and back, his ass, his legs. He could feel that stare fixing on his stiff cock, bobbing aggressively in front of his body. She was sitting at just enough of an angle to be able to see it.

And he knew that Mattie loved his body. Oh, how she loved it.

Ron stretched out on the bed, arms crossed behind his head. Closing his eyes, he imagined Mattie's reaction to seeing the book. The thought coaxed a smile from his lips.

Curiously, with wary glances toward the bedroom, she'd lift it from the table. This was after she'd swung her legs over the side of the couch and sat up, her succulent, tight-nipple breasts shifting beneath her pink t-shirt. Wonder and delight would creep into her face as she lifted the book onto her lap…

Mattie rolled over as soon as she heard Ron's footsteps recede. He was nude, certainly just to tantalize her. And it worked. With a stab of desire that made her wet, she glimpsed his jouncing erection. Knowing she was responsible for it excited her even more. She gazed at his wide shoulders, tickled at their midpoint by his messy spill of hair. She watched the muscles of his back glide fetchingly beneath his skin. She took in his firm, smooth ass and long, taut legs. Damn, that gorgeous body could deliver the most indescribable pleasure...

And then she saw the book on the coffee table. Her features blossomed into a smile as her fingertips skimmed over the embossed and gilded title. *Cheer Givers & Mischief Makers.*

Almost reverently, Mattie lifted the slim volume onto her lap.

Book construction was Ron's special talent and passion. He'd mastered the arts of papermaking, calligraphy, leather tooling and stamping and hand-binding. He could even produce quirky illustrations if he felt moved to do so.

But when Mattie opened the cover of this, her Valentine's Day present, she saw that Ron hadn't just made the book, he'd written it. He'd decorated each page with dried flowers and elaborate calligraphic flourishes. He'd even included some stylized erotic illustrations.

The book was dedicated to her.

Through a film of tears, Mattie began to read...

Introduction

ဢ

In the secret world of the Fae Rhy—as multifaceted in its translucent beauty as the most intricate crystal born of the Earth—there exist many races. Each has its own traits, and each has its own place and purpose.

The Cheer Givers and Mischief Makers are but two of the crystal's facets. Although related, they are as much at odds as the two poles at opposite ends of a magnet. Although both must regularly interact with humans, they must do it in entirely different ways.

Every *fer ny gerjagh*, or Cheerer, and every *olkeyr*, or Maker of Mischief—and I give the Manx names, for this story concerns the Fae Rhy of that place—must enter the mortal realm on every holiday beloved by humans. Whether religious or secular, and regardless of country or culture, none of these special days is overlooked.

Each Cheer Giver and Mischief Maker must seek out a male or female Recipient and, though that person, play out her/his purpose. The Cheer Givers must do what they can to enhance the special qualities of the holiday and bestow happiness and fulfillment on the Recipient. The Mischief Makers must do what they can to undermine the holiday's potential and the Recipient's satisfaction. In short, the *olkeyr* must ensure that if something can go wrong, it will.

This is the story of a particularly lovely *fer ny gerjagh* who took the name Isabelle and found that she wanted to please two men on Valentine's Day. One, however, was not quite what he seemed…

Chapter One

୨୦

Isabelle liked the body she chose for herself. She liked it very much. It almost had an elfin look—from the glossy, deep-red hair that was cropped and artfully scrambled, to the willowy limbs, to the high, pert breasts. She'd kept her original eye color, a bright, sparkling green, because people seemed to find it hypnotic. Isabelle discovered that she enjoyed her womanly endowments during a Holiday Visit of some time past, when she had decided to work In Form rather than In Shadow. It saddened her that the she hadn't had much opportunity since then to explore the whole carnival of carnal delights the human body seemed capable of engineering. The circumstances surrounding most holidays weren't appropriate for indulgence in physical pleasure.

This Holiday Visit, however, would be different. It was Valentine's Day—the perfect time to put her incarnation to the best possible use.

Isabelle had decided to find her Recipient at "Come Together", a club where, for a fee, men and women could meet. The process was unusually orchestrated. Each couple could speak to each other for ten minutes. They were encouraged to take notes as they did so. When a bell rang at the end of that period, everybody found a new partner and went through another ten-minute period of mutual assessment. On and on this strange dance went. Depending on the number of people in attendance, it lasted one or two hours. For the first half of the period, the women remained seated and the men moved around. For the second half, the men were the prey and the women were the hunters. The whole point of the ordeal was ultimately to exchange contact information, with at least one person but maybe more, for subsequent private dates.

Isabelle sat in a wing chair upholstered in burgundy cloth and waited, pen and notepad on her lap, for the afternoon's activities to begin. People couldn't take matters into their own hands. They had to remain seated until the first bell rang. Their gazes, though, did roam the room, seeking out promising prospects. Isabelle found this urgency both amusing and exciting. She, of course, had a different set of criteria from the other seekers. Finding a man she fancied was only secondary. Of primary importance was finding one who needed her Cheer Giver services.

She noticed a shy-looking man with neatly trimmed hair and a magnificent physique. Must work out, Isabelle thought. She studied his face. Neither handsome nor homely. Unassuming. An almost surprising contrast to that powerful body. Continuing to study him, she hoped he would notice her interest and return it.

Finally, his restless gaze made its way to Isabelle. She returned the man's uncertain smile. For good measure she cunningly crossed her legs, directing his attention to them.

It worked. Isabelle silently congratulated herself on her choice of attire. She wore a dress with a print in sea-foam green and peacock blue. It showed her legs to advantage and nicely complemented her hair and eyes. Isabelle loved the lighter-than-air feel of the fabric. But she would love even more taking the dress off…in front of the right man.

She leaned to her left, lifted a glass of iced tea from a small table and took a drink just as the first bell tinkled. The muscular man headed in her direction, but someone else got to her first—a blond guy wearing a leather jacket and cocky smirk. He didn't look promising.

After they introduced themselves, Isabelle went directly to her first question. She urged the man, whose name was Jim, to give an honest answer. "What's your definition of the perfect Valentine's Day?"

Jim leaned over the chair arm as he angled his body toward her. "That's easy. Spending as little money as possible and getting laid as much as possible." Looking self-congratulatory, he sat back.

Isabelle's eyebrows rose. "Do you think women will appreciate hearing you say that?"

"You're the first one I've said it to." He raised his bottle of water in her direction. "Hey, you want honesty from me, you get honesty."

He had a point. But he didn't have Isabelle's interest. She began to realize this whole endeavor was going to tax her patience. Jim prattled on about himself — or, rather, about his ex-girlfriends, all of whom he found seriously lacking in some way — until the bell mercifully rang once more.

This time, the muscular man made it to Isabelle's station. He respectfully stood before her as he introduced himself and extended a hand. She read him as she shook it. The softness of his skin was another startling contrast to his physique. His shy smile was still in place, its disarming quality underscored by his politeness. Isabelle was even more intrigued.

As Bryce seated himself, Isabelle asked her opening question.

He seemed to ponder it. "Boy, I don't know," he finally said. "Ever since my wife walked out on me three years ago, I've kind of been a stranger to romance. I just sort of withdrew from that whole scene."

Isabelle warmed to him. "I imagine you were pretty devastated."

Bryce looked down and nodded.

"Why did she leave?"

He rested his forearms on his thighs. Isabelle liked the delicate pattern of golden hair overlaying Bryce's prominent, rock-solid muscles. "I guess she just didn't want to be married, wanted to see other guys."

Isabelle briefly covered his interlinked hands with her left hand. "I'm sorry." Not wanting to seem fawning, she withdrew her hand. "No one's been special to you since then?"

Bryce glanced at her. "Not really. So I guess I'm here to get back on track...or try to. And maybe give romance another chance." He sat back. "Why are *you* here?" He watched her a bit more boldly, obviously encouraged by her sympathy.

Isabelle had already concocted an answer to this question, which she knew would be inevitable. "I'm in town on business and didn't want to spend Valentine's Day alone, that's all." She gave Bryce her most charming smile.

Bryce's attention seemed to sharpen. "Really. Where are you staying?"

"I have a suite at the Crown Belgian."

His eyebrows shot up. "Wow. Your company knows how to treat its people right. Where are you from? Who do you work for?"

This was where things got dicey. Isabelle had to come up with a profession that wouldn't generate too many questions. "I'm a fashion designer. I have to go on the road fairly regularly to sell my lines to retailers." She said nothing about where she came from, and Bryce didn't seem to notice the omission.

His gaze tripped along her outfit, as if gauging the level of her talent. "I don't know the first damned thing about fashion," he said with a self-effacing laugh. His voice lowered, became more seductive. "But you do look...well put-together." The shy smile had been replaced by one distinctly suggestive.

"So do you," Isabelle said with the same tone, the same smile. Spending the evening with this man's sweet face and hard body wouldn't be *too* onerous, she thought.

They talked for the rest of their allotted time about Bryce's job—he customized vehicles, mostly vintage ones— and a little about their likes and dislikes. As the bell sounded, he gave Isabelle's hand a meaningful squeeze before moving away.

That's when she spotted the other man, the black-haired man, sitting in a far corner of the room. It seemed he'd been watching her. Isabelle couldn't be sure, but she definitely got that impression. A very slight smile lay on his enticing mouth, which was ringed by five o'clock shadow. He looked perfectly at ease, with his right ankle resting on his left knee, and he took his time getting up and ambling over to another woman's station. Isabelle couldn't seem to take her eyes off him. The man was tall and lean and devilishly handsome, his dark good looks softened by shallow dimples and arresting blue-violet eyes. Not to mention those molded-for-pleasure lips.

Although he didn't approach Isabelle and certainly didn't look directly at her, she sensed she had some connection to his bemused smile.

The man did not look needful, not by a long shot, but Isabelle knew she would have to investigate him.

Refocusing on her mission, she paid polite attention to the next three men who came to her. One *may* have been a candidate for her services, but Isabelle thought him wimpy and boring. She knew she couldn't perform to the best of her ability with humans she didn't like.

Worse yet, she found herself increasingly chagrined by the tall man's avoidance of her. What was that smile all about if he had no intention of approaching her? Did he find her silly somehow? Did she inadvertently do something to amuse him?

Isabelle would have to find out. Strong curiosity was part of her fae nature. The man likely didn't need cheering, but Isabelle couldn't rest easy until she determined what had provoked his peculiar reaction to her.

When it was time for the women in the crowd to circulate, Isabelle unabashedly went straight to him. Had she been less fleet-footed, three or four other females would have gotten there ahead of her.

The man, still looking uncannily relaxed, had his elbows propped on the chair arms. He rested his chin on steepled forefingers and silently regarded Isabelle as she stood before him. The barest hint of his earlier smile lay both on his mouth and in his eyes. Very slowly, almost meticulously, his gaze slid down her body then up again. He didn't seem to care if this languid scan might be interpreted as rude.

Isabelle's nipples tingled into tightness.

He dropped his hands to his lap. "And you are...?" His eyes were fixed now on Isabelle's eyes.

"My name is Isabelle." She didn't offer her hand. "Do you mind if I sit here?"

"I don't have much choice, do I?"

Isabelle bristled. "Of course you have a choice. If you'd rather not waste your time on me, I'll go away."

The man's smile broadened for an instant. "I don't mind wasting my time on you." With a slight inclination of the head, he indicated the chair on the other side of the end table. "By all means, have a seat. I'm Daniel, by the way." He rested his head against the back of the chair and simply kept watching her.

Isabelle fidgeted, adjusting the bodice of her dress. Her nipples still plagued her, responsive as they were to Daniel's cool scrutiny. "Well," she asked, "don't you want to ask me anything?"

"Yes. Are you afraid of me seeing your breasts?"

Heat flared in Isabelle's cheeks. "No," she snapped. "What's the next thing you want to ask?"

Daniel lazily turned up his hands. "I believe it's your turn. I'm sure you have some trenchant questions."

Isabelle felt thoroughly flustered. What was his game? Why was he here? "What's your definition of the perfect way to spend Valentine's Day?" she murmured, then steeled herself for some saucy rejoinder.

But it never came. Instead, Daniel surprised her by pulling his chair around the end table so they were sitting almost knee to knee. He leaned forward. "Spending the evening, maybe the whole night, with a lovely woman who delights my senses and warms my heart." His voice, its sardonic edge gone, drizzled over Isabelle like warm maple syrup.

"Oh," she said, but no sound came out.

"I'm so sorry. It appears I've left you speechless." Daniel's fingers uncurled and drifted lightly over Isabelle's knees. She didn't even have time to react to this gesture before he straightened and moved his chair back into place.

By the gods, this man was diabolical! His direct gaze, his low voice, his casual masculinity had undeniably aroused Isabelle. Her nipples strained painfully against the tight fabric of her dress. Her pussy secreted more moisture. Oh, how she'd love to feel his silken tumult of black hair on her breasts, her stomach, the insides of her thighs. She suspected Daniel was well aware of the effect he was having on her...which strengthened that effect all the more.

"Do you think you'd enjoy my company?" she asked, her voice uncharacteristically meek.

He answered without hesitation. "I know I would — you've already met half my criteria — and I believe you'd enjoy my company, too."

Isabelle's heart was hammering. "What if I choose not to follow up on this meeting?" She wanted to find out if he would pursue her, persuade her.

Daniel shrugged. "There are bound to be other women who will. Besides, if I can't find someone here, although I'm certain I can, there are other options."

"Such as?" Isabelle asked. Her mind wasn't really on Daniel's "other options". More mystifying questions dogged her. *How can he be so passionate one moment and so lackadaisical the next? Why is he here if he doesn't really need to be?*

The man's behavior was inexplicable.

"Bars, parties..." Daniel turned up his hands and flashed a smile. "I'll have my Valentine. Even if it's just for the night."

Isabelle had to look away from him. She couldn't think straight while she looked *at* him.

She knew she was in quandary. Bryce needed a Cheer Giver much more than the confident Daniel, but this dark-haired enchanter strongly appealed to her. Way too strongly. She wanted to talk with him, learn about him, bare her body beneath his smoldering gaze and share it with him. And she wanted to enjoy *his* body. Daniel's physique wasn't as pumped up as Bryce's, but it was nevertheless beautifully tended.

Problem was, this mission had nothing whatsoever to do with Isabelle's desires. It was about bringing happiness to someone who needed it. She had to put her personal preferences aside.

"So," Daniel asked, "are there any gentlemen here who've caught your eye?"

"A few." Of course, Isabelle couldn't tell him eye appeal was more or less irrelevant. If that weren't the case, Daniel would be her hands-down first choice.

"And what's *your* definition of the perfect Valentine's Day?" he pressed on.

Isabelle had to look at Daniel, at least when she spoke to him. It was a matter of courtesy. He did have a wickedly perceptive gaze, in addition to wickedly seductive, and it made her squirm.

"Making each other feel appreciated, feel special," she said. Suddenly, that task seemed considerably more daunting than it had before she met him.

"Ah. That's very sweet."

Did he really think so or not? Isabelle couldn't tell.

Daniel continued. "But what about romance? What about sex? How special will you or your partner feel if it turns out you're not all that compatible? How appreciated will you feel if one of you gives the other the heave-ho after your big date?"

Isabelle felt her face slip into a frown at these unwelcome possibilities. She didn't doubt she could please her chosen Recipient. Men were quite easy to please...on a temporary basis, anyway. As long as their egos and cocks were stroked, they were content. But what if her Recipient wanted to carry their relationship past Valentine's Day? What if he saw her as a long-term or even lifetime antidote to his loneliness?

Isabelle realized she would have to give this contingency some thought. She could *not* make a human sad. It was forbidden. If she fostered misery, much could be taken from her by way of punishment.

Maybe she *should* have opted to work In Shadow. It was certainly safer. She could have targeted a couple who needed help and simply pulled some magickal strings from behind the scenes to give them a perfect day.

"Well?" Daniel prompted, his dark eyebrows raised expectantly.

"Two people can enjoy each other's company for an evening," Isabelle said, "without getting romantically involved. They can still make each other feel good."

Daniel pulled back in surprise. "Hmm. Now *that's* an odd twist. An anti-commitment woman who's indifferent to sex and romance." Again, his mouth assumed that taunting smile. "I would *love* to put you to the test."

This provocative and utterly baffling statement left Isabelle dumbfounded. Stymied, she realized she also felt a peculiar thrill. Damn it, she certainly had to avoid *this* man.

But she just as certainly didn't want to.

In her daze, Isabelle almost didn't respond to the jingling bell—a summons she suddenly resented. "I'm not indifferent to sex and romance," she muttered. Nearly bolting out of her chair, she hurried toward the first available man she could find.

Isabelle felt exhausted when the evening finally ended. The attendees milled about, exchanging their contact cards along with parting words and final flirtations. She impulsively glanced around the room and saw Daniel surrounded by four women. Not that it mattered how many wanted him, but the sight seemed to goad her.

Isabelle made a beeline for Bryce, as if he offered the only salvation from her wayward impulses. And actually he did. She felt grateful when he grinned as soon as he saw her approach.

"Would you, um, like to meet me at my hotel tomorrow?" she asked, making a concerted effort not to sound like she was merely settling for him. "We can go to dinner, go out dancing, do whatever you'd like."

"Yeah?" Bryce's grin shrank to a sly smile. "What if we just stay at the hotel, in your room?"

"You mean my suite," Isabelle said, still feeling distracted.

"Better yet."

"Would you like that?" Isabelle knew he would. This seemingly insecure man suddenly had very aggressive eyes. They were already undressing her.

He nodded as he took the contact card from her hand. "I'd like that a lot. A few drinks and privacy."

"All right then." Isabelle forced herself to concentrate on his broad shoulders and chest, his ingenuous face. Maybe, just maybe, Valentine's Day would end up being her favorite holiday.

After they decided on a time, she prepared to leave the club. But not before she caught another glimpse of the man who, truth be told, she *really* wanted to be with tomorrow night. The maddening, alluring Daniel had obviously been eyeing her interaction with Bryce. He slipped Isabelle another mysterious smile before turning back to the big-breasted woman whose hand already rested possessively on his arm.

Chapter Two

ஐ

Isabelle opened the door to her hotel suite. An explosion of red roses in a crystal vase nearly blocked her visitor from view. Nearly. It would have taken a full-grown lilac bush to hide Bryce's bulk.

"Right on time," Isabelle said with a demure smile. She took the vase from his hands. "These are beautiful. Thank you so much. I *love* flowers." She meant it. All fae folk loved flowers.

Bryce returned her smile. "Well, I had to bring *something* special for the pretty lady who was nice enough to take in a stray tonight." He leaned forward and lightly kissed her cheek. "Oh, can't forget this." A bottle of pink champagne, its neck gripped by Bryce's meaty hand, rose into the air.

"What a coincidence. I just happen to have ice to chill it, right over there." Isabelle did a graceful half-turn and indicated a silverplated bucket on the cocktail table. "Please, come in."

Isabelle not only felt flirtatious, she actually began to feel wanton. All day she'd been in a froth of anticipation about this evening's events. Beneath her skimpy black dress she wore an even skimpier semi-transparent teddy of the palest green. Soft music drifted through the suite, which was lit only by clusters of scented candles she'd bought earlier in the day.

Bryce, all scrubbed and glowing, had already stimulated Isabelle. A slick of moisture dampened the teddy's thin crotch. It didn't matter that his looks were ordinary. All Isabelle needed to see was the breadth of those shoulders, that chest. Even his cable-knit sweater couldn't conceal his extraordinary physique. As soon as he appeared in the doorway, Isabelle's imagination immediately stripped him down to smooth skin stretched over hard muscle…driven by animal instinct.

"God, you look delicious," he said, one hand gliding hungrily down her back as they walked to the couch together.

The heat in his fingers, the coarsened tone of his voice made Isabelle wetter. An almost painful tension gripped her private parts. The silkiness of the teddy seemed to abrade her nipples. She wondered if she should even bother with small talk and other pointless preliminaries. It wasn't as if Bryce and she were launching a relationship.

As Bryce rolled the champagne bottle into its bunting of shaved ice, Isabelle purposefully carried the flowers into the bedroom. She brushed her thumbs over her nipples to make them stand out even farther. "How do you like my accommodations?" she called out, luring her guest closer.

"First class," he said, walking to the bedroom doorway. "You sure travel in style." Watching her, he braced his arms on either side of the doorframe and crossed his legs.

Isabelle still stood beside the nightstand, where she'd set the roses. "The suite pleases me. It's like living a fantasy." She knew her eyes and voice had gone sultry. She knew her nipples pushed out the cloth of her dress.

Bryce's chest heaved more noticeably beneath his sweater. A distinct hump had formed at his groin. Darkening, his gaze slid over Isabelle's body. "And what are your other fantasies?" he asked gruffly.

Without averting her eyes, she answered, "To be taken forcefully by a large, strong man."

He licked his lips then took a few steps into the room. "You mean raped?"

Isabelle nodded. "When I'm in the mood."

Pulling his sweater over his head and flinging it aside, Bryce strode up to her. He wore a white tank top that strained across his pectoral muscles. His harsh breathing sawed through the air.

Before Isabelle could form another thought, Bryce caught her around the waist with one massive arm, partially lifting her off the floor, and crushed her body against his. He jammed a hand into her hair and forced her head back. "Are you in the mood?" he whispered, his breath hot against her ear. "Judging by your tits, I'd say you are. I'll bet your cunt is wet, too."

Isabelle tried to push him away. It excited her further to fight back, to feel his impassioned ferocity grow as she struggled. Her high, tight nipples filled with searing heat as they ground against the damp mounds of his chest. Bryce lowered his hand from her head and with one firm motion pulled her dress down past her breasts. It soon slipped off her body. He palmed and kneaded her breasts through the filmy fabric of the teddy, the sensitive flesh helpless beneath his hand.

Isabelle groaned as moisture oozed from her pussy. She writhed within his grasp, shoving at him, pounding at him.

"If you fight me," he hissed, "I'll have to punish you." He twisted one of her nipples. As Isabelle gasped, he held it firmly between thumb and forefinger while he pushed her away from himself. The nipple flared like a struck match and sent an exquisite jolt of pleasure-pain down to her pussy.

As Isabelle rolled onto her side, Bryce delivered a sharp slap to her ass. He flipped her onto her back and roughly pulled the teddy off her body, his knuckles intentionally digging into her breasts as he did so. Kneeling over her, looking like a lustful titan, he pulled something from his pocket then undid his pants and shoved them down his hard thighs and off his legs. He frenetically pulled his shirt over his head and flung it to the floor. Candlelight gleamed on his turgid cock, a dense column more thick than long.

Isabelle wanted to feel it inside her.

Bryce leaned over her and, grasping her by the shoulders, raised her up against the headboard. Again, she tried pushing his arms away. He delivered a stinging slap to each of her breasts. Isabelle moaned and arched her back.

"Suck me," he grated. "Pump me and suck me until I tell you to stop."

She eagerly curled her fingers around the turgid shaft and slipped its soft head into her mouth. Instinctively, she stroked and sucked as if she could make nectar spill from the man's body. Within ten or fifteen seconds he pulled away from her, breathing hard.

"I want to fuck you. Now." Bryce reached for something that lay on the bed beside his legs. A small packet. Frenetically, he tore it open and handed it to Isabelle. "Put this on me," he said, "then turn around and get on all fours."

Infected by his urgency, Isabelle quaked as she tried to remove the condom from its package. He certainly didn't need to wear it—given her nature, nothing could be transmitted between them—but it made no sense to bring that up now. She meticulously unrolled and smoothed the tube down the length of Bryce's cock until it fit him like a second skin. But it actually enhanced his cock, Isabelle noticed. It had a series of ribs she couldn't wait to feel massaging her insides.

"Hurry!" he barked.

Isabelle turned away from him and assumed the position he wanted. Immediately, his fingers dug into her butt cheeks and he guided his rod into her vagina. He grunted as he thrust—harder, faster—then reached beneath her to feel her hanging breasts, to palm and pinch her nipples. Isabelle felt rippling contractions, the heralds of orgasm, and tried to move her hips so her clit would be stimulated.

But Bryce came too quickly. Grabbing her pelvis, he let out a brute growl and gave one, two, three powerful thrusts before he jerked and shuddered. Isabelle felt the pulsing of his cock. She squeezed it, trying to extract every last bit of pleasure for herself, but he was already wilting inside her.

That's when she heard the knocks.

Chapter Three

ఈ

Isabelle inclined her head, trying to hear past Bryce's panting. She hadn't been mistaken. Someone was knocking on the front door of the suite.

"Did you send for room service?" Bryce asked, frowning.

"No." Isabelle got off the bed, went to the bathroom and lifted her robe from one of the door hooks. She slipped it on and tied the sash as she hurried through the bedroom and sitting room. "Who's there?"

"Delivery."

"Delivery of what?" she muttered, irritated, as she unlocked the door.

A tall, handsome man was leaning against the jamb, his arms crossed over his chest. He flashed a charming smile as soon as Isabelle opened the door.

"Daniel!"

"Hi. Am I too late?" Lightly running a hand down Isabelle's arm, he stepped past her into the sitting room. "I'm sorry, but it couldn't be helped." He took off his coat and tossed it on a nearby chair. "I had a dinner date. It ended rather badly."

Stupefied, Isabelle continued to stand beside the door and stare at him. "Daniel, you can't —"

He pointed across the room at the champagne bottle sitting in the ice bucket. "Oh, you *were* expecting me."

"No, I wasn't." Isabelle finally found volition. She trailed after him as he moved toward the couch. "If you'll recall, I never invited you here."

Bryce appeared in the bedroom doorway, a towel around his waist. He scowled at the intruder. "What the fuck…?"

Daniel amiably lifted a hand in greeting. "Hey, Bryce. Want to bring your ass over here so I can use that towel to open this bottle?"

Bryce didn't move. "What are *you* doing here?"

Isabelle walked over to Bryce and placed a hand on his forearm. "I swear, I had no idea—"

She jumped when a loud pop sounded. Daniel had managed to extricate the champagne bottle's cork without using Bryce's towel. "Well," he said, filling a glass, "shall we chat for a while…or just pick up where you left off?" He watched them as he took a drink, his eyes glimmering wickedly over the rim of the glass.

Bryce turned to Isabelle. He was obviously too befuddled to catch his rival's implication. "Which one of us is supposed to be here?"

"Uh…" Isabelle shot a glance at Daniel, who'd already made himself comfortable on the couch. She looked up at Bryce and distractedly patted his arm. "Will you excuse us for minute, please? I'll try to get this straightened out."

He hesitated, then ambled back into the bedroom and soundly closed the door. Isabelle marched over to the couch, took the glass from Daniel's hand and set it on the cocktail table. "Come with me."

"Gladly."

Without looking at him, Isabelle walked to the rear of the room, opened a pair of sliding glass doors and stepped onto the balcony. Both chagrined and—she hated to admit— thrilled, she kept wondering what the bloody hell Daniel was up to. Within seconds, he stood on the balcony with her.

"At least the weather's mild," he said.

Isabelle turned to face him. "How did you find out where I was?" She tried to sound stern, but just the sight of him was already weakening her.

Daniel inclined his head toward the interior of the suite. "Your bed buddy was boasting at that pick-up club after you gave him the nod. Said he'd scored a cute fashion designer with a suite at the Crown Belgian. I said, 'Oh yeah, I remember her. I talked with her a bit. What was her name again?' So he told me."

Isabelle hung her head and let out a sigh of exasperation. Damn it, another bigmouthed braggart. Apparently Bryce wasn't all that much of a shrinking violet...or a gentleman. Well, at least she was fulfilling her duty by making him feel good. And he'd excited her, too—although it rankled that he'd overlooked some important steps in the process. Isabelle just wanted to get on with it and bring this evening to a satisfactory resolution.

Mustering determination, she lifted her head. "Daniel, you need to—"

Strongly and surely, his arms curled around her. Reflexively, Isabelle returned the embrace. She looked up at him and held her breath. All traces of Daniel's impishness were gone. He lowered his head.

Isabelle closed her eyes. In excruciating slow motion he feathered his mouth against hers. The kiss intensified by small degrees, Daniel gently flexing and ultimately crushing his sumptuous lips against hers. Isabelle was transported by both the feel of him and his startling finesse. She hungrily parried the delicate, firm movements of his mouth. Soon, his tongue met hers. Their mouths kept gliding and pressing and pausing, then gliding again, as if passion had a heavenly taste and they could not stop savoring it.

Their bodies, too, were sealed tightly and perfectly together. Isabelle noticed how warm and lithe and graceful Daniel's was. And the feel of his mouth—incomparable! She couldn't get enough of it. His delicate, dark peppering of whiskers, which lightly sanded her cheek, was a wonderful contrast to the cushiony feel of his lips.

Isabelle felt mildly delirious...and, in her sweet delirium, thought how easy it would be to love this man. How easy, and how utterly maddening.

It could have been minutes or hours before they finally pulled away from each other. Isabelle realized her hand was in Daniel's hair. She relished the feel of that as well — thick and silky, like threads spun from a balmy summer night.

"I hope that's just the start," Daniel said, looking into her eyes. "Now what else do I need to do?"

Isabelle could think of a hundred things she didn't need but certainly wanted him to do. More important, though, she had to conclude her mission. She *had* to. And she couldn't do it by kicking Bryce out because she preferred another man's company. Not only would that humiliate him and thus be contrary to her purpose, it would also be unacceptably selfish of her.

"I can't just tell Bryce to leave," she said, unable to keep regret from creeping into her voice.

Daniel immediately answered, "Then don't."

"But..."

"I'll go talk to him." Daniel took Isabelle's hand and led her back indoors. Smiling enough to show his dimples, he tenderly ran a hand over her hair and down the side of her face. "Just give me a few minutes."

Isabelle watched him walk to the bedroom door, knock, then step inside. By the gods, he had an enticing body. That butt was irresistible. She went to the couch and dropped onto it. Glimpsing the open bottle of champagne, she lifted it from the ice bucket and poured a glassful. She quickly downed it, glanced at the bedroom door and poured another. When she'd had her second infusion of champagne, Isabelle set the empty glass on the cocktail table so she wouldn't be tempted to fill it a third time.

I hope Daniel doesn't say anything cruel or do anything rash. Bryce's contentment is my responsibility. She wondered if she should intervene.

Soon, the bedroom door opened. Bryce walked directly to the couch and swept Isabelle up into his arms. Although startled, she said nothing. Her hands once again enjoyed the mountainous contours of his back and shoulders as she waited to see how this capture would play out.

Bryce carried her into the bedroom and lowered her onto the center of the king-size bed. Daniel stood on one side of it, Bryce on the other.

"It appears you have a decision to make," Daniel said. He unbuttoned his shirt, unsnapped his jeans and lowered the zipper by a few tantalizing centimeters. He seemed to wait while Isabelle's appreciative gaze swept across his partially bared chest and abdomen.

She couldn't seem to keep from ogling him and saw no need to. He obviously wanted her to look. Daniel didn't have the rugged, body-builder physique Bryce had, but his sleekness excited her just as much...perhaps even more. The mounds of his chest and the bands of muscle across his abdomen were not as pronounced but were just as solid. Even more fetching was the delicate pattern of dark hair that flared out slightly from his sternum and crept in an unbroken line down his torso. Within the narrow V of his open zipper, the path of hair widened and thickened. Those black swirls looked luscious against his flawless, tawny skin.

Already aroused by Daniel's kisses, Isabelle thought she'd go crazy if she couldn't have more of him. Especially after this tempting glimpse of his body.

She shifted her eyes to Bryce. Magnificently built, yes, but he had no hair on his chest or torso, and his bland looks had nothing in common with Daniel's untamed beauty. And she realized Bryce had never bothered to kiss her. Still, his overpowering strength titillated her.

Daniel sat on the edge of the bed. He leaned over Isabelle. This time, his marvelous mouth played against her throat and slowly glided up to her ear. She sighed raggedly as the humid warmth of his lips seeped into her pores, as the very tip of his tongue drew the most intricate, precise curlicues on her skin and the ridges of her ear. She put one hand in his hair, the other on his chest.

This was an impossible decision.

When he was through with his persuasions, Daniel sat up. "Well, do you want Bryce...or me...or both of us?"

"Both?" Isabelle breathed. If she'd heard him right, it was too good to be true. She glanced at each man. Each of them nodded.

That prospect alone was nearly enough to give Isabelle an orgasm. Trembling with anticipation, she lifted herself and knelt on the mattress. She untied the bathrobe's sash.

"Wait. Let me." Daniel reached out to stop her hands. "Bryce already had his turn." Peeling off his shirt, Daniel got onto the bed. He knelt facing Isabelle, his legs bracketing hers. For one agonizing moment he did nothing but look into her eyes.

He reminded her of a sorcerer. He was gorgeous and self-possessed and wickedly alluring, and Isabelle wanted him so much she thought she would faint.

With his fore- and middle fingers, Daniel grasped the edge of the robe and eased it down one of Isabelle's shoulders then down the other. It barely clung to her body, but he moved it no further. Her eyelids drifted shut.

With a lighter-than-air touch, Daniel glided the fingertips of both hands over her forehead and eyebrows, cheekbones and nose and jaw. They tripped like tiny insects over her lashes. Two fingers slid over her lower lip and gently, for a fraction of a second, pulled it down. But he didn't kiss her. Instead, the ball of his thumb glided across both her lips as if setting them just right. Isabelle had the fanciful impression

Daniel was both memorizing and adoring her face. His spring breeze of a touch continued down her neck to her collarbone, both lengths of which he caressed with his thumbs.

The feel of this leisurely exploration drove her to distraction. How could be so patient? Didn't he feel her desire lapping at him like so many greedy tongues of flame?

Then, as if reading her need, Daniel ever so softly nudged the top edges of the bathrobe until it slipped down her body. Fully bared to his gaze, Isabelle could virtually feel it beating like wings against her flesh.

"You're so lovely," he whispered.

His palms slid down over her breasts, and two deft fingertips circled her taut, aching nipples.

"Hold me," she said in a papery voice. "Just hold me against you."

Daniel obligingly drew her toward him. Wrapping their arms securely around each other's back, they continued to kneel, their bodies pressed together. Isabelle ground her sensitized breasts against his chest. Her blood had become a lava flow. Feverishly, her hands caressed Daniel's muscle-plaited back as her lips branded his smooth, dusky skin—face, throat, shoulders, chest. For the first time, Isabelle noticed Daniel's scent. It was both provocative and evocative, somehow familiar to her. Ferns, oak leaves, rain. Maleness. Dear Mother, how she *craved* him.

Soon, their hands were scrabbling in each other's hair, their mouths moving wildly over each other's lips and face. Isabelle lowered her hands to the loosened waistband of Daniel's jeans. She dropped down to her haunches as he continued to kneel, letting her undress him. Almost desperately she forced his jeans and briefs past his cushion of pubic hair. She nuzzled her face in it, relishing its springy coarseness, ingesting the musky aroma entwined in it, an irresistible aphrodisiac. But the greater treasure was yet to come.

Driven as she felt, Isabelle nevertheless realized his still-hidden erection must be handled with care. Slipping her eager hand inside his zipper, she had her first, shocking feel of his stony cock, wedged at an angle within his briefs. It triggered an almost painful pulsing deep inside her abdomen. With as much caution as she could manage, Isabelle freed his hard-on.

Daniel had a larger cock than Bryce — just a shade less thick, perhaps, but definitely longer — and it stood like a javelin at a steep angle from his body. She wanted to take it all in, all of it. She wanted to make love to it with her mouth and tongue, her breasts, her vagina and ass.

Just as she thrust out her tongue to lap at the swollen head, Daniel cupped a hand beneath her chin. "Not yet," he said. "I want this to last for a while."

After kicking off his jeans and briefs, he slid down onto the mattress and lay on his side. Isabelle immediately lay beside him, on her back. She was a bit surprised to see Bryce reclining on the other side of her, stroking his own restored erection. She'd completely forgotten about him.

"You two are making me hotter than hell," he said in a gruff voice.

"Enjoy us," Daniel murmured in Isabelle's ear.

His luscious mouth closed over her left nipple as Bryce's closed over her right. Isabelle let out a thin wail as an excruciating current of pleasure mainlined from her breasts to her pussy. Bryce sucked forcefully, squeezing the base of her breast and drawing her entire areola into his mouth. Daniel practiced his usual erotic artistry. His sucking was firm and rhythmic, but it was unexpectedly punctuated by pokes and licks from his tongue, nipping little pulls by his lips. He seemed to be stimulating each individual nerve.

Isabelle writhed. Her movement made the men's ministrations all the more arousing. As she pushed one breast against one man's mouth, she freed the other. He would then have to reclaim it, perhaps trapping the high, tight nipple with his teeth. The keen sensations were ever changing, and their cumulative effect was beyond her control.

Then she felt a new sensation. Bryce was jabbing the head of his cock against her distended nipple. Isabelle began panting. Within seconds his thick cum spurted onto her breast, dripping sluggishly down its sides. Her nipple was nearly hidden beneath his cream.

His ejaculation so turned her on that she felt the first creeping ripples of orgasm. Daniel must have sensed she was nearing climax. His left hand slipped between her legs. Isabelle felt his long fingers move down the inner sides of her labia. As two or three or even four of them burrowed into her vagina, he expertly played her clit with his thumb.

It was unbearable. But she wanted his long, hard cock inside her. She wanted it to fill her so she could feel it throb as she throbbed. "Take me, Daniel," she gasped.

He needed no further prompting. His body moved like quicksilver between her spread legs. Lying on top of her, his body slicked with sweat, he rammed his cock deep into her body as his lips lowered onto her mouth. Isabelle grabbed the smooth globes of his ass. Daniel pumped with such power and grace, kissed her with such inflamed passion that she had no hope of holding out.

An orgasm ripped through her, its prolonged, regular contractions gripping Daniel's erection as her whole body stiffened and quivered. Then Daniel made a strangely provocative sound, a soughing sound of surrender and release, and Isabelle felt the strong pulsations of his own climax as his cock sent jet after jet of hot cum into her welcoming body.

Breathing hard, he was about to roll off her when Isabelle grasped his shoulder blades. "Stay with me, baby," she murmured against his damp hair. "Just for a minute."

His face fell against her neck. "You're wonderful," he said, his lips flexing against her skin.

When they finally did part, Isabelle saw that Bryce had brought the champagne and glasses into the bedroom. He sat against the headboard, holding a full glass. "If I hadn't just shot my load," he said, toasting Daniel and her, "that would've done it for me. Shit, that was some hot fucking." He took a drink. His free hand dropped to his flaccid but still thick penis and curled around it. "I can't wait for this bad boy to get hard again. Shouldn't take long."

Daniel sat cross-legged, facing him across Isabelle. "Don't get too greedy, Bryce."

Isabelle gave him a curious glance. His tone sounded acerbic, maybe even a bit menacing. *Now* what was going on with Daniel? This whole arrangement had been his idea, after all.

She lay on her back, braced on both elbows. Bryce offered her his glass of champagne. She took a drink and returned it.

"Pass that bottle and extra glass over here, would you?" Daniel took both from Bryce's hands and put them on the nightstand next to his side of the bed. Leaning toward Isabelle, he stroked away the damp hair that clung to the edges of her face. "How do you feel? Do you think you want more?"

Shifting onto her side, Isabelle faced Daniel. She felt a little wrung out at the moment, but stray tingles and pulsations still coursed through her body as she looked at him. They were her answer. "Yes, I want more." *Especially from you. Maybe* only *from you...*

Daniel smiled down at her. "Then you shall have it."

Isabelle couldn't seem to stop looking at him. He was a marvel to her. She couldn't imagine lovemaking being much better than his lovemaking. She wanted to roll around the room with Daniel, fly through the air with him, keep pulling his body against and into hers. Even now, after being satisfied, she still yearned for his touch.

"I think it's time for a little refreshment," Daniel said. "Lie on your back," he told Isabelle, "and put your sweet ass on my thighs."

He helped Isabelle reposition herself, grasping her legs and easing her butt up onto his lap. Her legs, bent at the knees, bracketed his body. Isabelle didn't question him—at this point, she probably wouldn't object to *anything* Daniel did—but she watched him expectantly. Her upturned cunt was fully exposed to him, and her excitement was mounting again.

"Honey, would you mind passing me that bottle and glass?" Daniel asked her.

Isabelle reached for the nightstand with her left hand. She gave him first one, then the other. Bryce had moved down the bed, apparently to get a better view of her pussy. Both his and Daniel's cocks were filling again, and those tandem erections coaxed a fresh flow of moisture from her body.

Bryce reached over and parted her labia. Two fingers glided along either side of her ripe clit then slipped inside her vagina. "God, you're wet," he whispered. He withdrew his glistening fingers and swiped them over Isabelle's right nipple, slicking it with her own juice. Then he lowered his head and began sucking.

Moaning, Isabelle clutched Bryce's head to her breast just as she felt the cool lip of the champagne bottle tease her clit. Daniel, his glorious cock hardening into a stiff bone, kept playing her cunt with the top of the bottle—rubbing it over and around her clit, circling the opening of her vagina, slipping it inside by an inch or two.

Isabelle arched and rotated her hips, welcoming the unlikely invader. She began to feel the luscious ripples of impending orgasm. Again, she yearned to have Daniel's cock inside her. But he was obviously taking his time, exploring her, enjoying her. He nestled the stemmed glass against the lower curves of her butt cheeks. Carefully, he drizzled champagne over the delicate folds of her cunt. Isabelle half giggled, half whimpered.

"Hold still," Daniel said with a smile. "You'll make me spill it on the sheets."

Bryce lifted his head from her breast. He moved back slightly so he could watch what Daniel was doing. The champagne continued to trickle between Isabelle's pussy lips, over her clit. Finally, Daniel lifted the glass to his mouth and drank.

"Delicious," he whispered, then seductively ran his tongue over his lips.

Bryce scrambled to put on another condom.

Daniel leaned over her, his hands cupping her breasts, his thumbs flicking her nipples. "Would you like to suck me off while Bryce fucks you?"

Breathless, Isabelle nodded. The prospect thrilled her — Daniel's sleek, dense cock in her mouth, his cum jetting into it, while another rod filled her vagina and pounded her toward climax…

"Lie on your side," Daniel said. He quickly put the bottle and glass on the floor.

Isabelle did so, bending at the waist to give Bryce access to her pussy. Bryce lay down behind her, one muscular arm curled over her rib cage. Isabelle could feel his hard-on already probing between her legs, seeking out her cunt. His hand furiously fondled her breasts. Daniel stretched out in front of her, his hips before her face.

Isabelle hungrily pulled Daniel's engorged cock into her mouth. She loved the feel of its plump head passing between her lips, and she took a moment to relish it with her teeth and tongue — giving it quick, assertive sucks, nibbling it, tracing its voluptuous contours. Then Bryce plunged his cock into her from behind. The dual sensations of one cock claiming her mouth while another claimed her vagina filled Isabelle with a branching current of passion that seemed to burst from every pore. Her whole body was quivering.

As she pumped Daniel, drawing deeply to take in his rich, heady essence, her tongue caressed the network of soft ridges beneath his satiny skin. It was so taut it seemed ready to tear. Isabelle not only filled her mouth with his delicious cock, she let it slide into her throat, too. She synchronized her sucking with Bryce's thrusts, and that honed her excitement to an unbearably keen edge.

The two men's groans and growls intensified...and so did Isabelle's arousal. Daniel stiffened. Hips jerking spasmodically, he emptied himself into her mouth. She eagerly swallowed as his strongly throbbing cock delivered each spoonful of cream. Apparently set off by Daniel's orgasm, Bryce came too, thrusting hard, clawing Isabelle's breasts.

She couldn't withstand the torrent of passion crashing over her, into her from both sides. Overwhelmed by it, Isabelle surrendered to the tight clench and rolling release of her own climax, which seemed to go delectably on and on and on...

Gulping air, Daniel and Bryce withdrew their spent cocks from Isabelle's generous body. Daniel slid farther down on the bed so he faced Isabelle. Bryce rose and padded off toward the bathroom.

Feeling a swell of emotion, Isabelle gazed into Daniel's midnight eyes and stroked his face, his hair.

"Am I melting?" he asked.

"Could be. You're damp enough."

He chuckled silently. "I don't think I want this night to end...even if it kills me."

"I don't either."

Rising up slightly, Daniel eased her onto her back and kissed her. Isabelle held him tightly, not wanting to let go, losing herself again to those marvelous lips that worked such magic...not just on her body, but somehow on her spirit, as well.

"I want to be alone with you," Isabelle guiltily confessed. Her fingertips adoringly stroked his mouth, his eyebrows, the strong line of his nose.

She figured she had fulfilled her obligation to Bryce. Certainly he'd had a satisfying Valentine's Day. Certainly she'd brought him cheer. Now this beautiful man who gazed down at her, this man who filled her vision and her heart, was the only one Isabelle wanted to be with. She couldn't divide her attention any longer. Every shred of desire she was capable of feeling clung to Daniel, only to Daniel.

His eyes glimmered. "Do you mean that? You want just the two of us to spend the night together?"

"Yes. Just the two of us."

Bryce cracked open the bathroom door and stuck his head out. "Hey, I'm gonna catch a quick shower." He ducked back inside.

"Now I just have to figure out how to break it to *him*," Isabelle said. "I don't want to hurt his feelings."

She *couldn't* hurt his feelings — not if her mission was to be considered a success.

"Don't worry about it," Daniel said. "Maybe he'll get the hint and leave. Maybe he's getting ready to leave as we speak. Why else would he be taking a shower?"

"To prepare himself for the next round?" The possibility depressed Isabelle. She couldn't deny that Bryce's presence had enhanced her enjoyment of the evening, but he'd pretty much worn out his welcome. Now he was a fifth wheel.

"I repeat, don't worry about it." Daniel gave Isabelle another of his enigmatic smiles. "I believe the situation will resolve itself to our satisfaction." He crawled across the bed and pulled a long-stemmed rose from the vase on the nightstand. "I assume Conan brought you these."

Isabelle felt another stab of guilt. "Yes, he did."

"Makes *me* look like a slouch," Daniel said. "And you probably love flowers, too."

"Yes, I do."

"I should've guessed," Daniel murmured. Falling silent, he suddenly seemed introspective. "Well, I'll just have to make up for my thoughtlessness." He idly fingered the flower's stem. "Thorns. Every rose has them."

"And wouldn't be a proper rose without them." Isabelle watched him, wondering what he was thinking.

Sitting over her, Daniel lowered the stem to her breasts. He lightly rolled it over her erect nipples, now achingly sensitive. Isabelle gasped as the thorns pricked her flesh. Spearheads of flame shot from her breasts to her cunt, stimulating another flow of moisture.

"You like the thorns," Daniel whispered, his eyes darkening. He eased her legs apart. Tenderly, he slid the rose's head between her pussy lips, stroking her clit with its petals.

Isabelle's eyelids fluttered and closed. The feeling was exquisite. Her breasts as well as her cunt felt hot, heavy, swollen with desire.

"You like the flower, too," Daniel said in a throaty voice.

He dipped down and gathered Isabelle in his arms, urging her body into his lap. Before she realized what was happening, his cock sank into her, fully. They twined their arms around each other, gasping and kissing, giving in to a raw rush of spontaneous passion that engulfed them like a tornado. Their unrestrained cries of pleasure came out in heated counterpoint. Clutching each other's sweat-glazed body, they both came unexpectedly, explosively. Isabelle's orgasm was so sharp and sudden it was like an ecstasy of pain. She collapsed against Daniel, shuddering and whimpering. He stroked her back.

Still embracing, they fell bonelessly onto the tangled sheets, laughing in astonishment, laughing in sheer joy.

"Can we possibly take any more of this?" Daniel asked.

"I think we can." Isabelle kissed him, wondering how she could bring herself to part from this man, wondering why she felt not only addicted to him but bonded with him...in ways that had nothing to do with sexual magnetism.

Bryce emerged from the bathroom. Isabelle forced herself to sit up.

"I, uh...I think I'd better get going," he said, gathering up his clothes and putting them on. He avoided looking at her.

"Why?" Isabelle asked, startled. The last thing she'd expected was so abrupt a departure. She got off the bed and slipped on her robe.

Daniel sat up, his expression completely impassive.

Bryce hopelessly shook his head. "Well, I think you wore me out, girl."

"You mean—" Isabelle had no idea what he meant. She began to feel alarmed. Had she displeased him somehow? She caught a glimpse of his shrunken cock before he pulled up his briefs. It looked red...or at least a deep, torrid pink.

"I mean," Bryce said with a self-conscious laugh, "my dick feels like one of the war wounded."

Isabelle circled the bed and went up to him, putting her hands on his massive arms. "Did I hurt you somehow?"

"No, no, not at all." Bryce waved the question aside. "You were great, darlin'. You gotta be the hottest babe I ever met. It's just that...I don't know, maybe it was the rubbers. But my dick is all kind of rashy and burning. I just wanna get home and soak in a tub full of warm water and Epsom salts." He kissed Isabelle on the cheek. "And daydream about you."

"I'm sure it will clear up overnight," Daniel said, getting off the bed. "It's happened to me too."

"Yeah?" Bryce seemed to find this encouraging. He didn't look quite so miserable anymore.

Daniel nodded and clapped him on the shoulder. "You'll be good to go by morning, big guy. Guaranteed."

The two men shook hands.

"You still gonna be around?" Bryce asked Isabelle. He wiggled his eyebrows.

"No, I'm afraid I'll be leaving fairly early."

Bryce put an arm around her shoulders. "That's a damned shame. I really get off on you."

Isabelle walked with him to the front door. Still nude, Daniel stood in the bedroom doorway, his arms and legs casually crossed.

"Thank you for a wonderful evening I won't forget," Isabelle said, smiling sweetly into Bryce's face. "And for those beautiful roses. I'll be sure to take them with me."

"Hey, thank *you*, pretty lady." Bryce lifted a hand in Daniel's direction. "Enjoy, man."

Daniel waved back. "I will. Thanks for being such a good sport."

"My pleasure." After giving Isabelle a farewell kiss, Bryce left the suite.

Isabelle closed and locked the door and briefly rested her forehead against it, sending healing energy at the afflicted man. She heard Daniel mumble something.

"Rhon'en the Master strikes again. Wins big."

The words hit Isabelle like a lightning bolt. She whirled around. "What did you say?"

Daniel seemed to tense up. "Shit, you have good hearing. I was just...congratulating myself."

"But you referred to *yourself* as Rhon'en the Master."

"Well, you know, I was...I was being facetious. I just sort of made up a...a magician kind of name. You know, like...Cosmo the Great."

Eyes narrowed, Isabelle cautiously approached him. "Rhon'en the Master is the most infamous *olkeyr* in the world of the Fae Rhy. You couldn't have simply pulled that name out of the blue."

"The most famous who in the world of what?" Daniel asked as he backed away from her.

Isabelle wasn't amused. She was bewildered and shaken and on the verge of high-voltage anger. "Let me see the back of your right earlobe."

"Why? Do you expect to find three sixes?"

Isabelle dove at Daniel, knocking him off balance. He toppled onto the bed. As he lay on his back, Isabelle scrambled to sit on his hips and keep him pinned down.

He began tittering like a naughty child who'd played a trick on an adult. "Insatiable wench! At least let me get warmed up first."

"What happened during your dinner date earlier this evening? What went wrong?"

"Why do you care?"

"You know damned well why I care." Isabelle bounced on Daniel's genitals. Still chortling, he let out an *oomph* and tried to fold up his body, but Isabelle was in the way. "Now tell me," she said. "Or I'll *really* crush those precious jewels of yours."

"You wouldn't dare. They're precious to you, too."

Isabelle rose up, ready to drop down on Daniel again.

"Wait!" he cried, grasping her hips to stop their descent. "Okay, I'll tell you. First my companion's false eyelashes fell into her soup. As she tried to retrieve them, the bowl overturned onto her lap. A female staff member tried helping her sop up the mess, but that woman's ass was in one of the restaurant's traffic lanes. So a passing waiter bumped into her, and a couple of raw oysters slid out of their half-shells and got lost in my date's considerable cleavage."

He made it all happen! Worse yet... "You made Bryce's penis burn!"

Daniel's laughter freshened. "I think it was...an allergic reaction to the condoms," he sputtered. "I'm sure Bryce is fine now."

"Allergic reaction, my ass." Isabelle grappled with Daniel, trying to turn his head. "Let me see your earlobe, dammit!"

He grabbed her wrists. "And why the interest?" he asked archly, holding Isabelle's arms away from his body. "Are you a serious student of folklore? Or, kind and giving soul that you are, might you be a *fer ny gerjagh*?"

Gaping at him, Isabelle froze.

"I very much like the body you chose," Daniel said in a molten voice. "I like how responsive it is. I like the joy you take in it. And I like the joy *I* take in it."

"Did you know all along?" Isabelle whispered.

"About your body or about your identity?"

Isabelle refused to answer so impertinent a question. He knew damned well what she was referring to.

With a sigh, Daniel released her wrists. "I *suspected* all along. That's one of the reasons I came here—to find out for sure. I've never had a close encounter with a Cheer Giver. And I've certainly never made love to one." He smiled. "It was quite a pleasant surprise—certainly made *my* day."

His confession only provoked Isabelle's ire. "So this was only some kind of challenge for you? Or contest? You just wanted to win over a gullible Cheerer and best another man in the process? Do you feel like some kind of conqueror now?"

Daniel's face fell. He immediately grasped her hands. "No, no," he said fervidly, shaking his head. "I mean, I might've had motives like that at first. But even then only partially so. I felt very drawn to you. So maybe...maybe in a way I resented the hold you seemed to have on me. Maybe I resented being rejected by you in favor of Bryce the barbarian. Damn it, lady, I do have an ego and it can be bruised!"

Isabelle felt flushed. Any *olkeyr* should be anathema to her. Yet, this Mischief Maker had thoroughly bewitched her.

And he certainly didn't seem as despicable as she'd thought his kind would be. In fact, he didn't seem despicable at all.

"What are the other reasons?" she asked, feeling desire for him stir again.

"For what?"

"For your coming here."

"Don't you know?" Daniel, still reclining beneath Isabelle, slipped a hand between her parted legs and, like a whisper, caressed her clit with one finger. Her hips jerked faintly in response. "I'm so attracted to you it's driving me mad," he said. "And it's an attraction that takes on more dimensions the longer I'm with you. I can't really explain it to myself. I just know it's there, and it's too damned powerful for me to resist."

His declaration suffused Isabelle with a warmth that came close to melting all her defenses. "So you *are* Rhon'en?"

"Will you hate me if I am?"

Isabelle tried to suppress a smile. He actually seemed...vulnerable. "It's too soon to say."

Daniel turned his head on the pillow to give her access to his right ear. Brushing aside of few wisps of his ebony hair, Isabelle dipped down to examine the lobe. As soon as she folded it forward, she saw the red symbol of the *olkeyr*.

Drawing in her breath, she simultaneously sat up and slid off Daniel's body. She wasn't as prepared for this shock as she'd thought.

"What, did it sting you or something?" Daniel asked, teasing her. He rolled onto his side. "What's *your* name, by the way?"

Isabelle was wary. Should she tell him? Could he somehow bedevil her beyond tonight if he knew who she was? Would he be inclined to?

Daniel grew serious. "How do you feel about me, Isabelle? Not about *what* I am but *who* I am."

Considering this, she touched his face, looked deep into his beautiful eyes. She sensed no lurking threat or imponderable evil. Rhon'en was what he was—a maker of mischief, not a vicious wreaker of havoc. It was his lot.

"First," she said, "I need to know if *you* can feel. At all."

His eyebrows drew together as if she'd unjustly accused him of some misdeed. He looked wounded. "It's a well-kept secret," he said softly, "but, yes, we can feel. Sometimes too deeply for our own good. The *olkeyr* are supposed to be eternally playful and devoid of regret or remorse. I assume you can see how ours is a very lonely and thankless existence. It's difficult *not* to feel, under those circumstances."

With a pang of shame, Isabelle lowered her eyes. True to her nature, she began to feel compassion for him. Compassion…and so much more. "I'm sorry. I know nothing about the *olkeyr* except what I've been told by my elders."

Daniel sat up and took her hand. "How do you feel about me, Isabelle?"

She suddenly wanted to hold him. Her gaze skipped uneasily to and from his face. "Earlier, when you first kissed me, I thought how easy it would be to love you."

"You did?" He sounded hopeful.

Isabelle nodded.

"And now?"

"Now I think I *am* falling in love with you…and it doesn't seem so easy anymore."

"Why? Because you think the same can't happen to me?"

She hesitated. "Yes."

"What do my kisses tell you?"

"That you're a very adroit lover," Isabelle murmured.

Daniel laughed. "Thank you. But that's only because you inspire me." He moved closer and tenderly delivered another kiss. "Whatever is happening to you is happening to me too."

Isabelle dropped her face to her hands. "Oh, I wish you hadn't said that!"

She wanted to cry. This was by far the strangest and most confounding turn her life had ever taken. Could she trust this creature? Was he being sincere? Or was he simply playing the ultimate prank? She didn't know *what* to believe.

Lowering her hands, she gazed at him, knowing the wretchedness she felt was reflected in her face. She was never good at hiding her feelings.

Daniel raised one hand and made a configuration with his fingers that Isabelle knew well. He touched it to his solar plexus. Symbolizing an oath sworn on one's honor, it was a Fae Rhy sign held in the highest regard. Any whimsical or deceitful display of this sign would result in severe chastisement. "If you give me a chance," Daniel said, "I will strive to be worthy of you."

"And you didn't put that rash on Bryce's penis?"

Daniel shrugged. "Well…yeah, I did," he said sheepishly. "He was turning into more of a liability than an asset. He was getting in the way. I didn't want to share you anymore."

Isabelle's sniffles gave way to giggles. Tittering, she rocked back and forth until new tears came, happier tears. "I just can't fight this," she said, tossing up her hands in concession. "Yes, I will give you a chance."

Daniel's face brightened like the sun emerging from a cloud. "Do you know, dear lady, what a coup we've just staged? Without even trying?"

His words sparked a realization…and suddenly, Isabelle did know. For opposites to come together through love, to become *united* through love, was one of the greatest achievements in the world of the Fae Rhy. And if ever there were opposites, they were the Cheer Givers and Mischief Makers.

By sunrise, when Isabelle's and Daniel's respective missions officially ended, the most extraordinary things would happen to them...

Epilogue

ಐ

Smiling wistfully, Mattie stared at the last line for a few moments. It would sound cryptic to anybody but her.

Extraordinary things had indeed happened to Rhon'en and Matirya. Their unlikely but ever-strengthening union was both celebrated and rewarded in the world of the Fae Rhy. Many privileges were bestowed on them. As long as they remained a couple, they could move at will between the world of humans and the world of their own kin. They could shift between their human and fae forms as much as they liked. They could take on whatever missions they chose, whenever they chose, as long as those endeavors had no evil or destructive intent.

Then something occurred to Mattie—the story didn't have an appropriate ending. Impulsively grabbing a pen from the coffee table, she carefully wrote in one more line before closing the book. Satisfied, she caressed its cover.

It was the perfect Valentine present.

Tonight, Mattie decided, she and her sweetheart would resurrect the spirit of their first night together. They would make love with a passion both tender and furious. They would worship each other. And from this day forward, nothing as silly as his undiplomatic remarks about her bad cooking would stand between them, even for a second.

Carrying her gift, she padded into the bedroom and crawled into bed beside the truly incredible fae-man she was honored to call her mate. Of course he was still awake, waiting for her.

"You forgot something," she said, stroking his brow. "In the book, your beautiful book."

He cracked an eye to regard her. "Oh? And I thought you'd object to all the poetic license I allowed myself."

"You might've taken a *few* liberties with the facts, not to mention my point of view, but I really don't object to much of anything you do. At least I won't anymore. You're too precious to me."

He lifted her hand from his forehead and pressed it to his lips.

Mattie opened the book to the last page and showed him her insertion.

He smiled that mystery-tinged smile she'd always adored. "I love you, Isabelle."

"I love you too, Daniel."

~ And they would live happily ever after ~

Also by K.Z. Snow

∞

Cemetery Dancer
Plagued
Wing and Tongue

About the Author

ɞ

K.Z. Snow (formerly writing as Kate Snow) is the daughter of Milwaukee tavernkeepers and learned her first words off a Wurlitzer jukebox. Nine years of higher education, resulting in two and a half English degrees and a stint as a teacher, did not dampen her enthusiasm for beer, Green Bay Packers football, classic R&B, and various forms of political incorrectness.

She's been many things in her life, including a varsity debater, a Catholic, a hippie, a Girl Scout, a junker, a fag hag, a gardener, an editor, a saxophone/ bassoon/tambourine player (not all at once), a damned good dancer, and a companion to most species of domesticated animals, including men.

One thing she has never been is a Republican. One thing she will always be is a writer.

She now lives in rural Wisconsin, not far from the birthplace of surrealism, a.k.a. "The Dells." Her imagination and her hips continue to grow unchecked.

K.Z. Snow welcomes comments from readers. You can find her website and email address on her author bio page at www.ellorascave.com.

Tell Us What You Think

We appreciate hearing reader opinions about our books. You can email us at Comments@EllorasCave.com.

DISCOVERY

Cris Anson

ဆ

Chapter One

ഔ

"I'm not sure if I can go through with this."

"Of course you can. It's what you wanted."

"But this...I didn't expect this to be just...a house." Becca's glance took in the brick and timber façade, a sprawling English Tudor in the middle of suburban Philadelphia, with its manicured, estate-quality grounds. "I thought we'd be going to, well, to a Dungeon."

"The effect will be the same." Her friend Glynnis nudged her up the steps, leaving the keys in her Lexus for the valet to move. "Here you will discover your true nature."

Becca opened her mouth to utter one more token of resistance, but the massive front door opened. Her jaw dropped. A giant, for so he seemed to her as she looked up at him from her five-foot-three height, skimmed his gaze over her as if she were nothing and settled on Glynnis, his eyes lighting up in recognition. Without a word he jerked his head in a quick nod then turned.

"Follow him inside," Glynnis hissed as Becca stood rooted to the flagstones of the portico.

"Is he — will he —" She couldn't finish the question. Was this the man who would be her Master for the weekend? A knot of unease lodged in her throat. Although bald, he looked to be in his middle thirties, six-six if he was an inch, with shoulders that had blotted out the interior of the house from his position in the doorway. Black leather gloved his massive thighs, thick-soled boots shod his huge feet, and weight-lifter arms jutted out from a black leather vest that also exposed a bare chest the size of a specimen tree-trunk.

145

With more than a little trepidation, Becca followed the giant through a spacious foyer furnished with a wooden settee and tranquil landscape paintings on two walls, and into a book-filled room containing a glass-surfaced mahogany desk and club chairs in a red-and-black plaid. He gestured for her to sit at a black leather sofa facing a cheerily burning fireplace while Glynnis joined him at the desk, completing the required paperwork amid the soft murmur of words she couldn't make out.

"Becca."

She jumped at the reverberating sound of his voice. The giant beckoned her to stand alongside Glynnis' chair. She stood uncertainly, gnawing at the inside of her mouth as she endured his long, thorough scrutiny. She knew what he was seeing — almost forty, overweight, dressed in muted colors and shapeless fabrics, her long brown hair pulled back and rolled into a bun at her nape. The only thing Glynnis had insisted she wear was a pair of three-inch heeled sandals, footwear she'd long ago consigned to the back of her closet.

But she was desperate, so she stood with her spine straight, her green-eyed gaze trained on her host, and took a deep breath.

His eyes narrowed as the motion drew his eyes to her bosom. Instinctively she hunched her shoulders to hide her large breasts amid the drape of her loose overblouse.

The giant's mouth twitched then flat-lined. "The rules here are simple," he said, the voice deep and vibrating. "A sub does not look her Master — any Master — in the eye unless invited to do so."

Immediately she lowered her eyes to the floor, seeing from her peripheral vision the satisfied nod of his head.

"You can do nothing without permission. Is that understood?"

"Yes, Master."

"You are in no danger here," he continued. "You will have a safe word. When you speak that word, all activity concerning you will cease and you are free to leave." A smile ticked up one side of his mouth. "Or stay."

Becca felt her eyelashes flutter, as did the moth-wings in her stomach. Of course she would stay. She had to stay.

"Becca?"

Eyes downcast, she whispered, "Yes, Master?"

"You may look at me." When she did, he said, "Your safe word will be 'moonlight'. Is that acceptable?"

Her heart jumped then went back to its normal rhythm. Their favorite song had been "Moonlight" —

"You may speak directly."

"Moonlight. Yes. Thank you," she added hastily.

"Good." He thumped massive palms on the leather blotter and pushed to his feet. "Follow me." He turned on his heel and strode through an archway at the back of the library. Becca glanced at Glynnis, who nodded and made shooing motions with her hands. *Go ahead*, her eyes said. *Enjoy your weekend, and find what you're looking for.*

Becca hurried her steps around the sofa and through the doorway into a far more Spartan room. Dim recessed lighting barely illuminated polished oak floors, benches with no cushions, bare walls. Two men stood one on each side of a thronelike wooden chair, a gloved hand on the back slat. Immediately she lowered her gaze to the floor, but the sight of them registered vividly in her mind's eye. Both looked to be a shade under six feet tall and in good physical condition. Both wore black leather pants, black long-sleeved turtlenecks.

And black hoods that hid all but mouth and chin.

The giant sat on the chair, which had apparently been built to his specifications, as it accommodated his size and girth with room to spare. "Come stand before me."

She did.

"The first part is always the hardest," he said, his voice surprisingly gentle for a man so huge. "But it must be done. And done quickly. Do you understand?"

"Yes, Master."

"Good. Take off your blouse and skirt."

Her breath caught. Dear Lord, this was the acid test. If she could take the first step, she might be able to recapture—

A crack like a rifle shot sounded in the air around her. Becca dared a glance up. The giant held a long, supple whip in his hand and had apparently just wielded it. "You are to obey your Master without question," he boomed, his deep voice echoing across the bare floors and walls.

With fumbling fingers she reached for the buttons of her beige silk blouse.

"Because you are a novice and this is your first offense, I'll let you off with a warning." The giant leaned forward, arresting her fingers at the second button. "Whenever I issue you an order, you are to acknowledge it."

"Yes, Master. I'm sorry, Master, I didn't know."

"The next offense will incur a punishment."

Becca bit her lip but resolutely nodded while working open the third button.

Without warning the giant jumped to his feet, tucked a massive hand around her jaw, thumb on one side and fingers on the other, and lifted her face to look at him. "You did not," he murmured, "say, 'Yes, Master' that I would know you heard me. I can only assume you want to be punished."

Unbidden, her eyes flared at that outrageous statement then, realizing her mistake, she bit her tongue to stifle any comment. She was an intelligent woman, a lawyer in fact, so she should have been able to follow directions the first time. She wanted to be a sub. She had to obey her Master, not contradict him or argue with him.

She lowered her gaze. "As you wish, Master."

Underneath her lashes she could see his posture relax, as if she had pleased him. Tiny tingles skittered up her spine. Until his next words.

"One of my assistants will be assigned to keep track of your punishment. And who knows? Maybe to dole it out." He turned. The man to his right took a step forward and nodded, the ghost of a smile just visible in the soft lighting.

"Please continue disrobing," the giant said, returning to his throne.

You can do it, she urged herself. *For years you've dreamed of flaunting yourself before a roomful of men.* She would never have admitted it to anyone, but she admired strippers and go-go dancers, women who displayed their perfect bodies so as to arouse lust in their audience, sexpots who allowed men — and women — to stuff bills in their G-strings, giving them the opportunity to surreptitiously fondle them in public. But Becca's daydreams had stopped there. She'd never had the body to be really sexy. Never had the guts for it either.

That's why you're here, she reminded herself. To see if she could be a sub who fired a Dom to lust.

As she unbuttoned the fourth and fifth buttons, she let her gaze creep up the legs of the assistant who would keep track of her punishment. Was it her imagination, or did it seem his cock had grown to push against the leather at his groin?

At last the blouse was free of its restraints and she slipped it off her shoulders and let it slide down to her feet in a puddle. She could feel her nipples harden beneath her plain white nylon bra, knowing that three pairs of male eyes were watching. Sure, some men might like the abundant top of her — she wore a 38-DD — but her waist and hips also held the same kind of extra padding, making her less than runway-model caliber.

The giant raised the hand holding the whip, its flexible length gripped along with the long thick handle, tail skimming the floor, and flicked the resulting loop of leather up and down over one nipple.

Becca gasped as the sensation shot straight down to the point where her legs met.

"Now the bra. The whip wants to feel bare skin."

Her throat dry, Becca reached for the front clasp and unhooked it. She could feel her cheeks burning as the cups fell to the sides, exposing her soft skin. Her breasts were full and round, swaying gently as she moved. She slid the straps down her shoulders and let the bra fall on top of the blouse.

True to his word, the giant nudged at her breasts, back and forth from one side to the other, raking the edges of her nipples to hard points with the looped whip.

Both assistants took an interested step closer. The one counting her punishments dared to lift a gloved finger and make a lazy circle around her areola. Becca arched her back, felt her chest swell out to him, thrusting her breast closer to his stroking.

"Go ahead," the giant said. "Give it a kiss."

The man made a deep sound in the back of his throat. Becca could see the brown flash of his eyes inside the mask before his head dipped and his tongue gently lapped her hard nipple then closed his mouth around it. Becca shuddered at the feeling. She wanted to cradle his head close to her and keep him there. But all she could do was close her eyes and tremble at the feel of his moist tongue, the inner softness of his mouth as he pulled and suckled at her with other men watching.

"Enough."

The man stepped back. Becca felt somehow bereft.

"Now the rest of it," the giant said, impatiently gesturing with the furled whip.

Having seen the glitter of lust in all three men's eyes, Becca felt a little more sure of herself and her feminine power.

She reached behind her, unhooked the waistband, pulled down the zipper, and wiggled the skirt off her hips, her bare breasts swaying and bouncing as she did so. The audible gulp of the Punisher, as she was coming to think of the man counting her offenses, goaded her into making her lips into a slight pout as she stepped out of the skirt.

Oh it was hard, very hard to stand still, arms at her sides and not crossed over her bare breasts or at the crotch of her translucent panties that teased the eye with a shadow of her dark pubic hair, as they scrutinized her.

"One more," said the boss.

Becca let out a harsh breath. "Yes, Master." Before she allowed herself time to second-guess her actions, she looped her thumbs under the elastic, raked the white nylon down her legs then bent down, breasts hanging free and swaying avidly, to pull the garment off one high-heeled foot then the other.

"Give it here." The giant reached for her panties before she had a chance to toss them onto the growing pile.

Her breath stuttered. "As you wish, Master."

The sight of her panties all but engulfed in his huge hand sent a shock-wave of misgiving through Becca, and more so when he lifted them to his nose and inhaled. Was she out of her mind?

"Mmmm. An aroused woman. Good." Tucking her panties into an inner pocket of his vest, the giant sent the other man to scoop up her clothing. "You won't need these for the rest of the weekend."

She stood stoically as the man disappeared with the remnants of her everyday world. Oh God, she was stark naked with three huge, virile-looking men in the house! Perversely, the thought started the juices flowing between her legs. *They'll know*, she thought. There would be no fabric to catch and hide the dribbles.

"Come, my dear. You will serve us dinner." The giant stood, casually touched her shoulder and turned her toward another door. His fingers glided down her backbone in the lightest feather-touch all the way down to the start of her cleft, raising the fine hairs on the back of her neck. She was sublimely conscious that the Punisher walked behind her, she could almost feel his eyes on her plump buttocks as they pulsed and bunched with her stride, as she swayed slightly in the unaccustomed heels. She was also conscious that the skin of her naked thighs brushed along her feminine juncture, teasing her labia and making her even wetter.

Oh God.

The giant led her to a cozy dining room with a table set for three—gold-rimmed china and etched crystal wineglasses, sparkling silverware, lighted candelabra and a spill of red miniature roses in a silver vase.

As they sat down, she was exquisitely aware of her pink nakedness in contrast to their black-garbed, masculine forms, their matter-of-fact attitude versus the sensual tenterhooks that gripped her. She could smell her own arousal but there was nothing to do about it, her panties were gone.

He gestured to the sideboard, which displayed several covered platters. She lifted the lid of the largest and bit back a smile. Chicken breasts. *What else would it be but breasts?* she thought.

Expertly she placed two on each platter, aware that her own breasts grazed each man's shoulder as she leaned forward. Then came a heavenly smelling mushroom sauce in a gravy boat, which she ladled onto each breast in a slow drizzle. Baby carrots flecked with fresh dill, twice-baked potatoes nestled in their skins and redolent of cheese, artichoke hearts marinated in olive oil and spices.

The giant had poured white wine, she noted as she offered the last dish, a cranberry relish fragrant with citrus peel and orange liqueur.

When all were served she stood by the sideboard, arms at her sides, eyes lowered, waiting for her next directive. Suddenly the rich aromas made her stomach rumble.

Three sets of eyes jerked to her, three mouths tilted up.

"Hungry?"

"Yes, Master," she said, the heat creeping up her throat to her cheeks.

"Would you like something to eat?"

"If it please you, Master."

"Then come. Sit on my lap."

She swallowed. "Yes, Master." And stood at his chair, uncertain how to proceed.

He pushed back his chair a bit and patted his thick thighs. "Right here. Face the table."

"Thank you, Master." Gingerly she lowered herself onto his lap, her knees primly together as she tried to stabilize herself.

"Another lesson without penalty, slave. Whenever you sit, you will spread your legs wide open. Whether you're on a chair, a bed, a lap or whatever. And keep your hands on your knees. Now straddle me."

Becca didn't think her cheeks could get any hotter, but she was sure they were the color of the roses on the table. "As you wish, Master." Perforce, she had to scoot back to keep herself upright, her toes barely touching the floor in her too-high heels. The cleft of her buttocks came to rest at the massive bulge of his cock underneath his leather, and an involuntary shiver slid over her.

Music played in the background, with a soft, sexy blues feel to it. The candle flames danced lazily, lulling her. The giant casually draped his left arm around her waist, his massive hand dropping smack in between her outspread legs. With his other hand he forked up a small chunk of chicken with mushroom slice and brought it to her mouth.

She closed her lips around the fork. The delicious blending of flavors burst in her mouth at the same moment a thick finger pushed its way into her damp slit. "Nice and juicy, huh?" he said, so nonchalantly that he could have been referring to the chicken in her mouth, but she knew, and he knew she knew, that he wasn't.

"Carrot?" This from the man who had hidden her clothing.

"Thank you, Master," she said as she leaned toward him for the tidbit. Too late she realized she had inadvertently invited the giant's finger to plunge farther into her passage, which he did with alacrity. She felt her knees closing instinctively, but they tightened only as far as the immovable thighs on which she sat.

Another piece of chicken coated with excellent sauce, a scoop of potato, and so it went, the three men taking turns in feeding her bit by bit while the giant played with her most private parts, sliding his thick middle finger deep inside then pulling out to circle his wet digit around her clit, driving her slowly higher and higher. She wondered how feminine juices affected leather, for she was almost flooding now—would he have to have it cleaned? Then stifled the urge to laugh. If this was his home, he obviously had money to spare for such mundane chores.

The Punisher bent forward, his brown eyes under the mask boldly watching the giant's fingers plunging and withdrawing from her woman's core, and offered her a forkful of the cranberry compote. By now Becca was so turned on she could barely reach for the morsel. Each time she bent to either of the assistants, the giant did something delectable and unexpected, like pinch her labia or twang her clit with a fingernail or, once, pinch the nipple that brushed his knuckles. She opened her mouth and the Punisher upended the fork into it, spilling tiny chunks of diced cranberry and bits of gelatin on her breast.

The coolness of the spilled salad felt heavenly on her heated skin. She closed her eyes to savor the contrast. They popped open when she felt her skin being drawn upward into the warm cavern of the Punisher's mouth as he sucked and licked the sweet relish off her breast. He moved to her nipple, tonguing it then suckling, strong and rhythmically, as the giant followed his rhythm with his fingers inside her pussy.

"Hey, me too," said the other assistant, and she felt herself being pulled backward as the giant leaned back in the chair, allowing both men equal access to her breasts. In between their sucks she could see how turgid and red her nipples had become, how peaked and hard.

Oh God oh God oh God, she could feel her fingernails digging crescents into her knees as the sensations piled one on top of another, both of her breasts being suckled and teased, three fingers of one hand now inside her while the giant's other hand circled and pinched her clit, the smell of leather sharp and intoxicating, the melting candlewax, the wine on their breaths, the scent of her arousal surrounding all of them...

She felt herself gathering, rising higher and higher as shards of electricity rocketed to every inch of her, inside and out. She was going to come. She'd never, ever felt like this, she knew the top of her head would blow apart like a volcano in just seconds—

Suddenly she was standing on her wobbly feet, the giant's hands holding her up by the waist. "I did not give you permission to come!"

Dazed, Becca forgot herself and looked dumbly at the Punisher, who was standing only inches away from her. His eyes were glazed with passion. The bulge inside his trousers made it seem as if he'd stuffed it with a pair of heavy sport socks. His scorching gaze held hers, and she licked her lips, her wet tongue slowly rimming her upper lip then the lower.

His eyes snapped to her mouth. She could see how much he wanted to kiss her, how much—she hoped—he wanted to fuck her. God she wanted to be fucked, she was so close, so close! And he'd stopped her, the bastard.

No. Her Master. Not a bastard, he was only teaching her how to be submissive. This was her first experience at it, and she had to try hard to do only what was asked of her.

But, dear Lord, she was horny. Her skin tingled from ears to toes with primitive desire. She could see how rosy her skin was, how aroused. A light sheen of perspiration gave her a glow in the candlelight. The casual bun of her hair was half askew, making her want to rip out all the pins and let the strands fall on her naked shoulders, caressing her the way the men's eyes caressed her.

As if reading her mind, the Punisher raised his hands to her neck.

"Go ahead," said the giant. And the Punisher pulled out pin after pin, setting them on the tablecloth until no more could be found. With the giant's hands still holding her loosely at the waist as if needing to keep her upright, the Punisher ran his fingers through her hair, sifting it until it flowed like warm honey around her. He cupped her skull in his strong hands and leaned forward. He ran his tongue over her softened mouth and a shiver ran through her body.

Kiss me, she thought.

Instead he withdrew his hands and again she felt bereft.

"I think you've charmed one of my assistants." With a gentle push, the giant moved Becca away from himself and toward the Punisher. "Let's see what she can do with her mouth."

With that he put his massive hands on her shoulders and pushed her to her knees, her eyes level with the Punisher's crotch. Close up she saw that the leather breeches weren't zippered in the center like normal trousers. They had buttons on either side, allowing a six-inch-wide panel to drop down and expose—

Holy Hannah, the size of his cock! The flickering candlelight made the purple head look even darker, with the long, thick shaft standing straight out, beckoning her to...to...

He did it for her. Standing with his feet planted wide apart, the Punisher grabbed her head between his hands and inexorably drew it forward. To keep her balance, Becca slapped her hands on his thighs. Strong, muscular thighs that could easily hold hers apart while he opened her to his onslaught —if he wanted to fuck her. Please, yes, make him want to fuck her!

Tentatively she licked the drop of pre-come that oozed from the very tip of that beautiful male appendage and heard a gratifying intake of breath. Emboldened, she licked all around the rim that flared out from the stem then moved slightly to encase the entire head in her mouth. The heat of him made her gasp, made her want to take all of him, to suck him as he had suckled her breast. She pulled deeply, feeling the tip of his cock touch the back of her throat, and she fought the urge to gag. He tasted and smelled very male, spicy and pungent and musky. And she was extremely aroused, even more so now than she'd been moments ago, with the heady feeling that she was in charge of this man's orgasm.

She thought she could come too, just sucking his cock. And would, by God, since by some cruel depravity they'd stopped her before. The thought galvanized her, raised her arousal another notch. She slipped his cock in and out of her mouth, gripping the base of his shaft in one hand, her other hand reaching behind him to squeeze his buttocks, her breath coming in shorter and shorter pants, and she was on the verge, and so was he, she could feel him pulling tight, his balls gathering up hard against her fist and her juices flowing unimpeded down her thighs, and —

And she was jerked off her knees and to her wobbly feet as his come splattered all over her breast and belly, shooting in wave after wave of sticky substance until his knees buckled and he leaned heavily against the table, gasping like a steam engine.

She was almost too enamored of the power of the orgasm she'd provoked to be pissed that she'd again been deprived of her own.

But she didn't dare be pissed. The giant held her upper arms in pincer-like fashion, almost behind her back, forcing her breasts — her dripping, slippery breasts — closer to him.

As if in slow motion, the Punisher pulled off his gloves, dropped them to the floor then raised his hands to smear his come all over her breasts, her waist and on to her back and buttocks. He kissed her navel, which had been spared his fluid, then moved to nip and pinch a path down her belly with his teeth, until he reached her neatly trimmed pubic hair and buried his face in her crotch. His tongue licked and his teeth nibbled.

It was too much. Her knees buckled and she yanked her arms from the giant's grip and grabbed the Punisher's shoulders to steady herself. She wanted to stay that way forever, with his mouth on her pussy, his come all over her, and her hands cradling him, even if she didn't herself come.

"You'll want a bath now," the giant said, interrupting her warm and fuzzy feeling. "Come."

"Thank you, Master," she said dutifully, although her skin felt as though thousands of butterflies were tiptoeing over it. She was as energized as she'd ever been. She could leap tall buildings, she could stop bullets.

But dammit, she couldn't even come.

Be patient, a part of her whispered. Just think how good it will be when they finally *do* let you come.

Yes. That's what Glynnis had told her. As she followed the giant up a wide, sweeping staircase, she wondered idly if her friend was experiencing similar sensations, if she was a sub or a Domme, or indeed, if she was even still here.

All thought of Glynnis fled her mind when the giant halted her at the top of the steps and one of the assistants came up behind her, still slightly taller than she while standing one step lower, and skimmed his fingers across her hips, down her buttocks and the sensitive backs of her thighs. Then he lifted her heavy hair from her neck and nibbled at the delectable point where neck and shoulder met.

She knew it was the Punisher because she'd already inhaled and memorized his unique scent. And her body already knew the feel of his fingers touching her.

Yes. If she could be his sub, she would be happy.

Chapter Two

છ

The Jacuzzi was sized for a party, set into a luxuriously tiled bathroom off what must surely be the master bedroom, with its bed even larger than king size. She'd been made to sit on a cool, marble-topped stool—legs widespread again, damp palms on her knees—while the other assistant unbuckled the ankle straps holding her shoes to her feet.

While moving from one shoe to the other, he stared at the sight between her legs, her pussy lips swollen and red, aching and throbbing and unfulfilled, her juices still seeping onto the marble. He bent forward and inhaled her sexual essence, making her blush. He lightly ran two fingers across the edges of her swollen lips, making her gasp. Then he moved even closer and lapped his tongue directly into her slit, from where it touched the marble all the way up to her clit, making her eyes close and her body shiver. While she savored the myriad sensations, she felt a hard pinch of her labia and fought not to jump, not to cry out, for fear of reprisal.

But he only soothed the spot he'd pinched then tucked her hair into a towel to keep it dry. He helped her step into the tub and ordered her to sit so a jet pulsed directly onto her wide-open pussy. The constant stimulation was overwhelming. She shuddered and gritted her teeth in an effort not to come.

Shucking his vest and leaning over the tub, the giant took over and washed her, using his huge hands to gently massage her body with a soap that smelled like lilacs and freesia then stood her under a warm showerhead to rinse her off.

Disappointment speared through her to see that it was again the second assistant who held the fluffy blue towel to dry the beads of water off her now even pinker skin. He sported a slightly less massive bulge under his leathers than she'd noticed on the giant. But what she really wanted was the Punisher. She'd bonded with him.

Still, the giant was her Master and her teacher, and she had to bend to his will.

"One more item before you are dismissed for the night. You haven't received your punishment for your offense." With that he motioned with his arms. The towel assistant sank to the tiled bathroom floor with alacrity, legs spread wide. He ripped open his crotch panel to allow his engorged cock to spring free almost to his navel and tucked the leather under him so that his balls spilled out onto the tile.

"On your knees, slave. Elbows on the floor. Take him in your mouth."

Becca's face flared into heat again. If she did that...she tried to envision what she'd look like, what would be exposed to them, and her face got even hotter.

"That's another offense. I'll say it again. You must obey immediately."

"Yes, Master," she said meekly, not sure how much more difficult any new punishment could be than withholding her orgasms. Slowly she positioned herself as directed, her elbows and palms on the floor in a V with her fingertips coming together where his balls rested tight against his shaft, her ass high in the air, her mouth on the head of his rampant cock. And waited for permission to fellate him. She wouldn't commit another punishable offense.

The giant sat down alongside them in a lotus position, knees out, ankles tucked one under the other near his groin, situated so he could watch her mouth on the man's cock. "Three strokes for each offense," he ordered.

A soft *whoosh* through the air then she yelped as a line of fire striped both globes of her backside. The Punisher! Standing behind her. She felt his booted feet nudge her knees farther apart, knees and elbows almost touching in order to balance herself over the huge cock without sinking over it. Her cheeks flamed as hot as the punishment stripe. The Punisher could see every inch of her most private parts, from the rosebud of her anus to the plump lips of her pussy and, she was sure, the tiny head of her clit standing straight out from all the stimulation she'd received.

Oh God. It felt wonderful.

A second then a third lash and a fourth, each one harder than before. With each stroke, the force of the pain drove Becca forward, impaling her mouth on the man's stone-hard cock, but she kept her mouth as tight as possible to blunt the impact on the back of her throat. If she couldn't speak the safe word, she just might strangle from her involuntary movements. She could feel the tension in the man's thighs as he held himself still, for her sake she hoped.

"Perpendicular for the last two." The order barked out by the giant evoked a small groan of—rebellion?—from the Punisher. In her peripheral vision Becca could see sweat beading on the giant's brow, a haze of lust over his eyes. Damn him, he was loving it!

Then she realized what the order meant. She tried to clench her buttocks to steel herself against the blows, but her knees were as far apart as they could be without cracking her like a wishbone.

The lash descended directly onto her pussy, wrapping around her cleft from anus to navel, hitting her clit and her inner lips as well. Becca cried out around the engorged cock but kept her mouth firmly attached to it.

The last one burned a flame through her pussy, pain and pleasure mixing, melding, making her juices flow again. She hadn't known she could enjoy pain.

She slumped to the floor and the giant tenderly raised her in his arms.

* * * * *

"Sleep now."

Sleep? Becca wasn't sure she could. Her arms and legs were stretched in an X with wrists and ankles bound to the bedposts with silken ropes, and a tight blindfold had been tied around her eyes. More importantly, her pussy still ached with desperate desire, tingling and aflame.

She waited for the next order, a word, a sound. But many moments later, she still heard only silence. Not even the ticking of a clock. She hadn't heard them leave, as footsteps would have been deadened by the thick carpet. She hadn't heard a door close. No matter how hard she tried to concentrate, she couldn't hear breathing so didn't know if one or all three of them stayed in the room to watch.

Watch? What did they think they'd see? Her masturbating to orgasm? How could she? Did they want to see her squirm and suffer? To watch her seeping juices stain the bedsheet? Perhaps that was all part of being a sub. Of never knowing when, or if, your needs would be met. Or when pleasure and release would come. Perhaps the pleasure was supposed to be in the anticipation.

She dozed fitfully, her sleep never deep enough to dream, her muscles cramping with the tension of her tethers, her unfulfilled longing to be fucked deep and hard until her clit and pussy were raw and satiated.

She rose to a slow consciousness, aware of a tingling on her inner thighs. Someone was in the room with her, in the bed, stroking her skin with soft touches. Fingers, she was sure. Then something else. A feather?

A puff of air directly on her clit made her hips rise. A moist tongue laved one side of her labia, then the other, teasing, whispering. Total darkness greeted her eyes as she tried to open them against the tight blindfold. Nothing, not even a slight hint of light around the edges. She could see nothing, could only feel.

The man—she assumed it was a man by the slight scratch of whiskers against her tender flesh, although some of the whisper-soft touches were very feminine—rose up to lick and bite around her hip, her belly, her waist. *Please, please,* she silently begged, *either my breasts or my clit, but not in between where it only teases more!*

As if in answer to her plea, the body reared up, knees on the mattress between her legs, hands palm down near her upraised arms, and gently dragged what felt like a real live cock between her legs. Hard, hot. And yes, throbbing. It couldn't be a dildo, for if it was a mechanical throbbing, wouldn't she have heard the motor whir? And would it be so hot?

Please, please, she begged again in her mind.

It was the Punisher! The unique scent of him wafted up to her nostrils as he moved, a dizzying combination of spice and musk and man. Perhaps she could take the chance that he wouldn't punish her if she asked. Beg, if she had to. Hadn't he already shown he wanted her? Hadn't he been reluctant to administer those last hard strokes?

"Please, Master," she squeaked out before she could stop herself.

"Please what?" he growled, his voice a harsh, unrecognizable whisper.

"Please fuck me. Or at least let me come." To emphasize her need, she raised her hips as high off the bed as the tethers allowed.

For a moment he didn't move but stayed rigid above her, every nerve vibrating. Had she done wrong? Did he have his own orders from the giant? Did he really want to fuck her or was he just teasing her according to a set plan?

With a groan he eased down, allowing the full weight of him—gloriously naked!—to rest on her equally naked body. She bucked and rubbed against him, trying to get her clit to rub against his cock, but her pitiful efforts were hampered by the lack of leverage offered by her tied extremities.

"Hush," he whispered, his mouth finding a distended nipple in the dark—although, she thought with a touch of hysteria, maybe he could see her just fine, it was only she who wore the blindfold.

He laved it, worshiped it with his mouth, then tended to the other breast equally well while his cock ground up and down against her clit and the outside of her pussy.

Inside, she almost shouted, I want your cock *inside* me!

Suddenly he raised his hips, and she almost whimpered at the withdrawal. Then, in one harsh thrust, he seated himself deep inside her. With a raw sound of need that she couldn't stifle, her inner walls contracted around him, milking him with greedy spasms. She wanted to dig her heels into the mattress, to push her hips into his, but her legs remained immobile.

And so did he. Damn him!

"Please," she moaned again.

He withdrew totally and, with a muffled curse, moved off the bed.

This time she couldn't help it. She cried out. "No! Damn you, don't leave me!"

But it did no good. He didn't come back. No one did.

* * * * *

"Did you sleep well?"

Becca roused to the deep voice of the giant. Her throat felt dry and raw, her muscles ached from being stretched, her wrists and ankles ached from being tied. Her pussy, she was chagrined to discover, still throbbed with unfulfilled desire. At the sound of his voice her juices began to flow in wild anticipation of possibly, finally, attaining an orgasm.

"Yes, thank you, Master."

He chuckled deep inside his diaphragm. "Little liar."

Biting her lip, thinking discretion was best, she made no response then felt the mattress dip heavily on one side. As near as her blind senses could judge, he was kneeling on the bed inside the angle made by her splayed right arm and right leg.

Suddenly she felt his breath on her face, his big hands lifting her head to one side. "Let's get rid of this, shall we?"

A moment later Becca blinked at the harsh glare of light as the blindfold fell away. Morning sunlight, she realized, streaming through a row of lace-curtained windows that, last night, had been hidden behind heavy draperies.

The giant was indeed on his knees. Naked. His cock rampant and impossibly huge, rising from between massive thighs and a forbidding thatch of thick, black hair.

Oh God, would she have to service *him*? No, her mind cried out, she wanted the *Punisher* to be her Dom, not this…this hulk of a mountain!

"One more thing a sub must do," he murmured, "and that's trust that her Master will not do anything to hurt her. Remember your safe word and use it if you really, really need to stop."

Becca tried to swallow through her dry throat. He had read her mind, knowing that his huge everything could be—was—frightening. "Th-thank you, Master, for your concern. I-I'll be all right."

"That's a good slave. Now let's take care of your straps." To her great relief, the giant reached up to her right wrist and untied it. "Careful. It will hurt less if you move slowly." As he guided her arm downward toward her side, he began kneading the muscles, from her wrist all the way up to her shoulder and neck. Then he did the same with her right leg, slowly unkinking the tension in her calf, her thigh, the muscles attached to her hip and groin.

Then he climbed over her body, his cock bobbing obscenely close to her face, balls hanging free and massive like a stallion's, and tended to the limbs on her other side.

She sighed deeply and closed her eyes. "Thank you, Master. That felt wonderful."

He settled down next to her, on his side, torso bent at the waist as he leaned on an elbow to look down at her. "You're such a beautiful woman."

Her eyes sprang open to capture his gaze. "Me?"

"That's another offense, you know," he said, chuckling.

"Oh." Immediately she lowered her lids. "I'm sorry for looking at you, Master. It's just…"

"You may speak freely." His fingers trailed idly along her waist to hip, down her outer thigh and back up again.

"I thought we were all supposed to be honest," she said in a small voice.

"I honestly think you're beautiful. Look at how perfect your skin is, how rosy, how delicate." His fingers trailed up to skirt the underside of her breast and she made an involuntary move toward him. "How responsive you are."

She bit her lip.

"And your breasts. They're so perfectly shaped, so heavy in my palm." He matched action to word, cupping one and watching it overflow even his huge hand.

"Your eyes." He bent to kiss one then the other as she fluttered them closed. "So expressive. So green like the finest emerald. You can't see the way the sunlight makes all the shades of your hair glow. Gold and red and bronze and what-all. Don't ever feel you're not beautiful. I forbid it."

He rolled one nipple between thumb and forefinger then tugged it sharply, making her hiss with pleasure. "You have my assistants salivating. They're both panting to do this to you." He bent his head and pulled the nipple deeply into his mouth, giving it a nip with his teeth. "But that's for later."

The thought of what the assistants had already done to her made her ask, "May I speak, Master?"

He took so long to respond that Becca was tempted to look up and see what emotions crossed his face, whether she'd spoken out of turn. But she didn't move.

"You may."

With no small measure of relief that she hadn't committed another offense, she said shyly, "I rather fancy...the one I think of as The Punisher." Heat crept up her face to blaze in her cheeks.

"And you think that a slave has any choice in the matter?"

Sharp tears pricked the backs of her eyes. She shouldn't have spoken! Now he'd punish her by withholding the very Master she wished would dominate her.

Instead, he chuckled. "Punisher, eh? Good name. Does that mean you can tell them apart underneath those leathers and hoods?"

She bit her tongue. Should she tell him she could pick out her man's unique scent without seeing his face? "I think so," she equivocated. "I mean, he's the one who keeps track of my offenses and administers the punishment, right?"

The giant made a noise in his throat. "And what about my other assistant? Have you a name for him as well?"

"Um, well he did pinch my," she blushed to say it, "my lower lips almost to the point of pain, so maybe...Pincher?"

"That's a great name. And me?"

"The Giant, of course," she blurted out.

He threw his head back and roared with laughter. "Surely you can be more inventive than that?"

Was he testing her? Had he something specific in mind that she should say? "Well, I could amend it to say 'Gentle Giant'."

"Thank you." He kissed her on the tip of both breasts then slid his arms underneath her shoulders and knees, lifting her, naked skin to naked skin, changing the subject totally. "Coffee? Tea? Orange juice? Cocoa? What do you favor in the mornings?"

"Whatever you want to give me, Master," she said shyly.

He grunted his satisfaction at her quick learning.

As he walked, he held her just low enough for her to feel the bouncing snap of his engorged cock on her rump with every step. One arm around his massive shoulder, she bit her lip, regarding it as just another tease-punishment.

Since he'd placed her in position to look directly at him, Becca indulged. She realized his bald head had been shaved — she could see the same shadows in his smooth pate as in his jaw. A fairly large diamond shone from one ear and she noted long black lashes surrounding his steel-gray eyes. Oh how she longed to see the features of the Punisher in daylight, without his hood! She remembered the fever in those sexy brown eyes last night and almost whimpered with need.

He stepped into an adjoining room lambent with light from windows on three walls and skylights in the ceiling. Flowers grew riotously in pots scattered in between wicker chaises and sofas and a breakfast table with four chairs. Gently he settled her on one of the chairs.

Becca relaxed into it then remembered the rules. Quickly she pulled her legs wide apart and sat with palms on knees.

"Very good," the giant said from behind her. He kissed the top of her head then poured steaming hot, sinfully fragrant coffee into the cup at her hand. "Please help yourself to anything and eat heartily. I'll be back in a minute."

If she was alone, Becca wondered, did she still have to sit with legs splayed wide? It was an awkward way to eat.

She solved that by pulling the chair close to the table then spreading her legs again. Under a domed cover she found fat slices of French toast and browned breakfast sausages. Warm maple syrup waited in a delicate pitcher. Sliced strawberries added to the decadence of the breakfast. She piled her plate high and began to eat, suddenly ravenous from all the exertions of the previous evening.

That plate held nothing but scraps on it by the time the giant returned, clad once again in the tight black leather pants, boots and open vest.

He stroked her cheek. "Ready for some more fun?"

Becca forced herself not to look into his eyes. "Yes, Master. And thank you for such a delicious breakfast," she added quickly, hoping it wasn't an offense to do so.

"You're most welcome."

As the giant pulled back her chair, she stood, eyes downcast to see only the feet of the two assistants, clad once again in black leather. The giant led her back to the bed, nudged her onto it. "We'll get your punishment out of the way first."

He positioned her near the foot of the bed, on knees and elbows, forehead touching the mattress. "Punisher," he snapped.

Heat flared throughout Becca's body at the voicing of her name for the Master she wanted. She felt his hands settle on her hips then spread her ass cheeks wide open. His tongue rimmed the rosebud of her anus, stroking wide wet swaths until he began to push that tongue into her opening. She felt her sphincter contract, open, contract again as his tongue set up a rhythmic fucking of her anus, forcing his saliva into the opening to lubricate it.

This wasn't punishment, she thought, this was nirvana! She strained to raise her hips to meet his thrusts, squirmed her hips to seat his tongue more firmly.

Suddenly he withdrew tongue and hands. Becca wanted to shout the loss, her pussy quivering with need and her breaths coming hard and fast, but she stayed silent.

A new pressure against her anus tightened her muscles. She heard a soft mechanical sound as the object was inserted a millimeter at a time until it was seated as far as the safety handles allowed. A butt plug. She'd never seen one, but the feel, the sound of its low vibration, were unmistakable. Oh God, she wanted him to move it in and out of her hole, wanted his own cock to supplant it and fuck her that way, she wanted—

Smack! The crack of a hand on her fleshy ass cheek stunned, stung, brought tears to her eyes. "She's moving too much, boss," said the voice of the assistant who had hidden her clothes. She felt the sharp pain of a pinch on her labia then another, and another. "I thought I'd slow her down a bit."

Oh God, she'd pulled the name Pincher out of a hat when the giant had asked her and now he was taking it too much to heart.

Fingers delved into her pussy. "Wet as a lake," Pincher pronounced then shoved an object into the passage his fingers had explored.

A dildo. Also vibrating. Sensations rocketed through her as both butt plug and dildo vibrated with a higher, faster pitch. She needed to feel a body slamming into her, not inanimate objects just teasing!

"Stand up." The giant lifted her off her knees and set her, barefoot and naked, on the plush carpet. "How do you like your punishment?" he crooned.

"I...it's...too much," she managed to blurt out. "I need—" Damn, she wasn't in any position to *ask* for anything, and she'd best remember that!

He twirled her around to face the room and the two assistants, each of whom held a remote control switch whose wire disappeared into one of toys lodged in her orifices. Both wore smiles on their faces. Both had lust in their eyes, and damn if she wasn't going to look at them!

One of them stepped forward, knelt before her, nudged her thighs open.

She complied automatically, balancing herself as best she could with both vibrating devices driving her crazy.

Holding his remote so as to leave thumb and forefinger free, the man used both hands to lift the hood of her clitoris. He began to lick it, suck it. He put his teeth around it and bit gently. The Punisher! She could smell him, knew the feel of his tongue on her. *Yes, please,* she wanted to cry out. *Take me, make me come! Devour me!*

With both devices now vibrating loudly, her clit being stimulated almost beyond bearing, she struggled between needing to obey and needing even more to allow this man to bring her to what she desperately craved.

His assault on her clit strengthened. His remote fell to the floor as he grasped her ass cheeks with both hands, pushing her closer to his face. He sucked, plucked, bit. His tongue picked up the vibrations from the dildo and transferred them to her wildly throbbing clit.

"Master, please! Please let me come!" Without conscious volition, her hands grabbed the Punisher's head and held him to her. Her knees bent as she rocked her hips to and fro into his face. "Master...yessss!"

She could no longer hold back the tsunami. The smell, the feel of him, the exquisite, embarrassing pleasure of so many men watching her sexual need explode into an unstoppable flood, broke her will and she climaxed again and again and again, the noises in her throat as feral as a wolf's, her juices rolling unchecked down her thighs, until she slumped against the Punisher and he rose to a half-crouch to keep her from sliding, boneless, to the floor.

"Thank you, Master," she whispered, looking directly into the deep, lusty brown eyes of the Punisher behind the hood.

Then everything went black.

* * * * *

Later, much later — or so it felt to Becca — she opened her eyes to discover she lay on the oversize bed she'd been kneeling on earlier. The concerned gaze of the giant touched hers and she instinctively lowered her lashes.

"Are you all right?" he asked, voice subdued.

Becca couldn't help blushing. It had been the most potent, mind-blowing orgasm she'd ever experienced. No wonder she'd fainted. She wondered if her Punisher had climaxed along with her, or if he'd jerked himself off after, or if he was still as hard as that dildo and butt plug, which, she decided as she surreptitiously clenched her inner muscles, had been removed from her person.

A decadent smile broke out on her face as she luxuriated in the feeling of utter satiety. "I'm delicious," she murmured, stretching like a sinuous cat, back arched and arms raised over her head.

The giant's laugh boomed around her. "You certainly are." Then his demeanor changed. "But now it's time to continue your lessons."

Her eyes snapped open. Her arms came down to rest at her sides. She stared at the door on the far wall facing the huge bed, hoping her peripheral vision would pick out the shadowy form of the Punisher in his black leathers.

But they were alone on the bed, the sub and her Dom.

Her giant Dom.

Her heart started beating a faster tattoo against her chest wall. Was this the litmus test? That she would obey whoever called himself Master at any given moment? That wasn't what Glynnis had told her. She wasn't sure she wanted to be a sub, if that's what the rules were. She'd thought she would be able to choose whom she would offer herself to. And she wanted the Punisher. Not the Pincher or the giant.

The mattress tilted as the giant eased himself off onto the carpet and stood so she saw his profile. He bent down and shucked off his boots. Next he pulled his massive arms through the armholes of the vest and discarded that.

Becca swallowed but stayed motionless.

He unsnapped the panel at the front of his pants, eased the leather garment off his ham-hock thighs and kicked it aside. His cock jutted out like a missile awaiting launch, purple and red and laced with veins along its formidable length.

She gulped. "Are we—" *Are we alone,* she wanted to know. *Is the Punisher here,* she wanted to know. Biting back her questions, she said instead, "Master, may I speak?"

"No, you may not." The naked bulk of him sheened lightly with sweat, he climbed back onto the bed. He threw one leg over her torso and knelt straddling her, his cock obscenely huge and intimidating. "You've had your stimulation, your introduction. You've had three men touching you, arousing you, lusting after you. You've learned that holding back your own pleasure, giving up your right to make a decision, can lead to a most rewarding conclusion."

He leaned forward, one arm outstretched to rest his hand on the headboard. The movement placed his cock little more than an inch from her mouth. "You've even snuck in an orgasm without permission. Now it's time to pay the price."

With his free hand he grasped his cock, squeezing it at the base, which made the shaft even thicker. "Open your mouth, slave."

A shudder made Becca's skin feel cool and clammy. No, not him! Not someone so huge! That had never been her fantasy. But still, her rational mind argued, he was someone that Glynnis had vouched for. And hadn't the giant himself told her that a true Master would never hurt his sub?

On the other hand, if she took all of his huge cock into her mouth, if she gagged, if he rammed it down her throat until it hurt, how could she say the safe word if she needed to?

Another, more positive thought edged into her mind. Maybe he was testing her true desire to be a sub, to make sure she submitted to his every wish, before pronouncing her ready to be turned over to the Punisher. With a small inner sigh, she decided she'd have to play this out.

Hesitantly she let her mouth fall slack then with more determination opened it wide and lifted her head that last millimeter to show him her willingness to obey.

"Lick it."

Obligingly she stuck out her tongue and licked the drops of pre-come oozing from the eye of his penis. Then she rolled her tongue around the edges of the purple head, moistening it with her saliva.

The giant let go of his cock to grab a handful of her hair. He pulled her head closer. "Suck it now. Take it deep."

Not waiting for her to take a preparatory breath, he thrust his hips forward so that her mouth was suddenly filled with hot, pulsating flesh. She could feel the rim of the head slide against the roof of her mouth, pushing deeper and deeper still.

Instinctively she tightened her cheek muscles to keep some semblance of control as to the depth of his thrusts. Above her, the giant groaned, giving her the impetus to continue offering as much friction, as much braking, as much protection to her throat, as she could summon.

With a sudden clarity of purpose she made a fist around the base of his cock, realizing it would limit the depth of his thrusts and still offer him the sensation of coverage. Gradually she relaxed the back of her throat, allowing his cock to penetrate deeper into this secondary passage, deeper than she'd thought possible, yet not nearly taking the full length of him.

She concentrated on her Punisher, imagining that it was his cock in her mouth, his body straddling her, his hot brown eyes branding her with their lust, and she was able to continue working her head up and down, her mouth and hand varying the pressure on the giant's cock, until she felt the tension in his body ratcheting up several notches. Perhaps the Punisher was watching from some unseen observation point, with his hands sliding along his own hard cock and imagining that he was the recipient of her efforts.

The hand fisting in her hair slackened off, easing the pressure against her skull. He pulled himself slowly upright then sat back on his haunches and ran his fingers from her shoulders to her breasts, brushing the nipples absently. "You're a natural, Becca. You suck cock like a high-priced call girl."

He scooted backward on the bed then maneuvered her knees apart just enough to allow him room to kneel between them. "Now," he murmured, "put your hands under your knees and lift your legs up then spread your thighs as far out as they can go. I want to see every inch of you."

Was this any more threatening than having his gigantic cock in her mouth? What would happen when he wanted to fuck her, to put that huge tool inside her pussy? Or, more worrisome, into her anus?

Was being subservient to him being disloyal to the Punisher? She was close to reaching the line she didn't want to cross. It was all well and good to have them all toying with her, to have them all watch while she sucked their cocks. But to be alone with him, knowing that he was going to fuck her—

"Master," she tried again, "may I speak?"

"In a minute. After you spread your legs the way I ordered you to."

Becca bit the inside of her lip but complied. He couldn't order her not to speak after he'd all but given her permission. Trembling slightly, she lifted her legs as directed, feeling the sweat of her thighs against the sweat of her hips as they came together, felt the deep heat of her shame as she exposed her pussy, her anus, to his view. She squeezed her eyes shut.

"Master?"

The giant crouched down between her legs, lowered his head and began to lick her slit, from back to front, his thick tongue reaching both sides of her labia in one swoop. "Mm-hm," he said.

She assumed his moan meant permission as much as pleasure, and blurted it out before she could consider the consequences. "Will your assistants be joining us?"

It took a moment before he answered, a moment in which he licked and sucked and nibbled. He shoved his tongue inside her pussy and a finger inside her anus. "You're not as juicy as you were before," he murmured. "Why's that?"

"Master?"

He raised his head, peered at her through her splayed legs, his gaze traveling up her belly, to her ample breasts now slightly flattened, up to her face, seeing her teeth worry her bottom lip.

"What?"

"Please, Master, if you would answer my question?"

He fingered her pussy idly, slushing in and out as if his thoughts were elsewhere. "Where's the woman who couldn't wait to come? Where's the sybarite who loved to be sucked and pinched and butt fucked? Do you need an audience?"

With some asperity, she retorted, "Did you hear my question?"

"Yes, I heard your question. I sent both my assistants home." His two fingers slid out of her pussy as he sat up on his haunches. Absently he put his slick fingers into his mouth and sucked them as though contemplating her juices, or lack thereof. "So you're not really a sub. You're an exhibitionist."

"I—I don't really know what I am, Master. I think you're a very caring person, very gentle. But I have to say it." Becca took a deep breath. "Moonlight."

The giant reared back as if stung by a swarm of wasps. "Your safe word?"

"I'm sorry. I can't do this. Not with you."

After a silent moment during which he was no doubt marshalling his thoughts—or perhaps his pride—the giant slid off the bed again and offered her a hand. "Come. Sit up and I'll arrange for Glynnis to pick you up."

Chapter Three

&

"Where the *hell* have you been?"

Becca halted in the doorway of her living room and studied her husband of ten years. Tufts of dark hair stood up on his head like a crown of thorns, as though he'd raked his fingers through it too many times. In a pair of tailored, belted black slacks and blue shirt with sleeves rolled to the elbows, he looked too calm, too controlled. Brown eyes, however, flashed daggers at her.

Answering that loaded question depended on whether she'd been right in her assumption. She'd told him she and Glynnis were having a spa weekend and she'd be home on Sunday noonish. But it was Saturday night, four hours after Glynn had picked her up at the giant's home, and Steve looked royally pissed.

"Glynnis—" She cleared her throat. Her voice sounded like a child's. Consciously she pitched it lower. "Glynnis and I had a drink or two after—"

Steve took a step closer. She could see the vein in his temple throbbing. A bad sign.

"Go on. After what?"

She tried a smile as she stripped off her coat and flung it onto the sofa. "After the event. What did you do this weekend?"

"The 'event'." He came even closer, walked around her in a circle, thoroughly inspecting her in her loose overblouse and long skirt. "What did you get at the spa? A facial? A massage? Got your toenails painted? Doesn't look like you got a new hairdo." He raised a hand, filtered strands of her long hair through his fingers.

"Steve." She reached out to touch his arm. "I know that was you."

His brown eyes narrowed. "What do you mean? What was me?"

She met his cold gaze with her own intense one. "You look good in tight black leather. All except the hood."

"Jesus, Becca!" He flung her arm off him, plowed both hands into his hair, rearranging the spikes. "I didn't know whether to kill you or…"

It was admission enough for her. The tight muscles in her stomach relaxed. "Which guy did you know?"

"Both of them," he answered between clenched teeth. "Lucas was one of the partners in that land deal I worked on. Warren was his attorney. But the more pertinent question is, how did *you* know about the Platinum Society?"

"Platinum…what's that?"

"It's an exclusive sex club where anything goes. As you well know."

"I don't know anything about any sex club." She brought her chin up in her characteristic attorney's stance. "Are you a member? Did you bring your *friends* Lucas and Warren there for a treat?"

"Whoa! Wait a minute! I got into this deal because Lucas told me Glynnis suggested he invite me over for something special. He said she told him it was a surprise for you. So of course I went. But I certainly never expected to see my wife naked and getting it on with a bunch of guys!"

Steve spun on his heel, paced away from her, raking his hands through his hair again. Becca's gaze snagged on how good his tight butt looked in those staid, traditionally styled trousers. He stood a moment then turned around to face her, his voice tense and low. "Lucas, that's the bald guy, he 'instructed' me—that's what he called it, 'instructed'—not to be surprised at anything, not to say anything, not to make waves. Just follow his lead, he said."

The look of pain in Steve's eyes almost buckled Becca's knees. Then he said, "When he stuck his finger in your pussy, I had to ball my hands into fists in order not to punch his lights out." He strode to her, grabbed her by the upper arms, his hands gripping her tight enough that she knew she'd have bruises. "Why did you do that?"

"I did it because...tell me, Steve, what day is today?"

"What?" He looked at her as though she'd asked him a question about Mongolian yaks.

"Today. Saturday. What's the date?"

Bewildered, he released her and looked at his chronograph watch. "The fourteenth. Why?"

"The fourteenth of what?"

"What is this, twenty questions? You're evading the issue."

"All will be clear in a moment."

He sighed, a heavy, put-upon sound. "February fourteenth."

"Yes. And does that give you a hint as to what answer I'm looking for?"

Incredulity replaced bafflement on his face. "I'm asking you why you were so eager to have sex with a crowd of men and you're carrying on about Valentine's Day?"

"You're damn right," she cried. "I wanted to give you something different, something special! Glynnis told me she'd arrange it for me. She said you knew a guy who'd take care of getting you there."

"I certainly didn't expect anything like that. I didn't know they were both Doms until Lucas laid it all out for me. But you came on like—like a wanton! You let three *strangers* see you naked!"

"You oaf!" she said. "There was only one *stranger* I was interested in. Don't you think, after ten years, I'd recognize you even in a costume? That I don't know the shape of your body inside those tight leather pants? That I wouldn't react to the unique smell of you?"

She began pacing. "I knew that our love life was getting stale. I knew both of us were working too hard, that we needed a spark. And good Lord, Steve. The first time I saw your eyes behind that hood, all chocolatey brown and full of lust, do you think I didn't recognize them? Did you even notice that I came without permission because you had your mouth on my pussy?"

Being the good lawyer she was, she didn't react at seeing the jump of his cock inside his staid woolen trousers as she spoke words she'd never had the nerve to say aloud before.

"But what about between the time Warren and I got ordered out of the mansion and the time you came home, huh? Do you mean to tell me you spent *five hours* in a bar with your friend? Or was that just an alibi and you fucked Lucas to ease your itch?"

Trying to hold on to her own temper, Becca looked him in the eye. "You ask Lucas what happened. Ask him how wet I was when he tried to use his finger to get me hot. Ask him how long it took me to say my safe word when he tried to stick that obscenely big thing inside me." She gave him a poke in the chest with one long finger. "Ask him *why* I said it."

After a long pause, during which Becca watched his jaw muscles work, he asked, "Why?"

She took a deep breath. "Because he told me he'd sent you home, that's why. Because up until then I thought you were watching. I thought he was preparing me to be a real sub, to be sure I'd obey instantly, and then he'd give his prize pupil to the Punisher. To *you*. To scratch my *itch*."

Steve looked inordinately pleased at that, until he glowered at her. "How long did it take you to get to the safe word?"

"About ten seconds after he said you were gone."

"Becca." He fell to his knees in front of her and buried his face in her crotch. "Becca. I was so jealous. I wanted to kill that bald son of a bitch for handling you like that, for sticking his fingers in your pussy when I couldn't, for making you obey him. And when Warren stuck that dildo inside you —"

"Oh God, Steve, Glynnis didn't say anything about having a third guy there. It was just supposed to be you and me and one other guy, the guy who would pretend to be the teacher so I could learn properly. I thought it would be more like play-acting. I didn't know he was a real Dom. And believe me, it disoriented me for a minute, to see that both of you were built the same under cover of all that leather.

"But I'll tell you this." She pulled him to his feet then closed her eyes and buried her face in the crook of his neck, inhaling deeply. "It didn't take long to tell you apart. *This* is the scent I know and love. You're spicy and musky and all male. In my mind I had to think of you as the Punisher so I wouldn't blurt out your name when you were touching me. I wanted you to wonder if I knew who you were under that hood."

"Christ, Becca. When I saw you take off your clothes in front of those two men, I got such a hard-on, I hated myself, wondering how I could be so horny when I knew what they were planning to do to my wife."

A delicious smile crossed Becca's face. "Really? Do you think we could do it again sometime?"

Steve gave her a long look. Then he said, "Take off your clothes. Right now."

"You're kidding. I'm too hungry to play games."

"I said take off your clothes, slave."

After briefly weighing her options, Becca complied. This could be fun, she decided. As she had done the previous evening, she slowly unbuttoned her loose overblouse and let it fall to the floor. She was gratified to hear his gasp when he saw she wasn't wearing a bra.

Nor panties.

Not taking his burning gaze off her, he pulled out a cell phone from his shirt pocket and pushed a series of buttons. She stood, shivering, in the living room in her three-inch heels and nothing else until he growled, "Sit down, slave."

She sat where he indicated, on a padded hassock, her legs splayed wide and her palms resting on her knees, as she'd been taught. He loomed above her, striding around her, arranging her lush, long hair on her shoulders, pulling said shoulders back to thrust her breasts out and up.

A devilish smile spread across his face on hearing a car's engine stop. He walked to the front door, opened it and said, "Come in."

Every nerve cell in Becca's body tingled. Following Steve into the living room was a good-looking man of the same general size and shape as her husband. "Meet Warren," Steve said. "The Pincher. I discovered he lives in the same town. Now get on your hands and knees on the hassock. Now!"

"Yes, Master," Becca said meekly, but her eyes sparkled as she whispered, "Happy Valentine's Day, my darling Master."

Also by Cris Anson

ℰℂ

Dance of the Butterfly
Dance of the Crystal
Dance of the Seven Veils
Mischief Night

About the Author

ଓ

Cris Anson firmly believes that love is the greatest gift...to give or to receive. In her writing, she lives for the moment when her characters realize they love each other, usually after much antagonism and conflict. And when they express that love physically, Cris keeps a fire extinguisher near the keyboard in case of spontaneous combustion. Multi-published and twice EPPIE-nominated in romantic suspense under another name, she was usually asked to tone down her love scenes. For Ellora's Cave, she's happy to turn the flame as high as it will go—and then some.

After suffering the loss of her real-life hero/husband of twenty-two years, Cris has picked up the pieces of her life and tries to remember only the good times...slow-dancing with him to the Big Band sound of Glenn Miller's music, vacations to scenic national parks in a snug recreational vehicle, his tender and fierce love, his unflagging belief in her ability to write stories that touch the heart as well as the libido. Bits and pieces of his tenacity, optimism, code of honor and lust for life will live on in her imaginary heroes.

Cris welcomes comments from readers. You can find her website and email address on her author bio page at www.ellorascave.com.

Tell Us What You Think

We appreciate hearing reader opinions about our books. You can email us at Comments@EllorasCave.com.

HEART ON HIS SLEEVE

Marissa Alwin

ɛ૭

Chapter One
England 1439

&

"I will toss the old woman from a catapult." Waryn stared in annoyance at the amount of people milling about in his bailey. Ignoring everyone, he continued with long strides through the outer courtyard to the ward. The inner courtyard teemed with even more people.

Now it was clear what the soldiers at the gate house had been murmuring about.

"What do you think your *dear* aunt is up to this time?" Sir Jacob, his friend and most trusted knight, asked with a smirk.

Waryn stopped walking and looked back toward the stables where his squire had taken his mount. He still had time to retreat. Truth was he was better equipped to face a charging warrior than his small aunt.

Lord, the woman tried his patience. The woman would try the patience of a saint, and he was no saint. Why hadn't he followed his intuition and sent the old woman to a nunnery? After all, his intuition had saved his life many times.

"Looks like those who aren't at war are eating you out of your coffers," Sir Jacob taunted.

"You want to sleep in the kennel this night?" Baring his teeth, he pushed by the man. He'd only been gone three weeks, and Alice brought together this…this gathering.

He wanted them all gone. "Toss them all out."

"It's getting late…"

"I want them all gone by dawn."

"I'll do my best."

Inside his hall, he didn't have to look long for his aunt. The old woman held court, smiling to the hovering ladies. Nausea turned in his stomach as recognition set in. Many of the ladies who vied for his duchy turned to look his way. Their fathers and brothers lifted goblets to him as his squire urged him out of his winter cloak and chain mail.

A serving wench rushed forward, handing him a tankard of warm mead. He drained it before glaring at Alice. Damn the old woman. His properties rivaled those of the royal families of Lancaster and York. Married once. Betrayed once. His aunt knew he wouldn't marry again even for either the crown or his family's wealth. He'd done so once before with disastrous results.

He'd done his duty to both crown and family. Besides, his brother Gregory and his own son John stood in line to inherit the duchy.

Laugh lines wrinkled the old woman's face as she came to stand before him. "It is so good that you arrived, my lord. I am ready to draw the last names from the St. Valentine's box."

He arched an eyebrow at her reference to the holiday. The old woman had set him up but good this time.

With bejeweled fingers, she withdrew two slips from the carved wooden box then peered down at the cards. She lifted her head with another smile. "Miss Sibil Carlisle."

A gasp from across the hall earned his attention. Eyes of summer green, full of curiosity and innocence, stole his breath. Lust like never before sent a jolt of arousal to his loins. His manhood swelled, thickening to a point where it was difficult to think straight.

Alice patted his chest to get his attention. "And you, my dear…Waryn Landelle, Duke of Lysky."

The old woman waved the young woman forward. Sibil hesitantly walked to him as the onlookers gawked. Something familiar about her…but it eluded him.

Then the name registered.

Sir William Carlisle's daughter.

The knight had lost to Waryn land he'd expected to gain from the King. Though the knight found him at fault for the loss, everyone who survived the Battle of Gerbevoy knew it was Sir William's own son who was to blame. The young man should never have been put atop a war horse.

His hands clenched by his side. Damn his meddling aunt.

The raven-haired beauty's nervousness showed as she curtseyed. "Good day, Your Grace."

Respectfully, he bowed. "Good day, Miss Sibil."

Her wide eyes held him captive. Nay, it wasn't nerves that shone through, it was joy. "Sibil, Your Grace, if it pleases you."

His loins tightened further. Her voice was rich as if husky with sleep. Oh the things she could croon to his ears in the dark of night. Her request as so many of the country's nobles looked on showed her innocence. If she were ever allowed at court, half the men would have her flat on her back, the King included.

"Sibil." He bowed. "Pardon me. I must see my son."

Lady Alice stepped forward, stalling him. "Oh we must finish with tradition." The old woman tied an embroidered ribbon around his upper arm. Sibil's name was scrawled across it.

He tried to keep his face impassive as not to embarrass Sibil or her family. *Damn* the old woman. Never before had he felt quite so trapped. Sibil's curious eyes watched him with an eagerness that stirred his lust.

"Sweethearts for a year." Alice patted his arm and kissed Sibil's cheek. "The duke will make the finest of protectors."

Murmuring rose and fell among the onlookers.

If his aunt had been a man at that moment he'd have kicked her arse all the way to Scotland.

It was clear by Sibil's blush she was no courtesan out for profit. Yet not once in all his life had he seen such longing or excitement in a person's eyes as he did in Sibil's. Not once in all his marriage had his wife wanted him with such openness.

Waryn wanted to toss Sibil over his shoulder and carry her to his chamber. They'd not be seen the rest of winter. He ached to plow her belly with his seed.

The situation wasn't half as unnerving as the emotions being invoked by the black-haired beauty. His heart thundered as she continued to pursue him with her gaze. Yea, she evoked far more than his lust.

"If you'd permit me, Your Grace, I'd enjoy doing a sketch of your son." There was the slightest of tremors in her voice as she continued, "I know it's not much...but I promise a fair likeness."

He nodded, having forgotten the tradition of gift exchange in celebration of St. Valentine's Day. In all honesty, this was his first Valentine's. Oftentimes war kept him away during holidays. He cleared his voice and spoke clearly. "I'll provide you with a wedding dower fit for a Duchess in exchange." He wanted there to be no doubt, they were not sweethearts.

And even if he ravished her during the holiday...she'd go to a marriage bed with a dowry no man would pass up.

"I'll join you for the evening meal." He bowed to a wide-eyed Sibil. Then he leaned over and whispered into Lady Alice's ear, "I want the majority of these people gone from my home before dinner." He gave her a hard look. "See to it."

* * * * *

Sibil stared after the duke, desperately trying to regain her breath. His presence filled the room more than any other man's. His dark brown hair, fallen free of its queue, hung just to the middle of his expansive shoulders. His solid body moved in a way that demanded respect. In a way that...she placed a hand to her dark green dress, pressing against the flutter low in her belly. When her eyes had first met his, warmth had started there and spread upward all the way to her face. Her other hand's fingertips touched where it still burned her cheeks.

When Lady Alice had insisted she enter her name in the box she'd seen her chance to experience what could never be. But she'd never dreamed — nay, that wasn't true, she'd dreamt of him often. How she had gotten any words out when he was near was beyond her. How was she ever going to muster the courage to propose her offer if she couldn't even speak of such a simple matter as drawing his son?

"Sibil!" her father bellowed across the great hall.

She turned to see her family hurrying toward her. She winced — he looked none too pleased. They stole her air as they circled around her.

"She cannot have a larger dowry," Margareta whined. "I am older, I should marry better."

"This is an outrage! How dare he presume I cannot see to my daughter's future! I will not accept charity from that man, especially since he offers what should have been ours to start with!" Though he kept his voice hushed, his face was a bright red and spittle formed on the corners of his mouth. "You will go and tell him you refuse to accept such an offer."

"Yea, Father," she agreed quickly. Sibil wrinkled her brows. She didn't want a dowry. There was no need for her to have one. She clenched her hands in the folds of her gown, her hopes sagging. If he had no intention of honoring a simple pretend romance, how could she get him to consider her request? This was not what she wanted at all.

"William, do not be too hasty."

Sibil looked to her mother, the one who had said repeatedly that with Sibil's constant dreaming, overwhelming opinions and curiosity, no man would have patience for her. The convent was the place for her to no longer be a burden and also assist her family's reputation with the King—having a member of nobility take holy vows, even with her family's title, added to one's influence with the Church.

Maybe the size of the dowry had changed her mother's mind but not her own. The convent was the one thing they had ever agreed on. Besides, the one man she had ever thought she could love was not only a duke and above her station, but didn't even remember her.

Yet she wanted to know a man intimately before she took holy vows. To have the memory of his hands, mouth and body possessing hers. She needed more than hearing the tales of chambermaids and kitchen staff. She'd seen the knights camping outside the convent, plunging their stiff shafts deep between the spread legs of local women. Their sounds of pleasure made her own body catch flame. She wanted to know what it was like. She closed her eyes, picturing the way the duke had looked at her with his brown eyes. *Please let it be him.* Her body grew heavy, pulsing with anticipation.

"I think we should accept the duke's gift," her mother continued.

Margareta's pouting lip quivered.

"Now, Margareta, calm down. Since we decided Sibil will devote herself to the Lord's service next year, we can inform your prospects that she has graciously donated the Duke's gift to you."

I should have known. Sibil almost laughed but the gasp from Lady Alice stopped her. She entered their little circle, smiling graciously.

"Sir William, Lady Johanna." Lady Alice nodded to her parents. "I hope you have been enjoying the festivities."

"Yea, thank you, Lady Alice." Her mother wrapped an arm around her father's.

"Fine. Why not go and continue to do so?" She linked her arm in Sibil's. "Sibil, my dear, you must be anxious to meet the Duke's son. Come, I shall introduce you."

Again Sibil stifled a laugh as her family's mouths hung open, but no one dared to say a word to their hostess. She wished she had a little of the older woman's commanding presence.

"Thank you, Lady Alice," she answered, already walking with her from the hall. For a woman of her age and stature, she moved swiftly. Sibil quickened her step to keep pace.

"So you are skilled with charcoal?" Lady Alice slowed her step as they began to climb the narrow stairs to the upper floor.

Sibil's face warmed. She hadn't planned on entering her name so she hadn't brought an appropriate gift. "I've been told I have some skill. I know 'tis not much…"

Lady Alice snorted. "Child, you offered to capture the likeness of the one my nephew holds most dear. I know he will treasure it more than any bauble those fortune-hunting cows would have offered him."

Lady Alice's remark made Sibil cough. The elderly woman experienced no difficulty expressing herself. She had the other women in attendance pegged perfectly. If only the woman's assessment of the Duke's interest was as correct.

The older woman chuckled. "My mouth has always been my best and worst quality."

"Mother often says the same of me."

"We have minds. I see no reason not to speak them." Lady Alice patted her arm.

She returned the woman's smile. If only everyone believed that. The glow of the setting sun lit the hallway passage of the upper floor through small arched windows. The opposite wall had three doors. The first would have been his deceased wife's bedchamber. The second was where he slept. Her heart jolted between her breasts. She forced herself to breathe and keep walking.

The last door before the causeway to the next tower was open and voices filtered out. A man's low pitch and a boy's higher one. Private places on Sibil's body started to pulse in time with her heart. Was it the Duke's voice?

"Tell me, dear, how long do you think it will take to make this sketch?" Lady Alice asked.

"I am not sure. It depends on how detailed I make it."

"Do this old lady a boon. Make it as detailed as possible. Perhaps include his new mount. I miss other ladies here, and I find you enjoyable company. I will arrange for you to stay as my guest until 'tis finished. Ah, here we are." Lady Alice guided her into the room before she could comment.

Sibil's heart was racing. Live here at the Keep? See the Duke every day? She didn't know why Lady Alice had taken a liking to her, but she was grateful. Her gaze adjusted to the room, tapestries hung over the stone walls and there was a large table covered with ledgers. What lined the walls in various manners of display made her breathless. Manuscripts — more than she'd ever seen before. How rare for a family to have such a collection. She noted at least five Psalters and many unknown works amongst the titles she knew, at least a dozen in all.

The sliding of chairs pulled her attention away.

"Lady Alice!" a cheerful voice greeted her companion. The young boy moved away from the ongoing chess game toward Lady Alice, but hesitated when he saw Sibil.

The man with him bowed slightly. "Lady Alice."

"Gentlemen." Lady Alice smiled. "John Landelle of Lysky and Sir Jacob Poins, may I present Miss Sibil Carlisle of Cumberland."

"Miss Sibil." The two bowed in greeting. Sibil responded with a small curtsey.

"Has your father been in?" Lady Alice asked.

John nodded and looked toward a door that connected this room with the duke's bed chamber. "He's washing some of the damned road off so he's presentable for the bloody banquet."

"My lord." Sir Jacob cleared his throat.

"That's what Father said."

She toyed with a jewel on her belt. The thought of him bathing behind the door made her belly flutter again, creating a strange sensation between her legs that made her shift restlessly.

"Miss Sibil is your father's sweetheart for the year, my lord," Lady Alice informed the boy. "She will be sketching your likeness as a gift."

Sir Jacob made a sound that quickly turned into a cough.

The young boy studied her. His slender frame, blond head and clear blue eyes showed nothing of his father's rugged build. Though the way he stood and the expression on his face was definitely his father's influence.

"Lady Alice, dear heart?" A matronly woman bustled into the room. "I was stalled by some divine pastries."

"Oh good, you found us." Lady Alice faced Sibil. "Sibil, I've asked Lady Joan to serve as your chaperone. She's grand company." Lady Alice leaned in close to Sibil's ear. "A jewel, but she tends to doze off at the most peculiar times and cannot hear well." She straightened and winked. "Make the most of it."

"Thank you, Lady Joan, for the company." Sibil curtsied. The elder offered her a smile before settling into a nearby chair.

Lady Alice gave her another wink then moved away from Sibil. "Sir Jacob, would you do me the honor of escorting these old bones back to the Hall so I can oversee the banquet preparations? We'll leave these two to get acquainted."

"'Tis my honor, Lady Alice, to have such beauty adorn my arm." The old knight smiled. "My lord, we'll have to continue our game another time."

Sibil squirmed more as Sir Jacob continued watching her. "Speaking of beauty." He approached them and held out his arm to Lady Alice. "Have we met before, Miss Sibil?"

"I do not believe so, Sir Jacob. I have been living with my mother's sister for several years."

Sir Jacob tilted his head, and then shrugged as Lady Alice physically coaxed him to the door. "I shall come see you later, John." Lady Alice smiled affectionately at the boy, and he returned the gesture. "And we will see you at dinner, Sibil," she called as they left.

"You're going to sketch a picture of me?" John bit the inside of his lip and fiddled with one of the chess pieces.

"Yea, Lord John. Lady Alice suggested I include your horse as well, what do you think?"

"So we can do this outside?" He sounded a little more eager and stopped shifting from foot to foot.

"I suppose we would have to if your horse is in it."

John went back to toying with the chess piece. He tilted his head and looked at her. "You're my father's sweetheart. Does that mean you are to marry him?"

"Oh...I..." If there was ever a man she wanted to marry, Waryn of Lysky was he. But she couldn't tell the boy that, nor was it likely to happen. "We aren't a suitable match," she said quietly. "This is for a holiday tradition."

They weren't of compatible station to be married and according to her mother, no one would ever see her as a suitable wife anyway. Besides she didn't want to be wed to any man who couldn't love her beyond the price her father would pay for a marriage. She was glad she wasn't going to marry at all.

Heat spread through her middle to pool at the joining of her thighs. Could Waryn be a man who loved her for just herself, if it were allowed?

Noting John's shift in attention, she looked back toward his door and froze.

Chapter Two

ಙಎ

After ordering one of Alice's cloaks to be fetched for Sibil, Waryn had stood watching Sibil with John for several moments before her discovery of his presence. It was a pleasing picture. "Son, collect your cloak and have a maid fetch Lady Joan hers. You shall play escort."

Lady Joan snorted in her sleep as she dozed in her chair. A small smile played on Sibil's lips and with shaking fingers she toyed with her belt.

"So you don't feel we suit each other?" He smothered a grin, confused as to why he wanted to tease this woman — other than this being the first time he'd heard the term *unsuitable* directed toward him.

Lashes lowered to shield her gaze and he regretted his words. He reached over and tucked a lock of black hair beneath her headdress. His fingers twitched with eagerness to remove the offending piece from her head. John dashed by with a shout as Waryn handed Sibil a woman's light cloak.

"You are a duke, I am only..." She looked up at him. "I have plans to enter an abbey."

A frown creased his forehead. That would be a waste. "And the dowry I'll provide you?"

"Oh..." Her hands fluttered once she was done with the cloak. "Margareta wishes to wed. Mother suggested I offer it to her."

"Is that what you wish?"

"I suppose." Her eyes dropped, she played with the cloak's opening. "There is one... I would like..." She fisted the material. "Your Grace, if I may ask a favor?"

She had his full attention. Her face flushed a heated shade of red. He could easily imagine her weak with the flush of passion. "Ask it."

"Father," John bounded into the room, "I'm ready." A quiet maid followed him and helped Lady Joan into a cloak.

"I see that you are." He turned back to Sibil. "Your favor?"

"Oh… 'Tis nothing. We can discuss it later."

"As you wish." He picked John up, tossed him over his shoulder and led the way down the backstairs in hope of avoiding visitors. Alice no doubt had no intention of asking her guests to leave since his squire hadn't noticed the number of people dwindling.

John laughed until they were out of doors and straightened up. Even knowing the boy was no longer a babe didn't prevent Waryn from treating him as one on occasion.

John's scrawny arm went around his neck. "I'm glad you're home, Father."

"Me too, my boy." He'd never cared to be away from his son. Upon his every return John appeared older by leaps. He hugged the boy closer. Yea, 'twas always good to be home.

"Your Grace, you'll catch your death with damp hair," Sibil said, keeping pace beside him.

You'll catch your death. Similar words echoed from his time at an abbey in Burgundy. Then, they'd been accompanied by a gentle touch.

Waryn stopped and set his son on his feet. "What did you say?"

"I… 'Tis not important, Your Grace."

Needing to see into her eyes, he clasped her chin. "Sibil, repeat your words."

"I was concerned for your health, Your Grace. I did not mean to offend you." Her voice was barely audible above the drone around them.

Lady Joan caught up to them, having been trailing a few steps behind.

"I am not offended." He released her and continued walking. Sibil couldn't possibly be the nurse who'd cared for him when he'd been at death's door. Wounded, he'd sweated out an infection as an angel tended to him. He'd sworn if he found another with the gentle ways of that angel he'd keep her for himself. In the years since no one had come close until… He watched the sway of his aunt's cloak around Sibil.

They continued on to the stable where John dashed off to see his pony. Several stable boys greeted them and left them alone.

Sibil moved to his side to stand improperly close. His cock stirred to life, declaring its need and want for her to be closer still. "You are very blessed to have such a lovely home."

He supposed so. He'd shed enough blood to keep what was his and to advance what land holdings he wanted. He led her away from the war horses toward the docile mares. Lady Joan wandered over to pet a stout, sleepy white mare.

Waryn stopped walking at the sight of the big red steed. His stomach churned at the recognition.

"Your Grace, is something wrong?" Sibil placed her hand on his arm.

His brother Gregory had returned. Why had the bastard appeared? Did he want John after these past six years? He closed his eyes… If Alice was behind this… Nay, the old woman wouldn't dare.

"Waryn?" The hoarse voice called from the shadows behind them. Instantly, Waryn's sword was in his hand.

"Brother…"

He pressed forward. "You no longer have the right to call me brother." His gut twisted. He'd never been so close to shedding blood outside of battle.

"Father?" John whispered.

"Take the boy to my rooms and keep him there."

"Yea, Your Grace." Fear strained Sibil's voice.

Cloth rustled. The sound of Lady Joan urging John along assured him both women had left. His heart thumped in his chest. Taking two steps forward, he pressed the deadly tip to his younger brother's throat and forced him back against a wall. "You dare to show your face here!" The bastard had left before John's birth. Noticing the stable lads nearby, he roared, "Get out!"

"You're my brother. This is my home." Sweat beaded on Gregory's upper lip. "I was so very young. Have you not ever done something you regret?"

"Nay, I have not." His arm trembled from the restraint he used not to kill the man standing before him. "You were old enough to know right from wrong. You were old enough to wield a sword."

"I was seduced. 'Twas not my fault."

An ache beat in his clenched teeth. Lowering his sword, he moved forward and took Gregory by the throat. He tightened his grip.

His brother didn't struggle.

"I could have forgiven you fucking my wife. But I shall never forgive you for abandoning John."

Nay. He'd not ever forgive the bloody bastard. Young or not, Gregory had to have known his actions were wrong.

"Waryn!" Lady Alice's cry racked his nerves.

"Pray...forgive...me." Gregory's words were strangled.

"Think of your mother." Lady Alice pulled at his arm.

With a snarl, he released Gregory who sucked in a breath. "You will get nothing from me. Now get off my land."

His chest heaved as he turned around. Sibil stood alone nearby. Briefly, he closed his eyes. *Fuck.* He'd lost his control. He never lost his restraint. For John's sake, he hoped no one overheard. "I will not be attending the banquet tonight."

He sensed her eyes on him. Oddly it calmed him.

* * * * *

Stripped down to just his tunic, Waryn sat in the darkness of his rooms. The castle had been quiet for some time. After he'd said good night to John, he'd confronted his aunt. Alice had sworn she'd had nothing to do with Gregory's appearance. Swallowing another long swig of ale, he cursed himself for believing the old woman.

Now for the first time in years he was heavily into the cups.

Bloody hell.

Had he come to twist the dagger of his betrayal even more? If it was money Gregory wanted he'd give it just to be rid of him. But Waryn would give him nothing more.

He lifted the jug to his mouth, only to lower it as the door eased open and the flicker of a candle glowed. As quietly as it opened, the door closed.

His nostrils flared. Sibil had entered his rooms. Blood rushed through his veins to engorge his cock hidden under his tunic. His ballocks tightened in anticipation.

From the deepest corner of the room, he watched her. As her fingers ran along his manuscripts, he palmed his thick manhood under the tunic. He ran his hand up and down the rigid shaft before releasing it. "Come to rob me?"

"Oh," she gasped and turned around to raise her candle up high, illuminating more of the room. "Your Grace…" One hand fluttered at the base of her throat. "Nay, I wanted to see if all was well with you. 'Twas so dark when I entered, I thought you were abed."

"Nay, I am well and fully awake. I welcome a distraction." Her concern stirred more in him than his lust. He could not recall the last time someone had asked after him. Not true—he once again recalled his angel's gentle touch and caring words.

He cleared his throat. "Now that we are alone..." The responsible Duke wanted to tell her she shouldn't be there. The man bit it back. He wanted this time with her. "Why not ask your boon now?" Besides John and Gregory, Miss Carlisle had been occupying his mind. Yea, Sibil's company would be most welcome.

She hesitated briefly. Then her determined exhale of breath flickered the candle's flame and she walked slowly to his chair, her cloak parting. She wore only a chemise underneath. Amazingly her hair was down, uncovered.

Her hips swayed. The white of her chemise taunted him from between the flaps of her open cloak.

Waryn swallowed, his mouth watered. "Do you know what would happen if you were discovered here? Now?"

"Yea," she continued on a breathless whisper, "but no one will miss me."

He groaned. No one miss her? *Fools.* A family of them. If she belonged to him he'd never want her out of his sight.

"Your Grace." She now stood before him.

He reached out, taking the candle from her and setting it on the table along with the ale. "Yea?"

"I want to know..." After a calming breath, the words rushed out. "I'd like for you to love me as a man loves a woman."

"You know not what you ask." His cock pulsed heavily.

Using surprisingly steady hands, she shook back the cloak and let it slide slowly to the rush-covered floor. "I know what I ask."

She stood before him in all her beauty. Her dark nipples peaked behind the white cloth. The dark hair hiding her pussy showed through the thin garment.

"I pray you, don't deny me. I want it to be you." Her full hips swayed as she moved to stand between his legs.

"You seek the wrong man." He clenched the arms of the chair. "There is nothing gentle to me. I know not what love is between a man and woman." Though he did know plenty about rutting. His cock twitched under his tunic.

Biting her lip, she clasped her long chemise in her hands and pulled it up over her knees, and then up to reveal the dark thatch that hid her pussy.

He swallowed. Her lush breasts bounced as she straddled his lap.

Lord, give me strength. He ached to plow her wet depth. Deep and hard. Yea, rutting he was prepared to teach the vixen.

Her delicate scent played havoc on his senses. Her gentle hands slowly roved up his forearms to his shoulders. Her hand slid back down to toy with the ribbon still wrapped around his arm. "You wear my ribbon still."

"Yea." Foolish or not, he hadn't been able to make himself remove it.

She shifted to rub her body against his cock. Again and again she rubbed her pussy along the rigid length hidden behind the worn lightweight tunic. He sucked in a breath at the thrusting of her wet folds upon his needy cock, her heat radiating through his worn tunic.

Pleasure—such a sweet promise. He wanted to be a greedy bastard and seek out his gratification. Instead, he kept a tight grip on the chair as she wiggled impossibly closer. He enjoyed the rise and fall of her breasts, teasing his chest through her thin garment.

Sibil clasped his face in her hands and placed a kiss upon his lips. His eyes opened on a moan. He'd only been kissed so one other time in his life, when his angel had kissed him goodbye and wished him well.

Nay, 'twas not possible. Long ago, he'd given up hope of finding the woman of his past, of his dreams.

She pressed her lips to his once more, softer this time, and he experienced the sensations of this moment. Eagerness for another taste swamped him. At the swipe of her tongue, he opened his mouth to accept her smaller, invading one. She was hesitant at first, but soon her hands tangled in his hair and clutched at his shoulders.

Every caress jolted through him. He'd never experienced this kind of tentative exploration before. He didn't touch her. If he did, he couldn't be sure he could stop from taking what he badly wanted.

His tongue teased back, causing her to moan and squirm against his manhood. His balls tightened more.

With rougher motions she caressed his shoulders, chest and arms. What she sought he couldn't say, but the touching aroused him to the point he could no longer control his breathing. One after another, she shared kisses with his hungry mouth.

She rocked her wet pussy along his rigid length.

He could barely think. He'd no desire to stop her. At the press of her lips on his jaw, chin and then throat he'd nearly come. He arched his hips, willing the pressure to retreat.

"Do I please you, Your Grace?" she whispered, running her moist lips along the column of his neck.

"We must cease."

"Nay. You want this as much as I." She moved to the other side of his throat.

Moaning, he rolled his head, relishing every sensation. No one had ever teased him such.

"Touch me. Please." Her plea was so urgent, so desperate for him. His heart wrenched in his chest.

With trembling hands, he released the chair and grasped her buttocks. "Lift my tunic out of the way."

Gasping for breath, she jerked it up to expose his cock to full view. Instead of impaling her, he pressed her hard against him. She was wetter than she'd been through the cloth. Using his hands, he slid her up and down along his thick shaft until she moaned and panted.

"Waryn," she murmured, her hips rocking with his hands. Her wet folds slid against his hard flesh, leaving him slick. Using fast motions, he worked her swollen button upon his cock. Her pussy juices flowed.

Her entire body tensed on a surrendering cry and he allowed himself to erupt, sending his seed along their bodies. He grunted, pressing her tighter to him as his pleasure faded.

Breathless, she laid her trembling body upon his. Roughly, he rubbed her back along her spine.

"Sibil?"

She lifted her head.

"You need to rethink your quest. Once I take you to my bed…I won't even share you with our Lord."

Nay. Not even with the Lord. He wanted Sibil Carlisle for his own.

Chapter Three

๑

"I think 'tis just your ale talking, Your Grace." Sibil's heart pounded under her breast. It would be beyond her wildest dreams if Waryn meant it.

She rested her head against his shoulder, nestling into his neck. Her entire body still quivered from the sensations he had caused to explode through her. It had happened before but never caused by anything other than her own hand and never with such heated passion. Oh she wanted more.

Closing her eyes, she inhaled his musky masculine scent, allowing her body to melt against his. She didn't know it was possible to feel so excited and so relaxed at the same time.

"'Tis neither a false tongue nor the ale speaking, Sibil." His massaging hands roved over her back and relaxed her more.

Her heart jolted. His deep voice vibrated from his chest to her breasts to straight between her legs. Her hips rolled in response and his hands clamped them, stilling them. His cock pulsed against her belly as her sex clenched, craving it.

"'Tis not possible, not conventional. Our noble society frowns upon it. Besides, Mother is right, I find it difficult to hold my tongue. I am not a suitable wife. I see how you react to your aunt." She wove her fingers into his hair at the nape of his neck, sighing against the column of his throat. "I would only make your blood boil. And you already made it clear you do not want another wife."

"You make my blood boil in other ways. In ways that have changed my mind."

She smiled against him and pressed a kiss to the soft place behind his ear. "If only the world were within these walls.

Besides, Father would never allow it, even if you were the King himself asking for me. He needs someone to blame for Simon's death. I am afraid it's you."

"Sibil, I —"

"I know you are not to blame. I know you risked your life trying to save him." She had seen her brother's dead body, had helped tend the wounds the duke had incurred as he and his knights tried to aid the young man. The pain of Simon's loss stung her anew. "He was not meant for battle, Father will not accept that." She rubbed her lips along his jaw, liking the way the coarse hairs tickled them. "Please do not deny me what everyone else wants to. Love me."

Waryn's fingers sifted into her hair and his hands cradled her to him. She swore she heard him growl. Her body was so heavy. Her eyes were barely able to open. She nestled closer, enjoying the feel of his heart beating along with hers. Oh the way the warmth of his body and being in his arms made her feel. If only someone might want her for who she was. That was what she truly ached for.

"Sibil, forget what your parents or even I have said. Tell me what you want."

His heart sped up. His hold on her tightened. Her own skipped a beat. She had been drifting away drowsily and not quite sure if she spoke her next words aloud. "I want nothing more than to stay right here with you." He murmured something she couldn't understand. She tried to ask what it was but sleep won.

* * * * *

Waryn woke slowly to a bare leg being rubbed against his thigh. He stirred. He was used to sleeping alone. Even married, he'd never shared the night with his wife.

This company he'd look forward to keeping in the future. Yea, every night after he claimed her, if she'd permit it.

Sibil moaned and pressed closer.

His arm that had replaced her pillow curled around her body as his manhood swelled.

He stirred from sleep at the feel of busy fingers as they brushed against his hipbone. He lifted his head. Sibil, wanton that she was, played in her own folds.

He groaned and rolled up onto an elbow.

Sibil lay back to spread her legs for his full view. The dark curls hiding her sex parted. Fingertips flicked the swollen pearl. With an arch of her hips, her fingers slid along her crevice to bury two into her wet opening.

Such temptation. Didn't the vixen know what she offered?

Groaning, Waryn closed his eyes for a steadying breath.

Sweat beaded his chest as he allowed himself the treat of watching her play.

She used quick fingers to work her glistening flesh. Sibil caught her lower lip between her teeth as she reached out to him. She wrapped her free hand around the crown of his manhood. Her thumb ran over the tip to collect the drop of seed.

She brought her thumb to her mouth and licked off his taste.

His shaft pulsed at her boldness.

Breathing harshly, Waryn moved her hand out of his way. He pressed the pads of his two fingers to her pearl and stroked. Sibil moaned, rolling her head. He increased the pressure and speed of his movements until Sibil panted for breath. Her passion further fueled his lust.

Controlling his passion, Waryn kept time to the roll of her hips as he settled between her spread thighs. He pressed his manhood into the mattress, wishing he was buried inside her depths, and lowered his head.

She cried out as he buried his fingers in her pussy and pumped. He then leaned forward and sucked her pearl into his mouth, wrenching another cry from her lips. Her hips arched off the bed as he sucked and fucked. He slurped harder at the feel of her inner walls clamped around his buried fingers.

Scrambling up onto his knees, he pulled her thighs up to his hips to hold her in place. His manhood slid along her dripping creases. Panting, Sibil reached down and rubbed along the top of his rigid length as he continued to brush back and forth along her wet sex. With her free hand, she pulled at the hidden peaks under the thin material that covered her breasts.

He clenched his teeth at the tightening in his ballocks. The hot eruption neared.

As if in tune with his needs, she applied more pressure to his manhood as he rocked back and forth over her slick folds.

She moaned.

The sound of her pleasure was too much, and Waryn groaned and spilled his seed atop of the skin on her stomach.

"Good day, Your Grace," she murmured breathlessly.

His chest heaved as he worked to catch his breath.

A smile played across her mouth as she rolled her palm around the head of his manhood. "One day you will fill me."

Swallowing, he moved her hand out of the way to rest his head on her shoulder. *Yea.* Sooner than she thought. Once dawn broke, he'd dispatch knights to deliver payment for a special license.

"I must return to my room." She sighed and wrapped her arms around his.

"Yea."

She pushed at his shoulders. He allowed her to move out from under him, but he grasped her arm before she could leave his bed. "'Tis a fine morning, Sibil." He placed a gentle kiss on her mouth and ignored the trembling in her limbs. Then he released her to watch her quickly leave his bedchamber before the sun could fully rise.

* * * * *

Sibil shifted on the stool and tried to concentrate on Lord John sitting atop his horse. Even in the cold crisp air of the morning, she grew feverish, liquid heat pooling in her belly each time she remembered her body rubbing against the duke's. How could she fall asleep in his arms when she was trying to convince him to lay with her? And then the early morning had brought nothing but more desire.

After she'd made it to her room she hadn't seen him at morning meal when everyone else had broken fast. Though after her clumsy attempt to seduce him then falling asleep she was a little relieved. Even more so when she finished before her family came to the hall too.

She'd rushed to leave the castle grounds before facing them. She and John had set up beyond the outer walls on the edge of an oak tree cluster. Lady Joan looked on, resting beneath a nearby tree. Lord John was just as excited as Sibil to be outdoors in this first spell of good weather after months of bleak winter.

Once they'd settled, Lady Joan's head soon nodded to her chest. Lady Joan had complained it was far too early to be out of bed.

Though the cold season still held the earth, she could feel spring approaching. The stream beyond the oaks swelled from the melting snows, and the days grew longer. The sky now shifted from dismal cloudy gray to a vivid blue as the morning progressed.

"Father said if my riding improves, he will take me on the next hunt." John shifted in the saddle. He had been patient while she outlined the portrait. Now he eagerly eyed the clearing spread out before them.

"Then why don't you and Sir Richard ride for a bit while I capture the trees' detail?" She looked back at the knight astride a large mount, keeping watch over them. He saw her and approached, and John's face lit up with a toothy smile.

"Shall we start with a trot, my lord?"

She sharpened the charcoal as they rode away.

"Nice blade," a voice wheezed into her ear.

She gasped, nearly dropping the dagger. Gregory stood at her side. He was breathing heavily and despite the chill in the air, a slight sweat beaded on his upper lip and brow. After the scene in the stable, she'd assumed he'd taken his leave. No doubt Lady Alice was behind his lingering.

"Thank you. My brother crafted it for me." She studied Gregory, who looked pale and leaned against the tree as if for support. "Is all well with you, my lord?"

"Yea, only slightly short of breath from my walk," he rasped. "Your brother is a fine craftsman."

"He was." She smiled, smoothing her finger over the jeweled hilt. "He was gifted much more in forging the weapons than in planning a strategy for their use." Too bad her father hadn't wanted that talent in a son.

She looked up at the man next to her. What could he have done to cause Waryn's inflexible ire? He had the blond curls and blue eyes of an angel, albeit a tired one. Curiosity was her strength and her weakness—she wasn't sure she wanted to know the answers to the questions in her mind.

"And you have a good eye." He nodded toward the stretched parchment on her lap.

"Thank you, my lord." Her face warmed. Her heart raced some as she asked, "Have you been away from the duchy long?"

He coughed. His hand moved to his chest. His breath wheezed, causing a twinge of concern to strike her. "Just over six years. As you saw yesterday, I did not leave on the best of terms." He drew in another breath. "I have returned to make peace with my family."

His eyes moved to the approaching horses, a painful longing crossing his face. John and Richard galloped to a stop before them. Excitement shone from the boy's eyes.

"Well done, my lord. Your father will be impressed with your progress," Sir Richard praised.

"Yea, Lord John, you ride quite well." Gregory had pushed himself away from the tree. "You will be an asset to any house who takes you as a page." A chill went through Sibil. She couldn't ignore the similarities in their appearances, identical blond curls and blue eyes. Given what she'd overheard in the stables, she realized she already had the answers. Her heart ached for Waryn.

John shifted in his saddle, his breath fast and his cheeks ruddy from the ride. "Father says he's not sending me away. Whatever I need to learn to be a proper knight and duke, I can learn right here."

Sibil's heart flipped. Was it possible Waryn wasn't bound by the nobility's dictates? Was it possible the words he'd spoken to her last night were true? Still, to break from the rules for his son and heir was one thing. Would he do the same for a woman?

"Your father always does what is right. You'd do well to listen to him." There was a hint of anger in Gregory's rough voice.

"Shall we go again, my lord?" Sir Richard asked.

John shot a look at Sibil. She laughed at his pleading eyes. How could she deny him? "Go on." The words were barely spoken before he turned his mount and rode off.

"Waryn will do anything for those under his protection. But never wrong him. He does not forgive." Gregory suddenly started coughing, unable to stop. Bending over, he brought the material in his hand to his mouth. Blood appeared on the threads.

"My lord!" Sibil rushed to him, grabbing him as his knees buckled to the ground. The man beneath the cloak was skin and bone. She knelt beside him and touched his cheek and forehead with the back of her hand. "You are feverish. You should be abed."

"Is everything all right, Miss Sibil?" Sir Jacob called, approaching rapidly.

Her heart pounded in her throat. She'd seen this before. The sisters at the convent had tended to those suffering from diseased lungs. "His lordship is not well, Sir Jacob. He needs to be in bed and tended to."

"I'll see him to his chamber and inform Lady Alice." He hooked his arm around Gregory and helped him stand, all the while watching her.

"I should..." She started walking with them but then looked back to John and Sir Richard.

"You should stay here with them and enjoy the day." Sir Jacob took halting steps, supporting Gregory.

"He should try to take some broth." She adjusted Gregory's cloak. "This cold air will only encourage fluid to your lungs, my lord."

Gregory's hand darted up and grabbed her wrist. "Not a word." His hoarse voice was only a whisper. "I pray thee, not a word to Waryn nor the boy."

How could she do what he asked?

* * * * *

Waryn stood in the warming sun doing his best to ignore Jacob. Alice had gotten to the man. A sure way to win over any of his knights was to offer them fierce competition. When the men weren't at war, they'd enjoy playing at it instead.

"They expect you to join the games."

A private Valentine's tournament held at his home. What an utter waste. Too many had already died for the sake of showing off their prowess. He should have known Alice had put more together than a simple gathering—singing, dancing, the neverending feast. If not for Sibil's company, he would...

"Your Grace."

He turned his head to glare at his knight.

"You've no need to make a name for yourself...some of your men wish to participate in the war games."

Waryn nodded. He had no need to prove anything to anyone. "Very well." He clapped Sir Jacob on the shoulder and leaned over. "Make sure the Baron Atwood gets knocked on his arse."

The knight snickered before rushing off.

He grunted. What were the chances all his knights would come through the following melee unscathed? Fools, the lot of them. No doubt they would all join in on the upcoming free-for-all.

"Your Grace?" A hesitant feminine whisper came from behind him. There was no mistaking that sultry voice. His groin stirred to life.

He braced an arm against the wall and turned. "Fare well this morn, Sibil?"

A blush spread up her pretty face. The look in her eyes encouraged him to drop to his knees and bury his face under her skirts. He refrained, noting the rousing crowd below them.

Damn his aunt. What he wouldn't give for some much needed privacy.

"'Tis a fine morn. And you, your Gra—"

He cut her off by pressing his fingertips to her full lips. "Waryn." He regretted avoiding her the past day. But after the intimacy they'd already shared, he'd wanted her to be sure of what she wanted. Never before had a woman perplexed him so. Sibil was a mixture of a wanton and an innocent. "Thoughts of you kept me awake once more."

Her expressive green eyes widened. "I thought we might share a walk and a meal. I've noticed you avoid the crowd."

"Yea." He waved her ahead of him. "Your company and a meal."

"In the forest we might have privacy." A deeper flush spread across her face. "Would you like that, Waryn?"

"Yea." His manhood pulsed with eagerness.

She fled into the trees before he could say more.

He summoned Sir Jacob to follow. They often raced their horses at this time. Only this morn he didn't turn back at the line of the forest but dismounted. "Miss Sibil will join me. I want a few minutes alone with her. Call out if any others approach."

The knight hid a grin. "Yea, Your Grace."

Thankful the performers kept the crowd engaged, Waryn moved off into the forest. He didn't have too long to wait.

Sibil was breathless when she reached his side. "Sir Jacob directed me."

He glanced around a final time and then beckoned her to his side. "Sibil, come here. I can't risk being seen here with you for long." At all really, but all of England knew he was a bastard.

The nobles could go to hell for all he cared. He didn't mind what they'd say about him, his only concern was her, and the lure of being with her was too great to resist completely.

He thought his heart would thump from his chest before she made her way to where he stood between two giant trees. Gently, he pulled her into his arms. "I have no wish to—"

The innocent vixen kissed him, cutting off his words. His hands buried under her cloak, trying to get closer to her body.

He had no wish to ruin her. But now, raw lust clouded his mind.

Sibil's small tongue played its way into his mouth, enflaming his appetite. Her eager moans provoked his arousal to something brutal.

Oh how she incited sensations within him. When she touched him so, it was clear she wanted him for more than his duchy.

A groan vibrated in his chest at the tug of her hands in his hair. His breath turned harsh as her mouth continued to toy and suck at his.

She panted between kisses as her hands explored his neck and shoulders. His cloak parted and he shuddered.

A gulp of air rushed into his lungs as she scooted from his arms and onto her knees. He already missed her warmth as he gazed down at the top of her hat. Dazed, he could do no more than stare as she freed his manhood.

Heart pounding he glanced around. "Sibil…" What a brazen little vixen she was! He sucked in another breath at her tongue licking the crown of his cock.

"Shh…we must hurry." Her tongue lapped at him.

Hurrying wouldn't be a problem. Sibil on her knees had him on edge. At the scrape of her teeth, he closed his eyes and experienced the sensations. Another rub of her teeth on his rigid flesh brought forth a low moan.

She'd never done this before. She was no paid whore, nor a lusty wife out for what they could gain or to ease their boredom. Her inexperience, her eager touch and tentative sucking had him on edge more than any experienced woman. That she was pleasuring him because she wanted him, not his name or his wealth, heated his blood even more, sent it surging into his cock.

"Do you like this?' She ran her tongue up his shaft, swirled it around the engorged crown.

"Yea." His breath caught. He eyed their surroundings. He'd behead anyone who interrupted. And Sir Jacob too, for being a poor guard.

"And this?" She slid a hand along his thigh and over to the base of his cock, where she clasped him in a palm. She squeezed and stroked upward. "And this?"

"Yea." His chest heaved.

Licking her lips, she dipped her head to suck his cock. Her teeth caught him once more before she gained a smooth sucking rhythm. Her free hand cupped his sensitive balls. He arched his hips and fought to hold back the eruption.

"Oh you like that as well." Her tongue swirled around the shaft. Then she lowered her hot mouth back down his cock as her hands worked to increase the pressure.

"Sibil," he groaned between his teeth.

Lord, he was about to flood her mouth. His pleasure burned hot as his ballocks tightened.

The slurping sounds she made around his cock drove his lust. Her head bobbed up and down as she worked as much of his manhood as she could between her lips and into the heat of her wet mouth. Her firm grip worked his shaft to meet her descending lips. The hand cradling his balls never ceased its play.

"Sibil!" Desperately he urged her away only to have her suck harder.

Tensing, he moaned as his seed burst forth into her mouth.

Sibil sucked hard then raised her head, gasping for breath. "Oh my...I wasn't..." Her chest heaved, her face flushed scarlet as she ran her tongue over her swollen lips. "I wasn't expecting that."

His hands shook as he refastened his clothes. Through lowered lashes he watched her stumble to her feet and smooth out her skirts. She straightened her cloak and hat.

"Where in bloody hell did you learn that?" he growled.

Wide-eyed, she gasped and stammered.

At her look of shock, he pulled her into his arms. That had come out wrong. This had been the second best sexual experience of his life. "I only meant you surprised me."

She smiled and kissed him deeply. Their tongues played until he broke her kiss. "Do you have any idea the risk we took?" He tried to disentangle her hands from around his neck. But the vixen simply wiggled closer. He was tempted to shake her for her recklessness.

"We're sweethearts." She caressed the ribbon he still wore. "A few stolen moments won't be noticed." Her soft lips continued to play with his mouth and he caved like a young boy. The kiss was long and hot. His manhood once again pressed into her with eagerness. Gasping for breath, she smiled almost shyly at him.

His breath matched hers. "I don't understand this game you play." Innocents had never sought him out. Not ever. Bloody hell, his wife had barely tolerated him touching her even as she'd welcomed his brother's touch.

"I'm not playing games." For a moment she looked offended, only to have her eyes soften to what he was accustomed to seeing. "I'd never done that before..." She wrapped her arms around his neck. "I'd seen it done once. I only wanted to please you."

Something in his chest tightened. He didn't understand her. Not for a moment. What was she doing to him? His manhood swelled, telling them both he was willing to allow her to please him all she wanted.

He briefly returned her embrace before forcing her to move away. "I must go." He had to get out of there before he said something foolish. Before he admitted he wanted her for more than the selfish bastard he was.

"You'll meet me at my family's tent?"

"Yea." He could tell by the expression in her eyes, she was about to say something. Her look made him edgy. Quickly, he left her before she could say more.

Chapter Four

෨

The midday meal had been a pleasant and a quiet affair with only a few attending. Waryn's manhood was still swollen thickly. The little vixen had twice touched his thigh under the table away from seeing eyes. The first time her foot had caressed him, he'd nearly spilled his drink.

Waryn hadn't made it six paces from the tent before Sibil called to him. "Your cloak, Your Grace."

He winced. *Bloody hell.* Would the vixen not ever think before she spoke? He nodded to the nearby ladies.

Smiling, she rushed to him. "I do not want you to catch your death from the chill."

There wasn't a worry for that happening. His body still burned hot for her. Her concern caused a new heat to spread through his chest. It made him feel bloody good.

"Lysky!" bellowed Sir Clement, one of his knights, momentarily distracting him from Sibil. "Your brother is about to go against Atwood."

The milling crowd broke into murmurs.

Waryn's brow creased. He had thought his brother had gone. Alice had assured him…

Sibil rushed past him with a cry.

Glaring, he watched her race away until he realized she was running toward the two men ready to joust on the field. He dropped his cloak with a roar and bolted after her with Clement beside him.

"Sibil!" he roared as she weaved her way through the crowd.

Damn it. He knocked onlookers out of the way as he shouldered past. If the vixen entered the field, he swore to all that was holy he'd toss her skirts up and beat her arse. The woman would get herself killed.

Sibil ducked under the ribbon dividing the lists seconds before he jumped over it. Finally, he caught her on the field.

It was almost too late.

Gregory and Lord Atwood raced toward one another, their lances swinging into position.

Heart pounding, Waryn pulled Sibil away from the jousters as she cried out.

Atwood's lance took his brother squarely in the chest.

Waryn stared. Had his brother even bothered to prepare himself? His shield hadn't been in place.

Gregory landed hard on his back as Atwood rushed by with a shout of victory.

The crowd erupted. Sibil pushed out of his arms.

Slowly, he followed her. His anger burned hot as he watched her kneel at Gregory's side. Huge tears swelled in her eyes, angering him more.

Tenderly, she removed his brother's helmet and pushed back his hair. Gregory coughed but didn't open his eyes. For the first time since his arrival, Waryn looked carefully at his brother, noting the hollow cheeks. Still, he could tell John was the exact likeliness of him.

Sibil met Waryn's gaze as her tears overflowed. "Gregory shouldn't have been part of the games."

Waryn shuddered. His fists clenched. *Gregory.* Sibil had called his brother by his Christian name.

Lord, he wanted to roar his displeasure as jealousy ate at him. This time was different. While before his brother had betrayed him, this time he'd thought the impossible. He'd thought the little vixen had wanted him above all others.

With a deliberate stride, he walked over to the pair.

Sibil looked up once more. She clasped Waryn's leg. "Your brother has come home to die. And I fear Atwood has rushed it along." She rested her forehead upon him as a sob broke from her throat.

"What?" He could barely breathe.

Die? Nay, sure he was just winded.

"I'm so sorry, Waryn."

He dropped to his knees beside Sibil. He checked his brother's throat for breath with shaking hands. "Nay. It couldn't be."

Damn it. His hands shook so badly he couldn't tell if a pulse beat or not. He pumped a fist before trying once more.

"Waryn." Sibil's arm entwined with his. "Waryn, I'm so sorry."

"Nay." He shook his head. Sibil kept a tight hold on him. Gregory hadn't come home to die.

"Shh…" Sibil tried to calm him.

He moaned. He refused to believe it. There had been too much unsaid between him and his younger brother. All the times he had protected him from their father's rages, taking the brunt of his fury, yet Gregory had betrayed him. But this, this wasn't what he wanted for his brother, traitor or not.

He groaned. *Damn it. He needed her.* His arm came around her to bring her closer. "Sibil."

"I'm here. Let's get him inside."

His eyes burned. *Fuck.* He should have chased Gregory down all those years ago and gotten it over with. Instead, he'd let him go and his brother had abandoned John without a bloody word.

"This isn't your fault."

Bloody hell if it wasn't. Atwood had challenged Gregory because he hadn't been in the tournament. If he had, he would have been the one on the field with Atwood. Hell, he'd have had more challenges than he could have handled in a day. Everyone wanted to see him knocked on his arse.

"Let's get Gregory inside," she urged. "We need to get him off the cold ground, Your Grace."

He looked around with only one thought — *Atwood*. He'd challenge the Baron himself.

"Your Gr — Waryn, listen to me. Let's get Gregory inside."

He trembled in fury.

"I pray you, let's get him inside." Her trembling fingers caressed his face.

He looked down as Sibil's father bellowed her name. The man rushed to them. "Compose yourself. You look like a common milk maid clinging to the Duke."

Waryn balled his fist. He'd knock the man's teeth down his throat.

Sibil discreetly clasped his hand, giving it a squeeze.

"Sir Jacob. Sir Richard. Take Gregory inside." Her eyes blazed as she faced her father. Without another word, she brushed past him to march after the knights carrying his fallen brother.

* * * * *

"You handle a man's armor well, Miss Sibil," Sir Jacob said respectfully.

"I have had experience aiding injured knights, Sir Jacob."

"Where was this, dear?" Lady Alice asked, soothing Gregory's head with a damp cloth.

"My aunt's convent was in Burgundy. I spent the last five years there. Many battles between Normans and Saxons brought injured to their doors. The nuns were oftentimes shorthanded, so I had to come to their aid." Her face heated under Jacob's stare as she concentrated on removing Gregory's boots. "The convent was damaged along with the cathedral.

Those cloistered were moved to other convents, and the lay were sent back to their homes during repairs."

"The Cathédrale Saint-Maclou de Pontoise?" Sir Jacob shifted around the side of the bed.

"Yea." She nodded though she didn't meet his gaze.

"Then…perhaps we have met before."

"Perhaps, Sir Jacob." He could have been among those with Waryn but Waryn was the only one who had held her attention. He'd been so concerned for his men. He'd kept trying to get up from the bed to make sure they'd been fed and had shelter, that arrangements had been made to return home to Lysky. He'd wanted to be with his son. It was that selfless strength she fell in love with, though she hadn't known it was love…until now.

"It must have been dreadful, dear." Lady Alice shook her head as she held a cup of tea to Gregory's lips. "All that bloodshed over land and power. I am sure you were a source of comfort."

"It tore my heart to see the wounded, yet I learned what true strength and valor were. They left more of an impression on me than I on them." Her heart clenched, wishing Waryn remembered her.

"I shall leave Lord Gregory in your hands and return to the duke," Sir Jacob murmured.

Armor removed, Sibil tore open Gregory's tunic. She and Lady Alice gasped at the reddish-purple stains on his chest. Sibil applied an ointment to ease the pain and bruising. They wrapped his chest with linens.

He stirred, moaning.

"You foolish boy, whatever possessed you to accept Lord Atwood's challenge?" Lady Alice scolded.

Gregory coughed, wincing at the pain. His answer was barely above a whisper. "Waryn would not forgive me. I could not leave. I've no wish to die alone… Better here…in battle."

Sibil stared at him in disbelief. "You entered the tournament to die? You selfish man!" She could only imagine the guilt that would have left Waryn with. "When in the last five years have you given him the chance to forgive you? When did you come to him and utter an apology? Even now you only utter excuses! He was the one that was wronged, and you act as if he owes you!"

"Sibil, dear." Lady Alice gently touched her arm.

Silently, she wiped the tears that fell for both men.

"'Tis all right, dear, 'tis refreshing to see someone bare teeth for Waryn for a change." She smoothed Gregory's covers like she was tucking in a child. "You'd do best to consider what Miss Sibil has said before your brother visits you." Lady Alice kissed his forehead. "Rest now."

Exhaustion and the herbal tea helped ease Gregory to sleep. Lady Alice settled into a chair near the bed. "Sibil, do me a favor. Fetch a manuscript from the library. Gregory enjoyed when I read to him—his favorite was *The Green Knight*."

"Certainly, Lady Alice." Her heart raced, thinking about entering the library. Once it would have been because of all those manuscripts. Now it was because of what had happened between her and the Duke last night in those very quarters— and then today in the forest. Need pulsed between her legs, beating in time with her heart, something occurring more frequently as the days passed.

Exiting the chamber attached to Lady Alice's, Sibil turned toward the causeway that connected this tower with Waryn's residence. She froze in her steps, her heart falling to her stomach.

"Sibil!" Her father stood before her. "How dare you cling to Lysky that way! Do you have any idea the disgrace you may have brought me? First he offends me with that obscene dowry, then adds insult by not escorting you to the banquet, and yet you continually throw yourself at him like a whore. Have you forgotten you take your vows at year's end? I will not have you bringing any more shame onto my name! We leave on the morrow, you will be with us."

"'Tis always how your children's lives will best benefit you, Father, isn't it?"

Her father took a step toward her with cold eyes.

She ignored his warning look. Her independent, unconventional thinking had frequently earned her that stare. "First Simon, whom you could not allow to be a craftsman, was forced into the knighthood. Then Agnes, married to a baron so ancient he is practically ashes already, in hopes the lands she inherits will gain her a more prominent husband! And Margareta, who is so frightened she will face the same fate, whines and schemes for a larger dowry so if she can't have love at least her husband will have money."

An angry red hue blazed on her father's face.

She continued fearlessly. "Since there wasn't enough left for my marriage dowry to improve your situation, the convent is to be my fate, which is fine. Not only because I accept it as my duty... I do not want to marry a man like you, Father. I learned here, as well as in Burgundy, Father, that not all men are like you! Now excuse me while I continue what else I was taught there—to care for the injured."

Her eyes left his and caught Waryn's and Sir Jacob's behind him. Her heart thundered, tears threatened the last of her restraint. She may never be allowed to be with him, especially now, but her heart was his no matter what vows she took. She swallowed a sob and turned, rushing across the chilled causeway.

Chapter Five

പ

Sibil ran her fingers over the manuscripts, searching through blurred vision for the one Lady Alice had requested. It wasn't a title she had heard before. She yearned to explore all of them. She ached to explore all Waryn could have shown her.

She drew in a ragged breath.

It was over. Tomorrow, she'd have to leave. The precious moments she'd shared with him would have to be memories enough.

"Why do you cry, *mon ange*?" Waryn's voice caressed her.

My angel, he had called her.

A sob mixed with a laugh escaped her throat as heat coursed through her. 'Twas what he had called *her*. The door closed. A latch slid into place. Clothing rustled. She continued to walk the room, afraid to turn around. "You remembered me?"

"Only by listening at Alice's chamber door and to Sir Jacob at my ear." The heat of his body burned her as he lifted her capped veil from her head. It dropped to the floor as he placed his hands around her waist. He pressed a palm to her lower belly, starting a fire within her womb. He dragged her earlobe through his teeth, his actions deliberate, determined. "I remembered the whispered voice and touch of an angel pulling me back from death." His touch and the vibration of his voice made the nub between her legs throb.

Her head fell against his shoulder. Her breathing raced. Her jeweled belt dropped to the floor next.

"My fever and wounds kept me from recalling a face. Disbelief kept me from recognizing your voice." The hand on her waist moved up and cupped a breast through her gown, teasing it to a full ache. She moaned, arching back against him.

"Why did you not tell me who you were?" His voice was rough. His hand unlaced her short-sleeved over-gown, her body tightening as the fabric around her loosened, pooling around her feet.

"It would not have changed anything. I did not wish to embarrass you or myself if you did not remember." He turned her to face him. His eyes were so dark, so hungry. They devoured her.

"It would have changed everything sooner. I swore if I ever found another woman like my angel I would never let her go. I had decided you were the woman most like her. Now to find that you are one and the same." His throat forced a swallow as his nostrils flared. "Do you still wish to know how a man loves a woman, Sibil? No matter the consequences?"

"Yea." He stood before her in only his leggings and boots. She reached out and touched his muscled chest, ran fingertips over scars she instantly recognized. His manhood strained against the fabric, against her belly. The hot ache between her legs beat as wildly as her heart. "Teach me."

His mouth crashed against hers.

Her breath rushed from her lungs into his as his tongue thrust into her mouth, branding her his. He tugged at her under-gown, tearing it open.

"Waryn!" She grabbed his arms, startled by the roughness. Excitement tingled over her skin, made her nipples strain to painful peaks.

He growled. "Women wear far too much clothing. I will commission you a wardrobe."

"I do not wish—"

"'Tis why you shall have it."

His kiss gentled but it was still searing, melting her all the way to her knees.

Sliding her hands from his neck, he moved her chemise down her shoulders, kissing newly exposed skin as it lowered. Her sex clenched tightly as the garment passed over her breasts and fell.

Pleasure throbbed in her loins as he sucked a taut nipple deep into his mouth. She cried out, thinking she might explode. As she gripped the table behind her, he crouched and kissed her belly. Her womb contracted under his lips. He tugged her undergarment down and lifted her slippered feet from them. His rough hands slid up over her stockings, the soft flesh of her thighs and the swelled crease of her sex.

His touch left her gasping for breath.

"Your womb weeps for me." He slid his fingers into his mouth, tasting her on them. "*Mon ange.*"

The walls of her passage spasmed. She parted her legs, boldly exposing more of herself, wanting him to touch her to relieve the pulsating ache. "I'm afraid I do not always behave as an angel." She wet her lips.

"I enjoy the vixen as well as the angel." His fingers parted the coarse hairs, the swelled creases. A moan escaped them both as he kissed her there, drew his tongue around the nub. Her hands tangled in his hair wanting to push him away and pull him closer at the same time. He continued to lap at her hidden pearl. His finger circled her opening then slipped inside her, rubbing her folds as he slid in and out of her.

The sensation built, her body reaching for release. Her eyes caught his as he slid another finger into her, her body stretching to accommodate.

"Let me hear that sweet voice," he rasped. His tongue moved faster, his fingers more urgent. Fire spread through her. Her hips rocked. Her head fell back, moans becoming louder as her body tensed further until she shattered, and release raged through her.

Before her trembling legs dropped her to the floor, he had her in his arms and carried her through the chamber to his bed. He removed his leggings and boots. His cock stood erect, a bead of moisture on its tip. She wet her lips as her hips rolled in their own invitation. "Be sure?" He asked as he lay in the cradle of her hips, holding her gaze with his.

She nodded her answer, fear and excitement preventing her speech. Her body tensed as the tip of his hard shaft pressed into her. Fingers were one thing. This was something else.

"Waryn..." She wanted this moment more than anything but now that it had arrived she was scared. His cock was much thicker and longer than his fingers. Her entire body tensed when she felt it stretching her open. She needed his reassurance.

"Shh. 'Tis all right." He kissed her. Braced over her, he reached down and rubbed her nub with a thumb. "Open for me, won't you, Sibil?"

Her hips rolled toward his hand, pressing into his touch, her muscles opening as he slid in farther, stretching her even more than his fingers had done. Her body adjusted as if he belonged there. With each careful advance she experienced the gentle manner she knew was his, though he normally kept it hidden.

She tightened around him as he slid out and opened for him as he returned, going deeper each time. Her body coiled tightly for another release, her hips rolling in frustration when he stopped moving his cock inside her. Her hands on his buttock tried to grasp him closer. The pulse of their bodies beat together, his inside her, hers around him. A moment she would never forget.

Sweat beaded on his brow. His jaw clenched as he waited. The rough hand between their joined bodies urged her over the cliff. His battle-scarred fingertips toyed with her needy clit until her juices gushed. Her body tensed, tightened around him. "Waryn!"

Her release came and only then did he thrust completely into her. His mouth captured her startled cry as pain shot through her. It faded just as quickly as he thrust hard in and out of her welcoming body. Her audible breaths mixed with Waryn grunting the force of his brutal thrusts, which mingled with the sound of wet flesh slapping wet flesh. Pleasure engulfed her entire body as his manhood pounded into her eager depths.

Her hips eagerly met each thrust. Her fingers clutched at his shoulders and back, digging into him. The waves of her release didn't fade, only strengthened, in an unending tide of liquid heat. Her body burned, riding the effect of the glorious friction their motions made.

When she thought she could take no more of this bliss, he shouted. His body tensed, his hips jerked and his hot seed burst forth within her. Giddiness blurring her mind, she fought for breath.

His body collapsed on her. She wrapped him tightly in her arms, every muscle in her body twitching, quivering.

"I hope that is the only pain I ever cause you." His voice against her sensitive skin made her squirm.

"'Twas not too bad. I enjoyed the feel of you inside me so much, I barely noticed."

He chuckled, nuzzling her neck. "Good to hear since I intend to spend a lot of time buried there."

She sighed, inhaling his musky scent. If only morning didn't have to come. She'd never been so complete.

When she left her heart would stay behind.

* * * * *

Sibil's tongue followed the line of a scar across Waryn's chest. The remnants of a wound she'd tended. His heart swelled, her goodness had healed more than his flesh. He'd enjoyed her sleeping in his arms—in his bed—and not only for the way she awakened his body.

233

He did his best to ignore his thickened cock. He had no wish to make her sorer. "Are you sure you won't break your fast?" He eyed the tray that held bread and mead on a nearby table.

"Nay, I'm tempted only by you this night." Her sharp teeth scraped his nipple, causing him to inhale. "If only I did not have to leave you."

Regretfully, he caught her wandering hand. She still thought he'd let her go. He had much to say and wasn't finding the words easy. His heart pounded under where her head rested. "I wish you to stay, to be my duchess."

She quickly lifted her head to meet his gaze. How could he have ever forgotten those green eyes even in his fevered state?

"I've already asked your father."

Her pretty eyes widened. "You asked him?"

"Well…nay. I told him to name his price." He'd never ask that bastard for anything, especially where his angel was concerned. And he hadn't had to. The man had blustered and cursed him but in the end, he'd named an outrageous amount. It wasn't nearly enough to have the woman in his arms as his in name.

"But you are asking me?" A smile played around her mouth.

"I am if 'tis a yea you plan to give me." A grin tugged at his lips, and he bit it back. "Otherwise, I'll tell you to name your price as well."

Gasping, she struggled to sit up. He held fast. "Yea, Sibil, I'm asking. But there is something I need to say before you give me your answer."

She settled down on her elbow. His gaze lingered on her breasts pressing into his chest. He tugged on a swollen nipple.

She batted his hand away. "Your Grace…" Another smile spread across her lips. "Hurry and speak so I may answer."

Waryn closed his eyes before urging her to rest upon him once more. He swallowed. He'd never spoken to anyone about John, though he knew Alice had guessed the truth. He was no coward, and he suspected Sibil too had guessed the truth, it was still difficult to admit aloud. He held her fast along his body. "John...John is not my true son. But I know I'll never give him up. If we..."

Her arms tightened around him.

"If we have a child...a son..." His chest grew tight. "John believes me to be his father. I can't take that from him. I won't." In their lives, there was no telling who would survive to rule the army he'd built, the lands he controlled. "I will not take what John believes as his unless he gives me just cause."

When Sibil raised her head and scooted up to look down into his face, he opened his eyes.

She pressed her warm mouth to his. "Giving birth to an heir is not the reason I desire to have your child. I know you will do right by our family."

"Yea." He swallowed, having never known the peace he had at that moment. Sibil would be his wife.

Her soft thigh slid across his hip, pressing against his once again stiffening cock. "'Tis very hard to think with you lying atop me," he growled, lust growing hot in his loins.

"Hmmm." Her nails raked across one nipple, then the other.

"While you tended Gregory, my squire told me we'd been given a special license."

Her lip caught between her teeth. "So you put planning into this marriage."

"Yea." He gulped at the caress of her hand sliding down his chest and belly. His rigid flesh pulsed under her thigh. "The other night I spoke the truth. I sent a dozen knights to the archdiocese with a treasure chest for the special license."

Her gaze held his. "Without knowing my price?"

He arched a brow at her. "Pray tell."

Her face tinted and her lashes lowered. "Your heart, Your Grace. I want your heart."

He smiled. Such a simple request. Yet had it been anyone else it would have been impossible for him to give. "Sibil, I have been wearing my heart on my sleeve for you since you first gazed upon me. I swear I'll spend the rest of my days protecting you and what is ours." His teeth clenched as more of her delectable body slid across his.

Her pebbled nipples rubbed his skin. "Then I am yours."

He groaned. His cock pulsed at the feel of her wet passage caressing its crown.

Sibil pressed a slow kiss to his mouth before arching her hips, driving his shaft a bit farther into her silken walls.

His toes curled in anticipation of what would soon be upon them both.

Pushing up from his chest with her hands, she encased him fully with a cry. Inhaling, doing his best to take control, he cupped her heavy breasts in his palms. His heart pounded as he toyed with them. She moaned every time he pinched at her nipples, her passage walls tightening more around him. Roughly he massaged the swollen breasts for good measure. Her nipples caught between his fingers and he tugged until she cried out. The white flesh overflowed his hands as he squeezed and rubbed.

His sensitive balls tightened from her juices leaking on them. He clasped her soft thighs and lifted his head. Her tight pussy ground down on his buried length. Sweat coated his body. The need to come was stronger now than the moment before.

Letting his head drop back to the bed, a groan rumbled from his chest as she rose up to slide back down his manhood, her breasts swaying with every motion. With her tousled hair about her and the flush staining her face and chest, she looked every bit the wanton, the vixen. He pressed a thumb against the swollen pearl until the hot depths swallowing his cock stopped clenching so desperately. He grasped her hips, forcefully grinding her back and forth on his hard flesh.

"Waryn, please," she moaned, squeezing her breasts like he had done.

He sat up to hold her close. Using his mouth and teeth, he kissed along the column of her throat, all the while keeping up the friction of their heated bodies. Her fingers threaded tightly into his hair. His teeth grazed her rounded shoulder. Her nipples burned his chest on every pass.

"*Mon ange*." His ballocks tightened, threatening eruption. Frantically, he forced her up and down his cock until she panted, clutching at his shoulders. Her nails dug in as their bodies tensed. She keened her pleasure with each spasm of her muscles.

He came in hot bursts as his seed filled her.

Sighing, she rested her head in the crook of his neck. "I love you, Waryn." Her hot breath teased his skin.

"I'm a lucky man." He tightened his arms around her.

Yea. A very lucky man.

* * * * *

Waryn walked into his brother's room a few days after Gregory's collapse. He'd put off the visit as long as he could.

Gregory turned his head and pushed up on his elbows.

Waryn waved for him to stay still. Anger at the younger man's betrayal still had him clenching his fists. But it was time to let it go. The past couldn't be changed, and now he knew he wouldn't change a thing even if he could. He had no regrets about his life except that Gregory would likely die soon from lung disease. He'd make the best of the time he had left with his brother.

"Waryn." Gregory's voice was entirely too weak.

"Be still."

He walked to the chair near the bed and sat. "The boy — "

"Nay, wait…let me speak…" Gregory trailed off as a fit of coughing took hold. "You'll never know…how damned sorry I am." His breath wavered. "I was so young then."

Waryn's mouth twisted at the excuse he knew was about to be uttered.

"Nay, wait. I pray you…"

"John will always be mine," Waryn growled between clenched teeth. "I have raised him." Truth be told, he no longer cared about the past, only for his son.

"I know, Waryn. You make the best father," Gregory turned his head to meet his gaze, "like you were to me."

He grunted and looked away.

"'Tis true. For as long as I can recall, you were always good to me. Always getting between me and Father's fists."

Waryn exhaled slowly. He had no wish to romance about the past. Anyone else would have done the same for his brother. He shrugged. "I'm marrying Sibil this evening. I want to introduce you to John before the ceremony."

Gregory nodded. "I would like that. I do not wish to take him from you. You are his father."

"You are welcome to remain here as his uncle."

"I would like that as well."

The rustle of cloth drew their attention to the door, where Alice stood with Sibil. The smile Sibil flashed Waryn's way warmed his heart.

"I see the St. Valentine's Day tradition has resulted in a betrothal!" Lady Alice clapped her hands gleefully. The old woman was pleased with herself.

"Yea." He caressed the ribbon that still circled his arm. He would treasure Sibil's heart forever.

Chapter Six
1441

෨

Waryn shifted Sibil in his lap as Sir Jacob and John entered the room. She tried to stand, but he held her in place. He absently ran his palm around her stomach. Soon another babe would grow within.

"Father, Uncle has sent us a message from Constantinople." The boy's eyes were bright with excitement.

He met Jacob's gaze as the knight passed him a scroll. Sibil wrapped her arm around his neck.

"What does he say, Father?"

Waryn broke the seal and read aloud once Sir Jacob left the room.

Waryn

By the time this reaches you, I shall have moved on to Egypt. The old gypsy hag was right in her witchery. Though I did not expect to live this long my breathing has eased in these hot desert lands. But war is near, and I have no real part in it. Heathens, the lot of them. Your men Thomas and William have served me well. I owe you for their sword arms. Sir Thomas wishes you to send well wishes to his sister Sarah. Give Ladies Alice and Sibil my love. And let John know I will visit him one day if the Lord wills it.

Be safe, my brother.
Gregory of Lysky

Gregory lived. It was a good day.

The cry of an infant rang out as he folded the parchment.

Sibil brushed a kiss under his ear before she slid from his lap. "She's hungry, I am sure."

He grunted. The vixen had enriched his life in many ways, including birthing their daughter. The babe was always hungry and Sibil wouldn't hear of a nursemaid.

"Father, do you think my uncle will come back?" John leaned against his chair.

"If the Lord wills it, my son." He ruffled the boy's hair.

About the Author

ஐ

I am the alter ego of a Jersey Girl and a Midwest Hoosier. Both have a love of writing and reading romance novels with yummy alpha male heroes. They decided to combine these and I was born. I am the combination of their voices.

I write hot sensual romances. In them the sparks fly from the first heated glance to the fever of that passion fulfilled. The romance is mixed with adventure of all kinds, be it spine-tingling action, a mystery waiting to be solved, or a meeting of the unknown, in any time or place. Throw in an alpha hero after his heroine's heart and the possibilities are endless. I love the what-if's that throw twists and turns at the characters, that torture and bring out the best or worst in them as they search for their happily ever after.

Marissa welcomes comments from readers. You can find her website and email address on her author bio page at www.ellorascave.com.

Tell Us What You Think

We appreciate hearing reader opinions about our books. You can email us at Comments@EllorasCave.com.

SCREW CUPID

Arianna Hart

ဆ

Chapter One

ಬ

Happy Valentines Day!

Don't have a significant other to spend Valentine's Day with?

Who cares? Screw Cupid!

Follow the link for a sensual celebration and spend Valentine's Day like never before.

Reannah Mason stared at the E-vite on her monitor for the millionth time. She'd received the strange invitation over a month ago and still wasn't sure what she was going to do about it.

At first she'd thought it was from her best friend, Molly, until she'd followed the link. Molly might be a practical joker but even she wouldn't go this far. The directions included a medical form she'd had to have her doctor sign declaring she was on birth control and free of any and all disease.

Her face flamed as she remembered bringing that piece of paper into the office. Thank God her gynecologist had a sense of humor.

After she'd ruled out Molly as the sender, Reannah began discreetly asking around to see if anyone else received the anonymous invitation. She'd struck out there too.

Of course, if someone had asked her whether or not she'd gotten an invitation to what amounted to a Valentine's Day orgy she'd probably deny it with her dying breath.

Almost against her will, she clicked on the link again and reread the directions she'd practically memorized.

The party begins at ten p.m. and not a minute sooner. Your costume and mask will be delivered the day of the party. Anyone attempting to enter without either mask or costume will be refused admittance.

This is for consenting adults only and absolutely no coercion will be tolerated.

Transportation to and from will be provided. You may leave at any time—not that you'll want to.

And remember, what happens at The House of Eros stays there.

If this was a prank, it was a damn expensive one. Sending costumes and transportation—even if they were cheesy—wasn't cheap. Who would go through all that trouble and expense to stage such a joke?

"Screw Cupid? That sounds interesting." A deep male voice vibrated through her body and lodged in her pussy.

Reannah immediately closed the screen and spun around in her cubicle to face Kiefer Brown—her worst nightmare, and her darkest fantasy.

"Didn't anyone ever tell you it was rude to read over someone's shoulder?"

"You sit in a cubicle in the middle of fifty engineers and programmers. If you didn't want anyone knowing what you were reading then you shouldn't have opened it up at work."

His hazel eyes glittered with good humor—as usual. Kiefer always seemed to be laughing at some joke only he knew the punch line to. It annoyed the hell out of Reannah because she was sure the joke was on her.

"So, what was that, anyway?" He leaned a hip against her desk, invading her personal space.

"Nothing. Just a prank someone sent me." She tried to breathe as shallowly as possible to avoid inhaling his spicy fragrance. His cologne haunted her midnight fantasies.

"Looks interesting."

"Hardly." *If he only knew how interesting…*

"So I take it you're not into the whole Valentine's Day shtick?"

"What ever gave you that idea?"

"Maybe it's the fact that you're wearing black when even the most clueless geek here has at least a little bit of red on. Or it could be that you still have your Christmas decorations up on your cubicle instead of a bunch of foil hearts like everyone else. Or—I'm going out on a limb here—it might be because you have a picture of Cupid with a big 'X' through him on your laptop." He picked up the stress ball on her desk and tossed it from one hand to the other.

Reannah had to tear her eyes away from the hypnotic sight of those long fingered hands fondling the glob of plastic. *How would it feel to have those fingers on her breasts?*

Christ, she needed to snap out of it! "I always knew you were bright."

"So, what gives? I thought all girls loved getting flowers and overpriced boxes of candy from their sweethearts on V-day."

"You thought wrong." If she had a sweetheart she'd have loved to have gotten flowers and chocolate. Unfortunately, it had been so long since her last serious relationship she'd forgotten what it was like to celebrate February 14th with anything but dread.

"Don't tell me you're alone this year?" He put his hand to his chest in mock distress. "I don't believe it. With all these guys panting after one of the few women in the company you couldn't find a date for Valentine's Day?"

Being a technical writer for a computer software firm meant the male to female ratio was about fifty to one. Great odds on paper but the reality was slightly different. Half of the men she worked with were either too young or already in committed relationships. The other forty-nine percent were so consumed with computer games and cyber worlds they didn't have a clue what to do with a real, live woman.

That left the one percent currently sitting his world-class buns on her desk.

Kiefer Brown knew his way around a sales pitch but his value to the company went way beyond bringing in clients. With his good looks and charm to smooth the way between brainy geeks and savvy businessmen, Kiefer had helped make Zera Technologies Inc. one of the most sought-after software firms in the business.

Of course, half the time all he had to do was walk into the room and the bid was as good as theirs. Reannah had been at sales meetings with him and watched as he turned female accountants into putty in his hands. If his wavy, golden brown hair and hazel eyes didn't grab their attention, his killer smile and voice smooth as melted chocolate did. Before he even started the pitch he'd already closed the deal.

She knew the only reason he flirted with her so much was because she was one of the few females at Zera. To him it was as natural as breathing, it didn't mean anything. And if she ever responded to one of his blatant invitations, he'd run so fast in the opposite direction he'd leave skid marks on the carpet.

Been there, done that, outgrew the t-shirt.

"Earth to Reannah?"

"Huh? What? Sorry, I was thinking about something else."

"Then I'll ask again. Do you have plans for tonight?"

He wasn't asking her out, was he? No, he couldn't be. His little vulnerable act was probably just the set up to a joke. He more than likely had plans with that knockout he'd taken to the Christmas part.

"I'm going to a party." The words popped out of her mouth before she'd even realized she'd made a conscious decision to go.

Who was she kidding? She wouldn't have gone to her doctor and gotten the form filled out if she wasn't planning on going.

"Oh, well have a good time."

"I'm sure I will."

His face lost a little of its usual good humor and for a second Reannah thought maybe he really *was* going to ask her out and she'd blown it. But his smile snapped back in place seconds later so she must have just imagined it.

"I guess I'd better get going then so you can leave on time." He tossed her the stress ball and straightened from his perch.

"Thanks. Have a good weekend. I'll see you on Monday."

"If not sooner."

Now what did he mean by that?

Kiefer hustled to his office and shut the door behind him. Being the top salesman had its privileges and having his own office instead of a six-by-six cubicle was one of them. He scrolled through his inbox at a furious pace.

Ah, there it was. He knew the picture he'd seen on Reannah's monitor looked familiar. He'd gotten the same E-vite and almost deleted it as spam, but for some reason hadn't. Curiosity had made him click on the link to see what the deal was. After he'd read all the cloak and dagger directions, he'd thought it was a joke but saved it anyway.

Now that he knew Reannah was going, he was willing to revisit the idea. He skimmed through the oddball directions then glanced at his watch. If he wanted to make the deadline he had a lot to do in a short period of time.

His cock hardened as he thought about finally getting his hands on Reannah's delicious body. He'd been after her for months and she hadn't budged an inch. All his usual tactics and charm had failed miserably to get him more than a lunch date with her. That woman had him so tied up in knots he hadn't been able to concentrate on anyone else.

What was it about Reannah that captured his attention to the point of enforced celibacy? She wasn't *that* gorgeous. Granted, her red hair and green eyes were unusual and her body was pleasantly curvy, but so were a hundred other women that he had contact with on a regular basis.

But none of them made his mouth water and palms sweat whenever he got within five feet of them. Every time Reannah bent over in her low-slung jeans showing the scrap of lace peeking out from under her waistband, his libido shot through the roof.

A relaxed dress code had never been such a mixed blessing before. Maybe if Reannah was forced to wear a boxy suit instead of hip-hugging jeans he wouldn't be so consumed with her?

Kiefer pictured her with her wildly curling red hair pinned into a tidy bun, wearing a boring blue suit that came down to her knees. His imagination took off and the hemline jumped to mid-thigh. Instead of boring flats, she wore stiletto heels and garters.

Heat pooled in his crotch as he fantasized about her unbuttoning the demure white blouse to reveal a lacy black bra underneath. His erection threatened to split the zipper on his khakis as his dream Reannah stripped down to a lacy thong and straddled his lap.

The shrill ring of his cell phone had him jumping out of his leather chair like a scalded cat.

"Kiefer Brown," he answered a little breathlessly. He felt like he'd just been caught with his pants down—literally instead of in his dreams.

"Keef, that lawyer we've been trying to nail down wants to meet tonight. I know it's Friday and Valentine's Day but do you think you can get over to his office?" Paul, Kiefer's boss, didn't sound very enthusiastic about the meeting.

"Not this time. I have too much to do before tonight. In fact, I might knock off a little early."

"Got a hot date, huh?"

"Something like that."

"I understand. God knows Cathy would kill me if I canceled our reservations tonight. I'll tell him we'll meet with him on Monday."

Guilt nudged Kiefer. "If you think we'll lose the deal, I can try to rearrange things." He didn't know how, but Paul had been good to him and Kiefer didn't want to miss a million dollar deal because he was horny. It wasn't like him to push aside a potential business deal for his personal life but damn it, he wanted to be at that party with Reannah.

"Nope. Don't even think about it. This guy has been dicking us around for months. He can wait a few days to make us jump through another hoop. Have a great time and don't worry about a thing."

"I'll try not to," Kiefer replied, faxing the form to his doctor's office.

He had a feeling all his worries were going to be over very soon.

* * * * *

She couldn't do it. There was no way she could go to a party dressed like this. Reannah twisted in front of the full-length mirror and tried to pinpoint exactly what it was that made her want to run for cover.

The boots came up to mid-thigh and had heels like ice-picks, that was the first problem. Although, the long, button-down skirt covered most of the boots so she didn't look too much like a dominatrix. She didn't want to examine why one would provide thigh-high boots if they were just going to be hidden under a long skirt. The obvious answer—because someone would be seeing her without the skirt—scared the hell out of her.

The skirt was actually demure, if one ignored how it clung to her hips. It was the corset and shirt—or lack thereof—that made her nervous. The directions that came with the box of clothes were quite clear about how she was supposed to dress. The white silk shirt went on first, then the corset cinched up over it.

Since she didn't have anyone to help her get dressed, she tied the corset down the front. It was made of the softest black leather and red lace—and looked absolutely decadent. The bones sewn into it pushed her already abundant chest halfway to her chin.

A situation the shirt did nothing to hide.

The silk top was exquisitely feminine with cap sleeves and an indecently low neckline. It was the neckline that was giving her fits. Trimmed in delicate lace, the shirt showcased her enhanced cleavage. The edging barely covered her nipples, heck, in some areas pink showed through the lace.

With her red hair spilling over her pale shoulders she looked like she was waiting to get ravaged. Christ, she was freaking pirate bait.

But wasn't that the point?

Reannah picked up the black leather mask that came with the outfit and twirled it in her hands. Was she really going to do this? Common sense screamed *No!* but the lonely part of her soul shouted it down.

She'd been alone for so very long. Was it too much to ask for one night of companionship? No one said she had to do anything she didn't want to. The invitation clearly stated this was for consenting adults only and no coercion would be tolerated.

Once again, she wondered who could have invited her, boring Reannah Mason, to an orgy. Whoever it was had to know her damn well because the clothes fit perfectly. Even the boots were made to order, with the left one a half size smaller than the right. There were only a handful of people in the world who knew that about her, and she trusted all of them.

So, someone who knew her well and therefore knew how lonely she'd been, had arranged for her to go to this wild party. A party where she'd be disguised the entire time, as would everyone else.

No one would know she was boring Reannah Mason, especially dressed like this.

She didn't have to *be* Reannah Mason tonight.

A shiver danced down her spine and sparkled through her bloodstream. For this one night she could act on all the secret fantasies she'd hidden away from everyone. Sure, most of them had Kiefer Brown in the starring role, but she could pretend for tonight.

Wasn't that what this was all about? By wearing the mask and the costume she could pretend to be anyone at all.

And better yet, she could pretend to be with anyone at all.

With determined steps, Reannah marched to the bathroom and wet a hairbrush. Tonight she was going to be a vamp, a sex goddess, pirate bait even, anything but herself And the first step was taming her hair. If she wanted to be someone else, she couldn't have her distinctive red hair announcing her identity.

She yanked the wet brush through her curly hair repeatedly. When it was almost dripping wet, she slopped a handful of gel through the mess. The combination toned down the bright red color to a deeper auburn. To disguise herself further, she wrapped the sticky strands into a bun at the base of her neck.

The severe hairstyle accented her high cheekbones making her appear almost delicate. She looked nothing like herself. When she tied the mask over her green eyes, her own mother wouldn't recognize her.

Thank God.

Siren red lipstick completed the outfit just in time. The car her unknown host provided pulled up to her house as she fastened the heavy velvet cape at her throat.

"I can do this. Tonight, I'm only going to think about my pleasure and not worry about tomorrow." Nerves twisted in her stomach despite her pep talk. This just wasn't like her, no matter what happened in her secret fantasies.

"It's perfectly safe and no one will make you do anything you don't want to," she reminded herself.

But what about the things she really *wanted* to do and had never dared? Who'd stop her from doing those? And would she want them to?

Chapter Two

∞

The limo driver was silently polite as he escorted her over the icy walk and into the back of the long black car. If it seemed odd to pick up someone in a velvet cape and leather mask, he didn't show it.

As she slid into the plush leather seat, Reannah tried to figure out who her mystery host could be. The driver wasn't going to give her any clues, he'd closed the privacy window the second he slipped behind the wheel. She could always use the intercom but she doubted he would answer her questions.

Who could have sent her that invitation? It obviously wasn't random. The person had her email address and home address. Although, anyone who knew how to use a computer could probably figure that much out. No, this was someone who knew not only her shoe size but also her secret yearnings.

They also knew her well enough to realize she'd never go to a "sensual celebration" unless she felt one hundred percent safe.

As the nearly silent car purred through the darkened night, Reannah tried to let go of her fears. She'd told Molly what she was doing so someone knew in case her body turned up in a gutter somewhere.

Oh, that's comforting.

Maybe this wasn't such a great idea. She reached for the intercom button to tell the driver to take her back. As she moved, her cape knocked an envelope to the carpeted floor.

Miss Reannah Mason was written in flowing script on the front.

Her hands shook as she broke the seal and slid the heavy parchment out. After clicking on an overhead light, she read the note.

Dear Miss Mason,

I'm so happy you chose to join me tonight for my Valentine's Day celebration. Your every wish and desire waits at the end of this ride. Rest assured, your invitation has come at the bequest of someone who loves you very much. Your safety and pleasure are assured.

Regards,

Cupid

What the fuck? Cupid? This was ridiculous. Who loved her so much they'd arrange for her to go to an orgy? It wasn't exactly something she'd talked about at family gatherings.

The only person in the world who knew even a tiny bit about her deviant sexual desires was Molly, and she'd denied any knowledge of the invitation.

But she *had* encouraged her to go to the party. Repeatedly.

Reannah tapped the note against her chin. If she hadn't been so wrapped up in solving the mystery of her host, she'd have paid more attention to Molly's behavior. It had to be her. Molly would never encourage her to do something this stupid if she didn't know who was behind it.

Come to think of it, Molly had insisted she get a pedicure and bikini wax last week too, before she'd even decided to go to the party.

The sneak.

Relief flowed through her and the tension leaked from her shoulders. Now that she'd solved the mystery she could relax and enjoy the ride. The only other time she'd been in a limo had been for her grandfather's funeral. And that one certainly didn't have a stocked bar.

Helping herself to a vodka tonic, Reannah toasted Molly silently and knocked back the liquid courage. A night to explore her every wish and desire, huh? Heat spread from her stomach to her thong-clad pussy.

She had *a lot* of wishes and desires. Most of them centered around Kiefer and her in a bed. Hell, in a bed, on the floor, against a wall, anywhere. She'd been imagining him in a variety of positions and locations for the last year. But all of them had his cock lodged deep inside her by the end.

Just the thought of him had her nipples pebbling up against the silk and lace of her shirt. The combination of sensations made her squirm. She'd been celibate for so long, her body became aroused at the mere thought of Kiefer. Her thighs grew damp and she clamped them together to stop the ache.

Why not relieve it instead?

What? She couldn't do that. She was in the back of a car for heaven's sake!

She glanced at the privacy shield in place. There was no way the driver could see in, right? A thrill of excitement made her clit throb.

Could she really take care of the need burning through her right here, right now?

She caught her reflection in the window and almost didn't recognize herself. Her lips looked swollen and pouty and her cheeks were flushed with suppressed desire.

Yes. She could do this. She *wanted* to do this.

Her hands trembled with excitement as she spread the cape and lifted her skirt. The velvet felt cool against her rapidly heating skin as she pulled the hem up to reveal the leather thong that matched the corset.

Leaning back into the seat, she let her fingers drift over her mound as she visualized Kiefer wearing nothing but silk boxers. In her mind, it was his fingers pushing aside the scrap of material covering her swollen clit. His hand drawing moisture from her slick pussy lips, and his finger driving into her needy channel.

A gasp escaped her lips as the pressure built inside her. She swirled her thumb over her nub as she thrust harder. The scratchy lace teased her nipples as she writhed against the cool leather seat.

Hot, she was so hot.

"I've wanted you for so long. You're the only one I want." The phantom Kiefer whispered love words in her ear as he pressed kisses against her fevered skin.

"Let me touch you. Let me love you. Let me make you mine."

Her breath came in gasps as she spun tighter and tighter. Fire burned beneath her skin and sweat beaded up on her forehead as she lashed her head back and forth.

"You're mine!"

"Yes!" With a strangled cry she exploded.

Street lights shone dimly through the tinted car windows as the limo exited the city limits. Reannah was too boneless to worry about being taken so far from home.

She couldn't believe she'd just masturbated in the back of a car. Well, tonight was her night for firsts, and by God she was going to experience as many of them as she possibly could.

Her pulse had almost returned to normal by the time the limo turned onto a gated drive. Spotlights revealed an enormous mansion with fluted columns and a veranda on the second floor. The circular drive wrapped around a marble fountain complete with a water spouting Cupid.

Considering it was February in New England, the water pouring from Cupid's mouth had to be heated to keep it from freezing. Anyone who would pay to heat water for a decoration had to have serious money to burn.

As the limo crawled up the brick drive, Reannah gazed at the statues that were spotlighted along the walkway leading to the house. The first one was of two lovers entwined in a passionate embrace. Then next had two lovers in a classic "sixty-nine". Reannah's eyes widened under her mask as she realized the statues got more and more risqué the closer they got to the house.

She was almost afraid to examine the two flanking the ornate front door.

What did you expect? You're going to an orgy, not a garden party.

Nerves grabbed hold of her and shattered the calm she'd felt after her explosive orgasm. What was she doing here? Dressed like this?

The car slowed to a stop and Reannah reached out to tell the driver she'd changed her mind but it was too late. Before she could chicken out he'd opened the door and helped her out of the car.

If he suspected she'd made free with her fingers while she was alone he didn't show it. He was as silent and stoic as when he'd arrived at her door.

"Please allow me to walk you to the door, miss."

"T-thank you." *I think.*

She walked up the marble stairs to the front door on shaking knees. Butterflies danced in her stomach the closer she got to the house.

What if Molly wasn't behind this? What if it was a big mistake?

Her hand trembled in the chauffeur's grip as he handed her off to a uniformed doorman.

"Welcome to the House of Eros. May I take your wrap?"

The doorman held the door open and Reannah saw a tiled foyer with a curved staircase in the background.

"No thank you. I'm still a bit chilled, I'd prefer to hold onto my cape for now."

"As you wish. If you give me your handbag I shall secure it at the coat check."

Even though he phrased it politely, it wasn't a request. She'd forgotten she'd held her purse clutched to her chest. Did she want to give it up? It had her cell phone and wallet in case she ran into trouble.

"You may retrieve it at any time, miss. I assure you it will remain safe."

Was her anxiety that obvious?

More nerves danced along her spine as she held onto her bag. Obviously no one here wanted her emergency twenty bucks, but if she needed her cell phone to call a cab in a hurry she'd be out of luck.

"May I keep my phone in case of an emergency? It doesn't have a camera in it or anything, but it would make me feel a little better if I had it."

The doorman shifted his feet uncomfortably as she dug out her phone and showed it to him.

"Please," she implored.

"I assure you, you're safe in the House of Eros, but if you insist on keeping it please refrain from using it where others can hear you and turn it to vibrate."

Relief rushed through her almost making her sag against the textured wall. "Of course. Thank you." Before he could change his mind, she tucked it into the pocket of her skirt.

She handed her pocketbook over, feeling a little more at ease. If she had to make a run for it she could always replace her credit cards. At least with her phone on her she could call for help if she needed it.

"Please make yourself at home. The night is yours to do with as you wish. Refreshment stations are scattered throughout the house and any unlocked room is available for use. If you wish privacy, make sure you lock the door or others will assume you wish to either be watched or joined. Enjoy."

Reannah swallowed a gasp at the idea of someone watching her...do what?

Guess I'm about to find out.

Her heels clattered loudly on the tiled floor and echoed through the foyer. As she approached an arched doorway with a naked cherub emblazed upon it, she heard the low thump of music and the hum of conversation.

Now or never Reannah.

She took a deep breath and pushed the doors open.

And couldn't believe her eyes at the scene in front of her.

The sunken living room was easily the size of a grand ballroom. Low couches were scattered in shadowed nooks around the room while a full bar stood against wide French doors that led to a darkened patio. The lighting was dim and candles by the hundreds flickered throughout the room. The scent of vanilla mingled with perfumed bodies and the distinctive scent of sex.

A waiter wearing leather pants with a matching leather mask—and nothing else—approached her with a tray of champagne glasses.

"Refreshment?"

"Thank you," she took the delicate flute and downed it before the bubbles could finish tickling her nose.

The waiter didn't even blink, just took the empty class and handed her another before moving on. Reannah took a moment to appreciate his fine ass clad in tight leather before she moved off to the side.

She needed a minute to take in her surroundings before she entered the room fully. There had to be a hundred people in various states of undress. Everyone wore a mask like hers but that's where the similarities ended.

Some men were dressed as pirates, with wide sleeved shirts and leather breeches. Other men had gladiator costumes on, their oiled chests glinting in the firelight. One man was dressed as an English lord complete with ruffles and a codpiece.

Unless he had a pair of socks down there, the codpiece provided some serious advertising for him.

The women were even more spectacularly dressed. She saw a can-can dancer kicking her leg up over the shoulder of the pirate. Her frilly skirt flipped back to reveal her shaven pussy framed by lacy garters.

A statuesque woman wore a silken toga that left one large breast bare. A situation the gladiator was taking full advantage of as he swirled her nipple with the cherry from his drink.

In the corner by the bar, a woman wore a leather outfit that looked like nothing more than a series of belts strapped from her hips to her breasts. She had boots like Reannah's and carried a whip. Reannah watched in amazement as the belted woman used the whip to pull a woman in a peasant dress between her legs.

Apparently the peasant didn't mind because she unbelted one of the straps and began licking the whip wielder's pussy.

A rush of cream flooded Reannah as she watched the leather-clad woman writhe and moan as she sank to the floor. She had to take a drink of champagne to wet her suddenly dry mouth when the gladiator and toga-girl joined them on the floor.

The woman in the toga knelt over the belted woman's face with her silken sheet hiked up over her bare hips. While she played with the belts over the woman's breasts, the gladiator pulled off his skirt, revealing an enormous erection.

Several people cheered as he drove his cock into the woman in the toga while the belted woman alternately licked his balls and the woman's clit. Another man dressed in leather flipped up the skirt of the peasant girl and flogged her naked ass.

Reannah's face flamed with heat but she couldn't pull her eyes away from the titillating scene. Her pussy lips swelled around the leather thong she wore as she watched the peasant girl drive her finger into the leather woman's slit. The sounds of their moans mingled with the slapping of the gladiator's balls as he drove into his partner. The slick slurping of fingers and tongues inside dripping channels added to the auditory foreplay.

Her nipples pebbled up as she watched toga-girl suck on the leather woman's swollen buds. What would it feel like to have that many people giving her pleasure? Or watching her receive that much pleasure? Reannah shivered at the thought.

It might be exciting to watch but she didn't think she could ever lay herself out like that, in public. Showing up here today was about the most daring thing she'd ever done, and it was a far cry from public sex.

One of the women cried out her release and someone else joined her. The pirate and can-can girl joined the crowd surrounding the group and blocked Reannah's view. It was probably for the best anyway. She'd seen more than she could have ever imagined and she hadn't even walked all the way into the room yet.

Well, what was she waiting for? She said she was going to take tonight to do the things she'd always wanted to, why was she standing on the sidelines? If she wanted to ease the ache throbbing between her legs, she should find an attractive, willing partner and go for it.

But not quite yet.

She did take another step into the room. The plush carpeting cushioned her aching feet and softened her steps. These boots weren't meant for standing in that was for sure. Her toes were pinched and her arches ached from the stiletto heels.

Reannah looked around for a place where she could sit and observe for a little bit longer and get off her feet. A narrow hallway paralleled the living room. She saw a tiny room off to the side and went to inspect. It had a comfortable chair and a basin of warm water with a pile of washcloths next to it. It seemed safe enough. At least it was unoccupied and best of all, had a place she could get off her feet without, ah, *getting* off her feet.

The mask and flickering candlelight distorted her vision some so she missed the wide window opposite the chair until she sat down. What was a window doing in an interior room?

Her eyes practically crossed when she got her answer.

As soon as she settled into the chair the thin blinds covering the window rolled back to reveal a sparse bedroom containing an ornate, wrought iron bed with a blood-red comforter. A muscular man more gorgeous than any she'd seen outside of a magazine knelt on the bed as naked as the day he was born.

His cock stood out from a nest of light hair and practically pulsed with a need Reannah could see from her vantage point. She wondered if he realized he was on display and thought about vacating the room but remained frozen as another equally gorgeous man entered the room.

Reannah couldn't hear what they said to one another but saw the kneeling man laugh and crook his finger in a blatant invitation. The newcomer wore a loincloth over his ebony skin and his muscles gleamed in the dim light. His leather mask almost blended in against his tightly cropped hair, giving him a mysterious appearance that made Reannah's heart race.

Apparently, it did the same thing for the blond because his cock grew even larger. Reannah's mouth dropped open as the dark man dropped his loincloth and displayed the biggest cock she had ever seen. It was easily as long as her forearm and had to be as wide around as a beer can.

The thought of something that large piercing her brought a quiver of alarm as well as a tingle of desire but that was nothing compared to what it did for the blond. He hauled his dark partner onto the bed and pressed him flat. The contrast of his steely hard sable body against the soft red blanket was both incredibly beautiful and infinitely seductive.

She wished she could hear what they were saying but the window didn't allow noise to slip through. All she could do is watch — which was probably all her overloaded libido could handle right now anyway. Reannah settled back in the chair and let her hand drift to her soaking pussy as the blond stroked his lover's well-defined abs.

Her breath came out in a gasp as the blonde wrapped his large hand around the darker man's cock. She didn't want to blink in case she missed what might happen next. Fire sizzled through her veins and sweat popped out on her brow as she watched the blond draw the almost purple tip of the darker man's penis into his mouth.

The black man's head whipped back and forth on the silken bed as the blond moved between his legs. Reannah swallowed hard as she got a front row view of a tight ass and ropey thighs. Testosterone oozed from the room as muscles bunched and rolled in pleasure.

Reannah had never seen two men have sex before. Had never really thought about the sensuality of it, but now that she was a witness to it she couldn't look away. There was a masculine beauty to two such gorgeous specimens giving each other so much pleasure.

The blond's head pumped up and down as he sucked on his lover's cock. The darker man clenched the blanket in his fists making his arms bulge and the tendons on his neck strain. Reannah could see the sweat glisten on his chest as he arched up with release. His whole body shuddered and bucked with the force of his orgasm.

With her heart beating a rapid tattoo, Reannah swirled her fingers over her clit faster and faster. Pressure built inside her and threatened to explode but she held it off. She didn't want to take her eyes of the scene in front of her for even the few seconds it would take for her to come.

And what happened next made the wait so worthwhile.

The blond released the darker man's cock with a final lick and reached for something on the floor. The black man lazily rolled to his side, his cock still impressively large even when it was no longer fully erect. As Reannah watched in anticipation, the ebony man crawled to his knees and presented his seriously muscled ass to his partner. The blond coated his penis and his lover's anus with some sort of lubricant that he retrieved from the floor.

She couldn't hold off the onslaught of pleasure a second longer when the blond pushed inside his lover. From her vantage point she could see two sets of rock-hard thighs thrust in a rapid pace as they each strained to achieve their pleasure. Reannah's hips bucked her pussy against her fingers as her release tore through the thin control she'd used to hold it back.

Her eyes closed against her will, but branded on her eyelids was the image of two brawny chests pumping in rhythm as massive shoulders bulged with the force of their desire.

When she opened her eyes the blinds had closed over the window and she could see no more. Her thighs were sticky with her juices and her body felt boneless. Suddenly, she realized what the basin of water and washcloths were for and was grateful for them.

Her hands shook as she moistened the thick terrycloth square and washed away the evidence of her orgasm.

Cripes, I've come twice and I haven't even taken off my clothes. That's better than my last three boyfriends combined.

One thing was for certain, her feet no longer hurt. In fact, she wasn't quite sure she could even feel her toes. And she was definitely no longer nervous.

It was time for her to stop watching and start experiencing everything Cupid had to offer. As soon as she remembered how to walk.

Chapter Three

ഔ

Where was she?

Kiefer kept getting distracted in his search for Reannah as he spied luscious breasts and creamy thighs everywhere he turned. If this was what people were doing in public, he could only imagine what they were doing in the private rooms upstairs.

And he had a damn good imagination.

He thought he'd spied Reannah lurking in a corner watching the impromptu ménage earlier but by the time he made it across the room she'd disappeared. Damn it, he didn't rush around like a lunatic just to watch her go off with some other guy. Or girl for that matter.

Although, he wouldn't mind seeing that, come to think of it.

He was on his second circuit of the room and third beer when he spied her coming out of one of the viewing rooms. Blessedly alone, thank God. Her face was flushed and her chest heaved practically out of her shirt but she was alone.

Not for long.

He'd known it was Reannah the second she'd stepped into the living room. Even masked and with her beautiful hair disguised his body had reacted to her presence immediately.

As he drew closer to her, his cock practically burst through the leather pants he wore. Her shirt didn't so much cover her cleavage as display it. Her rosy breasts lay over the lacy shirt like a delicious buffet just waiting for him to dig in and enjoy.

And enjoy it he would, as soon as possible. But he had to be smart about it. If she suspected his identity she might turn tail and run. Or worse, refuse him. He'd gone to great lengths to darken his hair and figured he'd use a fake accent to disguise his voice.

He wasn't going to hide forever, just until she was so overcome with lust for him she wouldn't turn him down yet again. It might backfire on him but it was a risk he was willing to take to get a chance to be with her after all these months.

"A lovely lady like yourself shouldn't be alone," he whispered in her ear with his best Irish accent. "Can I offer my services as an escort?"

Her eyes widened under her mask as she looked him over from the tip of his wide-brimmed hat to the points of his heeled boots. He held his breath in anticipation. This was the moment of truth, would she see through his disguise and send him away or not?

"You look more like a highwayman than an escort." She smiled coyly at him and didn't move away.

Kiefer released his pent-up breath as quietly as possible.

Step one, done.

"I'm not sure if I'm supposed to be a highwayman or a rock star. Do highway men wear leather pants?"

"Maybe. I've never met one before, although I've had some definite fantasies about them…"

His cock tightened and his body tensed as she trailed off. "Then I'm most definitely a highwayman. A masked avenger in the night. I steal from the rich and give to the poor and make free with the ladies."

"Isn't that Robin Hood?"

"Who cares? As long as I get the ladies, or lady, I'm not particular about the details."

"And who says you're going to get the lady? I don't recall you asking?"

"I'm a rogue scoundrel, I don't ask." And with that he scooped her up in his arms and threw her over his shoulder.

Cheers rang as he carried her up the curving staircase to the private rooms above. Her hips were over his shoulder and he could smell her feminine arousal. The musky scent shot through him with all the effect of a bullet, destroying his composure and shredding his control.

He'd wanted her for so long and now he had his chance.

Please, Cupid, don't let me screw this up.

It took him three tries before he found an unlocked door and an unoccupied room but when he kicked open the door he knew he'd found the jackpot. Leather cuffs dangled from the headboard of the brass bed and various implements of delight littered the floor.

When he spied the whipping post in the corner near the balcony his brain almost caught fire. The image of Reannah's rounded ass sticking up while she knelt with her hands tied to the post danced through his head, tempting him mercilessly.

A little snicker sounded over his shoulder and brought him out of his lustful dreams.

"Do you think this is funny, wench? You won't be laughing when I have my way with you."

"Oh no, don't hurt me. I'll do anything you say." The effect of her plea was ruined by the laughter in her voice.

"You're damn right you will." He dropped her on the gold lamé bedspread and gasped as her breasts almost bounced out of her shirt.

"What do you want me to do Mr. Highwayman?"

"Take off your cape and let me look at you."

She climbed off the bed and waited until he lay back on the pillows. Once he was settled she unfastened the ties at her throat and let the heavy material fall to the floor.

Without the shielding of the wrap he got the full impact of her outfit and was dumbstruck. The blouse left her shoulders bare and the corset cinched her waist impossibly tight. She looked demure yet tempting as sin. His mouth watered at the thought of what she hid under the long skirt.

Time to find out. "Your skirt offends me, take it off."

"And if I refuse?"

"I'll tear it off you, wench."

She shivered and he was afraid he'd gone too far, then he noticed her chest rising and falling with her heavy breathing. Her nostrils flared with desire and tiny drops of perspiration glittered above her mask.

Reannah Mason, technical writer was a closet sub. Who'd have thought it?

Lust, hot and furious tore through him at the thought of dominating this woman he'd wanted for so long.

"Don't make me ask you again, slave."

"Y-yes master."

Her voice was thick with desire and her hands shook as she unbuttoned the skirt slowly, starting from the bottom.

Kiefer didn't live the BDSM lifestyle, but he wouldn't mind playing the game with a willing partner. And by the rosy glow suffusing Reannah's skin, she was more than willing.

It took every ounce of strength he had to keep his hands by his sides as she revealed first the thigh-high boots and then the leather thong hiding her pussy from his greedy gaze. For a moment all he could do was stare at the picture she made, standing in the dim light with her silken skin and black leather.

With his mind turned to pudding it was hard to think about what to do next. He wanted to throw her on the bed and lick every inch of her succulent body but didn't want to rush her.

His muscles clenched as he forced himself to keep his distance from her. Before he could decide what to have her remove next, the thong or the corset, the doorknob turned and started to open.

Shit! He'd forgotten to lock the door!

Kiefer pounced off the bed and slammed the door closed before the person on the other side could get a good look at his Reannah. After he made sure it was locked he turned to find she had slipped into the shadows. Apparently she didn't want any company yet either.

"Come here, slave."

She stalked forward, her creamy thighs gleaming above the black boots. "Yes, master."

"Hold onto the whipping post and don't let go until I tell you."

Her breathing hitched as she did as he directed. Heat came off her in waves, stoking the fire raging inside him to a fevered pitch. The scent of her perfume merged with the musky fragrance of her desire and drifted through his nostrils. He breathed deeply, wanting to inhale her very essence.

"Close your eyes," he ordered, his voice husky.

To make sure she complied, he picked a silken scarf off a nearby chair and gently secured it over her eyes.

Now he could feast on her beauty without fear of her discovering his identity.

And Lord was he hungry.

The lack of sight immediately heightened all her other senses. Reannah couldn't believe how turned on she was. The highwayman reminded her so much of Kiefer, except his hair didn't have Kiefer's golden highlights and his voice wasn't quite the same. But oh, his body. Not that she'd ever seen Kiefer in tight leather pants, but if she had, she was sure he'd look the same as the man standing behind her now.

Could that be why she was so willing to let go of her inhibitions so quickly? Because he reminded her of someone she trusted?

No. It wasn't because he reminded her of someone she trusted, it was because he reminded her of someone she *wanted*. She couldn't have Kiefer, but for tonight she could pretend that this sexy stranger was the man of her dreams.

Dreams? Ha! More like deepest darkest fantasies.

How often had she thought of Kiefer controlling her with ecstasy? Hundreds of times.

But she had no idea how much better the reality could be.

"Not so feisty now, are you wench?" He slapped her bare bottom hard enough to leave a sting but not hard enough to hurt. Much.

"No, master." She had to bite her lip to keep from laughing whenever she called him master. It was hokey, but very exciting too.

His warm breath brushed over her shoulder and made her nipples perk to attention. The corset restricted her air supply and she felt almost lightheaded. As his hands brushed lightly over her chest and slipped under the lace of her shirt she knew her dizziness had nothing to do with lack of oxygen and everything to do with the man touching her.

She waited breathlessly for him to make a move. Her knees quaked as she wondered what he'd do next. Would he tear off her clothes or undress her slowly? Would he fuck her from behind or maybe spank her again? She wasn't sure how she felt about that, but the initial slap had sent a bolt of heat straight to her pussy.

Her nipples tightened as he continued to fondle her breasts under the shirt. When he pinched one bud hard, she gasped at the sting but the pleasure that shot from the tender point afterward made the slight pain more than worthwhile.

"It's too bad you can't see yourself right now. Your nipples are as red as berries and your breasts look like the finest cream. I've never wanted dessert so much in my entire life."

Reannah couldn't answer, couldn't form words in her lust fogged brain. His warm voice caressed every nerve ending even as his fingers plied her breasts. The most she could do was let out a whimper when his soft lips nipped along her bare throat. She could feel a faint hint of stubble along his jaw and the slight rasp teased her with thoughts of what that would feel like on her nipples.

Or between her legs.

She clamped her thighs together to stifle the ache blooming there. The feel of his fingers manipulating her nipples caused ripples through her entire body. Her pussy quivered with every tug and stroke and she swore she was about to come from his ministrations.

Christ, I'd like my clothes off for at least one orgasm tonight!

"Not yet, my sweet. I have a lot more planned for you tonight."

Oh dear, had she said that out loud?

He stepped away from her, dropping his hands.

The air felt cool against her nearly naked ass without his body behind her. Reannah could hear him moving around but didn't know what he was doing. It sounded like he was gathering things onto the nearby table so they'd be in easy reach but she couldn't imagine what he was getting. The scarf covering her eyes frustrated her as much as it excited her.

Almost.

"Now, slave, you've been a very bad girl."

The crack of a whip made her jump half a foot. He wouldn't really use a whip on her, would he?

Of course he would. She didn't know anything about this man, hell, she didn't even know his name. Just because he resembled Kiefer didn't mean he was Kiefer. For all she knew he could be a sadistic bastard who loved to hurt women.

Nerves doused the raging fire that he'd built earlier. But before she could step away, he laid a gentle hand along her cheek.

"This is just fun and games, if you get nervous, just say the word and I'll stop. Okay, luv?"

"Y-yes."

Her shoulders relaxed and tension slid from her body, until he cracked the whip again.

Now she felt a tension of a different sort. Right between her legs.

"How should I punish you, slave?"

Her highwayman ran the whip over her chest, teasing her nipples with the handle. It felt like soft leather and not in the least bit uncomfortable. The tail slipped over her shoulder and skimmed her back.

"I think you need to be properly prepared for your punishment." Without another word he yanked her shirt down her arms, freeing her breasts from their silken confinement. "Ah yes, much better."

He eased her arms out of the sleeves and placed them back on the post when he was satisfied. The cool air brushed her freed nipples and sent tingles rippling through her. The whip snaked down her chest and her highwayman pulled it tightly between her legs. Reannah's breath caught as his fingers brushed her swollen pussy.

He slid the whip down her torso and over her clit, rubbing against the thong with enough pressure to tempt but not to push her over the edge.

"Bend over," he growled in her ear.

She did as he said without the slightest hesitation. Her breasts swung freely in this position. The whip wrapped around one mound and pulled tightly, not enough to hurt but enough to force the blood to her nipple.

The constriction made her throb with need with every beat of her heart. His hand kneaded her bound breast, heightening the burning sensation in the tip. It felt swollen and needy for his touch.

Just when she thought she'd explode, she felt his head slip under her upraised arms and his hot mouth latch onto her nipple. Reannah's knees buckled at the wet heat of his lips. Waves of hot lust radiated from that one small point throughout her entire body, obliterating any fears or concerns she might have once had.

His teeth grazed her skin lightly sending shivers down her spine. A whimper of protest slipped from her when he removed his mouth but it quickly turned into a gasp of surprise. He's eased a ring of some sort around her nipple and it amplified the pressure on her swollen tip.

The sensation increased dramatically when he released the binding of the whip from around her breast. All the blood that had built up under the tie rushed toward her be-ringed peak.

Reannah shook with desire as he repeated the process on the other breast. Sweat dripped off her face and her hands clenched the post like it was the safety bar on a roller coaster.

"What should I call you, besides master?" she asked weakly. She desperately needed an anchor to keep herself from flying apart.

He hesitated as he moved behind her and she wondered if she had blundered in asking him his name.

"Just call me Ian."

"Yes, master."

Ian. That meant his lilt was Irish. Was Kiefer Irish? She wasn't sure…

Any other thoughts flew out of her mind as his hot tongue traced the line where her ass ended and her thighs began. Cream gushed from her pussy and she had a moment of embarrassment about her state.

"Um, delicious." He lapped her juices with little flicks of his tongue along her thigh, inducing more fluid. "You're so wet. Is that all for me, little slave?"

"Y-yes."

"I can't wait to sink my cock into all that creamy heat. But not yet."

Damn it! She was ready to beg him to fuck her and he wanted to play? The rings on her nipples sent pulses of fire through her with every breath she took. The glide of the whip along her pussy tormented her with its light touch. And his mouth, God his mouth was an implement of torture if there ever was one.

"I think you'd better remove your thong before it gets lost in those pouting pussy lips."

"Yes, master." *Thank you God!*

Her fingers fumbled as she unclenched them from around the whipping post. It was hard to get the leather thong over the boots with her eyes closed. At one point she almost fell, but Ian was there to catch her against his rock-hard frame.

While she removed her thong, he'd stripped. Reannah felt another moment of severe frustration at the binding over her eyes. She could feel his bare chest and legs but couldn't see them. What would he look like without those leather pants?

Pretty damn good, she bet.

"Spread your legs," he ordered once she'd finally removed the hated underwear.

She did as told and shook in anticipation. Was he finally ready to end this game and fuck her?

Apparently not, because he moved between her legs and ran something along her inner thigh.

"Have you ever used a dildo before, slave?"

What? She didn't want a fake cock, she wanted *his*!

"N-no." A vibrator, yes, but never a dildo.

"Then let me tell you about this one. It's rather unique actually. Instead of looking like a fake dick, it's shaped like a cone. It's made out of some sort of plastic that has give to it but it's still hard enough to do the job." He ran the cool object over her pussy lips. "And do you know what job that is?"

"To go inside me?"

"Absolutely."

He slid the dildo just inside her channel. Reannah's inner muscles tried to grip the smooth material and pull it in deeper. God, she wanted to be filled. She was aching inside.

"Not yet." He slipped it out and she cried with the loss.

Her legs trembled with need and her hands ached from clutching the post so hard. She wanted to weep, to beg, to do whatever she had to in order to get him to push the thing back in. To push *himself* inside of her.

"What do you want, slave?"

"You!"

"Not yet."

She ground her teeth in frustration, ready to scream her impatience. How much building up could she take before she exploded?

The feel of his hair brushing her thighs spiraled her even higher. His breath on her pussy pushed her even hotter.

And when he drew his tongue along her needy clit while he shoved the dildo into her grasping channel she reached the outer limits of her control.

Her head twisted from side to side as she pressed her hips closer to Ian's magical mouth. He furiously pumped the rod in and out while he flicked his tongue faster and faster.

Reannah couldn't hold back the storm raging through her. Didn't want to hold it back. She let it thunder over her, igniting every atom of her being as she shot to the stars.

"Now that is a beautiful sight. But I'm not done with you yet."

"More?"

"Much more. On your knees, grab onto the leather cuffs and assume the position."

Position? What position?

He slapped her ass again and she got the idea. It took a Herculean effort to get to her knees but she knew it would be worth the effort.

With her ass in the air and her breasts hanging low, arms overhead, she waited for Ian's next delight.

He didn't disappoint her. His hand caressed her butt cheek, drifting toward the tiny bud she'd never explored. Her breath came out in rush as he traced the opening, setting that nerve-rich area aflame.

Just when she thought he was going to do more than flirt around the surface, he came down with a stinging swat. Reannah's heart almost burst out of her chest as heat seared from her rear end to her core. She wiggled her butt, eagerly awaiting another spank.

Ian complied, quickly peppering her derrière with soft strokes and stinging slaps. With every stroke her body grew more and more needy.

"Let go of the cuffs," he ordered before biting her ear.

Reannah let go of the cuffs and let her upper body fall to the floor. Ian maneuvered behind her, wrapping an arm around her waist and leaning her over it.

"Are you ready?"

"Yes!" she sobbed, more than ready for anything.

Ian plunged into her from behind, his cock sinking deeply into her pussy. Reannah reared back, trying to get him as deep as possible. He reached around and flicked her blood-filled nipples that were still constricted by the rings.

One hand worked its way down her stomach to her curls and parted them. Sobs tore from her throat as he continued to pound her very depths as he flicked her clit. It was too much for her to handle and she rocketed to completion with a scream.

As she continued to ride the wave to the stars, she could feel Ian's thighs against her own, hear his harsh breathing as he fought for his own release. His hands clutched her hips, pulling her tightly against him until with a muted groan, he powered out three quick strokes and collapsed against her back.

Ian kissed the back of her neck as her legs crumpled beneath her. She lay on the floor, completely boneless, and unable to move. As he eased the scarf off her face, he kissed her and she could taste her arousal on his lips.

His hands cupped her face as he gentled the kiss, teasing her with soft nips and flickering licks along the inner edge of her lips. Her heartbeat ramped up again at the sheer romance of his touch. He didn't even know her name yet he kissed her like the most cherished of treasures.

Too bad it wasn't really Kiefer.

Stop that! You can pretend for tonight.

Reannah poured all her longing for Kiefer into kissing him back. She reached around and dug her nails into his well-formed butt and pulled him closer. Surprisingly, she felt his cock growing against her leg.

"Do you want me again so soon?"

"How can you ask?"

Amazed, she stroked his chest, soaking in every inch of his beautiful body that she could finally see. Having sex blindfolded had been an incredible sensual experience. Watching his cock grow as she stroked his gorgeous chest was a veritable feast to her senses. He'd wadded up the scarf in a ball and tossed it back and forth as he watched her caress him.

Something about the action tweaked her memory but she pushed it aside when he wrapped the scarf around the back of her neck and pulled her on top of him.

"You're going to drive me insane, do you know that? That corset thing pushes your breasts up so temptingly. I don't know whether I love it or hate it."

"If it turns you on, I love it."

"Oh, it turns me on all right. Too much."

She raked her nails down his sides and trailed them over his pelvis. When she reached his steely cock, she eased it inside her still quivering pussy. Instantly, the barely banked fires flared to life.

Every cell of her body celebrated his entrance inside her.

"Wrap your legs around my waist."

She did and gloried at how much deeper he could get. Ian got to his knees and grabbed her ass, lifting her hips even higher to meet his thrusts. Reannah arched her back and stared at his muscled chest over her.

His eyes blazed through the mask, staring down at her with an intensity that burned her.

"You're mine now. Do you hear me? Mine!" He captured her mouth with a soul-stealing kiss and his spicy scent washed over her.

"Yes!" she screamed as another wave of release swamped her.

Her body convulsed, bowing her body with the sheer power of her climax. Hips bucked against hips as he ground into her clit to push her orgasm even longer. The pleasure rolled on and on like waves in the ocean, eventually slowing but never seeming to stop.

After an eternity, Reannah collapsed against the plush rug, too spent to come any more. She lifted her heavy eyelids to watch Ian reach his own peak. The muscles of his shoulders stood out as he supported himself over her. His chest glistened with sweat and again, his musky, spicy scent washed over her.

Her befuddled mind screamed at her but she was too passion soaked to make any sense of it. The vein in Ian's throat pulsed rapidly as he threw back his head with a roar of completion.

The dim light shone upon his beautifully sculpted cheekbones and jaw.

His very familiar cheekbones and jaw.

Chapter Four

ﾒ

"That was incredible," he groaned against her throat. "More amazing than I could have ever dreamed."

"And how long have you dreamed about having sex with me, Kiefer."

Reannah pushed his heavy body off her. She had to bite back a cry of dismay as his heavy cock slipped out of her. "Is this some kind of joke to you? Are you the one who sent me the invitation?"

She searched for her cape but couldn't find it in the dark. Needing something to cover her nakedness, she grabbed at the tacky blanket on the bed and wrapped it around her. Her face flamed in embarrassment as she pulled the nipple rings off and threw them on the floor.

"It's not like that, Rea. Honest. I didn't send you the invitation. Hell, I don't even know who sent it to me. I thought it was spam until I saw it on your computer today."

Kiefer pushed to his feet and reached for his pants. The muscles of his abdomen rippled as he jerked on the leather trousers and Reannah felt her body heat. It didn't care that she'd just been made a fool of. All her body cared about was repeating the mind-blowing sex she'd just had.

"So you decided to come to the party and what? See if you could get lucky?"

"I told you, it's not like that."

"That's what it looks like from my end. Did you think it would be funny to see me, boring Reannah, technical writer, in fetish wear?"

"No, damn it! I thought if you didn't know it was me I'd actually have a chance to touch you without you running away."

"W-what?" What did he mean?

"Don't give me that dumbfounded look. I've been after you for *months* and you run away whenever the conversation moves beyond work."

"I thought you were just playing me. You have women calling you constantly. They hand you their phone numbers at sales meetings. I've seen it happen."

"I wasn't playing you. And I throw those numbers out as soon as I get out of the meeting. I don't want a one-night stand with someone who only sees me on the surface."

"So you came to an orgy for a meaningful relationship?" she asked with a raised eyebrow.

"No. I'd hoped if you let me past your guard once, you might do it again after the party."

His eyes pleaded with her to understand and Reannah had to sit down to gather her thoughts. This was just too weird. Here she'd been dreaming of Kiefer for months but had stayed away because she thought he was a player, not to mention the fact that workplace relationships were always a nightmare. She'd honestly thought he just flirted with her because she was one of the few women at Zera.

"Rea, talk to me. Please. Tell me I haven't blown any chance I might have had with you, however slim."

"I'm just trying to come to terms with everything." Now *that* was an understatement. "Why me? I'm so boring compared to the women you hang around with."

"Who do I hang around with?"

"That gorgeous blonde you brought to the Christmas party? What was her name, Barbie? Bubbles?"

"Bitsy. I only brought her because you turned me down. I wanted to make you jealous."

Boy, had that ever worked. She'd seethed with envy over the stunning blonde bombshell for weeks.

"I thought you were playing a joke on me. If I said yes you'd laugh and tell me you were kidding." Humiliation made her face flame.

"I'd never do such a thing. That's terrible. I can't believe you'd believe I'd do something so juvenile and cruel." He paced in front of her, clearly agitated.

"Let's just say not everyone has your moral convictions and leave it at that."

"Oh man." Kiefer whipped off his mask and knelt in front of her, taking her hands in his. "I meant every word I've ever said to you. Meant every invitation and compliment. You've had me tied in knots for months now."

His earnest hazel eyes blazed into her and she couldn't look away. She was grateful for the mask to help her hide from his gaze. Could she really believe him?

Her brain screamed at her to remember how humiliating it was to be the butt of a frat boy's joke.

Her heart insisted Kiefer was different.

"Please." He rubbed her knuckles with his thumbs. "I know after this stunt I don't have any right to ask for your trust but I am anyway. I'd have done anything, *anything*, to get you to notice me. To let me touch you. Now that you have, I don't want to ever stop."

"Really?" Her heart flipped over.

"Really. Even when you didn't know it was me, I couldn't help but celebrate finally kissing you. Touching you. Tasting you."

Reannah's brain went down for the count. Her heart expanded until she thought her chest couldn't contain it anymore.

"I hated lying to you about my name. I wanted to hear my real name on your lips when I drove into you. When you flew over the edge."

He brought her knuckle to his mouth and twirled his tongue over it. Flames shot from her finger to her groin in warp speed.

She took a deep breath for courage as her stomach twisted at the risk she was about to take. Screw it, if she couldn't risk her pride for love on Valentine's Day, when could she?

"I-I went with you because you resembled the guy I've had a thing for for months."

"Who?"

She shrugged the blanket off her shoulders and knelt on the floor with him. "This sexy sales guy I thought would run in the other direction if he knew how I really felt. How much I wanted him and how often I fantasized about him touching me."

"I'd like to hear a little more about those fantasies." He untied the corset with blinding speed and pushed the contraption down her hips.

"I can tell you, they had nothing to do with boots that made my feet hurt this much." She made a face and tried to stand but got tangled in the blanket.

"Then by all means, take them off. But promise me you'll wear them for me again."

"Liked the dominatrix look, did you?"

"It almost gave me a heart attack."

Reannah sat back on the bed and unzipped the boots, grateful to get them off her aching feet.

Kiefer rubbed her toes as she eased off the second heel.

"God, that feels good. I may keep you around after all, you have great hands."

"Honey, my hands aren't the only great part about me." His eyes glinted devilishly over her foot as he sucked on one of her toes.

Fire. He must be part fucking dragon to have so much heat in his mouth. Molten lava ran from her foot to her pussy. Since when were feet erogenous zones?

"Take off your mask. I want to see all of you when I make love to you."

"And what makes you think you're going to make love to me?" She teased taking off her mask and undoing the binding that held her hair in place.

"I'm a salesman, I go into every pitch assuming I'll win the deal." He ran his thumb over the arch of her foot. "Take off your shirt, please. My hands are busy." His fingers feathered up her calves and stroked the backs of her knees.

"When do I get my turn? You've already seen all of me. I want my turn to play."

"Far be it from me to keep a woman from her playthings. Be gentle with me."

Kiefer lay down against the pile of pillows at the head of the bed without the least hint of embarrassment at his nudity.

He obviously didn't have a thing to be embarrassed about. Thick muscles bunched at his shoulders and pecs. He wasn't built up like the men she'd seen in the viewing room, but was firm and well defined.

Her breath hitched as she ran her fingers over his six-pack abs. Was there anything better looking than a well-built torso? Trailing her hand lower, she grasped his hardened cock and decided maybe one thing might be more attractive.

"It really wasn't very nice of you to keep me from seeing this before. I feel cheated."

"Don't lie to me, wench. You enjoyed every second of it."

Reannah moved between his legs, running her fingers over his hard, hairy thighs. "Maybe I did. But I'm enjoying this quite a bit."

"Me too," he gasped as she brought her mouth down to trace the smooth glans.

She tasted the mingled flavor of their earlier passion and rolled it over her tongue like a fine wine. Fresh cream gushed from her pussy and her breasts felt swollen with need.

Drawing him in deeper, she rubbed her nipples against the roughness of his legs and hummed her pleasure. Goose bumps chased down her arms as she bobbed up and down on his cock. Using one hand to wrap around his length, she cupped his balls in her other one and gently rolled them in her palm.

"I'm getting lonely up here."

"Are you complaining?" She lifted her head off his shafted and stared at him.

"No, but one taste of you wasn't enough. I want more. Come here."

Heat coiled in her belly and spread to her breasts and pussy. Her thighs quivered as she placed her dripping core over his mouth and lay across his chest. Their heights were so well matched she was able to draw him back into her mouth without straining at all.

Thank God.

"Are you using the dildo again?" she asked when she felt something press between her slick pussy lips.

"Nope, my finger. This time nothing is going in you but me."

Her inner muscles spasmed around his finger as he drove it into her and continued to lick her clit. It was almost impossible to concentrate on his pleasure when he was driving her out of her mind with his mouth. She sucked as hard as she could, pulling him deeply to the very back of her throat, wanting to give him as much pleasure as he gave her.

If his sudden exhalation was anything to go by, she thought she succeeded. And then she couldn't think anymore. Kiefer pushed a second finger inside her and stroked the bundle of nerves that pushed her over the edge. She barely remained conscious enough to release him before another screaming orgasm ripped through her.

She reached for his erection again as the tremors subsided but Kiefer pulled her away.

"I can't take any more. I want to be in you when I come."

Wordlessly, Reannah squirmed around until her pussy was poised to let his cock inside her. With no masks between them, real or emotional, she stared into his eyes and slid him home.

Kiefer let out a guttural moan and brought his hands up to knead her breasts.

"God, I've wanted to see you like this for so long. Your hair tumbling wildly over your naked body while you bounce on top of me. I can die a happy man." He reared up and captured a nipple between his teeth.

"Not yet you can't." Another orgasm threatened to push her over the cliff.

His chuckle vibrated through her rib cage right to her heart.

"I don't plan on leaving you any time soon."

He circled her clit with his finger as he pushed upward to pierce her to her very soul.

"Look at me, my lovely Reannah. I want to be the last thing you see as you go over the edge."

She forced her lids to open and was mesmerized by the emotions brimming in his hazel eyes. "Come with me," she whispered, barely able to speak.

"Always." He thrust up rapidly while she rocked against him, clinging to the edge of the cliff until she felt him tighten beneath her.

Letting herself go, she fell into Kiefer's gaze and didn't care where she landed.

* * * * *

"I know it's six o'clock in the morning but I had to thank you," Reannah babbled into the phone as she waited in the limo for Kiefer to get some things from his condo. They were headed back to her place for a weekend of breakfast, lunch and dinner in bed.

"What are you talking about?" Molly's voice was rough with sleep.

"For the party. It was more than I could have ever imagined. But how did you manage to get Kiefer an invitation too? What if he hadn't shown up?"

"Rea, it's six a.m. and I'm not a morning person on a good day. What party?"

"The Screw Cupid party? You know. The one you so conveniently convinced me to go to? I know you set it all up. I don't know how but I'm glad you did."

"Honey, I had nothing to do with it."

"Come on, Mol. The joke's over."

"I'm not kidding. I had nothing to do with the party. I just thought you needed to get out and stop moping so I told you to go. I didn't arrange the invitation though."

"But—but they had my shoe size right. And they invited Kiefer too..." she trailed off.

"Must have been someone else because it wasn't me. Glad things worked out for you though. I'm going back to bed."

Reannah hung up the phone, stunned as Kiefer climbed in next to her.

"What's wrong? Are you having second thoughts?"

"No, of course not." She gave him a lingering kiss, tasting the strawberries and champagne they'd shared earlier. "I just called Molly to thank her for getting me an invitation to the party and she didn't know anything about it. I was sure she was the one who invited me. Who invited you?"

"I have no idea. The E-vite came from Cupid2007. I didn't pay too much attention to it until I saw you had one too. Then I knew I had to go. I figured it must have been someone you knew."

"Trust me, other than Molly no one, and I mean *no one*, would ever believe I'd go to a party like that."

"I'm sure we'll find out eventually. But in the meantime, let's just enjoy the gift fate dropped into our laps. Or rather, our in-boxes."

He kissed her again, leisurely nipping at her lips and teasing her with his tongue. The ride passed in pleasurable silence as they explored one another in the dim predawn light.

It wasn't until a discreet cough and a cool breeze snapped them out of their spell that they realized the car had even stopped. With her face flaming, Reannah collected her purse and pulled the cape over her disheveled outfit before accepting the chauffeur's hand.

"Thanks again. And please pass our gratitude on to our host," Kiefer said to the driver as he captured Reannah's hand.

"Of course, sir." The driver tipped his hat and handed Kiefer a card printed on the same stationery she'd seen earlier.

Before Reannah could ask him about it, the driver climbed into the car and pulled away.

"What is that?" she asked, her breath clouding the frigid morning air.

"I don't know but why don't we open it inside. I'm freezing."

They shuffled into Reannah's kitchen and she put on a pot of coffee before Kiefer opened the letter.

"Well, what does it say?"

"You're not going to believe this."

"Try me."

"Dear Ms. Mason and Mr. Brown,

Thank you so much for attending my sensual celebration. I hope you found your every wish and desire in each other.

Sincerely,

Cupid."

"Get out of town! Let me see that." Reannah snatched the note out of Kiefer's hand and read it herself.

"How could he have known we hooked up? Everyone was masked."

"I don't know and I'm not going to worry about it. I've got you now and if Cupid is the reason why I'll happily celebrate Valentine's Day for the rest of my life."

"You and me both." She sat on his lap and held his face in her hands so she could control the kiss. "You know, this isn't going to be easy with both of us working at Zera. I know there's no rule about employees dating but it can still get awkward."

"I know. I'll talk to Paul and see what he thinks, whether I should be switched to another office or what. But I'm not giving you up."

"But—"

"But nothing. Let's deal with that when the time comes. For the next two days, the only thing I want to worry about is whose turn it is to be on top."

"I believe that it's yours, master." Reannah tossed her cape over his face and took off for the bedroom.

A thrill raced through her as she heard Kiefer in hot pursuit. Cupid really had given her every wish and desire.

And then some.

Also by Arianna Hart

so

Behind the Enchanted Door
By Honor Bound (*anthology*)
Convince Me
Ellora's Cavemen: Legendary Tails III (*anthology*)
Lucy's Lover
Pleasure Raiders (*anthology*)
Rebel Lust
Sable Flame
Silver Fire
Sloan's Heart

About the Author

ଧ

Arianna Hart lives on the East Coast with her husband and three daughters. When not teaching, writing, or chasing after her children and the dog, Ari likes to practice her karate, go for long walks, and read by the pool. She thinks heaven is having a good book, warm sun, and a drink in her hand. Until she can sit down long enough to enjoy all three, she'll settle for the occasional hour of peace and quiet.

Arianna welcomes comments from readers. You can find her website and email address on her author bio page at www.ellorascave.com.

Tell Us What You Think

We appreciate hearing reader opinions about our books. You can email us at Comments@EllorasCave.com.

SOUL KISSES

Aubrey Ross

ॐ

Chapter One

$\wp$

Awareness returned by degrees. Tazney absorbed the vibrant ripple of life. A trickle of water drizzled across her parched tongue, she savored the precious energy. More. She needed more. She stirred, reaching for the source of the blessed disturbance. Jumbled thoughts and fragmented images flooded her.

Too much! She couldn't make sense of so many.

How long had she been trapped on this derelict spaceship? Had it been years or centuries since she last stirred? Valentine's Day? Who was thinking about that ancient Earth festival?

It didn't matter. She didn't have time for speculation. She was too weak to join her people in their home dimension and too stubborn to disperse entirely. Her only hope lay with whoever had happened upon her cold and lonely cage.

Following the intensity of their energy trail, she located the visitors. They wore formfitting suits and helmets with clear faceplates. Their cutting tools and hover carts identified their purpose. Scavengers, come to strip the ship of anything worth recycling. If they required an artificial environment and generated gravitation, they were doubtlessly traveling in their own ship. How many did they number? Would they offer assistance to a stranded stranger or try to take her prisoner?

They spoke in a verbal language Tazney didn't understand. She had only interacted with a few corporeal species and all of them had been humanoid. These men were faintly reptilian, though highly evolved. Her levels were perilously depleted. She didn't dare squander this opportunity.

As the team fanned out through the ship, one of the men turned and excitement surged within her. Human! The faceplate distorted his features, but he was far different from the others. His long stride carried him down one corridor and into the aft cabin. He began disassembling an alloy housing, his actions dexterous and skilled.

She moved closer, opening her receptors to his emotions. Focused and calm, his being flowed into her and she was no longer alone. Joy rippled through her warm and intoxicating. She had been isolated for so long, adrift in this disintegrating ship. She sensed his stubborn strength, the brutal edge to his personality and — nothing else.

Confused and unnerved, she pushed deeper. Humans were complex beings, often concealing their true emotions. She found them fascinating, enjoyed unraveling their convoluted motivations and trying to understand how they thought.

The deeper she delved, the more guarded his spirit became. She sank past layer upon layer of artificial indifference and protective disassociation. Understanding pulsed through her, making her ache with feelings he had suppressed long ago. Only those subjected to the most devastating agonies found shelter in oblivion.

Rage accessed his proximity scanners and watched negative readings scroll across the bottom half of his faceplate. No alarm sounded, but the hairs on the back of his neck were standing on end. Someone was watching him.

Despite the Linusian technology integrated into his gravsuit, he slipped the laser saw into its compartment on his tool belt and turned around. The lights surrounding his faceplate adjusted for distance, illuminating the opposite wall of the derelict cruiser. He was part of a licensed salvage team, a rare breed in this rough-and-tumble sector of space. Few bothered with permits and authorizations when bribes worked just as well.

"Rage to Letto." His brainwaves activated the nanocom embedded in his skull, sending his voice to the other team members. "How's it going up there?"

"Smooth as a whore's ass." Rage could picture the young Linusian's face. His solid black gaze would dart about with stealthy precision, while subtle changes in his skin tone revealed his emotions more accurately than any Linusian was willing to admit.

Rage had spent so many years among the Linusians their reptilian appearance no longer affected him. It was far more unnerving each time he looked in the mirror and viewed his own haggard features. Did other humans still exist in the universe? He'd heard rumors of scattered rebels and outposts with integrated populations.

The possibility was irrelevant. Curiosity was a dangerous waste of time. He had three years left on his contract with Captain Stromn. The Linusians were members of the Kytinian Confederation, while humans were hunted and despised.

A light appeared directly in front of Rage. He dimmed his helmet, making sure he wasn't seeing some sort of reflection. He searched the fluctuating orb for a discernible pattern or shape.

Careful to deactivate his nanocom, he said, "So you were watching me."

He waited for the rush of excitement or fear, a tingle of curiosity. It had been so long since any experience moved him. Nothing happened. He shook his head. It was useless. He was officially numb.

The creature hovered for a moment, then lunged toward him. He twisted to the side. The entity countered and sped, stabbing into the center of his chest. Searing pain erupted then shot down his arms as the being explored his body. Pressure drove the breath from his lungs and stars danced before his eyes.

Rage reached blindly for something solid as reality careened around him. Images rolled and tumbled, fading in and out of focus. Supple skin, slender thighs, moist lips, and full round breasts. *Woman.* Was this creature tormenting him with what he desired most or attempting to communicate?

Elation burst without warning. He gasped and clutched his abdomen. Hope, aching and sweet, unfurled with blinding intensity. "Too — much." Joy crashed down upon him, forcing laughter from his dry throat.

Her focus shifted. The emotions were no longer pleasant. He was afraid. He was annoyed. Then he was angry. Fury exploded within him, but she reined in the flare before he could wrap himself in the familiar emotion. How was she doing this?

Tenderness swelled, driving the other emotions aside. He resisted. Everything she'd released so far he was confident he could control. Heat washed over him in comforting waves. He felt surrounded by kindness, embraced by caring and enveloped in gentleness.

Shaken and resentful, he struggled against the weakening. He'd fought too hard to purge himself of all emotion. Didn't she understand? Banishing these feelings hadn't been a choice. It had been a matter of survival.

Desire curled up through his belly, heating his blood, adding depth and texture to the softer feelings. He stumbled back against the bulkhead, his legs trembling. His chest burned as sensations zinged from his heart to his groin. She was in his mind. She knew how long it had been since he'd touched a woman, found pleasure with anything other than sensory stimulators or the desperate stroke of his own hand.

His cock hardened and throbbed, his balls tightened and ached. He closed his eyes, trying to picture a woman, any woman, as long as she was *real*.

"You're sure as hell thorough," he whispered. Even knowing an entity was triggering these reactions didn't alleviate the underlying emptiness. He wanted to share this experience, touch her and feel her touching him.

Tension banded his chest and his shaft pulsed as phantom ripples massaged his length. His hands closed into fists and he gritted his teeth. This was no different than the stimulators.

See me. A sweet, feminine voice sounded inside his head.

His eyes flew open. She'd spoken in ancient Earthish. He hadn't heard his native language in twenty years. "What are you?"

The light hovered in front of him like some deranged fairy. It flared for an instant, growing bigger, then dimming considerably. *I'm still too weak. I need you to finish. Can you do that for me?*

"You want me to stand here and —come in my gravsuit?" An especially powerful tingle responded to the question. "This is insane." He panted. His body more than happy to accommodate her needs.

The only time humans emit energy concentrated enough for me to absorb is when they have an orgasm or during strong emotional reactions. Would your rather I find a way to make you angry?

"Why do you need energy?" Space dementia. He was standing here talking to a flickering light who had given him the hardest erection he'd had in years.

I've been trapped in your dimension longer than you can imagine. I want to go home.

Freedom, now there was a longing Rage understood. He shook his head and leaned against the bulkhead. "What do you need me to do?"

Just enjoy my touch. Think of them as soul kisses. You're sharing a small portion of your being with me and I'll show my appreciation by giving you the most powerful orgasm you've ever known.

Worst case scenario, she sucked him dry. What did he have to lose? Besides, Rage had felt her moving through his mind. This was not a malicious being. Why not help her if he could. "What the hell," he whispered. "Carry on."

As soon as he closed his eyes the wonderful massage resumed. He concentrated on the rhythmic squeezing, and let his body have its way.

Be happy, little Fairy. Be free.

He used the spontaneous thought to fuel his imagination and pictured her there on her knees. Delicate and ethereal, her naked body pale and shimmering with otherworldly light. Long blonde hair flowed around her shoulders and down her back. Her lips formed a tight circle as she slid her mouth up and down his shaft, one dainty hand cupping his balls.

Yes! That was it. Hot, wet lips and an eager mouth! He took her head between his hands and thrust faster as her tongue swirled and her lips sucked. She tilted her head, allowing his aching cock deep into her throat.

Tingling heat curled up his spine. His balls tightened and throbbed. He focused on the sensations and the image he had created in his mind. Still he longed for the soft brush of tangible fingers and the warmth of real lips. The pressure around his cock intensified as the phantom mouth sucked harder. He shuddered and moaned. Pleasure burst within him, powerful surges of release. He grasped the bulkhead for support, breathless and shaken.

He slowly opened his eyes. Had that been enough to send her on her way? Another emotion surfaced as he looked around the cabin. Years of numbness had spared him this hollow ache. He was alone again.

* * * * *

Rage didn't release his pent-up breath until the detox scanner assured him the light being hadn't left anything behind. The gravsuits underwent a complete decontamination after every use, so no one needed to know about his bizarre encounter.

Letto chatted away as they stowed their gear in the utility lockers. Rage nodded and provided noncommittal sounds hoping the young man wouldn't realize he wasn't listening.

His chest still ached and spiky sensations crawled down his arms. Where had she gone? Maybe the boost of energy had been enough to send her back where she belonged. He pulled off his undershirt and tossed it in the recycler.

"What the fuck happened to you?" Letto rushed up behind him.

"Am I bleeding?" Rage craned his neck, trying to see what caused Letto's outburst.

The young Linusian circled Rage. "Holy mother of Ggirt, it goes right through." The skin on Rage's chest was red and welted, as if two acidic fingers had drawn a perfect Valentine's heart on his chest, then proceeded to fill it in with blood. The reaction intensified as it neared the center of the wound. "Did you burn yourself? What caused this?" His fingers hovered over Rage's chest. "It's not as bad in back, but it's the same strange shape. Does it have some significant meaning?"

Rage pressed his lips together. Letto was the closest thing to a friend he had on this ship, but he was still Linusian. "Did you see her, Letto?" Rage watched his face carefully, waiting for a telltale darkening in the green tint across his sharply angled cheeks. "When you met me at the airlock you asked me what I'd seen, not what I'd found."

Snatching his hand back, Letto looked around the utility room before he lowered his voice to barely a whisper. "It attacked you?"

"If she wanted me dead, I'd be dead. I don't think she meant to hurt me. I have no idea what caused the heart."

"We have to tell the captain. Maybe this is what he was—Why are you convinced that thing is female? Do you think it was trying to communicate with you?"

"Report!" Rage snapped to attention beside Letto. They'd both been so engrossed in their conversation they hadn't heard the captain enter the utility room.

Rage knew better than making direct eye contact with Stromn. A select few Linusians were able to project an incapacitating mist that left their victim paralyzed and temporarily blind. Not surprisingly, these same select few were generally found in positions of power among the Linusian military. Captain Stromn prided himself in the concentration of his mist.

"Preliminary scans indicated nominal levels of radiation. Once we got on board the other ship the readings began to spike." Rage kept his explanation vague without being evasive. He always chose his battles carefully. The strategy had kept him alive for almost forty years.

"What happened to your chest?"

"I'm uncertain, sir."

"Guess."

"Probably a spike of radiation."

Stromn chuckled, a decidedly unpleasant sound. "Rather exact shape for random radiation. Isn't this the shape you described this morning? You said it was part of some ancient mating ritual on your home world."

"Valentine's Day, sir," Letto volunteered. "That's what the holiday was called."

Stromn accepted the information with a barely perceptible nod. "And if *she* had spiked you with radiation a second time, you believe you'd be dead?"

Taking a subtle step to the side, Rage tried to draw Stromn's attention away from the younger man. There was no need for Letto to be involved in whatever punishment Stromn had planned. "I saw a light as I was searching the aft cabin. I thought it was my imagination and continued the search until I saw it again."

"What is standard protocol for first encounters with an alien life form?"

"Contain any immediate threat and contact the team leader," Rage recited. He imagined kicking Stromn's legs out from under him and flipping him onto his belly before he had time to fire off his toxic mist. If he could actually move that fast he would have kicked the shit out of the condescending bastard a long time ago. Stromn was responsible for rescuing Rage from the Kytinians. A debt the captain never let him forget. So the violent fantasy kept Rage from going insane.

"And as team leader, what should your response have been?"

"If I'd been certain I was dealing with a life form, I would have contacted you immediately. I saw a ball of light, sir. That's all. I'm still not sure it was a life form. I might have triggered an automatic defense mechanism for all I know."

"Right." His sarcastic tone indicated his disbelief. "Both of you report to the infirmary. You're getting invasive bioscans for Valentine's Day."

Tazney moved closer to Rage as he hurried through the corridors of the functional ship. His name was tragically fitting. He'd been so consumed by anger there had hardly been enough of his spirit to restore.

Be happy, little Fairy. Be free.

The conviction in his thought had caught her off guard. This life-hardened human wanted her to be happy. Why would he care about her happiness when he was indifferent to his own?

And the pleasure! She had forgotten how exhilarating exchanges could be. Her being still vibrated with sexual energy. She felt herself starting to glow and strengthened her shields.

She hadn't realized their joining would mark his flesh and she hadn't created the odd shape intentionally. It must have resulted from the thoughts that flooded her upon awakening.

They entered a room with padded tables and odd machinery, perhaps a medical facility. Had their exchange done more than mark his flesh? Was he injured?

His protective suit had prevented her from seeing his face while they were on the other ship. She paused in front of him, assessing his chiseled features. Ice blue eyes stared straight ahead without expression or emotion. If she hadn't felt his barriers crumble, she'd wonder if he felt anything at all. His scalp had been shaved recently, leaving only a shadow of dark stubble. Was he required to shave his head or did it make him feel less different when surrounded by the hairless Linusians?

An image flared without warning. She imagined Rage thrusting hard and fast between her thighs, her pussy stretched tight around his thick cock as she rubbed her hands over his shaved head. Tingles erupted and again she intensified her shields.

Sleekly muscled with smooth skin and strong limbs, his lean body beckoned. She wanted to memorize every contour and swell with her hands and her mouth. It had been so long since she'd taken on shape. She might use more energy solidifying than she was able to gain from the exchange, but, damn, she was tempted to try.

Her attention focused on the ridge of flesh outlined beneath his uniform pants. His cock wasn't hard now and it still created a distinct and appealing shape. He hadn't touched himself on the other ship. He'd just surrendered to the sensations. Despite his emotional reserve, Rage was passionate and uninhibited. The contrast fascinated her.

She eased into his mind and insinuated her thoughts with gentle care. *I didn't mean to harm you.*

Ah, you are still here. His reply came strong and articulate across their telepathic link.

An odd combination of pride and possessiveness warmed her being. Her human learned quickly. *Her* human? She was certain he wouldn't appreciate the title.

You didn't indicate I'd caused you pain, she told him. *Do you understand your body's reaction?*

I don't understand any of this. It's rather decorative, don't you think? I keep telling them it doesn't hurt. No one believes me.

If you pretend to be fatigued, will they allow you to rest?

The third man asked Rage several questions, preventing him from responding to her. She watched the bunch and flex of his muscles as Rage was instructed to raise his arms and roll his shoulders. Many of her people considered corporeal beings beneath them and only took on shape when it was absolutely necessary. Tazney had always craved the intensity of physical sensations. Rage made the longing more acute, more pronounced than ever before.

What exactly do you need from me now? Rage sent the grumbling thought when the third man turned his attention to Letto.

His annoyance was understandable. She was asking him to risk his safety, perhaps his health, with only fleeting pleasure in exchange. She needed to give him something that would mean as much to him as her freedom meant to her, which meant she had to understand him better.

I need to be alone with you. I promise I'll make it worth your while.

Chapter Two

ഏ

Rage looked around his drab little cabin and wanted to rail against the injustice. He finally got to be alone with a woman after two decades of abstinence. The setting was dismal and the female was non-corporeal.

Are you still here? he asked, not wanting to drive her away with his discouraged thoughts. He might not be able to touch her, but he could sense her vibrant energy, a mesmerizing presence. It was as close to a woman as he'd been in more years than he cared to remember.

Can the others see us? Is it safe to appear to you here?

Desire washed over his body in a slow, intoxicating wave. He splayed one hand against his tense abdomen and closed the other into a fist, ignoring the rapidly growing bulge in the front of his pants.

She'd "appeared" to him on the scrapper. Why would the possibility of seeing a glowing ball of light arouse him? *The device in my head that allows me to communicate with the Linusians also allows them to track each other. Visual surveillance is considered rude.*

Then they'll be able to hear you if you speak?

No. I deactivated the transmitter. They'll know if I leave this cabin. I'm under quarantine for the next forty-eight hours, but we're basically alone.

Good. Had he only imagined tingling warmth radiating from the word?

He scrubbed his face with one hand, feeling oddly self-conscious. The captain had ordered him to the infirmary while he was half dressed and no one had offered him a uniform top since. The red heart was already starting to fade and there had never been any pain associated with the discoloration.

A slow curl of light rotated from the ceiling to the floor, creating a glowing nimbus. Rage crossed his arms over his chest, captivated by the light and tormented by anticipation. It had been so damn long since he saw a real woman, much less touched one, kissed one, fucked one. His gut clenched and his cock bucked. Was he going to survive long enough for her to solidify?

An outline formed within the light, tall and slender, graceful as it swayed. His heartbeat doubled. He hadn't dared to hope she'd be beautiful. In truth it didn't matter. Long strands of shadowy hair fluttered in wild disarray. She arched and twisted as if fighting to escape the light, or absorb it into her shape.

Full breasts thrust forward as she arched her back. Rage watched in helpless wonder. His palms itched to cup those soft-looking mounds and tease the rosy nipples beneath his thumbs. Pants identical to his rested low on her hips and a contract collar encircled her neck. He absently touched his own throat, his teeth set, jaws clenched. She was mirroring his apparel. She didn't understand the metal band's significance.

With a few stubborn sparkles, the light blinked out and she stood before him breathless and smiling. Her long silky hair flowed to her waist, concealing one of her breasts. She had copied the color of his eyes as well, but hers glowed with hope and wonder.

"Get rid of this." He reached for her contract collar, but his hand passed right through her image. Shock slammed into his gut like a sucker punch. "You're still not real." He could barely force the words past his unresponsive throat.

She licked those supple lips, disappointment flickering within her pale blue eyes. "I guess I'm not strong enough to solidify. It's been a very long time since I tried. I want this as badly as you do."

Dragging his gaze away from her half-naked body, he moved to his bunk and sat. "You've got forty-eight hours to assimilate my energy as many times as you can. After that Letto will be sleeping on that bunk and— Can you absorb energy from the Linusians?"

"If there's no alternative." She spoke quietly and avoided looking into his eyes. He hadn't meant to upset her, but this was worse than the simulators. "Would you rather not help me now that you can see me? I thought this would make it more pleasurable for you."

She moved to Letto's bunk and sat facing him. If Rage hadn't passed his hand through her neck, he would have sworn she was solid. The sheen of her ivory skin, the subtle hint of red in her wavy hair, every detail of her image combined to convince his mind she was corporeal.

"You've chosen an incredibly beautiful form." He couldn't allow himself to forget she was intangible. She was an interactive daydream, a semi-amusing way to pass the time until she had drained enough of his energy to rejoin her people. "Did you find that image in my subconscious? She looks sort of familiar."

"I combined elements of several images and added details from my interactions with others of your kind. Are you pleased with the result?" She smiled and Rage thought his treacherous heart would break free of his chest. Had she completely obliterated his emotional detachment? He was acting like a sex-starved schoolboy. "My name is Tazney."

No, your name is Trouble. The thought was out before he remembered she was telepathic. "So, Tazney, how did you end up trapped on that scrapper?"

"My people are largely nomadic." She gathered a thick lock of hair and curled it around her index finger. He could think of all sorts of erotic uses for those long, silky strands. He would tease her nipples and the underside of her breasts. Brush her belly and her inner thighs. "We move from dimension to dimension, taking on whatever form is most appropriate to the situation." Her soft voice only partially distracted him from the images forming in his mind. "We always travel significant distances in our non-corporeal state. As we passed through this dimension, we encountered the trap."

Despite the allure of her voluptuous body several things in her casual explanation caught his attention. "Are there others of your kind trapped on the scrapper?"

Her gaze filled with regret and she tucked a lock of hair behind her ear. "Not anymore."

Tension banded his chest and only the futility of the impulse kept him from dragging her into his arms. Did their telepathic link allow her emotions into his mind? Sorting through his resurging emotions was challenging enough without this overwhelming need to comfort her.

"The wise passed their knowledge to the strong and the strong…" Her lips trembled as her voice trailed away.

He didn't know what to say, didn't know how to ease her sorrow. If only he could touch her, maybe kiss her with tenderness and… He forced away the useless longings. He couldn't touch her. He could only *want* her.

"You were the last to survive?" She nodded, her crystal blue eyes brimming with tears. This was torture. He rubbed the fading mark on his chest. "How many were trapped on the ship? How long were you over there?"

"Eleven of us were caught in the trap. The others in our party did everything they could to free us, but everything they tried to weaken the trap only drained energy from us as well."

"Who set this trap? This doesn't sound like something 'my kind' would know how to do."

She nodded, composure returning to her pale features. "We have enemies as well as allies. Is it not the same with all forms of life?"

"I suppose so." He scooted back on the bunk until he pressed against the cold alloy wall. "Humans certainly have their share of enemies." The momentary shock to his nervous system only slowed the confusing emotions muddling his brain. She was the personification of everything female, lush, desirable, wild, with just a hint of vulnerability.

Resting his head against the wall, he kept his gaze fixed on her lovely face. "Take whatever you need from me. I'm glad I'm the one who found you."

As if to mock his determination not to ogle her, she sent her hair tumbling behind her shoulders with a rebellious toss of her head, then placed her hands on the bed on either side of her hips. Both breasts were exposed now, full, round and topped with sweet, pink nipples.

"If you could touch me, what would you do?"

"Don't! I can't touch you and we both know it. Just take my energy so you can go home."

She cocked her head to the side and smiled her siren's smile. "I didn't say you would never be able to touch me. I'm simply too weak to solidify right now. After a couple more bursts of energy, I'll try again to accommodate you."

"You're such a fucking tease." He shot to his feet hands clenched at his sides. "I get myself off a couple more times and you're out of here."

"No." She stood as well. Less than an arm's length separated them, yet they were worlds apart. "I promise. I will not leave this dimension until you've been inside me *physically* at least once."

He stared into her eyes as savage hunger spiraled through his body. "You can solidify? If I give you more energy, I'll be able to touch you?" He'd never wanted anything as much as he wanted her.

Except freedom! Some nearly forgotten portion of his psyche slapped him in the back of the head. At one time he'd wanted freedom more than life itself. Then life had become the worst cruelty of all.

"I want to see your cock."

Her husky statement jarred him from his muddled thoughts. With an exasperated sigh, he accepted the compromise. "Well, my cock wants to do a whole lot more than see you, so let's get this over with." He unfastened his pants and pushed them past his hips, amazed to find his shaft already half hard. His mind might not be into these creative alternatives, but his body was more than ready to play. "Your turn."

She dragged her gaze away from his shaft and shed her pants with a little shimmy that made her breasts jiggle. That was all it took to take his erection from semi-hard to breath-stealing pressure.

He sat on the edge of his bunk and closed his fingers around his shaft, no longer caring that the main event had been postponed. She turned around, shifting from one position to the next with fluid grace. He focused on her rounded ass and she bent forward, offering him a better view. His fist pumped faster. God, she was beautiful!

The delicate folds of her pussy were just barely visible. An instant after he wished he could see more, she moved her legs apart and arched her back. "Stop reading my mind."

She looked over her shoulder, her eyes wide and guileless. "Then tell me what to do. What will heighten your pleasure?"

"Turn around and get on the bed." She did. "Lean against the wall and spread your legs wide." She grasped the backs of her knees and angled her legs out, offering him an unobstructed view of her cunt. He wanted to howl with frustration. Her dusky folds parted and her slit shined with cream. He wasn't the only one turned on by these games. "Touch yourself and don't be gentle. I sure as hell wouldn't be."

Tazney watched Rage's fist pump the thick shaft of his cock, aching for its fullness inside her. Cream soaked her fingers and trickled into the crack between her ass cheeks. She shifted, thrusting her fingers faster and rubbing her clit. This was a piss-poor substitute for what they really wanted.

His gaze burned, transfixed by the motion of her fingers. "I want you here," she whispered. "I'm imagining your cock filling me, stretching me until I can't take any more."

He groaned. His hand moved faster and so did hers. "I want to fuck you with my tongue first. I want to feel you come against my mouth and taste all that cream."

"I want that too. Oh god, how I want it!"

She pushed her fingers into her passage as far as she could and gently tugged her clit with her other hand, simulating his mouth's careful suction. Pleasure curled up her spine and she sent it across their telepathic link.

He gasped, shuddering violently as her release triggered his. Energy flowed back across their link intensifying her sensations and rejuvenating her being. Strength swept through her, pulsating and alive. He withdrew from the meld as his orgasm ended and she felt a pang of sadness. For one blissful moment they had been joined, united, whole.

She stretched out on her side, confused by her reaction. She had exchanged energy countless times before. Why did this surly human make her feel complete?

He wiped up the mess he'd made and she hid her smile. There were advantages to being female. "Thank you," she said when he sat down again. "I know this isn't easy for you."

"I've always enjoyed foreplay. This is just a bit extreme." He swept her body with a lingering gaze before he asked, "Are you ready to try to solidify again?"

She sat and swung her legs over the side of the bunk. "Each attempt expends a lot of energy. I think it's best if we have one more adventure first."

"Anything that doesn't involve masturbation is fine by me."

She smiled. "I can help you relive a memory that was particularly pleasurable or we can share one of my memories." His gaze narrowed and their emotional link constricted until she could barely sense him. Why was he troubled by the suggestion? "I'm not trying to embarrass you. Images are easier to control if they already exist. When I have to construct them, it takes more energy."

"I understand." His tone became stiff and emotionless. "Let's play in your mind. My memories aren't worth revisiting." A spike of resentment emphasized his point.

If she pressed him for details right now, he might well shut down entirely. She knew his past had been unpleasant, almost assuredly abusive. Why else would he have retreated into an emotionless void?

"My existence has spanned many of your lifetimes and has taken on different forms. Would you rather experience something sweet and tender or — "

"Extreme. Don't we need to generate intensity?"

"Tenderness can be just as intense as animal lust."

His gaze lowered to her breasts. "I'm not in the mood for tenderness."

She suspected tenderness was exactly what he needed, but she wasn't going to argue the point. A smile curved her lips as she accessed a particular memory and reached for Rage's mind. It would be far more effective to demonstrate.

Rage immerged from the light with a disconcerted gasp. A rush of information inundated his mind. He was the ruler of this primitive planet, a barbarian who controlled through brutality and fear. Rage was aware of the king's thoughts and perspectives, while the king was oblivious to him.

Torchlight illuminated the small courtyard in which Rage sat. A swath of starry sky was framed by tall palm trees. Naked couples lounged in the shadows, indulging in all manner of carnal delights. Their gleaming skin and breathless sighs aroused the king as he reclined on his cushions and enjoyed the uninhibited display.

A particularly creative group came into view. A man lay on his back with one woman straddling his face, enjoying the attention of his mouth, while a second eagerly impaled herself on his hard cock. The second woman's sharp cries were what drew his attention. She squeezed her own breasts and slammed down over him again and again, obviously lost to everything but physical gratification.

Rage could feel the balmy night breeze wafting across his naked chest. Long dark hair spilled onto his shoulders, though he had been shaving his head for years. His cock hardened, tenting the simple garment secured around his hips. It was odd, yet incredibly evocative to steal a glimpse into someone else's life.

An angry shout drew his attention to the archway leading to his palace and anticipation twisted through his groin. *Tazney.* No one else infuriated like Tazney. No one else aroused like his little firebrand. He had granted her time, hoping she would accept the inevitability of their joining. She had only grown more determined to resist him. Well, her stubbornness ended tonight. She would learn in no uncertain terms what it meant to be given to a king.

Rage's mind buzzed with thoughts and realizations. He understood the king's fascination. Who wouldn't be attracted to Tazney?

The king shifted against the cushions as his guards dragged her into the courtyard. If she hadn't warned him that she utilized many forms, Rage might not have recognized her as the same entity. This Tazney was petite, with large dark eyes and golden hair that barely reached her shoulders.

"Why am I here?" the new Tazney demanded.

"You know why you're here." He pulled a plump grape off a nearby tray and tossed it into his mouth. "You were given to me as part of a peace treaty, yet you refuse to share my bed."

"How can my body be part of a negotiation when I am not included in the—"

"That is a question for your father, not me. He agreed to my terms."

"Then fuck my father!"

Rage braced himself for the fury he expected to feel. Any ruler would be incensed by such belligerence. Instead the king paused and then threw back his head and laughed. "If you continue to be so amusing, I might never give you back." He nodded toward a table-like contraption Rage hadn't noticed before. "Prepare her."

Tazney writhed and kicked, twisted and screamed. The guards ignored it all. Across their telepathic link, she shared the emotions driving her frenzy. Her fear was genuine, but it wasn't rape she feared. This was some sort of test. She was required to remain in this form or be shamed by her weakness. Rage didn't understand the details. Her emotions were too complex, but her determination in the face of her fear only made him admire her more.

And threaded through her fear was a tantalizing ripple of arousal. Their strong hands and unyielding purpose turned her on in a way she hadn't anticipated. She was aching to be dominated by the king, her body craved his aggression.

Rage tried to slow the exchange, but Tazney didn't seem to notice. She was lost in the memory, overcome by what she knew would follow. Tension intensified until Rage could hardly breathe. Did she realize how well he related to this scenario, how long he'd ached to experience his lover's complete surrender?

The guards stripped her and lifted her to the table, pushing her legs through padded loops that spread her thighs and kept her knees bent. Then they bound her wrists and ankles in stout cuffs and stepped back to survey the result.

"You said you wouldn't rape me." She panted, her small breasts quivering with each ragged breath.

The king stood and approached her, circling her slowly, savoring the view from every angle. Torchlight gleamed off her skin and gilded her hair. Her gaze followed his movements, bright with desire and uncertainty.

"I have never forced myself on a woman and I don't intend to start with you." He trailed his fingertip from the pulse pounding in the base of her throat, down between her breasts and circled her navel. "Before the sun lights this courtyard you will beg for my cock."

A sharp, nervous laugh burst from Tazney. "I think not."

He unfastened his garment and showed her the long, thick shaft he was promising her. "This will fill you and you will scream as you find release."

"If the sun rises and I haven't begged for that splendid example of male virility, will you let me go?"

"Of course not." He moved between her wide spread legs and grinned. "We'll simply begin again at dusk tomorrow. I will fuck you, Tazney. Your stubbornness serves no purpose." Before she could argue further, he traced her slit with the head of his cock.

Rage felt the silken heat of her folds surround him, yet he also felt the gentle pressure of the king's cock against her body. Extraordinary. As if all that weren't stimulating enough, the guards joined the play, one on either side of the table. They stroked her arms and caressed her breasts, perfectly mirroring each other.

She tossed her head and arched her back. Rage wasn't sure if she was trying to avoid their skilled fingers or move closer to their teasing touch. They rolled her nipples, working them into hard little points before they lowered their heads and suckled her together with slow, deep pulls.

The king chuckled. "You like that, little firebrand. See how your cream flows now." He continued his simple slide, up and down, up and down, rubbing her clit at the top of each stroke.

"Make them stop," she cried, her frustration rolling across their link and slamming into Rage. "I can't…"

"You can't bear the emptiness?" He parted her folds with his thumbs, letting the night wind tease the very heart of her need. "Are you ready to feel real pleasure? Just say please. That one word will end this foolishness."

Her pride demanded she fight, while her body had already surrendered. Rage understood the battle far better than she realized. Her core throbbed, her nipples ached and spasms of tension gripped her abdomen. She whimpered, tilting her hips in silent demand.

The king stepped back. "Not good enough." He signaled his guards to stop, his gaze boring into hers. "Ask me now or you'll find out why they call me a barbarian. I can do things to your body no civilized woman should enjoy." He paused for a provocative smile. "And I can make you crave every one of them."

Tazney focused, controlling the concentration of the energy stream. She hadn't expected the memory to be this intense. These events had occurred so long ago. Still, sharing it with Rage was making it seem new again. Spread before Chaz Tin, she had never felt more alive, or more helpless. Rage had wanted animal lust and this could be described no other way.

Apparently Rage had never been with a lover capable of transmitting sensations before. The multidimensional aspect of this exchange fascinated him. Not wanting to distract him from the scene, Tazney kept her thoughts carefully shielded.

"How could you be any more barbaric?" her past self sneered at Chaz Tin.

"That sounds like a challenge." With an abrupt hand motion, he set his guards in motion. They unfastened her cuffs from the table without releasing her from the restraints. One guard lifted her into his arms, while the other made several adjustments to the table.

Struggling against them was useless. They were fast and incredibly strong. In a matter of minutes, they stood her on the ground and attached her ankle cuffs to the table legs. Her arms were raised overhead and secured to a crossbar that stretched her onto her toes, tilting her hips forward. One of the guards knelt in front of her and looked to the king for further instructions.

Tazney looked at Chaz Tin as well. Would she be whipped for her insolence? She didn't quite understand his threat. Rage felt her uncertainly and responded with an immediate wave of reassurance. She accepted the warmth with a wistful sigh. He would be a fierce protector, of that she had no doubt. But she didn't need protection. She needed energy. Refocusing the memory feed, she continued.

"I don't think she's a virgin, but be careful until you're sure." Chaz Tin looked into her eyes before he added, "You will watch all of the pleasures awaiting an eager slave, but you will know only the burning hunger of the unwilling."

The guard parted her folds with his thumbs and gently circled her opening. She bit her lip to keep from crying out. They had teased her so close to orgasm before, the embers fanned to flame with hardly any encouragement.

Chaz Tin selected a black-haired woman and positioned her in front of Tazney, then he motioned to the other guard. They kissed her and stroked her breasts, teased her nipples and caressed her belly. Tazney closed her eyes, but the guard in front of her pinched her clit until she opened them again. The other woman arched and moaned, kissing Chaz Tin and then her guard with equal enthusiasm.

An eager slave receives pleasure. The guard in front of her slipped his middle finger into her aching passage and Tazney moaned, tightening her inner muscles in greedy response.

He shook his head. "Too late for that tonight. I can't let you come."

She closed her eyes as he lowered his head and circled her clit with his tongue. If she held perfectly still, maybe he wouldn't realize —

I can feel your pleasure, silly firebrand. We are not as barbaric as you think.

With that simple statement she knew she was doomed, at least until the following day. He licked her folds and suckled her clit as he slowly pumped his finger in and out of her slick pussy. Each time she felt the tingling tension begin to gather low in her abdomen, he stopped until the sensations receded.

The black-haired slave, on the other hand, cried out again and again as Chaz Tin and the other guard took turns pleasuring her.

Tazney's guard used his mouth with ruthless skill. When her core became too eager for his finger, he worked her cream into the seam between her bottom cheeks and circled her tightly puckered hole.

She felt Rage resist the memory. Was he responding to the rise in her anxiety or was there something about anal sex that he found particularly arousing? She was too far gone to consider it at more length.

"Stop it!" she gasped, trying to twist away from this new invasion.

She glanced at Chaz Tin and gasped again. They must be communicating telepathically. This was all choreographed to torment her.

The woman straddled the other guard's face, while she arched over his body. He was devouring her pussy while she slid his cock in and out of her mouth. For a long moment Tazney just watched, transfixed by the carnal beauty. The guard gripped her hips, his face moving back and forth faster and faster.

Chaz Tin scooped a glob of something shiny out of a nearby bowl and smeared it over his cock. She knew men used the anal passage for sex, but why would a man take a woman that way? He knelt behind the slave and pushed his finger into her ass.

The guard in front of Tazney pushed inside her body at exactly the same instant. She gasped and shuddered, but the stimulation had just begun. Chaz Tin positioned himself against the slave girl as the guard closed his lips around Tazney's clit. She watched Chaz Tin's cock sink into the other woman as the guard dragged his finger nearly out. Her core contracted painfully.

I don't want that. You can't make me want that! She had no idea who she was trying to convince. The guard in front of her didn't move his finger once he got it lodged inside her again. It was a punishing reminder of all she was depriving herself. He licked her clit whenever she started to relax and nipped her if she closed her eyes.

Chaz Tin moved strong and steady inside the slave girl's willing body, while Tazney ached, empty and unfulfilled. The guard came first. He arched into the slave girl's mouth and shuddered beneath her. She stayed with him until the last tremor passed, then he crawled out from under her.

The guard in front of Tazney moved aside, leaving her bound and alone.

After that there were no distractions. The barbarian king fucked his surrogate slave. Tazney watched his muscles flex and his savage features strain. Tears ran unchecked down her cheeks, but their gazes never faltered.

She'd expected Rage to lose himself completely in Chaz Tin, but she sensed him there, worrying about her, wanting her with an intensity that transcended anything Chaz Tin had ever felt for her. Chaz Tin's eyes turned blue and Tazney gasped.

How was this possible? He shoved the slave girl into the waiting arms of his guards and stalked toward Tazney. She wrapped her hands around the chains extending from her wrist cuffs. Chaz Tin's features hadn't changed, but this was Rage, only Rage.

As he knelt to unfasten her ankle restraints, he pressed his face again the juncture of her thighs and inhaled deeply. A primitive thrill raced up her spine. Many species recognized their mates by scent. She didn't know what to expect. This wasn't how it had happened before.

Without a word he hooked her legs over his brawny arms and stood. She tightened her hold on the chains as the position pulled on her shoulders. Then he thrust into her, his cock stretched her so suddenly she threw back her head and screamed.

"Easy, love. I won't hurt you."

She dragged her muddled gaze back to his face. "More! I need more."

Freed by her frantic admission, he supported her weight with his arms and pounded into her. She tightened her inner muscles, reveling in the fullness and the demand. Each of his forceful thrusts rocked her body, jostled her breasts and ground his shaft against her swollen clit.

She came hard, her body gripping his cock with a long series of ripples. He kept right on going. His fingers dug into her ass as he adjusted the angle of each thrust. Harder, deeper, he claimed her with savage aggression.

"I never want to stop." The words sounded strangled as if he forced them out between clenched teeth.

Another orgasm claimed her and then another. His frenzy intoxicated her, decades of suppressed desire released in an intoxicating rush. Rage finally began to slow. Shifting her legs to his waist, he pressed her against his chest and covered her lips with his.

His tongue moved in her mouth, the same long, steady strokes that his cock had taken up. Tazney closed her eyes, picturing his lean features and shaved head.

Come again and you'll take me with you.

She squeezed him tightly and tilted her hips, increasing the pressure on her clit. Her last orgasm was gentle, comforting. Gathering the sweet, tingling warmth, she channeled it across the link to Rage.

His cock bucked and throbbed inside her and energy burst forth again and again. She absorbed it with greedy abandon. Even as the exchange overwhelmed her senses, a bittersweet temptation echoed through her mind. *Take me with you...*

Chapter Three

ෆ

Unable to bear the emotional tempest any longer, Rage fought the images flooding his mind until Tazney ended the transmission.

"What's the matter?" The patient calm in her tone only added to his agitation.

"Just get the fuck out of my head!" He shot to his feet and stomped across the room. Unfortunately the cabin was so bloody small it only took four steps. "I don't want to watch some barbarian king enjoy what I'm denied." Her warm hand touched his arm and he spun to face her. Fingers trembling, he stretched out his hand and touched her shoulder. Warm, soft, solid. "How?"

"I told you it was just a matter of —"

He pulled her against his chest and buried his face in her hair. If this was all a delusion, he honestly didn't care. He cupped her butt with one hand and pushed his fingers into her hair, making a loose fist. He had to kiss her just once before reality returned.

Tilting her head back, he found her lips with his, carefully at first, then with ravenous fervor. Real. He was holding, kissing a real woman, and she was kissing him back! Their lips slid, clung, nibbled and slid some more. He traced her lower lip for a long time before venturing into her mouth. Her tongue curled around his and he was lost. He explored, drawing her sweet scent into his lungs and imprinting her taste on his brain.

Long minutes later, he separated their mouths. His hands lingered against her skin, partly because he couldn't get enough of her softness and partly because he feared she'd disintegrate.

She looped her arms around his neck, rubbing her nipples against his chest. "How did you do that?"

He laughed. "You've never been kissed before?"

"You took control of the memory transmission. Chaz Tin didn't take me until the following night and even then that's not how it happened."

"I was tired of watching." He swept her into his arms and carried her to his narrow bunk, sitting down with her soft body cradled against his chest. "And now I'm tired of talking." He cupped one of her breasts and gazed into her eyes.

"I just need to know if you did it intentionally. It's not something most humans can do."

"Why does it matter?"

"It might be important."

He blew out a ragged sigh. "Yes. I intentionally took control of the transmission. The Kytinians used a form of telepathic torture that... The only way to combat it was to learn to control the images they were forcing on you, to reshape them into something less horrific." Laying her back across the bunk, he left her legs arched over his lap. "Can we do this for real now? I'm *really* tired of mind fucking."

He reached for her thigh, but she caught his wrist then touched his contract collar with her index finger. "What is this? You told me to get rid of mine right after I first appeared."

"You've been in my mind, Tazney. You must know the kind of life I've lived. Why do you need to hear it?" Her hair fanned out creating a silken backdrop for her ivory skin. He looked everywhere but at her perceptive gaze. He'd been hard and aching since he encountered her on the scrapper. Now that he could touch her, she wanted to talk?

"Touch me. Just talk to me too. I need to understand more about you."

"Why?" He pulled her arms above her head and held them there with one hand as frustration twisted through him. "I'm nothing to you. A power source. As soon as you're strong enough you'll..."

"Leave?"

"Yes!" he snapped, infuriated by the admission. "You'll return to your people and I'll be left here with the Linusians."

"I'm not sure what you want me to do."

"But you expect me to help you." He shoved against the bed and sat, pressing his back against the cold alloy wall. He'd spent so many nights with his back pressed against this wall, wishing he was somewhere else, *anywhere* else.

She sat as well and folded her legs in front of her. Drawing her hair over her shoulders, she covered her breasts. "You'll receive sexual gratification for the energy. That was our agreement. Beyond that I can't promise you anything." Her voice broke as if she was bothered by the admission. "I'm not unfamiliar with your culture. This sort of pleasure has been used as a commodity since time began."

"*My* culture?" He scoffed. "Are you talking about humans, scavengers or contract laborers?"

"I was speaking of humans." She drew her legs up toward her chest and wrapped her arms around her knees. "Was I wrong in concluding that you are descended from one of Earth's outposts?"

"I have scattered memories of my mother. She taught me how to find food and where to hide during Kytinian raids." A gentle smile and a hushed, urgent voice. Regardless of how hard he tried, memories of his mother remained hazy and jumbled.

"Who are the Kytinians?"

"They united the warring forces across this section of the galaxy and created a confederation so powerful governments either bow to their will or are obliterated."

"I take it humans refused to bow."

He could feel her presence in his mind. Why didn't she just extract the information she wanted and leave him alone? He rested his head against the wall and closed his eyes. The hate had festered for so long. Perhaps it was time to release some of the pressure.

Tazney heard his thoughts and decided to accept the invitation. She crawled onto his lap, smiling when his eyes opened wide. "The memory exchange can flow in either direction. Do you trust me to—how did you put it—play in your mind?"

"If I can play with your body, you can play with my mind." He cupped her breast with one hand and her bottom with the other.

"Kiss me," she whispered. "It helps me concentrate." Actually it helped distract him from how deeply she was delving, but he didn't seem to mind.

Images and information inundated her being. Year after bleak, hopeless year of slavery and abuse. He'd been captured by the Kytinians when he was little more than a child, treated with contempt and brutality.

His fingers tightened on her nipple sending a short spike of pain into her chest. She moved on. He was older now, a tall lanky lad, filled with resentment and hatred. Though there were females among the slaves, they were greatly outnumbered by the men.

Tazney tried to gentle their kiss, to show him compassion and tenderness. His mind remained open, but he drew her arms behind her back. "Go on," he growled and lowered his mouth to one of her breasts.

He punished her with pleasure-pain while she continued her search for understanding. If she was going to consider transforming him, she had to be certain of his character. His mental abilities increased their chances of success. Still she had to be certain he was worthy of the change. Once transformed he would be virtually immortal.

After beating a man into submission, Rage won the right to fuck his first woman. It was a shocking reality, but it was the world in which he lived. The woman lay beneath him sobbing, so he accepted defeat and sent her away. Even in his violent world, abstinence was better than rape.

Tears escaped the corners of Tazney's eyes as she scanned through more of the same. Beatings and starvation, isolation and want. Stromn had bought him from the Kytinians. Other than the lack of physical abuse it was hard to tell the difference between Linusian contract labor and Kytinian slavery.

His hand moved up her thigh and she opened for him, eager to comfort him in any way she could. So much pain. He parted her folds and slipped two fingers into her core, rubbing her clit with his thumb.

His mouth returned to her face and he stiffened. "Why are you crying?"

"No one should have to endure—"

He jerked his hand back and glared at her. "I don't want your pity."

"I don't pity you. I care about you." If only she could offer him hope, a way of escaping this dreadful existence. She knew others had transformed humans, but she was barely recovered. "How long have you served Stromn?"

"There are three years left on my contract."

Three years before he would know freedom for the first time in his life. She traced his lips with his fingertips, then guided one of his hands to her breast. "Tell me about Letto."

"Why are these things important to you?" He tried to snatch his hand away but she covered his fingers with hers. "Didn't you see it all in my head?"

"I've stolen enough from your memory. Thoughts surrounding Letto seemed to be pleasant. I didn't think you'd mind." Actually it was a test. She needed to see how truthful he'd be and the small deception made her feel guilty as hell.

"Letto is the closest thing to a friend I've ever known." He glanced away, then reinforced his calm with a deep breath. "His grandmother was human, so they stuck us together. The rest of the crew ignores me, but they torment him."

She took his face between her hands and looked into his eyes. "If you and Letto have found comfort in each other's arms, there is no shame in that. In my natural form I am pure energy. It is only when I take on form that gender becomes an issue. I have found through past experience that I prefer men to women, but I have shared physical pleasures with females."

"It's not that simple." After a pause, he went on, "Linusians only mate with females when they're ready to reproduce. They prefer spending time and finding pleasure with other males. Letto is no exception."

"And as his cabin mate, you had no choice but to watch Letto with his lover or lovers?" She moved her hands to his shoulders, amazed by the tension bunched in his muscles. Why did he find the subject so uncomfortable? She'd already told him she wasn't bothered by the concept of men sharing pleasure with each other.

"I tried to schedule sessions in the sensory stimulation booths whenever Letto was going to have visitors, but he likes to fuck. If I stood in the hall or slept in the shuttle bay every time he felt the need to rut, I'd never see the inside of this cabin." He pressed a kiss against her temple.

"Go on. I promise you won't shock me." His lips teased her skin and he combed his fingers through her hair, luring her away from the conversation.

"I walked in on Letto and Stromn. Letto was struggling and I reacted without thinking. I dragged Stromn off Letto and punched the captain in the jaw."

"You punched Stromn in the face?" She rocked back on her heels and covered her smile with her hand, afraid her amusement would annoy him. This was the second time she'd seen evidence of his tattered nobility.

"Stromn came after me, but Letto grabbed him from behind. I was so confused by then I didn't know what the hell was going on."

"Stromn likes to subdue his partners?"

"I don't know how Letto found out, but Stromn didn't want anyone else to know. A captain can have any partner he wants. It's considered an honor to share your body with a person of power. Maybe that's how it started. Stromn got tired of everyone literally prostrating themselves before him. Letto made it challenging again."

"That makes sense." He stroked her cheek with the back of his fingers and she waited for the rest of the story.

"Stromn told me to sit on my bunk and keep my mouth shut. I thought I knew what to expect. They were more or less fucking when I walked in and it wasn't anything I hadn't seen before. But this was different. Stromn wasn't just arousing Letto, he was arousing me. Everything he did, everything he made Letto do was designed to make me lose control."

"What did you do?" She felt foolish asking, but there were several possible outcomes.

"I'd rather show you." He framed her face with his hands as he leaned in close. "I think I need to share this with you." Then his mouth sealed over hers, not so much a kiss as an invitation.

Rage was open and waiting. Tazney was humbled by his trust. After enjoying the warmth of his embrace for a moment, she eased into his mind.

The cabin dimmed for a moment, then the Linusians appeared. Tall, muscular Stromn, fierce-eyed, yet controlled. He stood at an angle so Rage could admire every contour and ripple of his sculpted physique. Though their features and coloring were far different from humans, they had fantastic bodies.

Letto stood beside Stromn. The younger man had his hands clasped behind his head and Stromn stroked his cock with one hand and Letto's with the other. Letto's eyes were closed, his features tense with pleasure as his hips rocked to the rhythm of Stromn's fist.

Rage tried not to watch. This was just Linusian sex. He'd seen it hundreds of times before. Stromn turned and used both hands to arouse the younger man. Letto's face darkened, his lips parted and he panted. He was literally trembling. Fascinated by the intensity of Letto's reaction, Rage glanced at Stromn's face. The captain watched Letto carefully, possessive pride glowing in his dark eyes.

Stromn pushed Letto to his knees and rubbed the head of his cock against the younger man's lips. "Suck me hard."

The whispered command sent a hot, melting sensation sinking through Rage. His cock had been more or less hard since he'd walked in on the lovers. The treacherous appendage throbbed with renewed demand. They were both men and they weren't human. How could he be turned on by this?

Letto wet his lips and sucked on the head of Stromn's cock, pulling until his cheeks drew in. Stromn groaned and caressed Letto's hairless scalp, the motion oddly tender. "My pet has the most talented mouth in the confederation, *human*. I challenge you to prove me wrong."

Rage's gaze flew to Stromn's face. The captain's skin was nearly as flushed as Letto's. How did he respond to this without insulting the captain? "No challenge is necessary, sir. I can see that he's quite skilled."

Stromn growled and pulled his cock out of Letto's mouth. "You didn't even hear my challenge."

"Sir, I'm human." Rage spoke each word with careful emphasis. "Our ways are not your ways."

"What would you know of human ways?" Stromn strode across the cabin and stood before Rage fists planted on his lean hips. Savage and spectacular in his nudity, he reached down and boldly stroked the bulge in the front of Rage's pants. "I've wanted to feel you writhing beneath me since I first looked into your eyes. My challenge is simple. Allow Letto to suck your cock. If he can't make you come in five minutes, you have my protection until your contract ends. But if you lose control, you willingly kneel before me and offer me your ass."

"I don't have sex with men."

Stromn grabbed his face and sneered into his eyes. "It is my right as captain to fuck every member of this crew. Contract laborers are usually passed from man to man. It is only my desire for you that has kept your precious asshole safe."

Rage knew Stromn's claim was true. He'd felt lustful gazes following him and wondered what held back numerous attacks. Letto often flirted as well, drawing unwanted attention away from Rage. On any other Linusian ship he would have been ship's whore.

"All right," he forced the words out. He could endure anything for five minutes.

Letto knelt on the floor in front of Rage and offered him a playful grin. "Relax. This won't hurt a bit."

Tazney felt Rage's emotions wash over her, excitement, dread, fear and uncertainty. It had been so long since another person touched him in a sexual way he wasn't sure he could control himself for five short minutes and he really didn't want Stromn to fuck him.

Letto unfastened Rage's uniform pants and took out his cock. "Very nice." Letto closed his fingers around the shaft and Rage groaned.

Digging his fingers into the pad on his bunk until his knuckles turned white, Rage tried to ignore Letto's warm tongue and firm lips. The interior of his mouth was hot and silken just like a woman's, just like a *human* woman's. His cock pulsed and his balls tingled. He was in serious trouble here.

Rage shook his head and clenched his teeth. "Please, sir. I don't want you to fuck me." His voice was harsh and breathless. He felt desperate, half-crazed.

Stromn growled and knelt behind Letto. "Then watch me, Rage. Look into my eyes and surrender a bit of that human pride."

After smearing lube on his massive cock, Stromn glanced up to make sure Rage was watching. Letto continued to slide his mouth up and down the aching length of Rage's cock while Stromn positioned himself behind Letto.

Rage stopped resisting the inevitable pleasure and moved his legs farther apart. Tazney understood his struggle. This was not that different from what she had experienced with Chaz Tin.

Letto raised his ass, pushing out as his lover shoved in. Transfixed by the graphic spectacle, Rage watched the thick column of flesh disappear into the slender Linusian, then slowly emerge again. Letto shivered as Stromn pulled out then gasped when he rammed deep again.

"Look at me," Stromn snapped.

Rage raised his gaze and Stromn moved in earnest, thrusting into his lover while Letto sucked Rage fast and hard. With their gazes boring into each other and their bodies locked in sexual combat, Stromn used Letto to fuck Rage.

They came in a sudden burst of pleasure that knocked Tazney out of the meld. She rocked back on her knees, shocked by the furious explosion of sensations. Her core fluttered and she blinked, dazed by the stark, masculine perspective on sex. Energy flowed into her, darker and richer than ever before.

"Wow," she whispered, then blew out a shaky breath.

"It's never happened again, but I know they'd both love to include me in their little wrestling matches." He turned his head and kissed the palm of her hand. "Now you know everything."

Telling her about Letto and Stromn had left Rage feeling liberated and eager to move on. He'd felt more in the past few hours than he could ever remember having felt. He helped her to her feet, while he remained on the edge of the bunk. Gathering her hair at the nape of her neck, he dragged the entire mass behind her back and bared her breasts to his ravenous gaze.

He sucked her nipple into his mouth and she smiled. He'd had enough of talking, of sharing memories. Tazney was tangible and willing and he intended to savor every moment they had left.

She splayed her fingers against the back of his head and moved her legs apart. No pretense, no demure, she needed this joining as much as he craved the physical connection.

Moving from one breast to the other, he licked and suckled, nibbled and caressed. She arched her back, pressing deeper into his mouth. Each time he closed his teeth around a tender crest she gasped and a shiver shook her body. Even in reality she liked a little edge to her pleasure. He pushed the sensations higher, built the intensity. He circled her waist with one arm as he continued to suckle her breasts. Soft, warm, woman, he would never tire of touching her.

She teased the head of his cock with her fingertips, then closed her fist around his throbbing shaft. He groaned. Her hand left his shaft and he clenched his teeth to keep from crying out. He needed to lift her onto his lap and impale her with one firm thrust, but he wanted to prolong the pleasure as long as humanly possible. All their shared fantasies had left him ravenous for the hot slap of flesh against flesh and the unmistakable smell of passion.

Splaying her fingers against the back of his head, she kissed him and let her thoughts flow into his mind. *We can take as long as we like. If you come too fast the first time, we'll just do it again.*

The thought made him tremble as she sank to her knees. "Is that all right with you?" She licked her lips and smiled.

He managed one stiff nod. Tension rippled through his abdomen. He could relax and enjoy this. She wasn't going anywhere — at least not yet.

She touched him with the tip of her tongue, keeping her gaze locked with his. Her tongue circled his cock, laving the flared head and tracing the distinct ridge over and over until he clenched his ass cheeks. The urge to thrust into her mouth was nearly overwhelming. She dragged her tongue down one side and up the other, working her way around his entire width. Only then did she close her lips around him and slowly suck him inside. Her head bobbed as she moved her snug mouth up and down his throbbing length. Hot. Her mouth was incredibly hot.

Rage imaged Stromn standing across the room, leering at him as Letto eagerly sucked his cock. Replacing her mouth with the firm grip of her hand, Tazney looked up. "A rather vivid image just flashed across our link. I'm not intentionally invading your privacy."

Rage chuckled. "Privacy seems a rather trivial concern when my cock is in your mouth."

"Not to me." Her tone was soft and sincere. "I only want you to share those portions of yourself you're comfortable sharing and nothing more."

Her hand kept up its steady rhythm, so Rage indulged her curiosity. "Sucking and fucking, that's all they did. It became routine after a while—except for that night with Stromn."

She only missed one beat after his admission. "Are you attracted to him? Do you wish he had taken you that night?"

He caught her wrist and waited until she stopped. "Not in the way you mean. I was fascinated by his abilities, but I wanted to *be* him. I didn't want to be with him. I wanted to know how to touch a lover so skillfully that she would surrender everything. That's why I took over for your barbarian king. You were exactly what I'd dreamt of all my life and I didn't want to share you with him."

She smiled, her gaze warm and luminous. "You might have been using his body, but Chaz Tin never excited me like that."

"Well, let's see if I can do even better with my own." He lifted her in his arms and placed her on his bunk. She parted her thighs and bent her knees, making room for him to join her. He knelt there, mesmerized by her uninhibited beauty.

"You are unbelievable." His husky tone revealed as much about his desire as their telepathic link. He brushed his fingers from her knee to the crease where her thigh met her pelvis. Her hips rolled, obviously wanting more.

With just the tip of his index finger he traced her feminine slit. Moist heat radiated from her core, drawing his attention like a beacon. Her throaty little sounds grew louder as he circled her entrance. Did she want him inside her as badly as he needed the embrace of her tight cunt?

"Yes," she responded to his thought. "I ache to have you there."

"Soon." Holding her open from above, he circled her clit with his tongue. She angled her hips and tossed her head, panting helplessly. Her ragged breaths made her breasts quiver and her taste thrilled him, the salty-sweet essence of woman.

He pushed two fingers into her passage and she arched clear off the bunk. Her inner muscles fluttered with the first wave of her orgasm, but he wasn't satisfied. He needed more, *they* needed more. It simply couldn't end like this.

Tazney cried out as Rage drove his tongue deep into her core. His lips covered her mound as he pushed in again and again. She could feel his hunger, the demand in his spirit, his raw, aching need.

She came hard, trembling against his lips. He only growled and lifted one of her legs to his shoulder. Confused by the urgency building within him, she sent a soothing current along their telepathic link.

His mouth gentled, lingering over her clit for a moment before he kissed his way up her body. She clutched his shoulders as he positioned himself at her entrance. Energy sizzled around them, making her skin tingle and her nipples throb.

He eased in just a bit, then stopped. "Promise me," he whispered.

What? She was too distracted by the teasing promise of his cock head to remember to speak.

"If the only way for you to make it home is to destroy me, promise me you'll do it. I want to set you free." Then he opened to her as she opened to him. His shaft pushed into her body and she penetrated his mind. Her inner muscles relaxed, accepting his thick length as he took her deeper into his soul.

She gasped, amazed by his uninhibited acceptance. Beyond the fury, beneath the numbing indifference burned compassion and tenderness. She brought his mouth down to hers, filling her lungs with his breath before she thrust her tongue past his lips. Sharing, they moved and arched ever closer.

She wrapped her legs around his waist, her knees hugging his ribs. His hands never stopped moving. He caressed her breasts, her sides, her legs. He wanted her to make it home. She could sense his determination to give her what she needed to leave his dismal world.

Could she do it? Was she strong enough? Others had succeeded, but others were far more experienced. She couldn't ignore his willingness to sacrifice himself for her or the connection she sensed to him.

Heat erupted, shooting through her and passing to him. Rage cried out, but he didn't stop. He thrust harder and drove deeper, offering himself without reservation.

"More," she gasped. Intensity, momentum, they couldn't allow these sensations to ease. Filling his mind with graphic images, she showed him what they needed. He didn't hesitate or question the urgency shuddering through her spirit.

Wrapping his arms around her back, he pulled her up off the bunk, obviously loath to separate their bodies. "Are you sure?" The tender concern in his tone filled her with determination. She could not, *would not* leave him behind.

"I want to do this for you." He didn't understand what she was trying to accomplish. She needed him entirely focused on their pleasure. She slipped off the bunk as he frantically searched in a recessed compartment and found a packet of lube.

When he turned back around she was standing as she had seen Letto stand, legs spread, arms raised, hands clasped behind her head. Emotions sizzled across their link, lust, affection and possessiveness. He paused, chest heaving, eyes blazing with passion and tenderness.

"I don't think I can be gentle," he warned.

"I don't want you to be."

He took control and she reveled in his hunger, thrilled by his obvious need. Guiding her arms down and back, he caught her wrists at the small of her back and held them there with one hand. His mouth swooped down to claim hers in a savage kiss, while his other hand squeezed her breasts and rolled her nipples.

With one well aimed thrust, he pushed his cock between her swollen folds, rubbing against her clit, yet refusing to fill her. She squirmed, desperate to have him inside her again. Raising one leg to his hip, she tried to end his teasing slide. They couldn't slow down. They had to build the flames higher.

"Mine," he whispered against her lips. "Mine to do with as I wish." Turning her to face the bunk, he bent her forward and placed her hands on the pad.

A thrill shot through her. Yes! She needed his aggression. He didn't realize how much. His fingers stroked her, working her cream up and into her tight, puckered hole. A pause followed and she glanced over her shoulder. He opened the packet of lube and smeared it over his cock. She swallowed hard, excited yet unnerved. Rage was big and wildly aroused.

"If it hurts too much, I'll stop."

She quickly turned to hide her smile. He hadn't said "if it hurts I'll stop". They both knew there was no way to avoid the pain entirely. In truth she needed that too. Anticipation mixed with desire. Her pussy fluttered and tension twisted through her abdomen. He pulled her ass cheeks apart and positioned himself against her anus. She took a deep breath and arched her back.

Expecting a violent thrust, she moaned when he only pushed in far enough to seat the head of his cock. She needed to be ravished, to feel him lose control. He reached around and found her clit with his middle finger, circling the swollen nub.

"We'll take all the time you need," he whispered above her ear. "Relax and let your body accept me."

"I want this. We both need it."

He continued the tight, fast circles around her clit with one hand and stroked her breasts with the other. Mounted on the head of his cock, she could barely breathe. His arousal poured across their link, sweeping away the momentary sting.

Slowly he pushed deeper and deeper still, stretching her, filling her until she cried out and rocked back, driving herself onto his hardened length. His patience was almost cruel. She needed him to move, to force the pleasure higher and surround her with energy.

"Easy. I won't hurt—"

"Just move! It must be *now*." Grasping her hips, he pulled nearly out, then thrust deep. "Yes! Don't stop moving."

He quickly found the rhythm, hard steady drives that ricocheted through her entire body. She pushed back against him and reached into him, amazed by the bounty awaiting her there. She hadn't expected him to be this selfless, hadn't realized she'd be able to access him so completely. Taking all he offered, she inundated herself with his energy, building her strength and augmenting her control.

Light burst around them, disintegrating the alloy walls. She couldn't let him realize what she was attempting. If she failed, she would gently give him peace.

He stiffened. *Don't stop moving.* She sent a rush of urgency along with the thought. *Feel me. Think only of me.*

His emotions focused on her. His body resumed its strong, steady rhythm. She reached for him with her body and her mind, blending their beings into one.

Now let your soul kiss mine. Don't think, just let it happen.

They melded and then transformed. He flowed into her as she disintegrated their corporeal bodies, leaving only energy.

Passion exploded in dazzling bursts, gradually fading into gentle swells of peace. Tazney hung suspended, scanning, searching. Had she done it?

How is this possible? His awe and elation helped her identify where he ended and she began. With the greatest of care, she eased their souls apart. They were surrounded by glittering colors and welcoming warmth.

There was no way I would accept my happiness at the cost of yours, she told him emphatically. *We've both been alone too long.*

He flowed through her, infusing her with tenderness and gratitude. *It would have been a fair exchange for even one of your soul kisses.*

Hope shimmered all around them. *I have so much to show you.*

Then, lead the way, my love. Lead the way!

They sped beyond the physical dimension toward freedom and toward home.

Also by Aubrey Ross

ʂ

About the Author

෨

Aubrey Ross writes an eclectic assortment of erotic fiction. From power struggles between futuristic clans, to adventurous mystic guardians, her stories are filled with passion and imagination. Some of her recent awards include an EPPIE finalist, two Passionate Plume finalists, and a CAPA Nomination from the Romance Studio.

With a pampered cat curled on the corner of her desk, Aubrey dreams up fascinating words and larger than life adventures—and wouldn't have it any other way!

Aubrey welcomes comments from readers. You can find her website and email address on her author bio page at www.ellorascave.com.

Tell Us What You Think

We appreciate hearing reader opinions about our books. You can email us at Comments@EllorasCave.com.

Why an electronic book?

We live in the Information Age—an exciting time in the history of human civilization, in which technology rules supreme and continues to progress in leaps and bounds every minute of every day. For a multitude of reasons, more and more avid literary fans are opting to purchase e-books instead of paper books. The question from those not yet initiated into the world of electronic reading is simply: *Why?*

1. ***Price.*** An electronic title at Ellora's Cave Publishing and Cerridwen Press runs anywhere from 40% to 75% less than the cover price of the exact same title in paperback format. Why? Basic mathematics and cost. It is less expensive to publish an e-book (no paper and printing, no warehousing and shipping) than it is to publish a paperback, so the savings are passed along to the consumer.

2. ***Space.*** Running out of room in your house for your books? That is one worry you will never have with electronic books. For a low one-time cost, you can purchase a handheld device specifically designed for e-reading. Many e-readers have large, convenient screens for viewing. Better yet, hundreds of titles can be stored within your new library—on a single microchip. There are a variety of e-readers from different manufacturers. You can also read e-books on your PC or laptop computer. (Please note that

Ellora's Cave does not endorse any specific brands. You can check our websites at www.ellorascave.com or www.cerridwenpress.com for information we make available to new consumers.)

3. *Mobility.* Because your new e-library consists of only a microchip within a small, easily transportable e-reader, your entire cache of books can be taken with you wherever you go.

4. *Personal Viewing Preferences.* Are the words you are currently reading too small? Too large? Too… ANNOYING? Paperback books cannot be modified according to personal preferences, but e-books can.

5. *Instant Gratification.* Is it the middle of the night and all the bookstores near you are closed? Are you tired of waiting days, sometimes weeks, for bookstores to ship the novels you bought? Ellora's Cave Publishing sells instantaneous downloads twenty-four hours a day, seven days a week, every day of the year. Our webstore is never closed. Our e-book delivery system is 100% automated, meaning your order is filled as soon as you pay for it.

Those are a few of the top reasons why electronic books are replacing paperbacks for many avid readers.

As always, Ellora's Cave and Cerridwen Press welcome your questions and comments. We invite you to email us at Comments@ellorascave.com or write to us directly at Ellora's Cave Publishing Inc., 1056 Home Avenue, Akron, OH 44310-3502.

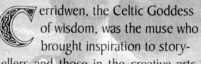

Discover for yourself why readers can't get enough
of the multiple award-winning publisher

Ellora's Cave.

Whether you prefer e-books or paperbacks,

be sure to visit EC on the web at
www.ellorascave.com

for an erotic reading experience that will leave you
breathless.